TURBULENT WATERS

Betty J. Vaughn

TotalRecall Publications, Inc.
1103 Middlecreek
Friendswood, Texas 77546
281-992-3131   281-482-5390 Fax
www.totalrecallpress.com

ISBN: 978-1-59095-175-0
UPC: 6-43977-41751-0

Printed in the United States of America with simultaneous printings in Australia, Canada, and United Kingdom.

FIRST EDITION
1   2   3   4   5   6   7   8   9   10

I owe my sister, Helen Brumbaugh, a debt of thanks for her unfailingly wise suggestions. She is a thoughtful and critical reader and my books are the better for her input. Our baby sister, Peggy Johnson Iacocca, has my eternal gratitude for being a vibrant and beautiful part of our lives. Her years were all too short, but how she did live them. You fill my heart, my sisters, my friends.

To my agent and editor, Rebecca Pratt, I owe you so much and I am so delighted I found you. Thank you for believing in me.

NC Society of Historians
Established December 1941

AWARD WINNER

"Vaughn's first book, MUDDY WATERS, was reviewed by our panel and selected as an award-winner in 2011. We reunited with memorable characters and were introduced to new ones as the saga continues in TURBULENT WATERS. The characters in this novel become real to the reader. We became swept up in the novel and didn't want to put it down until we had finished reading it. Vaughn captured the essence of the difficult reconstruction period. So smoothly did she work 'history' into the story, that we were taken aback at times when we realized the book was a series of 19th century life's lessons.

Vaughn can consider herself a seasoned novelist! Her work simply isn't just a flurry of words, dry and boring. She is a master of literary technique as she weaves together her tapestry of words to develop a picture that is complete, yet can be added to in the future. Each volume is self-sufficient but leaves the reader wanting more, hoping for more...and this volume is no different from the first in that respect.

This novel earns the 2012 Historical Fiction Award due to the unanimous decision of our panel."

--The North Carolina Society of Historians

Author's Note

Many of the characters peripheral to the story are true portraits of people who lived in New Bern, Kinston, Fort Macon and other North Carolina locations during Reconstruction. I hope that their descendants will find their characterizations acceptable and will gain some insight into the world of their ancestors. Where appropriate, I have included actual incidents and atrocities although some dates were changed by a few months in order to fit into the plot in a timely manner. I have tried to present both sides of the difficulties that ensued in the South following the surrender at Appomattox in a fair and historically accurate manner. I hope that you will enjoy the continuing saga of Penny, Ryan, Marcus and the others brought to life in *Muddy Waters*.

1

The clacking wheels of the train were a rhythmically noisy reminder of the increasing miles between Marcus and the home he doubted he would ever again see. Marcus Cauley hunched on the uncomfortable seat, cold, miserable, wanting sleep that eluded him. He had seen days without rest, yet the images cart-wheeling through his mind gave him no peace. Shifting to ease his back, he stared with disgust at the manacles that bound him hand and ankle.

He had ridden to Lena Rouse's house that Saturday night, arriving later than planned after stopping by the Henry Tull farm to see Joshua Dawson, whom he had heard was looking for another overseer's job. Not finding him home, Marcus continued on to Sycamore. It was almost bedtime when he arrived. After a cold supper in the kitchen and a couple of stolen kisses on the front porch, he had gone to bed dreaming of the day when a wife would be sleeping beside him. Sunday had been a repeat of so many spent with the Rouse family, first to church and then back to Sycamore for a well-attended and justly appreciated feast. He left late that afternoon satisfied that time would fly until their wedding. Lena stood waving to him when he turned onto the road to begin the ride back to Belle Terre, her promise ring sparking beams of light that reflected in her smiling eyes. Just before riding from view, he turned in the saddle and blew her a kiss. Contented with his relationship and the new direction of his life, Marcus sighed with pleasure as he rode home.

He thought little of the overseer Calvin Smith and his

scurvy-ridden family, certain that by his return they would have packed up and left. He was happy to be rid of the shiftless lot. It was dark when he reached his stable. Using the light of a full moon, he rubbed down his mare. After giving her fresh water and some oats, it was time to acknowledge the rumble of hunger in his own belly. Guided by dim light from coals still glowing in the hearth, he rummaged for a fat lightwood splinter to light the oil lamp that stood on the table. Marcus ate steadily until he finished the meal left for him, not really noting what it was in his haste to be done. It was not until he lifted his head as he pushed his plate away that he saw the note propped on the chest by the door. Dropping his plate into the pan of water left on the workbench, he crossed the room to the chest.

His heart began a drum beat of dread as he read what his friend and neighbor had written him:

> *Marcus, we thought we should warn you that sorry overseer of yours was found murdered in the field behind his house. His wife says you killed him and has gone to get the sheriff. I know you didn't do it. But with that damned bunch of Reconstructionists in charge, I don't know whether to tell you to run or to stay. Let me know what Pa and I can do to help.*
> *--Brett*

Walking back to the table he sank into his chair and reread the note. For a moment he was too stunned to either think or react. Blowing air through his teeth in disgust, he marched with determination to the overseer's house to find it dark and deserted, the empty rooms holding only debris and filth. Although he had hoped to confront Calvin's wife about her spurious allegations, it was obvious she had not waited around to face his wrath. In angry frustration, he stretched long legs in the direction of Lucinda's house. Perhaps, she would know what had happened during his absence.

The woman was sitting in the heavy shadow of her porch when he walked into the moonlight-washed dirt yard. Her grim voice came to him from the darkness, "I've been waiting for you to show up."

"For God's sake, Lucinda, can someone tell me what's going on around here?"

She studied the rugged planes of his face for several moments before answering, "That piece of garbage Calvin met with an untimely accident at the end of a knife blade. I didn't do it. I wanted to and I planned to. That man for sure needed killing. It seems someone got to him before I could. If it was you, I'm mighty grateful."

"I swear I didn't kill him. I went to see my fiancée and spent Saturday and most of today with her and her family. The last time I saw Calvin was yesterday morning when I paid him off and told him to be gone by my return."

"His wife says you did it."

"I can't help what she says. She's lying."

She gave him another cold smile, "Doesn't change anything does it? He's dead and you're accused. If you were a black man, I'd tell you to take to your heels. But you're not, so maybe you can prove you didn't do it. The sheriff will be here in the morning to get you." Lucinda shook her head and continued, "I'm grateful to someone for doing it for me. They'd hang me for sure if I'd killed him."

"Well, if I can't prove my innocence, they'll be hanging me for something I didn't do." Looking into the dark porch, he nodded to her shadowy form, "If you learn anything that might help me, I'd appreciate it."

"I'll do it. I owe you for the school. I don't forget my debts, white man." She watched him walk away, weariness and frustration making his feet heavy. Lucinda lifted her hand in silent goodbye but he did not see it.

****

"Mercy. Stop fidgeting or I'll never get this pinned right." Nancy Herring ordered around a mouth full of pins. Her voice was so sharp that Penelope Bartlett Kennedy looked down in surprise at her friend and companion. Ignoring the expression of shock on Penny's face, Nancy continued fitting the dress that Penny was to be married in.

"I'm sorry, Nancy. I'm as jumpy as spit on a hot iron. I can't stand still. Pa is furious with me. Marcus is livid; you're upset; and Rye is teething. I think Mammy Rena and Moses are the only people around here who're happy with me at the moment. On top of that, who knows the person responsible for throwing that rock through the dining room window last night? I feel as though the whole world is against me and frankly it scares me to death. I don't know what will happen next. It could just as well be a bullet as a rock." Penny's amber eyes snapped with frustration.

"For goodness sake! What did you expect when you announced that you're planning to marry a damned Yankee and an officer at that!" Nancy remonstrated.

It was apparent to Penny that the woman was ill prepared to ignore the suffering enemy soldiers had brought to family, friends and neighbors. Nancy's voice was stern when she added, "I don't mean to lecture you, but they did kill your husband and his father along with dozens of people we know."

Neither Nancy nor Penny would ever forget how the Yankees dumped poor sick Ann Herring into the yard and left her to die. Penny shuddered at the memory of Mr. and Mrs. Noble, their neighbors on British Road, who had been hung after soldiers raped Mrs. Noble with their children watching from their hiding place in the woods. And then, there were homes like the Waller's that were now nothing but chimneys looming over ashes like so many tombstones over graves. Too many neighborhood boys were buried or their poor bodies blown to bits so small they were never found, and too many others came home maimed. How could any of them ever forget with scars from the horrors they had lived through ever present?

"Nancy, I've forgotten nothing I assure you. Ryan Madison is a decent man even if he is a Yankee. He's going to make a life here because he loves New Berne and he loves me." Penny felt they all should be grateful for him and so many other good men who had stayed. Ryan had told her he understood what they had been through and that he never condoned the atrocities. Had it not been for him, who knows what might have happened to her father's home and her own. She wondered if her father in his anger had forgotten how Ryan had posted his own men to protect them. As far as she was concerned, the South could use men like him to help with building a bridge to a new kind of world. They could never return to the one they had before the war, and she for one didn't care to. She understood they would need men capable of dealing with the problems of a military government, roaming bands of outlaws, destroyed infrastructure and all of the other difficulties they faced now and in the foreseeable future.

"Give him a chance, Nancy. He's a good man and I do so love him. Will you try for my sake?" Penny pleaded, sighing as she smoothed her hands down the sides of the heavy white satin gown. It had been her mother's and she herself had worn it for her marriage to her first husband, Daniel Kennedy. Killed in Virginia, his body lay moldering beside the graves of his father and mother in the cemetery behind the plantation home her father's former overseer, Marcus, had bought.

Looking up, Nancy's voice softened as she watched Penny stroke the gown. "It is beautiful cloth. You're lucky you have it for you'd never be able to buy fabric like this now." Pausing she continued, "Penny, I don't mean to be cross with you. You know I appreciate all you've done for me. Your home and family mean as much or more to me than my own. I love your son as though he were the child I know I'll never have. I do want you to be happy. I just hope that this man is the right one for you. Marcus loves you so much and he's such a good man. I guess I'm just sorry that he's not the one you chose. It would make everything so much easier."

"I for sure know that. I'm sad about Marcus, too. And it just breaks my heart that Pa is so angry with me. If it weren't for Brett, I would despair of him ever coming around. Thank goodness, my brother doesn't hold this against me. He likes Ryan a lot. I just hope he can convince Pa to give us a chance." Penny sighed. When she had told her father whom she planned to marry, he had raised his hand to slap her. Quickly he had caught himself and dropped his hand limply by his side. But that had not stemmed the spate of furious words he threw at her. The words 'You're no daughter of mine' still rang in her ears and haunted sleepless nights.

John Barlett was a dignified, easy-going, affable man, not prone to losing his temper. Penny was shocked that in the depth of anger he would come so close to assailing her. Even as a child when her naughty capers merited a spanking, he had handed the switch to her mother, Sarah, and left the room while she applied a few stinging swats to their child's backside. With Sarah dead since the day after Christmas of 1863, John had continued to grieve. Only Brett's return and the daily antics of Rye had brought moderation to his mourning. Now with Penny's coming marriage to the hated enemy, he was once more morose and aloof, lost in an inner world of pain.

During the years of war when Ryan had been estranged from her, thinking that not he but the husband she said she no longer loved had fathered her son Rye, she thought she had lost him. Now she badly needed him near. Penny regretted that after their reunion he had returned to New Berne and his new law practice leaving her alone to close her home and prepare for their wedding. It would have helped to have him to lean on when the disapproval that radiated from those around her threatened to overwhelm her resolve to make a new life with him. Coupled with that was an equal relief that he was not with her. Ryan was too like his son. Penny feared her father and the others would see the truth of the child's paternity. The lie of omission, that allowed them all to believe that Daniel had fathered her son before his death, was a burden on her soul.

Even the child's name was Ryan, 'Rye' just the nickname given him by her father in salute to his favorite whiskey. Were the truth known about her child, the ripples of anger radiating from news of her marriage would become a flood that would wash away any path to future reconciliation. Remembering the brief pleasure and passion Ryan and she had shared during the Christmas of '62 when he was convalescing in her home, Penny blushed.

Marcus had already looked with suspicion from Ryan to Rye and she had seen the speculation in his angry eyes...that same dark hair, those sky blue eyes? Since he had stormed away, Penny found herself missing Marcus' steady support and warmth. The years of the war would have been unbearable without him. Now his cold anger left her bereft of one of her longest and best friends. Were it not for Ryan, she would have married Marcus months past. She could not blame Marcus for his anger. He waited for her for years, saved to buy a home so he would be a man of property and a peer, and declared his love for her and wish to marry. And, not knowing if she could ever reclaim Ryan's love, she allowed Marcus to dream and hope. Meanwhile she spun her own dreams around a nebulous future with Ryan. She was willing to settle for a life with Marcus and the possibility that in time she might come to love him until she realized that she did not have to compromise. Had she been fair to Marcus? She had to admit that she probably had not.

"Lord, Miz Penny. You sure is a sight for sore eyes." Mammy remarked as she entered Penny's bedroom, an excited Rye dashing in before her. The creamy satin of the gown enhanced Penny's auburn hair, perfect features, and curvaceous figure. Mammy stood for a moment admiring the woman she had known since birth. "I come to tell you Mistah Brett say he want to take Rye for a ride this morning if it all right with you?"

"Please tell him that's fine with me. But do ask him to see me when he returns," Penny said, as she scooped up her wiggling son to give him a resounding kiss.

"I do that." Shaking her head with pleasure, Mammy remarked, "My girl going to be the prettiest bride this state has ever seen. Uh huh, I sure am glad you marrying Mistah Ryan. He one fine man and a real good looking one, too."

"Yes, he is a good man, Mammy. How about telling the others that for me?" Penny swept the woman that had been with her since she was a child into her arms. Tears of gratitude threatened to spill from her eyes. Blinking them away, she smiled and waved as an excited Rye and the old woman left the room. She called a cautionary, "Be a good boy for Uncle Brett, darling."

"Well if that remark to Mammy was for my benefit, I get the message." Nancy commented as she took the last pin from her mouth and used it to pinch in the waist another notch. "Okay, Penny, it's fitted. I just have to redo the seams and you're all set."

"Thanks, Nancy. You're the best seamstress I know." She smiled with gratitude at the woman she had grown to love. Nancy was honest, hardworking, intelligent, witty and gifted in the household arts. Penny thought it was a shame that local men had not cared to look beyond an austere and homely countenance to the true beauty of the woman beneath.

"I may be the only one you know at the moment." Nancy snorted.

Penny laughed with her, "I think you may be right." She began to remove the pin-studded dress to re-don the one she had been wearing, flinching when errant pins pricked tender flesh. Deciding no time was like the present to broach a subject that had been troubling her, Penny began, "Nancy, I've been wanting to ask a favor of you."

"What's that?" From her tone of voice, Penny knew the woman was wary of what was coming.

"I asked Mammy and Moses to come with me to New Berne and I really hate to leave the house empty. Would you be afraid to live here alone for a while?"

Nancy's brows knitted in concentration. "I just don't know about that. You've heard the same stories I have about the Bushwhackers and renegade darkies. Without a man on the place, we're going to run a terrible risk here even if it's not sitting on the road like your Pa's house. That rock that came sailing in here last night is proof enough of that. There's no way I could hold off a bunch of good-for-nothings if they decided to rob the place. I think I would be mighty afraid here at night all by myself."

"I think they're calling themselves Regulators now instead of Bushwhackers," Penny offered parenthetically. "But, I do understand. I thought I would ask Brett to move over here for a while until we can find someone to run the farm. He could live in the overseer's house so you're not here all alone."

"I'll think about it. I don't know that I would feel safe even with Brett here. He's single and bound to be out and about as soon as he finds someone to court. I'm just not sure how much protection he would be."

"Do you know anyone that could come stay with you so you wouldn't feel so alone?"

"Right off the top of my head, no. But I'll think about it." Obviously uncomfortable with the conversation, Nancy busied herself lifting the dress from Penny's bed. "I'm going to start on this so we have time to make any last minute adjustments if we need to."

Penny knew it was an imposition to ask the woman to remain. As a spinster, she had served as companion and helper for several local families. But, Penny's family was the first that she had adopted as her own. For over three years she had been nurse and companion for Sarah Bartlett while she was dying, then friend and companion to Penny, and nanny to her child. It was an unspoken reality that Nancy's parents were old and soon she would be obliged to return to them.

Nancy was right to be worried about living alone in the house after the departure of Penny and her two servants. Already rumors were circulating of trouble brewing between townsmen and Negro troops manning the military government offices in nearby Kinston, North Carolina. While many of the troops were local and known to citizens of the area, the fact that former servants now had power over them rankled more than a little. Prideful Southerners were slow to accept the new relationship between darkies and whites. Of even greater concern were the bands of Regulators composed of outlaws, rebellious former soldiers, and darkies who roamed the countryside robbing and raping with essential impunity. Talk of citizens banning together to take law into their own hands was becoming more than idle speculation as atrocities increased. Penny had listened to conversations between her father, brother, and Marcus when they began to express their concerns about the state of things in the county. Even more worrisome was the fact that of late they halted such conversations whenever she approached.

She sensed that they were involved in something that they did not want her or the others to know about. What it was she had not yet surmised, but somehow she would. Although she fretted about it, she tried to credit them with the sense not to embroil themselves in some kind of unlawful group in order to control Regulator incursions on life and property. If they had joined such a cabal, Penny was determined to convince them to quit before they brought the wrath of the military government down on their stubborn heads.   Nor could she condone predatory actions against hapless Negroes that were as lost as whites in terms of their role in the new era. Penny had voiced without hesitation her opinion that they deserved greater dispensation considering their more limited resources and education. Marcus had sharply rebuked her by reminding her that he had little education and had begun with no resources either except his own determination and hard work as her father's former overseer.   Now as the owner of a large plantation, he was modernizing it to be more productive than it had been before the war when slave labor had worked it. He had little patience or sympathy for those less eager to seize the reins of opportunity.

Penny had bitten her tongue to keep from reminding him that not only was he white, but she had sold him the farm at a price below the current market value following her husband and father-in-law's deaths. She knew he had worked hard, saved, and could have paid more had she asked. But she had not asked, perhaps hoping to assuage her own guilt. Had she not led him on in order to keep him as a personal safety net when faced with a life without Ryan? Penny blamed herself for Marcus' anger and resentment. She deserved some of it, maybe all of it. And she owed him for her own farm's prosperity and the financial means to procure the modern implements that would make it more productive. During the war, she had funded their moonshining venture, but there her involvement in the actual process had ended. Had it not been for his labor, skill and devotion she could never have made the money she had from their illegal still on the banks of Southwest Creek whose muddy waters bound the edge of her plantation.   Although Marcus' knowledge of the process, his acumen as a businessman, and his quiet discretion had been far more important than her minor role, she had received an equal share of the earnings. She hoped in time that Marcus would find a good woman who would love him and that he could love in return. He wanted children and a family of his own and deserved them. She longed for the day when he would also forgive her and be her friend again.

With Marcus, her father and the neighbors openly hostile to her marrying a Yankee, the joy that would have been unalloyed was now tainted by their overt disapproval. She clasped her right hand over the ring that Ryan had given her on that fateful Christmas when she had conceived their child, but it could not bring him nearer. Those brief halcyon days of forbidden passion and joy had sustained her through the long years of war. She once believed their memory alone would have to be enough to last her a lifetime without him. Now she counted the days until he arrived for their wedding in the rose garden behind her home. Three more weeks seemed an eternity.

Penny stared out the kitchen window lost in thought, swallowing hard to keep tears of frustration from welling to the surface. She shrugged her shoulders to ease the tension and resumed the task of grinding herbs for a compound to relieve Mammy Rena of some of the pain that afflicted her joints. Hearing the clop of hooves, she again looked out the window and waited as Brett reined in his horse near the back steps to the kitchen.

Mammy's husband, Moses, took Ole Polly's reins and led her to the barn as Brett walked into the house to see Penny as requested. Penny smiled with delight as her excitedly bouncing son followed his uncle into the sunny room. "Welcome back, darling. Your mama missed her little boy."

"Oh, Mama. That was a good ride. You come next time. Then you won't miss me."

"Maybe next time, darling. Now run along to see Nancy

because I need to have a talk with your uncle."

Brett took a seat at the worn kitchen table and patted the place across from him. His normal jocularity missing, her brother lifted serious eyes to her own, "You sit down, too, Sis. I need to have a chat with you as well."

Sitting across from him she smiled at his good looks: dark brown hair, clear green eyes, trim and muscular body, and regular features. "Lord, Brett, with so many single women and so few men, I'm surprised you haven't been kidnapped."

"I run fast." Brett laughed, but was not to be put off. "Let's get serious for a moment. I didn't come over here to talk about the women in my life or the lack thereof."

"Of course. What's bothering you?"

"It's Pa." Brett looked into her eyes. "This marriage is too much for him to swallow. He won't be attending your wedding, nor will the neighbors and friends you've invited. You don't want a riot on your hands when you get married either. Things could get a lot worse than just a rock through your window and you know it. You need to consider moving this wedding to New Berne. It'll be easier for all concerned if you marry away from here.   I'll stand in for Pa if you want someone to give you away."

"You mean it? No one will come?" Penny gasped in shock. Looking down, she studied her hands as they rested on the table, watching the light glint on the emerald and diamond ring she had worn for the last three and a half years. She whispered, "This makes me so sad but I suppose I have no choice."

"No, you don't. I think it's for the best. Trust me, at some point they will all come around, but not now. It's much too soon considering the on-going problems in the community."

Heaving a resolute sigh, Penny agreed. "Very well. I'll write Ryan to arrange for a wedding service in New Berne and reservations for us at the hotel there for a day beforehand."

"Good." Brett continued, "It's better for you not to put this marriage too much in the faces of our friends and neighbors. I haven't wanted to tell you, but that rock through your window was just a warning. I've heard rumors of worse. Furthermore, you don't want to deal with the kind of hurtful remarks that Ella Swain faced." They'd both listened to the vicious rumors that circulated when the president of the University of North Carolina's daughter, Ella Swain, married the ex-Union officer, Smith Atkins. People spat on the invitations and few actually showed up for the wedding. They even accused Atkins of giving her jewelry stolen from Southern women during the war. Brett felt pity for Penny's predicament. He knew her heart was heavy that their father would not attend her wedding as she had always been his particular favorite. "Now, Mammy said you want to see me about something?"

"I know you have your hands full with Pa's farm, but do you think you could look after things here, until I can find an overseer to run things for me? I wouldn't even ask knowing how unfair it is to dump one more thing on you, but I don't know where else to turn." Penny clenched her hands under the table until the knuckles turned white as she waited for his answer. He could not know how much she was depending on him.

Brett studied her face for long minutes before replying, "You know I'll do what I can until we can find someone you can rely on. I know some fellows I served with that might be looking for something. Let me ask around and see who I can find."

"That would be a big help. I also asked Nancy to stay on but she's afraid to stay here alone. I took the liberty of telling her you might be willing to live in the overseer's house for a while until we can find someone, but she still doesn't seem too thrilled at the idea."

Brett nodded his head in agreement, "I can understand that. This is no time for a woman to be alone with no men about for protection." Glancing down, he worried at is lower lip for a moment before continuing, "Are you so sure that Mammy and Moses are going to New Berne with you? From what Marcus was telling me about Lucinda, I wasn't so sure they would be willing to leave her and their grandbaby here without them."

Penny's head jerked up in patent alarm. "As far as I know they're still going. Why, what have you heard?" She felt her spirits sinking even lower with this new potential problem. "Oh for goodness sakes, what more am I going to be hit with?"

"Hey, Sis. It's not like you to sound so down in the dumps. I really don't know anything in particular except that Marcus seems to think they won't go. Lucinda is kind of worried about them being so far away. Also it doesn't sit too well with some folks around here that you gave her fifty acres of your husband and his father's land after their deaths. Both Lucinda and Marcus think there're going to be problems. And it doesn't help that Lucinda puts on airs around people. If she would just back off and lay low for a while, she wouldn't be so hard for folks to take."

"So am I supposed to inform our nosy neighbors that I did it because my late husband was the proud father of her half-breed baby?" She had confessed the truth of her marriage to him months before. "After all, you well know that Jeremiah is the only blood kin the Kennedy's have left and that's why I did it. I can't tell people that without announcing that my own child is the bastard son of a Yankee officer, for Christ sake." Penny felt her anger rising at the mounting frustrations and struggled to regain control of her emotions.

Rising, Brett walked around the table and took her in his arms. "Penny, calm yourself. You don't want the others to hear you. Trust me to take care of things here as best I can. People will come around eventually. It's not easy to go from treating men as the enemy one day and an intimate the next. I'll try to talk to Lucinda and warn her to back off folks a little. Right now with darky troops controlling the area, many of them former slaves of the folks around here, it doesn't take much to touch off sensitive tempers. We're beaten, Penny, but we're still damned proud. All of the change being shoved down our throats is hard to swallow."

"I know and I am so grateful that you can rise above all of this." Penny smiled up at him.

"Dammit," Brett cried. "I beg pardon, but I'm not *rising* above it, Penny. I wish it were different and Ryan were one of us, but he isn't and I have to make peace with that because I love you and I don't want to lose you. You just have to trust that someday Pa and the others will accept it, too. It's up to Ryan to show them he's a decent man they can respect and relate to."

"I have no other choice, do I? It's just that it's so hard to feel like such a pariah after all I've done for so many people in this community. I guess they've conveniently forgotten all of that," Penny hated the petulant note in her voice. Recalling the long hours she had toiled preparing medicines and nursing them, she felt anger rising into a choking knot in her throat.

"It's not that they have forgotten. If they had, you might be dealing with more than just a thrown rock. It's just that at the moment this takes pre-eminence in their minds. If we had won the war, maybe it wouldn't be so hard to accept you marrying a Yankee. You're asking them to embrace the enemy that beat us and treat him like he's one of us."

"He's not the enemy. He helped us by saving our farms."

"Correction, he saved your farm and Pa's. But what about all of the others that were robbed, burned, or destroyed? Do you think those people have forgotten who did it to them?"

"It wasn't Ryan. He can't be blamed for the sins of the whole dad-gum Union army."

"Let it rest. You're not going to fix this mess overnight any more than you're going to convince Marcus that you've been fair with him."

"I know, I know. Don't remind me. I just can't deal with Marcus right now on top of everything else."

"He'll be all right. He's a fine man and he's going to have plenty of women to choose from with men in such short supply. He'll get over you and he'll find another woman and make a life for himself with her."

Penny laughed, "Don't think you're going to be overlooked either."

"I need to get accustomed to being alive and living in peace before I enter that particular battleground." Impishly Brett leaned over and pulled out the pin holding her hair, watching as it cascaded to her shoulders. They both laughed, remembering how he used to annoy and tease her doing the same thing when they were children.

"Well, some of us are still up to the same old tricks, I see." Penny's mouth lifted in a wry grin as she pushed her hair back into a messy chignon.

"Better talk to Mammy Rena and Moses, Sis, before you make too many more plans for them. Let them decide what's best for their family. They feel beholden to you, particularly Mammy, but Lucinda and Jeremiah are their blood kin. That needs to come first."

"I know. But I just can't imagine life without them. Mammy has always been there for me. To give up both Nancy and Mammy would be a real hardship on Rye, too."

"If it weren't for her parents, Nancy could go with you to New Berne if Mammy decides to stay. Moses and Mammy can do more around here to take care of things than Nancy can." Brett shook his head, knowing they would all sacrifice themselves out of loyalty to her if she asked it of them.

"Lordy, I suppose I know all of that. I just didn't want to think about it. It's hard on me to leave home too, and even harder if I have to leave everyone behind."

"You will have your husband and your son. You won't be

alone. I'm sure Ryan can find suitable servants for you. I remember him saying that his neighbor, Mrs. Framingham, can loan you someone if needed."

"I'll think about it."

"Do that. Now get Mammy and Moses in here and tell them they don't have to feel obligated to go with you. Let them decide what's best for them."

"I will." Seeing the admonishment in his eyes, she added, "I promise."

After the evening meal, while Nancy was reading a bedtime story to Rye, Penny asked her old retainers to join her at the kitchen table. When she told them that she knew their own family needed to come first, she could see the relief in their eyes. After that, she knew she could not ask them to go with her.

"Miz Penny, you know we going take good care of this house and plantation for you. It going to be done just like you still here." Moses nodded his head in emphasis as he made the pledge to her.

Mammy reached over and patted her hand, "You my baby just like Lucinda. I done pinned diapers on the both of you and took care of you when you sick. You and Brett like my own children, but I'd be mighty sorry to leave Lucinda and Jeremiah. Times are real tough for us darkies now, just like for you white folk. Lucinda and Jeremiah need us worser than you. I going to miss you something fierce and that boy of yours too, but you can come back to see us. Mistah Ryan say y'all going to be coming here a lot."

"I'll miss you both, too." Penny assured them with a sad smile. " I promise to come Christmas and every summer to help preserve fruit and vegetables and stay for a while with you. Please, take care of my house for me and my herbs."

"You know we do that for sure." Mammy and Moses promised in unison.

"I'm going to ask Nancy if she will be okay to stay, since you will be here as well. Brett says he will move into the overseer's house for a while if needed."

"It be good if Miz Nancy stay on to help take care of the house. Mistah Brett welcome to stay here, but it ain't necessary if he need to do something else." Moses assured her.

"Thank you both for so very much. You are so dear to me I don't know how I'll manage without you. You've been with me my whole life." Penny bit her lip to stop herself from asking them to change their minds.

"We be here when you come home and we take good care of this house for you. This is still your home no matter what." Mammy folded Penny into her arms.

Penny climbed the stairs to kiss her son goodnight wondering if she still had the courage to marry the man she loved.

2

Penny had visited her father to tell him goodbye and ask for his understanding. It had been an awkward visit and she knew that her father was far from happy with her decision, despite his grudging apology for calling her no daughter of his. During the previous Sunday's service at the Woodington church, hisses and sibilant whispers left no doubt about her neighbors' feelings. Their vicious remarks had buzzed in the air around her like angry bees as she walked from the church door to her buggy, their backs turned in rigid ostracism.

The last of the boxes of clothing, silverware, china and odds and ends she was taking with her to her new home in New Berne had been loaded onto the wagon that Ryan had sent for her. The wagon's driver, a black man named Custis, helped Moses load the last of the goods. Most of her household furnishings would remain, as she couldn't bear to lose this home before she found comfort in a new one. Taking a last look around the hall, she smiled bravely at Nancy, Mammy, and Moses who were waiting in the pre-dawn light to bid her farewell. After hugging each of them goodbye and pressing a parting gift of money into their hands, Penny lifted her son and prepared to face her new life with the man she loved. She did not see Marcus watching from the protection of the pinewoods beside the lane. She did not see the grimace of pain he wiped from his face with a shaking hand.

Penny handed Rye to her brother who was already seated in the buggy, reins in hand, before climbing in herself. Waving one last time at the trio in the doorway, they started down the path to the road and the thirty-mile journey to New Berne, the wagon following behind. Penny sighed at the thought of the long trek ahead. It would be late day before they and the wagon would reach, Fair Bluff, Ryan's new home on the banks of the Neuse River. Penny was grateful that Mammy had packed a generous fried chicken and ham biscuit picnic for the three of them, as well as Custis.

The weather was sultry, ripe with the promise of late afternoon storms. As the day progressed, she anxiously watched the gathering clouds and prayed that they reached New Berne before the fury of a summer storm assailed them. Mindful of the weather, they wasted little time on the noontime break and were soon back in the buggy. The horse sensed the coming weather and began to act skittish, causing Brett to hand Rye back to her so he could give his full attention to handling the horse.

Brett cast a wary eye at the darkening sky. "We're in for quite a storm. I sure don't like the looks of those clouds and apparently the horse doesn't either."

"Do you think we could find someone's barn or shed to wait under until it passes?" Penny looked about with mounting anxiety, but saw nothing that would provide shelter either ahead or immediately behind.

Clucking, he gave the horse's back a smart slap of the reins. "There's nothing behind us worth turning back for and I have no idea what's ahead. Judging by the distant rumble of that thunder, I suspect we'd better find something in the next twenty or thirty minutes or we'll just have to hunker down and sit it out in the open."

The birds grew silent as the wind began to flick leaves and small twigs into the road where they skittered about beneath the rapidly turning wheels of the buggy. Penny clutched Rye as the buggy sped down the rutted road bouncing them precariously about the seat. A sudden peal of thunder and a sharp crack of lightening added urgency to the need for shelter.

"Look, Brett." Penny pointed off to the left of the road. "That looks like a tobacco barn that's big enough to get the buggy and horses under. The wagon's covered so it should be okay."

"Hang on. I'm going to make a run for it." Brett called to her over the rising wind. Fat drops of rain announced the pending arrival of a deluge.

By the time they reached the dilapidated shed on the side of the weathered old barn, the pelting rain was beating against them in blinding fury. At first they did not see the body that was swaying gently under the rafters as the blowing wind pushed against it. Rye was the first to notice.

Looking up, eyes rounded with excitement, he pointed at the corpse, "Look, Mama. There's somebody up there."

"Oh, my God, Brett. Some darky has hung himself." Penny held her son to her to hide his eyes from the grim sight. She shuddered with revulsion as Brett pulled the buggy further under the shelter of the shed.

"Stay in the buggy and look the other way if it bothers you. I'm going to cut him down and put the body inside the barn." Brett extracted his knife from his belt as he stood on the back of the carriage, stretching to reach the body. Cutting through the rope, he lowered the body beside the buggy. It dropped to the ground with a heavy thud. "Right off hand, I'd say this was recent. The body's still warm."

"What does that rag pinned to his clothing say?"

"KKK, I think." Brett seemed reluctant to answer.

"What does that mean and why would it be pinned to him?" Penny asked in puzzlement.

Loud keening from Custis interrupted Brett's response. "Lord have mercy. They done killed old Jimbo. I ain't going to stay under this here barn in case they come back and try to kill me too."

Brett barked at the sweating man, "No one is going to harm you, Custis. As soon as the storm passes we're going to leave. Besides, I suspect whoever did this is long gone."

"I know this here darky. He own this farm here and white folk around here don't like it none. They say he uppity. I ain't staying, no sir. Y'all is going to have to get this wagon to New Berne yourselfs." Wasting no time, Custis climbed down from the wagon and set off into the woods at a trot.

"What is this all about, Brett? Who would do such a thing?" Penny cried, distress choking her voice.

"It's the Ku Klux Klan, Penny. It started in Tennessee and now it's here. Folks are tired of lawlessness and some have banded together to take matters into their own hands. It's not pretty for sure, but they feel desperate."

Penny rose in fury, "Desperate! Do they really think murdering people is not lawless, for Christ sake?"

A sharp crack of nearby lightening illuminated Brett's face as he struggled for a response. "Men cannot just sit by and do nothing when their families and homes are threatened by the hooligans that are running things around here. They feel they must do something to provide what protection and deterrent they can."

"From what Custis said, his crime seems to have been a lack of due servility to the local whites. Does that justify stringing him up in his own barn?"

"We don't know the reasons behind this. I'm not saying it's right, only that men feel forced into taking some kind of action."

"I've watched you, Pa and Marcus hush up when I enter the room. Are you involved in this mess, too?"

"Don't worry about us. We know better than to do anything stupid." Brett looked out into the rain. "It seems to be slowing up. We should be able to leave soon but I'm afraid I'll have to drive the wagon and leave the buggy to you. Can you manage the horse and Rye too?"

"Rye will be a good boy for Mommy, won't you honey?"

Her son looked up with sad eyes. "That man gone to Heaven, Mama?"

"I surely hope so, darling. Now, be a good boy so I can drive the buggy and we can go see your new daddy."

"I like my Daddy. He's fun." Rye grinned up at her.

Penny smiled back remembering those few days when Ryan had returned to her and they had planned their future. He had been so proud of this son that he had only just met, and so eager to marry her and claim him as his own. She also remembered the tenderness of their reconciliation. Despite his obvious desire to sleep with her during the three days that he spent, she had resisted. Reflecting on the previous consequences, she was determined any future children would be safely conceived within the bonds of wedlock. With the world around her still in chaos, mishaps on the way to the altar were still a possibility. This time there would be no convenient husband to claim paternity were that to happen. She would have liked to daydream her way to New Berne, to anticipate the house that awaited her beside the broad river, and the man she was soon to wed, but the rutted road pitted with deep mud holes and the bouncing child beside her demanded vigilant attention.

The sun had begun to sink low in the sky when the spires of New Berne's churches beckoned them welcome. As they turned onto Pollock street to make their way to Ryan's law office where he would meet them, Penny's attention was caught by a loud hello off to her right. There sitting in the shade of a tree with his horse Windfall standing by, sat Ryan. Another man waited with him. She waved to Ryan as he sprang to his feet, looped the reins over the saddle, and mounted his horse. Soon his horse was tied to the buggy and he was riding by her side. The other man walked back to the wagon and climbed up beside her brother.

"I was beginning to worry as I had anticipated you much

sooner. Did you have problems on the way?" Ryan inquired as he reached for the reins, unable to hide the anxiety that had been growing in him as the hours ticked by.

"We ran into a fierce thunder storm and had to wait it out under a tobacco barn or we would have been here earlier. The muddy roads slowed us down after that."

"We saw a dead man!" Rye exclaimed his eyes rounded with excitement.

"You did?" Ryan looked at his son in bemusement, not sure whether it were true or not.

"I'm afraid so." Penny answered, glancing at her son and back to him in silent message. "I'll tell you about it later."

Changing the subject before Rye could pursue the topic, she asked, "Are we going to your house first?"

"It's so late I'm going to have Kirby take the wagon on to the house and get it unloaded while I get the three of you checked into the hotel. My neighbor and old friend, Caroline Framingham invited you to stay with her, but my mother and sister are already there and I thought perhaps you would like time to rest up and refresh yourselves before meeting them all."

Penny smiled with weary gratitude, "Very much so. At the moment I feel bedraggled and more than a little exhausted."

"You're still a beautiful sight to me." Ryan winked seductively. "I would marry and take you home with me this minute if I could."

"Ryan Madison, I'll marry you tomorrow after I've had a good night's sleep, thank you very much." Penny laughed at him as she said it, feeling her heart soar with joy. She intended to be rested and fully ready to respond to his lovemaking. She blushed remembering the Christmas almost three years past when they had last lain together. Those memories had filled many lonesome nights.

Reading her thoughts, he smiled. "Yes, sleep well tonight. I fear you will get little opportunity tomorrow night."

"Hmm. I trust that's a promise?" Penny murmured.

"I assure you so."

"Hey, you two lovebirds!"   Brett called from the wagon. "Enough of the cooing. I'm ready to get out of this wagon and into a comfortable drink."

"Just a couple of blocks more, Brett, and Kirby will take over for you. The man working the hotel bar is waiting for us." Ryan called over his shoulder. "I even had them ice down a bottle of champagne for your sister, if you think that's permissible."

"I don't need my brother's permission. It sounds wonderful after the heat and hassle of today. Just get us there before I wilt." Looking into his blue eyes, Penny felt a jolt of desire sweep her body. It had been so long since she had desired anyone she had begun to wonder if that part of her life were over. Not yet twenty-five, she was glad to know she had not grown that old.

They drew to a stop in front of the Gaston House Hotel where Ryan handed the reins of the buggy to the doorman and arranged for a porter to carry luggage to the suite he had reserved. Reaching up, he lifted Rye from the buggy and handed him to his uncle before helping Penny descend. Pulling her into his arms, he hugged her close and whispered in her ear, tickling her with his breath. "It's been much too long since I held you. I don't intend to ever lose you again."

He sealed the promise with a discreet kiss, before leading her into the hotel. While they waited for rooms, Ryan fretted about what to do with Rye on his wedding night, as he wanted no distractions for his bride. A whispered conversation with Brett resulted in her brother's promise that he would spend a couple of nights at Caroline's until Rye felt comfortable staying a few days with her, Ryan's sister Isabel, and his mother, Martha.

Ryan had wanted to go to Wilmington or even New York for

a couple of weeks alone with his Penny, but an insistent request from the local military provost marshal had left him no choice about leaving. With increased problems from Regulators on one hand and belligerent whites on the other, the Union was having a difficult time restoring order to the area. With his foot in both camps as a former military officer respected by both the Federals and the local townsmen and as an attorney, he was an important cog in the machine that was trying to restart the workings of government in the district.

Eager to reach her room and change into fresh clothing, Penny wasted no time in the lobby once they had room keys. She wanted to look her best for her first evening in her new hometown. "Give me an hour to freshen up, and we'll meet you back here."

"I think I need to do the same." Brett remarked as he looked down at his mud-spattered clothes. "Tell that man with the liquor not to go anywhere."

"I'll make sure the horses and buggy are taken care of and get Kirby on the way to my house with the wagon. See you in an hour for that champagne and some supper." He walked out whistling as they ascended the stairs to their rooms.

With the buggy seen to, he waited for them to join him. To occupy his mind he made a checklist of the various arrangement he had hurried to make when the wedding was moved to New Berne. The bedroom at Fair Bluff where he would take his bride was newly furnished, aired and decorated with bouquets of roses. His mother and sister had booked the First Presbyterian Church for the following day and spent the afternoon arranging flowers on the altar. Caroline was busy supervising her servants as they prepared for the evening's wedding feast to be held on the lawn of her home. The grassy knoll had been trimmed and weeded, showing the riotous flowers to best advantage and reminding Ryan of the gardening still needed around his new home next door. He never rode up to it without remembering to send a silent thank you to Caroline who had deeded the land to him with his promise to establish a memorial garden for her and her husband on the remaining acreage.

At the appointed hour, Ryan was waiting in the lobby when Brett escorted his sister and Rye down the stairs. Looking up he watched as Penny descended each step, her eyes locked on his. She was magnificent. No other word quite described her for him. Her auburn hair was swept up, held at the crown of her head by sparkling emerald pins that matched her necklace, earrings and the ring that he had given her. She was wearing the green and gold silk gown that she had worn for him the Christmas he had spent with her in 1862. Knowing the deprivations in the South both during and after the war, he suspected she had few nice gowns and even fewer new ones. Despite its age the gown was spectacular and enhanced the lush curves of her body. He longed to remove it as he had done the last time he had seen it.

Watching him as he looked at his sister, Brett could almost read his thoughts. The electricity between the couple was palpable. He knew his sister was beautiful, not just in physical attributes, but as a person. He acknowledged that Ryan was as handsome a man as he had ever seen. He could only pray that he would be a good husband to Penny and treasure Rye and her as they deserved. As hard as he tried to forget, he could not ignore that they had fought on opposite sides. Although he liked the man, respected him for his calm and intelligent demeanor, he could not set aside the divided loyalties that lay between them as neatly as his sister had done. He wondered what Ryan would say if he knew just how involved Penny's kin were in the vigilante committees that were struggling to regain control of their local government, committees that skirted some of the laws that he himself made a living upholding. For that matter, he wondered what she would say.

Jimbo's body, now lying in the tobacco barn he had once

tended, was not the first to swing from a rafter or tree. He, his father, and Marcus had watched a hanging just two weeks before. The man had wet himself and cried piteously to be spared, but the KKK had turned a deaf ear. His crime: he had raped and robbed a widow woman and left her for dead. But she had not died and she knew him. Her sons had joined the group that extracted vengeance for the wrong done their mother. Even knowing the essential justice of the punishment, it sickened him that he and his father and neighbors had come to this. He had served for four years in the Confederate army and seen scores of men die of horrible wounds, had been present when deserters were hung. He had watched atrocities that had been unimaginable prior to the war. But nothing had so repulsed him as that swinging man, feet kicking, body jerking, tears flowing as he died from slow strangulation. Brett had stepped into the bushes at the edge of the clearing and retched until his stomach was empty. Even now, remembering, he could feel the bile rising. Shrugging away the ugly images, he walked with the others into the dining room.

Except for an occasional visit with his grandfather, it was Rye's first overnight stay away from home. The whole experience had him bubbling with excitement. The three adults watched with amusement as he pretended to read the menu, upside down. Long before the meal was finished his eyes were drooping. Ryan scoped him in his arms and stood. "Brett, if you'll grab that bottle of champagne and the other one over there on ice, we'll adjourn to your suite. It looks as though this boy is ready for his bed."

Penny and Brett followed Ryan up the stairs. When they reached their suite, Brett took the open bottle of champagne and handed the other to Penny. "This is for the two of you. I'm taking the open one with me, and tucking myself in for the evening. I confess I'm ready for bed myself."

"Are you sure you won't stay and visit with us?" Penny

asked but was not disappointed when he shook his head to decline. "Good night then, sleep well and I'll see you in the morning."

Ryan grinned. "You Rebs always did know how to decamp with admirable grace. I'll see you in the morning, brother."

"As long as you don't mean *retreat, brother...*"

Penny watched Brett begin to bristle at the unintended cut. "Of course he doesn't. Now rest up because I'm depending on you to give me away." Penny said as she pecked her brother's cheek goodnight.

After Brett left the room, Ryan began to apologize. "I'm afraid that remark was insensitive of me under the circumstances. I ask your forgiveness and his as well."

"Ssh. We Southerners are a proud bunch and it still hurts to be defeated even when we knew we would be."

"Permit me to put Rye to bed and then we'll visit for a few minutes. If I stay longer, I fear my intentions to be honorable may be severely compromised. That dress and what it conceals remind me of all that I have missed the last few years."

Penny sat on the sofa and fluffed her skirts around her like silken armor, then smiled at the silliness of it. She knew she wanted him as much as he wanted her. To distract herself from her mounting need, she looked around at the suite that Ryan had booked for them. It was beautiful in the faded way that so much of the South had become. The drapery and furnishings were once of the finest to be had, but now were dulled by age and use. Even so they represented the best available and she was grateful to him for arranging the wedding here without questioning her about the need for the change of venue. She had to stop herself from dwelling on the rancor she felt that it had to be so.

Ryan peeked back through the door into the adjacent room and announced, "Rye's sound asleep. I can't believe he didn't awaken even when I tucked him into bed. But then I don't know much about little ones at this point." Ryan's mouth twisted with wry humor.

"Not to worry. You'll learn fast."

"I think we need to get busy and make another baby so I can watch it grow. I regret that I've missed the first years of this one's life."

"I regret that too, Ryan," Penny said. "As for working on another, it will be my pleasure, sir."

Ryan studied the face of the woman who had taken him in and saved his life when he lay injured on the battlefield near her home. Lifting a glass of champagne, Ryan said, "Here's to our family, the one we have now and the ones we will make. And here's to the woman I adore with all my heart, now and always, only you, no other. Not now, not ever."

"I'll drink to that and to the man I'm going to wake up with every morning for the rest of my life." Penny drank of the champagne and then set her glass on the table. "Ryan, I'm really worried about some of the things that are going on around here."

Ryan merely nodded to her to continue before settling her against his shoulder. He leaned back on the sofa stretching his long legs before him and waited.

"Remember Rye telling you about the man that we found dead on the way here?"

Ryan nodded again as she continued. "He'd been hung, and judging by the sign left on him, the KKK is responsible. Brett knows about the group and says that people feel forced into this kind of vigilante-ism because of the abuses of the troops and the Regulators. I asked Brett about whether he and Pa are involved but he says they're 'not doing anything stupid.' I'm not sure that was an answer to what I asked."

"This is serious, Penny. I know because Lieutenant Colonel Augustus Boernstein, the military commander here, has asked me to represent the government in cases of this kind. Neither the military authorities nor the police under the mayor, John Hough, are going to just look the other way. Despite the on-going conflicts between the military and the local police, they are united in this. People that take the law into their own hands will be punished if they are caught. If Boerstein didn't already have so much on his plate, even more vigorous pursuit of these groups would be assured. I'll talk to Brett and try to warn him not to get involved." Ryan looked troubled when he added, "I'm representing the government now in a case where a Negro was hung for some offense by the local KKK. Unfortunately for the defendants, there were witnesses willing to testify. These men who feel more than justified in what they did to exact punishment for the man's crime are just as guilty of a criminal act. I suspect they're going to be facing a noose themselves."

"Gracious me, I don't think the war and all this mess will ever end. People are still so worked up about it all."

Ryan studied her face as she said it. Pausing to consider his words, he picked up her hand and looked into her eyes. "Darling, was there a problem with getting married in your home? Don't misunderstand. I'm more than glad that it's here. I just couldn't help but wonder, especially since your father didn't come."

"Let's just say, this seemed the better option." Penny bit her lips with embarrassment just before he leaned closer and planted a gentle kiss on them.

Ryan solemnly pledged, "I'll make it up to you. I promise. Someday your family and friends will accept me. I'll see to it."

"I love you no matter." Penny gave herself to the ardor of his kiss. When it threatened to weaken her resolve to wait for the sanctity of their marriage vows, she drew back. "You'd better get some rest. Friday, August 4, 1865 is going to be a momentous day."

"Rest yourself! We're both going to need it." Ryan stood and drew her into a goodnight kiss. "Tomorrow you'll be Mrs.

Madison. I'll see you at the church at one o'clock.

Long after Ryan left, Penny sat lost in thought as she sipped the remainder of the champagne. Worry for them all made her restless. She wished the War Between the States and the current hostilities could all be miraculously erased from the calendar of history, but she knew it could not. All of them must somehow find a way to cope with an alien world they could never have envisioned and dangers as deadly as those of any war.

3

Penny adjusted the train on her gown once more as Brett held her bouquet of fragrant pink roses. The church was hot despite the open windows. The few people in attendance were busy waving fans to create a semblance of a cooling breeze. July was a hot month under the best of circumstances and the tension of the moment only increased her discomfort. *Please God,* she prayed, *let me get it right this time. This time my parents aren't the ones choosing the man. This time I'll have no one to blame but myself if it is the wrong decision. Why am I thinking this way when I know I love this man and have never loved anyone else this way?*

She jumped at her brother's light touch on her shoulder. "Calm down, Sis. This is a wedding not an execution. If you've got any doubts, there's no firing squad to stop us from leaving."

Penny looked up with troubled eyes. "I know. It's not that. It's just that I was so miserable with Daniel. I don't ever want to feel that way again. It was so very alone even when I was with him. In fact, it was lonelier when I was with him."

"I can walk down this aisle and tell Ryan you need more time."

"No. I love Ryan. I know that, and I want to marry him. I just want it to be good this time."

Brett squeezed her hand, "Marriages come with promises, not guarantees. Whether it works or not will be up to the two of you. I can see you love each other and there sure are some sparks flying when you're together. You've got a son you made from those sparks. Now it's up to y'all to keep the old fire burning and make a good life together."

"So when did you get so wise, brother dear?" Penny gave him a fond smile.

"I think I was one of the fortunate few and was just born this way." He winked.

Penny squared her shoulders and turned to face Ryan as he stood waiting for her beside the altar. "Oh, for goodness sake, just walk me down this aisle and give me away before your head explodes from pure ego."

"Ego? Me?" Brett turned to Rye. "Okay my man, take hold of your mama's other hand. We're going to go hogtie you a papa."

"We hogtie a papa?" Rye looked at his uncle in astonishment.

"You can just explain all this to him later. Now, march." Penny looked at her brother in amused exasperation. "Just wait until you get married. I'll fix your old apple cart, my boy."

"No marriages in my future. I've decided to become a monk." He whispered under his breath as they started down the aisle.

"Better choose a church that's mighty free thinking then. One that doesn't mind women and liquor." She hissed back.

They arrived at the altar grinning. Ryan looked only at his bride. In the heavy satin gown with roses pinned in her hair, she glowed with radiance. He felt his heart burst with pride that this beautiful, exceptional woman loved him enough to be his wife. He smiled down at his son who was struggling to get away from his mother to reach a penny he had spotted on the floor under the front pew. Reaching down, Brett towed Rye from under the pew while the congregation snickered. The proud little boy emerged with the errant penny clutched in his sweaty palm.

When asked who was giving the bride in marriage, both Brett and Rye answered. "I am."

Penny stepped forward and took Ryan's arm. Neither of

them could have recalled their automatic responses after that. They stood lost in one another's eyes. With hands entwined, they waited for the words of the ceremony to be done. Penny offered tremulous lips for the kiss that Ryan bestowed as the preacher intoned, "I now pronounce you man and wife."

The organist pumped away with vigor as they made their way down the aisle, giggling like children when she missed a note. The playing of music during the wedding was a break with tradition that Penny was glad Ryan had requested, even if the woman delivering it was a little inept. When they reached the narthex with the strains of Mendelssohn's "Wedding March" ringing in their ears, a modest number of guests had gathered at the front door of the church to offer their congratulations. There they were engulfed by the people that Ryan held dear: first his mother, Martha, and then Isabel, his sister.

Caroline Framingham stepped up when they had finished welcoming her into the family. Penny studied this elderly woman who had so befriended Ryan and his family with interest, knowing that Caroline was returning the same scrutiny. Although the years had faded her looks, it was apparent her immense vitality and zest for life had kept her spirit youthful and her tongue tart.

"Well, girl, it's about time you married this boy. He's been missing you for one mighty long spell." Caroline ignored Penny's offered hand and instead gave her a long hug. "He's the son I never had. Now you're going to be the daughter I've always wanted, so just get ready."

Ryan could see his mother bristle at the presumption from Caroline and hastened to soothe ruffled feathers before some further remark from the two women spoiled the moment. "We're lucky, darling. We have not only my mother, but also my adoptive New Berne mother to spoil us. The trick of course is to avoid having them both bossing us around."

Every the peacemaker, Isabel smiled at the group. "Gracious me, I'm just glad to have another woman to share their orders. Penny, you're as gorgeous as Ryan promised and I cannot wait for you to teach me about herbal medicines. Ryan says you are a veritable miracle worker."

"He's much too kind." Penny instantly liked Isabel's open warmth. "I'd love sharing what I know and I could use an assistant to help me gather herbs and wild plants. I don't know what is available here so we'll have to go exploring soon."

"I'm the only thing wild here." Brett walked up to Isabel who's serene beauty appealed to him and offered his hand. "Brett Bartlett, brother to the bride. Now that we're sort of family, Miss Isabel, I have the honor of requesting your help minding this little scamp for a few days."

At the mention of the child, Martha looked in the blue, blue eyes of the small boy and blanched as though she had seen a ghost. Caroline saw the direction of her gaze and looked as well. The two of them stood agape as they stared at this child and the man that Penny had just married. Penny knew they both had noted the remarkable resemblance, as well as the name they shared. Realizing that Ryan had not told them the truth of the child's paternity, she felt a small frisson of incipient anger that he had not acknowledged his son to these people that formed the nucleus of his life. Lifting her eyebrow in unconscious imitation of the gesture that Ryan had seen all to often on Caroline's face when she was annoyed, Penny coolly tapped her brother's arm.

"Brett, do you think you and Isabel could manage Rye for a little while. I need to speak to Ryan for just a moment."

Ryan knew from her face she was upset and he knew the reason why. The women's exchange of glances from his son's face to his own had been too obvious to miss. When they rounded the corner of the white clapboard church, he took her in his arms and stroked her back. "I know you're upset, darling. I just didn't know how to tell them the truth. Since we didn't really decide what or how to say anything about it before I left, I hesitated for fear it would be the wrong thing and I would merely succeed in scandalizing them. Let's just let the dust settle a bit before we pile that on."

Penny took a deep breath and looked into those blue eyes she so loved. She could not blame him for saying nothing. She didn't know how to do it either. Her anger died as quickly as it had sprung to life. "I know. For a minute, I was upset but I'm fine now. Let's not let this spoil the best day of my life."

When they rejoined the group that was waiting at the front of the church, Penny noted that Brett was wasting no time in charming Isabel. He had his mouth to her ear and was apparently amusing her with something audacious. Her surprised laughter suggested that his sense of humor and good looks were not unwelcome. Ryan was happy that Isabel was enjoying herself with a man. Since the death of her fiancé, Phillip, early in the war, she had studiously avoided male attention. Perhaps her time of mourning had run its course.

Not waiting to be asked, Brett picked up Rye and joined Isabel, Martha and Caroline in Caroline's carriage. Ryan and Penny followed behind them on the road to Riverview and the celebration. The other wedding guests who had been invited to the wedding feast followed in their own buggies. On sudden impulse, Ryan detoured from the little parade of buggies at the entrance to Fair Bluff. He did not want to wait any longer to show Penny the new home of which he was so proud. He could only pray that she would love it as much as he. He was thankful that Isabel's trip to Baltimore to retrieve the family heirlooms he wanted and the one to New York to buy new furnishings had still left large gaps in the interior. Now Penny could choose the additional things she wanted for their home. He held his breath as they rounded the bend in the path and the house appeared through the embracing canopy of trees.

"Oh, Ryan! It is gorgeous. And what a beautiful view to wake up to every day! I'm going to love it here."

"Would you like to see the interior now or after the party?" Ryan waggled an eyebrow in blatant suggestiveness.

"Somehow in the interest of propriety, I think we had better wait for that tour," Penny said as she cupped his cheeks in a tender caress. Their son was enough of an incipient scandal that she did not intend to create another by appearing at their wedding supper looking rumpled and bedded before they had even entertained their guests.

Ryan heaved a mock sigh, "Okay, wife. I'll have to wait I suppose."

When they walked into the parlor at Riverview they were surrounded by guests waiting to meet the woman who had won the hand of the elusive Mr. Madison. Caroline's attorney, John Harvey, nodded merrily from across the room where he had ensconced himself at Martha's side. Ryan knew if John had his way, his marriage would not be the only one in the Madison family and by the expression on Brett's face it appeared as though it might become contagious. Despite his protestations of eternal bachelorhood, Brett was clearly smitten.

Ryan noted that Brigadier General Charles Paine, commander of the Eastern District, was standing with Post Commander, Lieutenant Colonel Boernstein, and Mayor John Hough. He was pleased to see Boernstein and Hough in amiable conversation. Despite some recent confrontations between the two factions they represented they seemed to be dealing affably enough with one another. Ryan led Penny over to the three men just as Boernstein was pontificating on the filth, the agitation, and the illegal gambling that plagued his soldiers. "I tell you, sir, much blame can be laid at the feet of those who disseminate liquor in this town. It is an abomination."

The blush that spread across Penny's face, when she took his hand on introduction, was not from shyness. She was glad they did not linger for more talk of liquor as she recalled her own past contributions to the area's liquor supply.

Penny spied an excited Rye chattering up at Caroline who had given him her undivided attention. As they watched, Rye reached up and patted Caroline's cheek. They did not hear what he said, but Caroline swept him up and held him cuddled against her. As she kissed the top of his head, a dreamy look suffused her face. Penny smiled at the sight and commented to Ryan, "It looks as though both Brett and Rye have made the conquest of two lovely ladies."

"That would make me happy on both counts. I don't know if I told you but Isabel was engaged at the beginning of the war. Her fiancé was killed not long after he enlisted. Any number of Union officers would have been happy to keep her company after she and mother joined me here but she would have nothing to do with them. I think Brett is just what she needs. As for Caroline, she and her husband never had children. I suspect Rye touches a part of her heart that has laid dormant all of her life. He will be good for her, too."

"And for Rye. I confess I have been so worried about how not seeing Pa, Mammy and Nancy will affect him now that we have moved here. They so dote on him and he absolutely adores them. Brett is a big favorite, too. Fortunately, I suspect Brett will do a lot of traveling back and forth." Penny looked fondly at her brother. "I never realized how very much I had missed my brother while he was away in war until he came home again. With Mama dead and Pa so upset with me, I feel as though he is the only family I have left."

"Although I have said it before, I do hope your father will soon forgive you for marrying me. Tell me what I can do to help make that happen. I didn't marry you to take you from your family but to add my family to yours."

"Don't worry, Brett will work on him. I really don't know what you can do other than give him time and not resent his animosity."

Brett walked up with Isabel on his arm, "I feel my ears burning."

"I was just telling Ryan that you have decided to become a monk. I wondered if he might know a monastery that would accept you." Penny couldn't resist teasing.

"Oh, Brett, I had no idea you were considering taking vows?" Isabel looked both shocked and crestfallen.

"I assure you, Isabel, at the moment there is no monastery that could hold the appeal that you do. Please don't pay my sister any mind. She enjoys teasing me." Brett turned to Ryan, "There are times when I find myself hoping you're a wife beater."

"I have far different ideas about what I'm planning to do to your sister, I assure you." Ryan returned his grin. "Besides, I suspect this sister of yours would beat me far worse if I ever tried."

Blushing in embarrassment, Penny turned to Isabel. "I think you're going to have some help with Rye for the next few days beyond that of this reprobate of a brother of mine. It looks as though Miss Caroline is really enamored of him. I hope your mother will take to him as much as she has."

"Don't worry about Mother, Penny. I'm sure Ryan has warned you that she can be difficult but she means well. It just takes Mother a little time to work through things in her mind and then get to the place she needs to be. Trust me, she is going to love both you and Rye. Besides, any woman that has made my brother as happy as you have is bound to be really special."

"Thank you, Isabel. Your brother makes me happy, too." Penny smiled up at her new husband. "I think you should introduce me to some of the people here."

Ryan took her by the elbow and led her around the room. Although she doubted that she would ever remember all of the names, she couldn't help taking note of Hattie, John Harvey's niece, who had all but sniffed when she was introduced. Not understanding the animosity, Penny had nodded and moved on. Ryan muttered in her ear, "Don't worry about her. She was congenitally afflicted with a case of contrariness."

"Remind me to steer clear of her then," Penny whispered back.

Ryan realized that Hattie still smarted from his continued rejection of her, despite her marriage to his former aide de camp. He knew the man adored her and could only hope that would suffice to encourage her to confine her venom to someone other than Penny. Had it not been for her husband, Bobby Richards, and her kinship to John Harvey, Hattie would not have been invited.

A far larger worry than Hattie lurked like a predatory animal on the edge of the group. He suspected Lizzy Berkely had not been among the invitees, especially since she had not been at the wedding. He could not imagine his family would have done so knowing her aspirations before he had announced his engagement to Penny. Perhaps he had led Lizzy on with his lackluster courtship in the waning weeks of the war. Despite not giving her reason to think that his ultimate goal was marriage, she had assumed so. Knowing how brazen she could be, he suspected either spite or intense curiosity...perhaps both, were responsible for her presence. He had no intentions of introducing her to his new wife. Lizzy, however, felt no need for the formality of an introduction. He saw her angling their way and tried to steer Penny away, but Lizzie caught up with them before he could assure their escape.

"Well, so you're the lady that took Ryan away from little ole me. I'm Lizzie Berkely, Mrs. Madison. Mr. Madison and I were very good friends during the war, weren't we, darling?" She asked as she purred at Ryan.

"Certainly we knew one another, Miss Berkely. However, I think you presume to make more of our acquaintance than justified." Ryan remarked with cold precision.

"Well, Miss Berkely, any friend of my husband's is of course a friend of mine." Penny's voice had a deceptive sweetness, but Ryan caught the edge of steel in the tone. "Ryan, do let's see what Rye is saying to Miss Caroline. Please excuse us, Miss Berkely."

"I'll see you around, Ryan." Lizzy called as they walked away.

"I have a feeling I'm not going to be seeing much of her if I can avoid it," Penny commented.

"I can assure you I have no desire to see her myself." Ryan echoed just as they reached Caroline.

Immediately that eyebrow arched over the sage old eyes. "No need to tell me who you don't care to see. I assure you she was not invited. I just hesitated to toss her out on her ear when I saw her arrive. However, I think I will have a wee word with that wayward bit of baggage, if the two of you will entertain this boy of yours for me." Caroline didn't wait for their reply or for a comment on the wording of her last sentence.

"Well, Rye, what do you think of Miss Caroline?" Ryan asked.

"She's fun and she asks lots of questions. She's nice."

Ryan watched the elderly woman make her way through the guests to where Lizzie had inserted herself into the group conversing with the Mayor. "I think we're going to need to have a little private meeting with Caroline sometime soon about Mr. Rye here. What do you think?"

Penny signed, "I think so, too. And your mother?"

"I think we may want to wait on that until I can tell which way the ground lies." Ryan smiled, "Don't worry. It will work out. Besides, we have two ready allies in Isabel and Caroline. They have already told me how thrilled they are that I married you."

"I'm pleased to hear it." Penny cast a longing glance at the buffet table, "This food looks wonderful and I am starved. I haven't eaten anything at all today so the champagne is making me a little giddy. Do you think it's all right to pause for something to eat?"

"Of course. I'm hungry, too. Then I think we need to say our goodbyes for the evening. I'm ready to take you home with me." And that is the understatement of the year, he thought. He ached for the want of her in his bed.

With demure lowering of her lashes, Penny whispered, "That sounds like a marvelous plan." The heat in his eyes made her burn with the need of him.

When they had eaten, Ryan and Penny bade the wedding guests goodnight saving Rye for last. Scooping him up in his arms, Ryan asked, "Do you think it would be okay if you stay here with your Uncle Brett and Aunt Isabel. Your mother and I are going to spend a few days with just the two of us. Then we're going to come get you and take you to our new house where there's a special room just for you. You can wake up every morning looking out at the river. Do you think you'd like that?"

Rye looked thoughtful for a moment. "Can we go fishing in that river?"

"That we can. Let's think: today is Friday. Would you like to go fishing Monday?"

"I would. I'll get Uncle Brett and Aunt Isabel to help me dig worms."

"Not I, my boy. I'm afraid of nasty old worms. But Isabel says she'll get them for you. Right, Bel?" Brett grinned at Isabel as she wrinkled her nose in distaste at the idea.

"I think you fish with baby shrimp or something like that, so no need to dig worms." Isabel smiled as Brett slid his arm possessively around her waist.

"If either of you need anything, do let us know. Rye should be fine but he's never spent the night away from me before."

Penny whispered in Isabel's ear.

Penny wasn't sure if she would be okay without *him* near *her*. For so long he had been the center of her world and the focus of her love. Now she had to learn to share herself with a husband as well as her son. Yet she wanted this time alone with her husband. Sympathizing with her anxiety but eager to begin their honeymoon, Ryan guided her to the waiting carriage. On the steps, Isabel, Brett, and Rye stood waving goodbye as they drove down the drive.

The early evening brought a brisk breeze from the water, cooling the darkened land. The moon was rising over the river when they pulled to a stop near the house. Caroline's servants, Beulah and Rufus, had come over earlier to help light candles and prepare Ryan's home for the arrival of his bride. Laying the reins across his lap and leaning over, Ryan kissed Penny gently on the cheek. Penny smiled up at her husband. Looking at the mass of the house, the golden moon, the twinkling stars, and the shimmering, light-flecked water beyond, she made a silent prayer this marriage would be blessed one for them both.

"I'm going to carry you over the threshold and show you the house. After that, I'll take care of the horse while you get settled. Our bedroom has a tub big enough for two filled with water. I told them to put in boiling water so the warmth would last awhile. It should still be a little warm." Squeezing her hand, he added, "I'll join you in it as soon as the horse is stabled."

"I remember what you told me at Pleasant Glade. You said then you intended to have a tub big enough for two someday. No more wash basins for us!" Penny smiled at the memory of that evening.

"Oh, I keep my promises. Especially that one." Ryan grinned.

"Now, Mrs. Madison. Stand up."

"Of course, Mr. Madison."

Ryan scooped her into his arms and mounted the steps of their home. Struggling not to drop her, he managed to turn the doorknob and kick the door open with his foot. Giving a quick glance around the foyer and adjoining rooms, he was pleased to see the house had been made ready for his bride. Candles were glowing in the sconces and chandelier. In the foyer, fresh flowers, gracing a tall vase centered on the antique pier table, were reflected in the gilt mirror hanging behind them. Through the open door of the parlor he noted that the few pieces of family heirlooms he had requested from the family home in Baltimore had been carefully unpacked and polished to a rich satiny sheen. He stood Penny on her feet in the foyer and gave her a minute to look around. Her gasp of pleasure was a welcome reassurance, as he had feared she might not like what he had done.

"You like it? If you don't, I want you to feel free to change it."

"I like it very much." She admired the spacious hall foyer leading to French doors overlooking the river. Penny ran her hand down the smooth top of the pier table. "This is exquisite. Is it one of your family's?"

"My father selected that for our house in Baltimore." Ryan could not hide a note of pride that it was now in his possession. Painted by a local artisan, Hugh Finlay, in 1820, his things were much sought after in the Baltimore area and beyond.

"Your father had excellent taste."

Ryan laughed, "Better than my mother's." Ryan had made it a point to select items chosen by his father or those inherited from his grandparents when they sold the Baltimore house.

"I see my luggage has already been unloaded." Penny spotted several of her boxes gleaming in the moonlight that spilled through the French doors.

"Those are household things. Your toiletries and clothes are upstairs in our bedroom. Shall I show you the way?"

"Why don't you take care of the horse? I'll find our room and get the things unpacked that I'll need for tonight."

"You won't need much." Ryan grinned at her, "Keep the bathwater warm. I'll be back as quickly as I can."

4

Marcus walked slowly down Queen Street looking at the new buildings going up and the repairs to old ones. With the war ended, Kinston was busy readying itself for a new era. Despite the frustrations of military occupation and the misery of defeat, there was an underlying sense of optimism in most of the people he met and talked with. He had come to town to visit the post office and buy some pantry staples. Such former luxuries as coffee, tea, sugar and flour were once more available on merchants' shelves.

In Peebles' grocery shop he selected the items he wanted and stood behind a young woman. His attention was riveted by her low musical voice as she chatted with the clerk. As he waited, he studied the riotous mass of silky black hair that she had caught behind her head with a red ribbon. Her slim figure was clothed in a drab gray dress that was worn but clean, enlivened with new red trim, and neatly pressed. Not many people had new clothes and those worn during the long years of war showed their age and extended use. It was obvious to Marcus she was making do along with everyone else.

Marcus found himself shifting from foot to foot and wishing she would turn around so he could see her face. He cleared his throat hoping that would cause her to look back. It didn't.

The merchant finished tallying her purchases and turned the paper for her to see the total. Pointing at the end of the column of figures with his stubby pencil, he announced, "That will be three dollars and twenty eight cents, Miss Rouse."

The young woman opened her purse and extracted three one-dollar bills and then began counting change. "Dear me," she exclaimed as she rummaged through her reticule. "I think I am a quarter short. Could you wait until I fetch my father to finish paying for this or put it on account?" She winced with embarrassment when she saw the strange man watching her in amusement.

Marcus handed her a quarter and said, "Permit me, Miss Rouse." He noted that she had a pert nose, clear green eyes, and cheeks that had reddened under his scrutiny.

"You know, sir, that ladies cannot accept gifts of money under any circumstances."

"Well then, shall we call it a loan until you pay it back? I could charge interest if you prefer?" he laughed at her hesitation.

"I will pay you back just as soon as I find my father, but if you want to charge interest, I suppose you can." She reluctantly handed the proffered coin to the merchant who was struggling to contain his mirth. All three were well aware that the store had always extended credit to frequent clients.

"Allow me to introduce myself, Miss Rouse. I'm Marcus Cauley. I'm from Belle Terre plantation over on British Road near the Woodington community."

"I'm Lena Rouse. Our house, Sycamore, is west of town."

Her items were in her basket and she was turning to leave. Quickly he sat his things on the counter. "Miss Rouse, if you will give me a moment to pay for this, I'll be happy to walk you to your buggy and carry that basket for you. It looks mighty heavy to me. Of course, I need to protect my investment in your purchases as well."

"Why, thank you very much. It is heavy." Her dark lashes swept down, shading her eyes.

Marcus knew then she was interested and flirting. She intrigued him. He was more than a little determined to find someone to fill the void left by Penny's departure from his life and this girl might just fill the ticket. He knew he wasn't over

Penny. A piece of his heart would always belong to her, but he would move on. At thirty-six, he looked younger than his years but if he wanted a wife and a home filled with children, he could not afford to wait. He'd already lost fourteen years mooning after a woman he could never have. By the time he had settled Lena into the wagon to wait for her father, he had secured permission to call on her the following Sunday afternoon to reclaim his quarter. Marcus walked off whistling.

His ebullient mood was short lived. Near the corner of King and Queen Streets he heard a commotion from the direction of George Taylor's tavern on King Street. Judging from the froth of men spilling from the doorway, tempers were high. Flying fists and crude shouts assured him he didn't need to join the fray. He had turned on his heel prepared to walk away when he heard his name shouted from the crowd. Looking back, he caught sight of John Bartlett. Penny's father was hurrying his way.

"Wait up, Marcus!" John called.

Marcus waited for the older man to catch up with him, then nodded his head in the general direction of the tavern, "What in tarnation is going on back there?"

"Hell. The whole blamed town is in a stew this morning. The train pulled in with a load of white Union soldiers that took a notion to 'appropriate' some bread from the government bakery before the train left. The Negro troops assigned to guard the bakery wouldn't back down. If it hadn't been for the train whistle blowing no telling what would have happened. Then a bunch of carpetbaggers in the tavern there bragged about how they were going to be running things. Some of the locals took exception to the idea." He shook his head, "While I might have swung a few punches in my day, I'm too old for those shenanigans now. Can't say as I blame them though. We're in for some troubled times, I can tell you. Major Edward Fuller, the commander of the post here, is going to have his hands full today."

Bobbing his head in agreement, Marcus said, "I'm afraid you're right. Any more talk about the KKK?"

"I heard they hung a darky over near Dover. I don't know what it was all about, though."

"I haven't heard anything about it either. Maybe Brett will know something when he gets back since he's got to go right by there." Marcus's mouth set in a grim line when he thought about the reason for Brett's trip to New Berne. He could see John's mind had followed the same path.

"Damnation. I can't believe I've got a damned son of a gun Yankee for a son-in-law. I'll be damned if I know what gets into Penny's head sometimes. She was always a willful one, but I never credited her with being a traitor to her own kind."

"In all fairness, John, I don't think she sees it that way." Marcus added cryptically, "I really think she loves the man and maybe has for longer than we know."

"There's a meeting of the KKK over at the Becton's farm the night Brett gets home. I'm planning to go and I suspect Brett will, too. You want to ride over with us?"

Marcus took a deep breath and hung his head, working his mouth before he answered, "I suppose so. It sure looks like we're going to have to do something sooner or later. It's so damned lawless at the moment there ain't no telling what's going to happen around here. The military government ain't worth a hill of beans and that passel of darkies that's enforcing things is pretty near worthless. Looks to me like they picked the worst of the bunch to lord it over us."

John grimaced, "It's not a pretty picture, that's for sure. I suspect it's going to get a bunch worse, too."

"I agree. I'm not sure the KKK is the answer, though." Marcus shook his head.

"Probably not, but when people get desperate they turn to anything that offers any relief. Right now there's not much else out there to cling to." John took a cigar out of his pocket and sniffed with appreciation. "Damn, I'm glad the war's over if for no other reason than smoking a good cigar and drinking a cup of real coffee."

"I don't smoke cigars so I can't remark on that, but I sure am glad to have coffee again." Marcus smiled, "If you're on your way home, I'll ride with you."

"I'd welcome the company. Where'd you leave your horse?"

Marcus pointed, "Round the corner. I see you've got yours here. Give me a minute and I'll be right back."

They had mounted their horses and were trotting down the street when the sound of police whistles announced a half-hearted attempt to break-up the melee. The carpetbaggers, who were getting the worst of it, did not have eager rescuers in the local police. The fighting didn't end so much with the police interruption, as just wear itself out. John looked back and laughed. "I reckon that trash will think twice before getting into it again with us locals."

"They have other ways of making life miserable. Don't think they won't get theirs back. After all, they're in the catbird seat now." Neither of them realized just how prophetic those words would be.

Marcus left John when he reached the lane into his own property. Jeremiah, Lucinda's boy who had been fathered by Penny's first husband was playing in the dirt in the edge of his yard. Marcus worried about the hostile and uncommunicative boy.

Both he and his mother had sizeable chips on their shoulders. Although Jeremiah was only six years old, he had a cold surliness around whites. Lucinda was worse. Attractive, well-spoken, intelligent and the owner of fifty acres Penny had given her at Daniel's death, the woman could have any number of local black men at her beck and call if she would not hold herself in frosty aloofness from them. She watched white men like an arrogant cat stalking a lowly mouse. Marcus worried that her ambitions, resentment, and haughtiness would create repercussions. Riding past, he saw her standing in the doorway of the former overseer's cottage that she had received along with the land. Lucinda sidled from the door, then lifted her chin at him and tossed her head. Her stance was both seductive and challenging. Her dark beauty and smoldering sensuality made him more than a little uneasy. There was a part of him that wanted what she dared him to take. It frightened him that he might. He needed to court Lena with haste he decided, as he rode past with only a cursory nod to the woman on the porch.

He suspected his failure to appreciate her overture would annoy Lucinda. The bang of her door assured him of it. He would need to be very careful to give her a wide berth to avoid any problems from that direction. Marcus forgot about her as he settled his horse in the stable, saw that the animals had been tended, and the overseer he had hired was getting settled into the new cabin he had built for him. Marcus had hesitated at the expense but knew the plantation was too large for him to manage alone. In the long run the man would make him more money than he cost. Or so Marcus hoped.

Calvin Smith stepped onto the porch of the overseer's cabin as Marcus walked past. His battered straw hat did little to hide the sallow yellow of his complexion, nor the greasy ends of blond hair protruding from under the brim. "Evening, Mr. Cauley. I got them animals took care of and been kind of settling myself in. I expect we're going to have to hire us some more hands to work them crops next season. You got a lot of land here we can get some good from."

"This spring with the war just ended, I didn't get the chance to get things rolling. However, by next spring we should be able to clear the weeds from the fallow fields if we can find the workers; maybe clear some more land." Marcus looked across his fields and visualized green crops growing there. He could not help the smile that stole across his face when he thought of it.

"By the by, just exactly who is that darky woman over yonder. She is one mighty high strung bitch, appears to me." Calvin rolled his chaw in his jaw and spat a brown stream of juice into the dirt at his feet.

Marcus scowled. "Steer clear of her and there won't be any problems. She's a fish out of water here. She's too educated to want to associate with most of her own kind who never got the chance to get her learning, and she's too proud to stoop. She's not a bad one, just angry at the world." Marcus added without considering the ingrained prejudices of the class of man he was addressing, "My neighbor, Brett Bartlett, and I thought we might see if we could build a little cabin over on the edge of the woods by the road and hire her to teach reading and writing to the neighborhood field-hand's children." When settling on the plan, they had agreed it was not only good for the children but might serve to keep Lucinda out of trouble. Brett, always sensitive to the nuances of others, had initially arrived at the idea of a school for darky children. John Bartlett had made his adamant dislike of the notion quite clear. Failing with him, Brett had come to Marcus and the two men had agreed to build the school together.

"Ain't sure that'll set too good with white folk around here. Giving darkies education and all." Calvin spat again, before commenting, "She sure ain't a bad looking piece of tail though."

"Don't even think about." Marcus' face quickly settled into a scowl. "If I hear tell of you making any trouble in that direction, you're out of here. Do you understand me?"

"Yeah. Reckon you make that real clear. I sure don't mean to get in the way if you're interested in her for yourself." Calvin spat another stream of dark brown juice.

"I'm not. That's not my point. I said leave her alone. And, I damned well mean it." Marcus felt his temper rising as he walked away. He could only hope that Calvin would not prove to be more trouble than he was worth. Maybe when his family arrived, he would be less tempted by Lucinda's obvious charms.

He sat at the table eating the supper prepared by his cook, Bessie, who had worked for the previous owner, Fitz Kennedy. He ate without thinking, still annoyed by the cracker overseer's comments. When he finished his meal he wiped his mouth with his hand and handed Bessie his plate. She took it without comment and turned her back to him. Marcus wondered what he had done to annoy her. For that matter, he wondered why her husband Bacon seemed cold and uncooperative the last week or so. Had Calvin crossed them, too, he wondered. Shaking his head in exasperation, he took his hat from the hat rack and stomped out the back door.

He had not planned his destination. It was with some surprise that he looked up and realized that he was standing in Lucinda's yard. He stood there a minute kicking at some acorns that lay at his feet. Her hound barked sharply and then stirred from his lair under the front porch before sidling up for a wary sniff of the man. Knowing him, the cur ambled back to his sandy bed and resumed biting fleas.

"Who's out there?" Lucinda called from her raised kitchen window.

"It's me, Marcus. Would you mind coming out to the porch? I want to talk to you a minute."

"Allow me a moment to put away the last of our supper, and I'll be right with you. Please make yourself comfortable."

Marcus never failed to be shocked at the proper diction and the elegantly gracious way the woman spoke. Penny's mother had schooled her well. Whether blessing or curse only time could tell, but so far it had been nothing but problematic for the woman. Now he wanted to waste no time putting the idea of the school to Lucinda. He also worried whether or not he should warn her to steer clear of Calvin.

While he waited for her to come out, Marcus propped the slat-backed chair against the wall, faded gray by time, and hooked his feet on the crossbar. Jeremiah slid around the corner of the porch and looked at him for a long cool moment. Marcus studied the face of the boy that looked so much like Penny's first husband, Daniel Kennedy. Once again, he wondered at the ways of the world and how twisted and mangled the lives of people could become when caught in the mesh of deceit and desire.

The boy's eyes were old, older than time and filled with the knowledge of evil and hatred. It made him shrivel inside when he looked into them and a chill crept down his spine despite his effort to control it. This boy was a small package of trouble waiting to grow big enough to exact revenge on those he targeted. Marcus wondered if Lucinda had seen that in her son, or perhaps, Mammy Rena or Moses, his grandparents. Perhaps if they recognized it in time, they might be able to fix whatever was broken in the child. He exhaled and then muttered, "I sure to God hope so."

"Well, Marcus, what brings you here this evening?" Lucinda inquired as she stepped through the door onto the porch.

Her coy smile accompanied the cool words, unsettling him. He found himself sputtering, unable to get the words out. Marcus felt his face burning with embarrassment.

"Did the cat get your tongue?" She laughed, enjoying his discombobulation.

"I'm sorry to disturb you this evening, but Brett and I have been wanting to talk to you about a proposition we would like to make to you." The moment he saw her lips curl into a knowing smirk he regretted the inopportune phrasing. "I mean, we'd like to ask you about a project we have in mind."

"Pray tell, what would this project be that you are both so

interested in?" The sudden flatness of her eyes gave no clue to her thoughts.

"We want to build a school for the field-hands' children so they can learn to read and write. Thought we'd put it over there," Marcus pointed to a plot by the road next to a grove of oak trees. "I suspect in years to come some schooling is going to be a lot more important for these children than it was before the war. We can't think of anyone around here more qualified to teach them than you are."

He watched in silence while he waited for her answer, unable to decipher her expression. It was so long in coming he began to fidget. "Of course, if you're not interested we could try to find someone else. It's just that you are one of the few among your people that's got any education..."

Her voice sharp, she interrupted, "Did I say I wasn't interested?"

Taken aback, Marcus replied, "Well, no."

Again she was silent as she watched him shift uneasily in the chair. After several tense minutes, she remarked, "You have succeeded in surprising me, mister white man. I never hoped to see the day when a man around here would be willing to build a school for my people. Are you planning to pay me for teaching as well?"

"Well, ah. Well, sure." Marcus hesitated, as they had not discussed the need for paying her. "I'll see if the other planters would be willing to contribute based on the number of their workers who have children in the school. In the meantime, Brett and I will cover the cost. The state might even be willing to help pay for it."

"Make it worth my while. I need some money to run things around here and pay my taxes." Lucinda smiled, and pausing, added. "This is the best job offer I ever hoped to have. I will do this so my child and the others will grow up able to do something besides labor in a field." Her face lit with animation.

She laughed delightedly. "I'm a happy woman. Let's build that school."

"Soon as Brett gets back here, we'll get right on it. I suspect he'll be home by tomorrow or the next day at the latest."

Marcus pondered his next words before continuing, "I think you ought to be careful to steer clear of that new overseer of mine until his wife can get here and keep him in line. He seems to think you might welcome his attention. I've warned him to stay away. Do you think you can handle him if he comes sniffing around?"

"If he values his manly parts, he won't come messing with me." Her eyes went cold when she said it. "He's a mean one. You'd be wise to send him packing tonight. If you keep him, there will be trouble...if not with me, then with someone else. Crackers like him hate us. In particular they hate someone like me who is more educated and better spoken. I've been waiting for a burning cross to show up in my yard some dark night. Once I start teaching my people, I'll be a bigger target."

Marcus and Brett had not considered that potential source of trouble when they dreamed up the school. He knew she was right and that it would be up to them to protect her. "Lucinda, I don't know quite how to put this, but I'm going to do my best to say it without setting you off like a firecracker." He worried his mouth a minute. "Some folks think you put on some mighty tall airs. There are others that think you're sending out some strong signals...I mean, they think you're kind of inviting them to indulge their, ah...ah..." Marcus gulped with embarrassment and continued, "...carnal appetites. If you can sort of change those perceptions, it'll make our job of looking out for your safety a lot easier."

"I'll live up to my end of this bargain and see to it they have no cause to mess with me. Now the rest of you live up to yours."

"I'll see to it." Marcus walked the dark path back to his

house. And owl hooting in the distance and whippoorwills calling in the pines added to the symphony of night noises generated by a host of cicadas. The stars looked bright enough to reach up and grab like fireflies. The peacefulness of the night added to his sudden feeling of satisfaction. After his conversation with Lucinda, he realized she was a lot more decent and approachable than he had given her credit for. Perhaps her air of provocation was mostly just plain boredom and the lack of any man she considered a serious suitor. For the first time he thought he could see beyond her obvious sensuality to what had so enamored Daniel of her.

Marcus went to bed dreaming of the girl he planned to court come Sunday. He didn't hear the creak of the overseer's door. He did not note the footfalls on the path to Lucinda's house. He didn't see the man crouching in the weeds on the edge of her yard watching the lamp-lit window until she extinguished the flame.

But, Lucinda knew Calvin was there. It was as if she could smell him. Even before the dog emitted a low-throated growl, she knew. Hearing the dog, she reached over to snuff out the light. Grabbing a butcher knife from the kitchen table, she took it with her as she padded on bare feet to her cot. It would be a long night with little sleep, but she would be ready if he came for her.

In the uneasy darkness Lucinda watched the moon carve an arc across the section of sky framed by her window. She sniffed like a hound. She was certain she could smell the scent of the man as he crouched there. After long wakeful hours, she heard a rustle as he slithered back to his own cabin. She pulled the sheet over her shoulders and rolled over. The last thought she had before surrendering to sleep was of the unexpected salvation that had come her way. She would be a teacher.

5

Penny had arranged her toiletries and was just stepping out of her chemise when Ryan reached their bedroom. She turned when he entered and stood there with only her auburn hair for covering. Sudden shyness caused her to reach for her robe but the heat in his eyes assured her it was a waste of time.

Ryan stood a moment in silent appreciation of his bride. "Well, Lady Godiva, as I live and breathe. You are one beautiful sight. Give me one minute and I'm going to climb in that tub with you."

"Please do. I need you to scrub my back," Penny said as she batted her lashes in blatant parody.

Ryan laughed as he removed the last of his clothes. "I plan to scrub more than your back, wife of mine."

In the small hours of the morning, Penny awakened to her husband's kiss as again he made love to her. Sated, they curled into a spoon and slept until Caroline's crowing roosters announced the beginning of a new day. She stretched languorously as she opened her eyes and looked past his muscled shoulder to the open doors that ushered the cool breeze of morning into the room.

Beyond the undraped French doors that led to a balcony, the blue water of the Neuse River sparkled in the morning sun. It promised to be a cloudless day. She loved awakening to the expanse of water and sky that lay beyond the bedroom, a view so different from the dark oak and pine forest that encircled Pleasant Glade. She surveyed the room that Ryan had crafted for them. The bed was an elegant Charleston rice motif bed draped with mosquito netting to protect them during the night from the yellow fever-carrying mosquitoes that infested the area. She mused that drapery was as needed as the netting, as it would darken the room on mornings when they might wish to sleep late. Suddenly her decorating visions were interrupted. She gasped with surprise when Ryan grabbed her in his arms and rolled her over on top of him.

"Mrs. Madison, I'm glad you're awake as I am planning to ravish your delectable self one more time before we go down to breakfast." Ryan smiled up into her eyes, "I have a feeling we're going to be one tired married couple for awhile. I can't seem to get enough of you."

"Well, rest assured, I'm not asking you to." Penny laughed as she rocked her body on his, eliciting an immediate response.

The sun was well on its way to midday when they arose from the bed. When they descended the stairs and walked to the dining room, Penny saw that the sideboard had been lavishly furnished with breakfast. Ham, biscuits, eggs and grits kept warm in chafing dishes were waiting next to strawberry jam, butter and sliced peaches. The aroma of coffee wafted through the open door.

"I'm delighted to see that food waiting for us. I was in no mood to go hungry until I could fix something," Penny remarked.

"I'm nigh unto starving myself. All that activity has made me ravenous."

"I think 'ravenous' is a pretty good description of you, Mr. Madison, my dear."

"You're not complaining, I hope?"

"Far from it." Her face lit with happiness. After her loveless first marriage with Daniel Madison, a union bereft of any real passion and warmth, Ryan's desire for her gave needed reassurance.

After breakfast Ryan took her on a buggy tour of the area

along the river. He pointed out local landmarks and explained Caroline's vision for the park that she had charged him with creating at her death. Penny listened with interest, interrupting on occasion to ask questions. "Obviously she adores you and puts much faith in you. I hope that I will become her good friend as well."

"I can tell she already likes you. If that were not the case, you would know it, trust me." Ryan laughed, "Miss Caroline doesn't pull her punches."

They rode on in companionable silence with the rhythmic clopping of the horse's hooves and the twittering of birds, providing a lulling counterpoint. After a few minutes, Penny inquired, "I can't help but ask where the wonderful breakfast came from. Do you have house servants already?"

"I do. They have only just started. Miss Caroline recommended them to me as they once worked for her. Kirby, the man you met day before yesterday, is my all-purpose man about the place and his wife Gerty is the cook. Since we are newlyweds, they are making themselves scare to give us some privacy. Miss Caroline's servants have been coming over to help out too, but still need to find someone to help with cleaning. I'll need to find a gardener, as well, as the grounds are somewhat extensive. At least they will be when the landscaping is complete. I also want another horse or two, as soon as I can find the right ones. However, so many were killed in the war that it's a problem finding any at the moment."

"Since I don't know anyone here, I'll leave that all up to you." Penny smiled and pointed over the water. "Look there's a sailboat out there. How I would love to be on it."

"Do you sail, Penny?" Ryan looked at her in surprise.

"Heavens, no. There was nowhere for that in Kinston. Not enough open water and not enough wind, but for some reason I've always wanted to. I'm not sure I'm brave enough for it though."

"I'll make you a deal. I'll take you sailing. I have a boat and I love it. If you don't like it, I'll take you back to shore then and there. Let's see what the weather is tomorrow. If it's good, we'll do it."

"Okay, I think." Not being a swimmer, she was suddenly dubious, "I think I need to learn to swim, too. That way I won't be afraid."

"My word, you're even more of a little rebel than I knew." Ryan grinned at her, "That's a good idea. We must make sure Rye learns. Living on the water this way, it is too dangerous for him not to know." Ryan looked at the expanse of the river and began planning an excursion.

The following morning dawned bright and beautiful with a suitable breeze for undemanding sailing. A strong wind that kicked up waves would not be a good introduction. He wanted her first sailing trip to be a positive one. If she enjoyed it, they would take future trips to some of the islands and sites that he had grown to love. He could envision taking Rye with them to Cedar Island to see the wild Outer Banks ponies, shipwrecked there in decades past. Rolling over, he cuddled Penny to him and whispered in her ear, "Wake up, lazy bones. I'm taking you sailing."

"Hmm. Give me a minute to wake up." Penny wiggled closer into his arms.

"On second thought, I think we need to stay in bed a few minutes more. After all we do need to get well acquainted."

Penny turned into his kiss and soon they were lost in a private world of bliss. When they had finished making love, she signed with contentment. "I do like being married to you, Mr. Madison."

Ryan kissed her a thank you. Rising from the bed he walked over to the window and admired the view. He suspected his wife, his family and his home were his new definitions of paradise. He turned from the window to catch her watching him. He smiled at the appreciative scrutiny she was giving his bare form. While he was tempted to climb back into the bed and return the appreciation in a tangible way, he said, "Up and at 'em. Do you have anything you can wear besides skirts and petticoats?"

Looking puzzled, Penny responded, "Why no. Is there some reason for something else?"

"I don't plan on having you fall in, but should you, heavy skirts would only drag you down. Besides, Miss Caroline went sailing with me in trousers. I'll get a pair of my old pants and we'll chop the legs off so you can wear them." Walking to the cupboard, he churned about for several minutes before pulling up a suitable pair. "These will do. I'll find the scissors while you start dressing."

The water slipped past the hull of the boat as seagulls wheeled in the air above them. Stretching slim pants covered legs in front of her, Penny marveled at their comfort and her daring. Leaning back against the gunnels, she lifted her face to the sun and closed her eyes, feeling the wind whipping in her hair. She had never felt so free. Kinston had never afforded experiences like sailing and she had never learned to swim. Women were not expected to learn and many of the men in her area could not swim either. She decided in that moment she and Rye would both learn to swim as soon as Ryan could teach them. "When can we start swimming lessons? I really want to learn."

"We'll do it tonight, just as the sun goes down. Since your most appropriate attire as far as I'm concerned is very natural, it might be best not to do it midday." He laughed at the shocked look on her face.

"You're not serious!"

"Darling, until we can devise a suitably modest swimming uniform that is also not an impediment, we'll keep it simple. Besides, it sounds to me like it could be a really fun lesson."

"Maybe my chemise?"

"Maybe." He looked doubtful, enjoying teasing her.

They ate the light supper that Gerty had left for them while sitting on the veranda watching the sun go down. With the light was still soft and not too dark, Ryan guided her to a spot on the bank of the river that was protected from view. Spreading a blanket on the ground, he tossed a couple of towels onto it. "Leave your clothes here. No one will see us, I promise."

"You didn't have to go to this much trouble to get me naked, you know," Penny remarked as she began removing her clothes. She surprised herself with her brazenness. Even though she had always been adventurous for a girl, she had been conscious of societal expectations and conformed to most of them.

"Lord, I can't decide if I want to make love to you or give you swimming lessons." Ryan muttered when she stood before him clad only in her chemise.

"There's no limit you know. Why not now and after our lesson as well?"

"That is one excellent suggestion." He commented as he lowered her body to the blanket. She arched to meet him, both ready with passion. Afterwards he taught her the rudiments of swimming until she could paddle about enough to keep from sinking. Watching her, Ryan decided she was a natural and with a little more practice would soon be swimming with ease.

"I think you promised another engagement," Ryan remarked when he could no longer concentrate for watching her body sliding through the water, the wet chemise hiding none of her charms. Grabbing her in his arms, he walked with her to the blanket. He luxuriated in making slow, teasing love to her as the moonlight illuminated the hollows and mounds of her body. They came together, crying one another's name.

The following morning the newlyweds drove to Riverside to collect Rye and say goodbye to Brett who was leaving. When they arrived, a beaming Caroline greeted them at the door. In the background they could hear Rye whooping with laughter followed by equal gales from Martha. Caroline remarked, "That boy of yours has won all our hearts. If he keeps this up, there won't be a girl in a hundred miles that won't fall in love with him when he's older."

"Oh, I do hope he hasn't been too much trouble?" Penny inquired.

"Trouble? I can tell you now, if you want to leave him longer, no one here will object."

"Thank you, Miss Caroline, but we're kind of missing him ourselves," Ryan said. "Where are Isabel and Brett? We want to say goodbye to him before he leaves."

"They're walking by the river. I think they are going to be seeing quite a bit more of one another, unless I miss my guess." Caroline smiled at Penny, "He's not only one charming, good-looking rascal, but what a great sense of humor. If I weren't too old, I'd toss my own hat in the ring for that one."

"He has my father's sense of humor, or at least the one he had before my mother died." The loss of her mother was still a keen pain for them all.

Brett and Isabel strolled into view around the corner of the house. Brett called, "Hey, you lovebirds, I thought you would still be in bed, ah, *resting*. After all it's only eleven o'clock."

Isabel blushed at his casual reference to the physical relationship between their mutual siblings. Watching her downcast eyes, Brett laughed and encircled her waist with one arm; with the other he pointed to Ryan. "I need to have a serious talk with you, sir."

"Of course. Walk to the stable with me and we'll see if your buggy is hitched."

When they were out of earshot, Brett said, "My buggy's hitched; it's my carcass I'm working on hitching." Brett grinned at Ryan before adding, "I'd like your permission to call on your sister.   She's one heck of a woman and I assure you my intentions, despite myself, are honorable ones.   I know it's sudden, but when someone like her comes along a man would be a fool to dally around."

"I'm happy for you, Brett, and I'm happy for Isabel, too. Any idiot can see that she likes you.   Besides, Penny and Rye would never forgive me if you didn't visit often.   As I see it, this gives one more guarantee that you will."   Ryan reached out his hand and shook Brett's.   "Don't worry about our mother.   She can be a little off-putting, to say the least, but she'll come around."

"It just so happens that Mrs. Madison is the one that suggested I approach you as the man of the family for permission to court Isabel.   I didn't need her encouragement, but it seemed to please her to give it, so I let her think she was talking me into it," Brett laughed.

"I will be damned.   Between you and Rye, the ladies have been conquered *en masse*."   Ryan shook his head in amazement.

When they drove the carriage around to the house, so Brett could take his leave, they were all waiting.   Martha, holding Rye by the hand, had just walked up to join Caroline, Isabel and Penny.   She wiggled an eyebrow at Brett as though to ask, *well, did you?*

Brett smiled and gave her a thumbs-up.   Turning to Isabel he asked, "Would you allow me to walk with you for a moment? There's something I need to ask of you before I leave."

Isabel's blush betrayed to Ryan that she knew what it was that the two men had discussed and was more than receptive to the idea.   His mother was beaming her approval as Caroline gave Ryan a smug I-told-you-so smile.   Martha remarked, "I'm so happy for her.   I worried that it took her so long to get over Phillip's death, but I think Brett has succeeded in winning her heart."

"We Madisons know our hearts well enough to spot the one

for us when she comes along. I know I did and in not much more time than it has taken Isabel and Brett," Ryan commented as he gave Penny's waist a squeeze.

"It seems the Bartlett's know a good thing when they see it, too," Penny added with a laugh. "At least now he's going to be visiting us regularly, for sure."

"Uncle Brett's coming to see me in two weeks. He told me," Rye said, holding up two fingers on his right hand and counting them with his left.

"Good boy, Rye!" Caroline congratulated. "We've been teaching him his letters and numbers. I hope you will allow him to come by daily as it has been so much fun for us all to work with him."

"I'm going to be an Eskimo, Mama. They live where it's freezing cold. Uncle Brett taught me how to Eskimo kiss. I show you." He reached up and tugged at his mother until she brought her face down to his, then he gently rubbed her nose. "See. I can Eskimo kiss."

"So I see, honey." Penny gave him a hug, realizing just how much she had missed him in the days away.

Rye chatted all the way to Fair Bluff. It was obvious that Martha, Isabel and Caroline were immediate favorites and he was excited about living on the river with new sights and new places to explore. When he saw his room overlooking the water he squealed with delight. His hobbyhorse and other favorite toys were all ready in place, Kirby and Gerty having worked to unpack his things as well as Penny's.

The following morning, Ryan made love to his wife before riding into his office to see what new cases might have arrived in his absence. His assistant, a fellow officer with some education but no real studies in law, was organized and efficient. Ryan knew under Charlie Morton's care things would have ticked along with no real problems in the few days without him.

While he was catching up in New Berne, Penny and Rye explored the gardens and woods that encompassed Fair Bluff. While they walked, Penny took the opportunity to survey the wild areas for needed herbs and plants that she could use for her teas and medicines. Noting each plant that would be useful in a small notebook that she carried, she was able to determine those that she would lack and need to plant. If New Berne were anything like Kinston, she suspected once word got around that she was skilled in home remedies, she would not lack for custom. She hoped not at any rate, as it was something that made her feel needed and gave her tremendous satisfaction despite the sometimes-arduous work.

Rye babbled as they walked, stopping to chase errant seagulls or to pluck a wildflower to present to her. He also picked a bouquet of them to take to the ladies at Riverside. When he walked over after the noon meal he presented the wilted flowers with the same confident assurance a beau would have presented a bouquet of the finest roses. Charmed, all three ladies cooed with delight that he had thought of them. Penny left him for his daily lesson with Martha and Isabel, as she and Caroline strolled the gardens that would someday form the nucleus of the park Ryan had told her about. It was obvious that Caroline was bursting to have a private talk with her.

"I trust you and Ryan are getting settled in over there?" Caroline began.

"Yes, we are. Kirby and Gerty are a big help. Thank you so much for finding them for Ryan. I wonder if you could recommend someone to help with cleaning and gardening? Ryan told me to ask if you know of anyone."

"I'll ask around and let y'all know so you can interview them."

"Thank you. That would be such a help." Penny pointed to a plant in the garden, "That's comfrey isn't it?"

"Oh, that's right, Ryan said you're an herbalist." Caroline turned to where Penny pointed, "It is that. If you wish, I'll share some with you so you can plant it in your own garden."

"I would like that. There are a number of plants I need growing wild in the woods here, however their are many others I'll have to plant. I thought later in the fall, I would return to Kinston to collect some bulbs and plants from my garden there. Any you could add are most welcome."

"Come over anytime you like and take what you need." Caroline swept her arm around the garden, "It could use some thinning out. Martha and I have done some of that but there's a lot more that can be done."

"I'm happy to help you. Just let me know when."

In companionable silence Caroline and Penny walked down to the water where they stood for a long moment watching the waves slapping peacefully against the sandy shore. Turning, Caroline lifted one eyebrow in a high arch and looked her in the eye. "You can tell me it's none of my business and dismiss me as just a meddling old woman, but there's something I've been wanting to ask. You see during the war, there were times when Ryan was very despondent. Once he let it slip that he had lost the woman he loved. I thought he meant that she had died in the war and he didn't correct me, but he mentioned her name. 'Penny' he said. Are you that Penny?"

"I am." She confessed and then taking Caroline by the hand and leading her to a bench, she proceeded to tell her the story of their meeting and the ensuing love affair. When she reached the part of her story telling of her pregnancy with Rye, Caroline just nodded sagely.

"I knew he was injured in the first battle of Kinston and spent some time convalescing there." Caroline winked at her, "Even my old eyes can see that the boy is the spitting image of his father. I'm just so happy that Ryan found you again and that you married. I'm happy your boy has his real father to love him." Caroline patted her hand comfortingly.

"We're going to have to talk to Miss Martha, too. It's such a scandal, I must confess we both dread the thought of disclosing the whole thing to her."

Caroline snorted. "Well, don't. Both Isabel and Martha have eyes in their heads. They know Rye has to be Ryan's son and they know you're the reason no woman around here stood a chance with him. Would you like me to tell them your story? It might be less embarrassing for you."

"I'll think about it and I need to ask Ryan how he wants to handle it. Since you all have it figured out anyway, it takes some of the pressure off trying to hide it. I confess we have both been embarrassed to bring it up. We realize that our actions were less than admirable."

Caroline winked at her, "There are bigger sins in this world than that. I'm glad that a new life came from that meeting between Yankee and Rebel. Rye helps make up for so many that were lost. And he is adorable, I must say."

When Ryan and Penny talked later, they decided dinner at Caroline's the following evening offered the perfect opportunity. They would sit the three ladies in the parlor and tell them how they had met and fallen in love. Feeling as though a great burden had been lifted from her, Penny settled in his arms that night, more peaceful than she had felt in days.

She awakened in the night, listening to the rumble of distant thunder that drew ever nearer. However, it was not thunder that aroused her, but a vivid nightmare. She prayed it was only that and not one of the visions that sometimes came to her in the night. In the dream, she had seen them all clinging to a boat in a raging storm. Suddenly a huge wave crashed over them. Ryan had grabbed for their son and held him fast, but she had been swept away. She left their bed the following morning tired from hours of restless tossing.

"Are you well, my dear?" Ryan asked with concern when he noted the circles under her eyes.

"I didn't sleep well. Just a bad dream and then that storm, I suppose..." her voice trailed off. "Ryan, help me to swim better and let's teach Rye, too. Soon."

"Of course. We'll do it this afternoon as soon as I return. And everyday until you both swim like fish. Now, un-knit that brow and stop worrying about that dream, I'm going to take good care of you both." Long before Penny had asked, Ryan had decided to teach Rye to swim. The river that swept across the front of their lawn was a shining magnet of temptation for any little boy.

6

Marcus sat at the family table surrounded by as many vociferous Rouses as could be packed in. Lena's mother was a prodigious cook and a tireless talker. He didn't worry about the need to respond, as any remark by him would have been as inconsequential to the flood of words as an autumn leaf floating in a stream. Occasionally Lena caught his eye from the opposite side of the table and grinned in amusement. He concentrated on the savory dishes that continued to circle around the table. Just when he felt his belt would burst if he ate anything more, Frances Rouse and her husband Wiley rose from the table signaling the end of the meal.

"Why don't you two young people, take a spin in the buggy," Wiley offered. "We came straight home from church and I didn't unhitch the horse yet so it's ready and waiting."

Surprised at the unsolicited offer and the subtle acceptance of his courtship of their daughter, Marcus hastened to respond, "Thank you very much, sir. I'm happy to take you up on it."

Lena placed her hand on his arm and he led her to the buggy where he assisted her in. Marcus swung himself up beside her and slapped the reins on the back of the waiting horse. It was a beautiful late October day freshened by a lively wind that stirred the yellowing leaves of the surrounding sycamores that gave her home its name. Marcus guided the buggy to the road and leaned back beside Lena who remained quiet. Content, he allowed the horse to amble at his own pace.

"That was a wonderful dinner your mama cooked. I don't think I have ever eaten so much."

Lena laughed, "Mama can sure cook and she for sure can talk. I do declare she could talk the ears off of a deaf mule. I hope you didn't mind being surrounded by so much family, though, every time you come to my house? It's just that there are a passel of us and it's traditional for everyone to wind up at our house after church."

"I don't mind. In fact it kind of makes it easier on me. I'm not much of a talker so I didn't have to worry about what to say to your folks with all the talking going on." Marcus cut his eyes at her and smiled. "Besides, you're the one I really want to talk to, but every time I look at you I plumb forget what it was I meant to say."

"And why is that, Marcus?" Lena asked, hoping she did not sound too coy.

"I think you know. I've been coming for these dinners for several weeks now, so I guess it's no big surprise to anybody that I am mighty taken with you."

"My goodness, I thought it was my mother's cooking that kept you coming back." Lena teased.

"Well, that sure doesn't hurt anything," Marcus chuckled and took a deep breath. He figured the time was as good as any to pop the significant question in his mind. He knew he wasn't over Penny and probably would always regret that she had spurned his love, but Lena suited him well enough and he assumed in time his fondness for her would become love. "Lena, I think you know by now that my intentions are pretty serious. I would like to ask your father for your hand in marriage, if you have no objections?"

Lena went still. She sat staring for long minutes at the puffy clouds in the sky before turning to him. Quietly she answered, "Yes, Marcus, I accept. I wish you could tell me that you love me as I do you. I hope in time you will. For now, I'm willing to wait."

Marcus started to protest and assure her of a love that he

knew he did not feel, but she stopped him with her finger against his lips.   A wistful smile crossed her face and slowly faded away. "Don't. Not now."

"I promise I will make you the best husband I know how to be. I'll take care of you and treasure you all of our lives. You won't regret marrying me, Lena. I swear it."

"I know you'll be a wonderful husband, Marcus. Now let's go tell Ma and Pa. They've been wondering when you'd get around to asking," Lena giggled.

"Oh, Lord. Am I that transparent?" He groaned.

"Well, when you told Ma you hoped she had taught me how to cook as well as she does, it was something of a clue to your intentions. By the way, I can cook but nowhere near as good as Ma, so maybe we should move into Sycamore instead of Belle Glade," she joked.

"You couldn't wedge me in here sideways with a shoehorn," he said with a snort. "So, I guess you're just going to have to come on over my way, Missy."

"You've told me so much about Belle Terre that I'm impatient to see it. Now that we're engaged, do you think I could ride over sometime and have a look? I could get my brother to drive me over."

"Of course. In fact, I should have invited you over myself long before now. It really is a nice house with plenty of room for a family."

"Let's get married, then we'll talk about how much room we'll need for children," Lena tittered nervously in sudden embarrassment.

Marcus rode home late that afternoon satisfied that come December his mission to marry and begin a family would reach fruition. Her father had smiled his pleasure when Marcus asked for Lena's hand in marriage. Wiley called an unsurprised Frances into the parlor and told her, too. Soon the entire swarming tribe had surrounded the couple, crowing with delighted remarks and jibes. Wryly, he wandered if the exuberant throng even realized when he departed. He looked forward to a happy family to surround him in his own home, if not quite such a large one as the Rouses' brood.

When he turned into the drive to Belle Terre at dusk that night his nostrils caught the scent of burnt wood wafting on the humid air. Puzzled, he lifted his head and sniffed like the old hound that hung around his back door. He knew something was either burning or had burned. Alarmed, he spurred his horse down the lane to his house, the scent growing ever stronger. When he drew near Lucinda's cottage, the source of the odor loomed against the darkening sky. Standing in the yard at a lopsided angle stood a crude cross. The last of the flames had died leaving smoldering cindered remains. He reined in and swung to the ground.

"Lucinda, Jeremiah! Are y'all in there?" he called in alarm.

"Just a moment, Marcus." Her voice wavered when she answered.

While he waited, he used his foot to shove the cross to the ground. It was obvious from the hoof prints that had churned up the dirt yard there had been a large party of KKK'ers on the property. Furious that they would threaten someone that was under his protection and that of the Bartletts, he kicked the charred wood with disgust. He pledged then and there that he would have nothing more to do with the clandestine group. For him, the nobly stated aims bore little resemblance to their acts. A piece of fabric lying nearby caught his attention. The torn dress told him what else had occurred. Just as Lucinda emerged from her door, he stooped to pick it up.

"Don't. Just leave it there," she choked. "I don't want that filth."

Marcus turned to face her, ashamed by what his neighbors and friends had done. When he saw the quiet fury on her face, swollen by the blows she had suffered, he realized any apology would be inadequate. "I'll get Mammy and Moses to come over and be with you. It's best you and your boy not be alone right now. I can see you've been hurt, but is Jeremiah okay?"

Lucinda grimaced, "He ran off while I was being violated. I haven't seen him since. He's hiding out there somewhere. I'd be grateful if you would find him before you go for my parents."

"Don't worry, I'll see to it." He heaved a heavy sigh and shook his head.

Lucinda's eyes glittered with suppressed rage. Pointing toward the shattered and charred cross, her voice was tightly controlled when she demanded, "You know why this happened, don't you?"

Marcus looked into the dark well of her eyes. "Tell me."

"Apparently they resent that school you and Brett are building. I don't think they wanted to tackle the two of you by burning the school, but they didn't hesitate to come after me."

"I'll find the bastards responsible for this. When I do, I'll see to it they're punished."

Her laugh was colder than January sleet. "You know that's not going to happen. Who do you think is going to arrest most of the white men in the county? Forget it. Just don't stop building my school. I'm damned well not going to be scared off. They only way they can stop me from teaching my people is to kill me. Now go. And please find my boy for me."

It was long past dark and he was ready to abandon the search when the rising full moon illuminated the fields behind his house. He found Jeremiah crouching among the dried stalks of corn. The moonlight glinted on the boy's face. Dirt-caked mucous glistened like silver on his dark skin where he had cried, smearing his nose with his hand.

When Marcus reached for him, he recoiled and struggled to push him away. "Come on, Jeremiah. Let's go home. Your mama is mighty worried about you." Again he tried to get the child to get up from the dirt and to come with him; again the boy pushed him away. "I tell you what, why don't you just follow me back to your house. That way I know you get there safe and sound. Can you do that?"

Jeremiah glared at him and without speaking, stood. Weary, Marcus walked in the direction of the cottage, judging only from the sound of the boy's steps whether or not he was following. When they reached the child's mother, she enveloped Jeremiah in her arms and began crooning to him.

Marcus felt compelled to ask, "Do you know who molested you?"

"I know him."

"Him? Only one?"

"Only one."

Immediately Calvin's leering face loomed in Marcus' head. He demanded, "Tell me and I'll see to it he's punished."

"Don't worry, he will be." She looked over her child's head at Marcus and waved him off. With reluctance Marcus left them on the porch and went for her parents not knowing what more he could do. It would be many months before her child spoke to anyone.

It was a weary man that lay on his bed that night not even bothering to undress or to turn back the sheets. Over and over Lucinda's parting words pounded in his head and he worried what she might do. With tempers so high, any effort on her part to punish the man responsible would only make matters worse for her. Sleep was slow in coming and fitful when it did. The weak light of a dawning day brought him to his feet. He walked to the chest in the corner of his room and poured water into the basin. Quickly he splashed it on his face, grimacing at the new lines that had etched his features overnight. With a determined step, he walked to the barn to saddle his horse. He was going to find Brett and see what he might know about the attack on Lucinda.

The last person he wanted to deal with was lounging against the barn door when he walked up. Marcus supposed the overseer was competent enough, but he just could not like the man. Even the arrival of his family had done little to ameliorate Calvin Smith's obsequious, yet at the same time, somehow surly disposition. "Morning, Calvin."

"You up mighty early, ain't you?" Calvin asked as he scratched at the crotch of his dirt-caked trousers intent on dislodging unwelcome guests.

"Lot of things to tend to." Marcus walked past, and then reconsidering, turned back to Calvin who was still acting like he needed to support the door. "You see anybody sniffing around here last night?"

Calvin stiffened. Casting wary eyes at Marcus, he asked. "What for you asking?"

"Lucinda had a visit from the KKK. I was just curious to know whether or not you saw anything." Marcus watched the man through squinted eyes.

"I don't go studying on that uppity bitch since you warned me off of her. I ain't got no clue what is or ain't happening over yonder." He looked off in the distance as he said it, and then spat brown juice into the straw floor of the barn.

Seeing no point in asking the man any more questions about the raid, Marcus ordered, "See to the fence in the back pasture. I didn't like the cows getting out down there last week. That repair you made was a little too makeshift. It was hard enough to buy those cows and I sure don't want to have to try to find more. Besides, they cost a precious lot right now."

"That ain't no lie. I'll get on it right after breakfast. My missus ought to be about finished fixing it by now." He heaved himself away from the doorjamb and shuffled off in the direction of his cabin.

Marcus shrugged his shoulders in weariness. He would have to look for someone to replace Calvin. He could feel a mean streak in him not far below the surface that boded ill for the future. Good overseers were out there, it just meant more time and energy spent looking for one. "Oh, well. I guess it just can't be helped," he muttered to himself as he finished saddling the horse. Again he wondered if Calvin was telling the truth about the attack on Lucinda.

Both Brett and his father were standing in the yard near the paddock talking when Marcus rode up. From the grim set of their faces, he surmised they were well aware of the events of the previous evening. Hitching his horse to the paddock fence, he joined them. "Morning John, Brett. Guess from the looks of you, you heard about the happenings over at Lucinda's last night?"

"Yep, her Aunt Delia told us about it this morning when she served our breakfast. She was some kind of worked up. Mess like this is sure stirring up the few darkies we got left to work for us." John shook his head. "Looks like we're in a fine pickle. In the absence of law and order around here, we form a vigilante group to protect ourselves and they just end up causing a bigger ruckus than they're worth, dam it to hell."

Brett added, "Some of the locals are fighting mad about our school. They're bucking like a bunch of jackasses with a bee up their ass. You notice the three of us weren't informed about last night's little get together. They know we would have argued against it since you and I are the ones behind the school in the first place."

"You know one of them raped Lucinda in front of her little boy?"

"Hell, that's the first thing Delia told us. You know we don't hold with that sorry business. I'm afraid you're going to need to be talking to that overseer of yours. Word from the darkies is he's the one that did the raping," John said with disgust. His eyes went hard as he added, "We take care of our own folks. I'm tempted to go kill the son of a bitch myself if the darkies don't get him first. Not that I'm all excited about that school, mind you. I just don't hold with messing with our darkies. Lucinda grew up in my own house, playing with my children. I feel responsible for her, even if I don't like some of her ways."

"I understand. And don't worry. I already decided to let Calvin go. He's nothing but trouble anyway. If you hear of anyone looking for his job, let me know." Marcus looked at the sky, watching a crow circling over the trees at the edge of the pasture. "God dammit! I'm tempted to kill the bastard!"

"Sure wouldn't be any great loss except maybe to his missus and young'uns, but he's not worth the gunpowder it would take to blow him to hell. If he were, I'd have already done it. Everybody knows the law is not going to get worked up over a darky that got herself raped." Brett laughed bitterly. "I don't know about you, Marcus, but Pa and I are finished with this KKK business. It's just too damned rotten for my taste."

"I made that decision myself on the way over here. I'm not backing off the school either. I don't give a damn who it hare-lips. I hope you're still in it with me?"

"We are. Don't worry on that score. I don't like the idea that you two started that school, but I'll be damned if a bunch of backwoods villains in white sheets are going to scare me and Brett from doing what we damned well please with our own darkies." John Bartlett pounded his right fist into his left hand in angry emphasis.

Marcus was in high dungeon when he rode up to Calvin's cottage. He had debated the wisdom of approaching the man when he was in a towering temper, but his fury was great enough he went anyway. Stopping in the yard in front of the cottage, he watched two of Calvin's brood of children playing hopscotch in the dirt yard. Dog-gnawed abandoned bones, leaves and trash littered a yard that his wife Abigail was too lazy to sweep. The children were dressed in the kind of rags that even Marcus's darkies would shun. His wife walked to the screen door and stood watching him for a moment. Finally she called, "You looking for my man?"

"I am. If he's in there send his sorry hide out."

"Just a minute, he was just finishing up his dinner," Abigail answered in a desultory tone. She wiped her hands on the greasy feed-sack apron that hung at her waist before crossing her arms over sagging breasts.

"I ain't going anywhere. Send him on out now. He's about to lose his appetite anyway."

Calvin stepped into view behind his wife's back. Pushing her roughly to one side he walked out into the yard. Judging from the shifty-eyed look Calvin cut his wife, Marcus figured he knew he was in for some trouble. Jerking the reins of his horse, he ordered, "Follow me aways. Your young'uns don't need to hear this."

Marcus rode his horse out of earshot of the house before reining him in. He swung from the saddle and turned to face his overseer. Struggling to get his temper under control he took several deep breaths before beginning, "Calvin, I want you and your family out of here by Sunday. That gives you nearly a week to find somewhere to go. If you're not out, I'll throw you out. Is that clear?"

"Mind if I ask what got you so hot and bothered?" Calvin looked up with a sneer, one eyebrow cocked challengingly at Marcus.

His eyes drilling into Calvin's shifty ones, Marcus declared, "I don't much care for low-down, sorry assed rapists. I don't intend to have one on my property. If it weren't for your family, I'd kick you out right now."

Calvin snarled, "Now wait jest a minute. I ain't no rapist and if that biggety nigger bitch says I am, she's pure damned lying."

"Nope. Somehow, I don't think so. Besides, don't you think it's kind of curious that you know who was raped before I even said anything?"

"You telling me you take the word of a sorry nigger ahead of mine?" he challenged.

"That's about the size of it."

Shifting tactics, Calvin demanded, "I want the money you owe me."

"You've been paid through last week. I'll pay you for this week and for next week. As far as I'm concerned that's a lot more generous than you deserve. You ought to be hung for the sorry scum you are. You'll be damned lucky if you get gone from here before somebody gives you your just deserts and makes your wife a widow." Marcus snarled.

"You trying to scare me, Mister Boss Man? You planning on killing me because your pet piece of ass had somebody get hold of what she was offering?" Calvin spat brown juice at Marcus's feet, missing his boots by an inch.

"I'm not threatening you at all. I'm telling you to git. You're finished here and good riddance to you. Now start packing." He glared at the man, clenching his fists to keep from bashing that snide face to a pulp.

Calvin walked off muttering about the unfairness of it all. Marcus swung into the saddle and kicked his horse into a gallop, leaving the disgruntled overseer to swallow his dust. By Saturday, Calvin and his family were packed. He came for his pay in the morning, his wife sniveling at his side. Sorry for her plight if not for her husband's, Marcus gave her an additional five dollars. He reminded them to be gone by the next day. The unpleasant chore done, he rode to Lucinda's.

"Lucinda, I wanted to tell you that Calvin and his family are moving out. If I have any say in it, Calvin won't find another job around here. That way you will no longer need to worry about him." She didn't comment, just gave a cold-eyed nod at his news.

That done, he began his journey from Lucinda's to the

Rouses' where he planned to spend the night and go with them to church the following day. As he trotted along he occasionally patted his jacket pocket, comforted to feel the promise ring that he would give Lena that night. It had taken him time to find one that he both liked and could afford. He planned to give her a better one once his farm started producing enough to warrant the expenditure. She seemed to be sensible and understanding about his priorities and he ranked that as another of her assets. Despite almost sixteen years difference in their ages, he thought they got along well enough. Both had similar values and were eager for a large family; both were hard workers and frugal; and while he liked her, he knew that she loved him. He thought many marriages had been forged from far weaker metal.

His biggest concern on the ride to Sycamore was finding a new overseer. It was fortunate for him that some of the Southern soldiers returning from war often had no standing home and no working tools and stock to run farms of their own. Brett had mentioned a former soldier in his unit who was looking for a position. From nearby Deep Run, the man would be familiar with the area and Marcus would have no problem learning something about him if he wanted. With Brett's endorsement he doubted that he would bother to check further. Fleetingly he thought of Calvin. Suspecting that he might seek some spiteful retaliation prior to leaving, he had taken Ben aside and told him to be watchful while he was away. A slave of the former owner, Fitz Kennedy, Ben was one of the most trusted and intelligent workers he had at Belle Glade. Marcus knew he could rely on him not to do anything rash and to be diligent in protecting both Belle Glade and Lucinda's property.

7

"Penny, wake up darling. You're having a bad dream." Ryan held her gently in his arms as she awakened. "Were you dreaming again about being swept away from a capsized boat?"

"No, not that. I keep seeing this man's face. He has stringy blond hair and he's lying in a field bleeding to death. I don't know him, but he's going to bring trouble. I can feel it coming..." At moments like this, Penny hated the visions that came to her in the night. The only one that had turned out well was the one that had led her to Ryan as he lay injured on the battlefield near her home. Saving his life and falling in love with him had been one of the best events of her life.

"Shh, darling. I'm sure it's nothing but a bad dream. We all have bad dreams from time to time, you know. It doesn't mean that all of your bad dreams are visions of something that is going to happen or is happening." Ryan tried to understand this gift of second sight that his wife possessed, but it eluded his sense of reason. However, with personal, firsthand proof that it was sometimes valid, he refrained from dismissing her visions.

"The moon is so bright tonight you can see everything in the room. This is the Harvest Moon. I've always loved it. It's so big and golden. Don't you just love it? I'm tempted to wake Rye up so he can go to the window and look out at the water and the yard. It's lit almost like daytime." Penny realized her nervous babble was a lame attempt to push the dream from her mind.

Ryan offered, "It's a trifle early to be waking the boy. Would you like for us to take a walk outside? The moon is getting low enough that it will go down soon and then it will be time to get up anyway. Why not get up now and enjoy the sunrise? I'm not sleepy any more anyway."

"Let's do. I'm too keyed up to sleep." Penny picked up her wrapper and pulled it over the sheer batiste nightgown. The pre-dawn air carried the first hint of the coming winter and she knew it would be even cooler by the water.

Penny leaned against her husband as they stood on the pier staring at the dark outline of the distant bank. She loved the view as much as Ryan. Looking back at their home on the knoll and the gardens that flowed down to the river, she could understand what had first drawn him here. The live oak trees on the lawn framed the house in lush green and the azalea bushes come spring would be aglow with vibrant color. The house itself was elegant but restrained, each part a necessary component of the aesthetic whole.

Her admiration of the house was interrupted by the sound of his sailboat bumping against the pier as it rose and fell on the shallow waves that slapped the shore. It reminded her of how much she had come to love sailing and being on the water. Not only had she learned to sail, both she and Rye were now proficient swimmers thanks to Ryan's diligent tutelage. Only the horror of her recurrent nightmare about the boat capsizing and her loss in the crashing waves spoiled her unalloyed pleasure of the water.

A rising breeze tugged at the flowing tendrils of her hair, chilling her. She pulled the robe tight and hugged her arms to her chest. Reaching over, Ryan pulled her against him to share the warmth of his body. They stood there, lost in one another's arms, watching the sun's first glow light the horizon.

"I'm chilly. Let's go make some coffee, Ryan. I think it's just what I need right now."

"That's sounds like a fine idea to me. I doubt Gertie is up yet. Do you think you could rustle up bacon and some of those fine pancakes you make?"

"I believe I can just do that. And as soon as Rye smells them cooking, he'll be downstairs in a quick minute. By the way, I love that maple syrup you had shipped from Vermont. I like it much better than the sorghum molasses we always used on our pancakes at home." Penny relished the fact that Ryan's wealth and contacts brought them so many of the pleasures denied during wartime, as well as new comestibles that she had never before experienced. Maple syrup and lobsters, brought on ice from Maine, now ranked among her top gustatory delights.

Ryan sat at the table as she prepared their breakfast, admiring his wife and once again gave a silent prayer of thanksgiving that she and their son were now a part of his life.

Both his personal life and his legal practice were thriving. Continuing friction between the locals, soldiers and police, as well as KKK activity provided him with a steady stream of clients. As proof of his growing acceptance and involvement in the local community, he had been elected in September to represent the district at the October 2nd convention in Raleigh. He had taken the train to the convention with high hopes. Under a directive from President Andrew Johnson, the State was forgiven of its war debts, the convention forever prohibited slavery within the State, and its secession ordinance was repealed. Most significant for returning the State to local rule, they had scheduled an election for November. Qualified voters would elect a governor, state legislators, U.S. congressmen and a number of local officials. Since the convention, both Lieutenant Colonel Boernstein and Mayor Hough, despite representing opposing factions, had approached him to run for the state legislature. After talking it over with Penny, he agreed, wondering if he would regret the increased time from home that the position would demand. Already he was spending several nights a month at Fort Macon interviewing and consulting with prisoners awaiting trial there, if elected there would be more nights away.

It was fortunate Penny made friends easily. Word of her expertise with herbs was also bringing people to her for help with various maladies. While he missed her when away, he did not worry that she would be lonely.

Rye was also thriving. His daily visit to Martha, Caroline and Isabel was yielding real results. At just over two years old, the boy already could write his letters and numbers and recognize a few words.   With the train now running smoothly on refurbished rails, Brett had been devoted in his visits to Isabel, coming at least once every three weeks. Penny and Rye looked forward to the visits almost as much as Ryan's smitten sister.

"What do you look so pleased about, Mr. Madison?" Penny smiled at the contented expression on her husband's face.

"I was just thinking what a lucky man I am. As you Southerners say, I'm as happy as a pig in slops."

Penny hooted with laughter at the incongruity of her urbane husband uttering such a homily. "I think you should just stick to Yankee expressions, darling."

"But I'm trying to fit in," Ryan protested.

"Judging from what folks are saying about how decent you were to them during the war and how much they appreciate it, you don't have to worry. I guess proof of that is you'll be representing them in Raleigh. I am so proud of you. I when Pa hears, he'll change his mind and accept our marriage. Brett says he's softened a little but I can tell it's not much. I hear Pa misses Rye sorely though, so maybe he'll come around. Besides, Isabel told me a big secret."

"So when is the wedding date?" he drawled.

"Oh, pooh! I wanted to surprise you," Penny made a little moue.

"Now, why would I be surprised when they make moony eyes at one another every time he's here? I don't know who is more smitten, Brett or Isabel. I do know I'm pleased as all heck at the whole idea. Isabel told me she and Brett are going to live at Pineview with your father after they're married. She doesn't seem to be put off by the idea of living on a farm after being a city girl all her life."

"You already know all my news," Penny remarked with feigned sadness. "So, do you know the date?"

"That I don't know."

"It's going to be during the Christmas holidays," she announced. Penny was quiet a moment before adding with a pensive sigh, "I do so hope Pa will come."

Studying her face, Ryan softly asked, "You talked of going to Kinston to help with preparing things for winter. Have you given it anymore thought?"

"I should have gone at the end of summer to help with the canning, but Nancy wrote me she had everything well in hand, so I didn't see any point. Besides, there was so much to do here to get settled in. And mostly, I couldn't bear the thought of spending so much time away from you."

"I have to go to Raleigh for a few days in November. Why don't you ride on the train as far as Kinston? You can satisfy yourself everything is fine there and let Rye visit with your father. When I come back through, I'll come to Pleasant Glade and spend a couple of days with you there before coming home."

Penny stood for a moment pondering the suggestion, "That sounds wonderful. I would so like to visit for a little while. Pleasant Glade is my home, too, and I really do miss it and everyone there. Hopefully, Pa will not only want to see Rye, but me as well."

"Good! That's settled then. Now kiss me goodbye and send me off to another day of hard work at the old salt mine," Ryan winked at her.

"Pooh! You love going to the office and you know it. Besides, you don't have to work. You work because you want to."

Laughing, he agreed, "Yes. I do enjoy being an attorney. I couldn't abide slothful idleness and I'm glad that I'm a part of rebuilding this community."

Rye walked into the kitchen just as his father swept Penny into a heady embrace. "I want pancakes, too, Mommy."

Ryan picked up his son and gave him a warm hug. "I saved you an extra special pancake, my boy." He sat his son on his chair at the table and gave Penny a final goodbye kiss, "I'll see you two later."

It was a weary remote man that returned home that night. Throughout dinner Ryan said little, responding to questions with a minimum of comment. Confused by the laconic mood, Penny fell silent. Wherever she looked up, she would catch him watching her, a worried frown puckering his brow. With the dinner cleared from the table, Penny stood and asked if he would like to go with her to tuck Rye in for the evening. It had become so much a ritual, that she was shocked when he declined.

"You go, darling. I think I'll sit on the veranda for a while. It's such a beautiful evening and with the mosquitoes gone, along with the heat and humidity of summer, it should be pleasant." Without waiting for her reply, he walked through the French doors onto the veranda.

Penny watched him reach the edge of the porch and lean against a pillar. She sensed his thoughts were far away as he stood there looking out at the silvery expanse of the Neuse River. Troubled by his uncharacteristic behavior, Penny went to Rye's room to tuck him in for the night and listened with distraction as he recited his bedtime prayer. Afterwards she walked onto the veranda, determined Ryan would tell her what was disturbing him. He wasn't there. She could see him standing on the pier looking down at the water. Sitting in the white iron chair that was still warm from his body, Penny waited.

With his head down, Ryan turned from the pier and walked toward the house. Dew had fallen on the grass scattering little diamonds of light across the lawn in the still brightness of the waning harvest moon. His footsteps left a dark trail on the glittering grass. With weary tread, he walked across the brick veranda and seated himself on the chair next to his wife. Reaching across he took her hand in his. Ryan drew a deep breath, releasing it in drawn out exhalation.

"Penny, I'm afraid I have some troubling news."

"How do you mean? Is it something to do with your work, my family, what?" Penny's voice caught in her throat as a thousand possibilities winged their way across the periphery of her conscious thought.

"Both, I'm afraid. I was assigned a new case today. Your neighbor Marcus Cauley has been charged with killing his overseer and is being brought to New Berne for trial. I've been assigned to prosecute the case." Seeing her sputtering indignation, he touched his finger to her lips, "Wait. Let me finish."

She nodded for him to continue, but her face had gone cold.

"There were warrants for the arrest of your father and brother, as well. However, with little evidence to support the warrants, I was able to squelch those, at least for the moment. It seems that there was a KKK raid on your former servant Lucinda. She was violated and a cross was burned in her yard. Some of your father's workers said that Marcus' new overseer was a part of the raid and the one that committed the crime. Your father, brother and Marcus were all overheard saying that they'd like to kill the man. That can just be the talk of an angry man and not necessarily the expression of any serious intent to follow through. Other than their words, there was nothing else to tie your father and brother to the murder of the overseer, Calvin Smith. However, the murder weapon with the man's blood on it was found behind the barn at Marcus'. It matches others in his kitchen."

"That's crazy!" Penny exclaimed in anger. "Those same darned knives are in the overseer's house and Lucinda's, too. They all belonged to my former father-in-law, Fitz Kennedy, who owned all that land before he died. I left those knives in the kitchen of the overseer's house, when I deeded it to Lucinda, and in Belle Terre, itself. I took very little from Belle Terre when I sold it to Marcus, only a few heirlooms that Fitz would have wanted kept in the family. Marcus had extras of everything which he used to furnish the new overseer's house that he built after I deeded the old one to Lucinda."

"Those are good points and I'm sure the defending attorney will use them when he prepares his defense. The biggest obstacle is the sworn testimony of the victim's wife saying that Marcus killed her husband. That kind of testimony cannot be overlooked by the court."

"She's lying. Marcus would never kill anyone. He's not that kind." Standing, she began to pace in agitation. Whirling to face her husband, she exclaimed, "How can you prosecute my friend? I can't believe you would do something so awful to me."

"Penny, I'm not doing anything to you. I will do my best to see that Marcus has a fair trial. I can't do more than that. I will find a good attorney for him if you would like. I'll even pay for it if Marcus is unable. Just don't turn on me, darling."

Ryan went to her and tried to take her in his arms, but she pushed him back with a warning, "Don't. Not now."

Penny stood leaning against the post looking out at the water in unconscious mimicry of her husband's earlier posture. Turning she commented, "It's that dream I had last night. I'll bet the man that was murdered had nasty blond hair. And he has for sure brought trouble to us and to my family and friends."

"It doesn't have to be trouble between us, Penny. Yes, it is trouble for your friend, and potentially for your father and brother. Although, I think that unlikely."

"You don't understand. Marcus helped me when there was no one else. He made it possible for me to earn the money I needed to survive the war and have the money to restore my farm. I owe him."

"It's more than that, I suspect. He was in love with you. Is that what this is about?" Ryan struggled to keep the sudden jealousy from his voice.

"Yes, he was in love with me. He asked me to marry him but I didn't, because I loved you then and I still do. Had you never come back for me, in time I might have married him. Not because I loved him, but because I didn't want to spend the rest of my life a lone widow with a fatherless child. This is not about that. I tell you, Marcus is not a murderer. Why would you agree to prosecute him? Surely you must know how very upset that would make me?" Penny glared at him. Her eyes snapped in anger as she awaited an answer.

"I knew you would be upset, yes. That's why I have struggled so to try to find a way to tell you that would help you understand my own position. I have an obligation here as a result of my military service in New Berne during the war. I know the people on both sides of the issue and I have friends in both camps. I will tell you again that I am the best choice to be the prosecutor. I will be as fair as I know how. If I can find proof of his innocence then I will make sure all charges are dropped. But if he murdered Calvin Smith, it is my duty to see that justice is done. The KKK and the vigilantism that is rampant here is the antithesis of what I believe in. I will work to see it come to an end. We cannot support these criminal acts, no matter how justifiable some locals seem to think they are." Ryan started to lift his arms to draw her close but at the expression on her face, he let them drop by his side. "Penny, I love you. I don't want to hurt you. Please try to understand."

"I gave up my father, my home, and friends and neighbors

to marry you. All I ask is that you not be party to further persecution of my people." He resented that she was being unfair. He reminded himself that it was worry for her family and Marcus that made her voice sharp. He knew on reflection she would regret the implicit accusation in her words.

"It is not persecution to seek justice through lawful means," Ryan fought to maintain his equilibrium. Taking several deep breaths to calm himself, he continued, "I would never hurt you willingly. Surely you know that? Just trust me, please."

"I do trust you. It's just that we see much of what is happening from two very different vantage points. You were a Union officer in the army that occupied my homeland. I am part of a conquered people that could only watch everything that we believed in either destroyed or irreparably changed. I didn't believe in slavery. I owned none. But I did believe in the right of the South to secede from a union it entered of its own volition. I do think we had the right to form our own government when the rule of the North became so confounding to our way of life. I hate the military government that has been imposed on us. I despise the fact that ignorant field hands have been put in the position of policing us. I abhor carpetbaggers that descend on us determined to pick our bare bones even cleaner. I resent the new tax laws enacted by these thieves that cause people to lose their homes and farms. I detest the whole mess that this war created."

"Many of your objections are valid. But you and all the other locals need to be patient. It can be resolved without the need to resort to violence."

"That vile man deserved to die for what he did to Lucinda no matter what the law says. Was anyone in the local police even trying to find who was responsible?"

"From what I understand, they didn't know except from rumor. The violation wasn't filed."

"Well, why would they worry about some poor Negro

woman? Besides, enough Southern women were molested during the war that we should all just be used to the idea by now."

"That's not fair. No one believes that this kind of behavior should go unpunished. The difference is that it is not up to vigilante committees to assume the role of judge, jury, and law enforcement." Ryan struggled not to reply with anger.

"Have they moved Marcus to the jail here?"

"He should be transferred here by tomorrow. The military police in Kinston are afraid of trouble if he's kept there."

"They well should be. Somebody would help him."

"It is not a help for his friends to take the law into their own hands. They would just end up in trouble, too."

"Could you arrange for me to see him tomorrow?"

"I'll do my best."

"Good. Then I want to go to Pleasant Glade. I want to see my brother and my father. I want to spend some time at my home."

"Your home is here with me, darling. Don't go away angry, please. Wait until November and go with me as planned when I make the trip to Raleigh."

"I don't know if I can wait that long."

"Tomorrow I'll take you to see Marcus if he's on the early train. If not, I'll take you the following morning as the last train gets in to New Berne so late they will not be allowing visitors at that hour."

"Very well." Penny ventured a contrite smile. "I'm sorry I was so angry. I know it's not your fault. Just please help him to be acquitted of these charges. Please, please don't make him guilty."

"I can make no one guilty that isn't," Ryan reminded her. "Let's go to bed. It's been a stressful day for us both and we were up early because of that bad dream of yours. I guess it wasn't as much a dream as I hoped, huh?"

"No, it wasn't a dream."

"I've never known anyone before that had visions like these. It's a lot for me to wrap my mind around. I'm glad *I* don't have them."

"There are times when I wish that I didn't. It hurts so much to know bad things are going to happen and have no power to stop them."

8

Jesse Kennedy, the new sheriff, under orders of the local military commander, Major Edward M. Fuller came in the morning along with the group of black soldiers that were sent with him. Riding with them, hands tied behind their backs, were John and Brett Bartlett. Marcus caught Brett's eyes and held them briefly as they came to a halt at his back porch. He stepped off the porch and walked up to the sheriff. "I don't know what's going on here, but I can tell you that these two men had nothing to do with Calvin Smith's murder and I didn't either."

"It's like I told John and Brett, I'm mighty sorry about this but I've just got no damned choice in the matter. Major Fuller sent me out here with these sorry-assed excuses for troops to arrest you for your overseer's murder. They've got a witness that heard the three of you say you wanted to kill him. They've got the knife from your kitchen that was in his back. And they've got a widow that says you did it." Jesse shrugged his shoulders in apology, "I'm afraid I've got to take you in, Marcus. Pack up some clothes. Better get someone to take charge while you're gone, too. Ain't no telling how long it'll be. We'll wait here for you."

"Why don't you untie John and Brett's hands? You know damned well they're not murderers and they ain't running, or they would have been gone already. I'm not running either, and I intend to prove I didn't do it, no matter what that lying, good-for-nothing bitch said."

Grabbing what he could and again asking Ben to see to things in his absence, Marcus walked back to the porch where he found his horse saddled and waiting. He swung himself into the saddle and edged his horse next to those of Brett and John. He was pleased to see that Jesse had untied their hands so they could at least ride more easily.

The three of them spent two uncomfortable days in the cell in the Kinston jail. They speculated about the potential murderer, but came to no answers that would free them. During the time they were held, they had been allowed no lawyers or visitors. The guard explained that visitors were forbidden out of fear that their friends would try to free them. It would not be the first time in recent months that local folks had freed people from the jail, either under the mantle of the KKK or anonymously. They were given no reason for the lack of legal counsel.

Wednesday morning Jesse came for John and Brett. "Y'all can go on home. John, it seems that son-in-law of yours has sprung you. He got the charges dismissed for you and Brett, at least for the time being. I'm sorry, Marcus, but with Mrs. Smith's identification of you as the murderer, there ain't much anybody can do. We got orders to ship you on to New Berne for trial. I 'spect you'll be going out on the train this afternoon."

"Look, Jesse, I done and told you and told you I wasn't even to home on Saturday night. I was over near Falling Creek at the Rouse place, Sycamore, giving my fiancée a promise ring. I can damned well tell you, I wasn't studying about any Calvin Smith Saturday night. Ask the Rouses. They can tell you I was there."

"I done sent somebody over there to come in and give an affidavit to that effect. However, I still can't let you just waltz out of here. This has got to go to New Berne now. And you've gotta go, too. They're afraid if you stay here the KKK will spring you. I don't need no more jail breaks around here."

"I'm not in the KKK, remember. I only went to a couple of their meetings. I've not been since. I can for sure tell you, the three of us weren't at that damned meeting that burned the cross at Lucinda's. Hell, they're pissed at us because we're building a school for the darkies."

"Shit, Marcus. You ain't telling me nothing new. I got a deputy that was at that damned meeting. He already told me y'all weren't there. That still ain't good enough for the military. They are some kind of worked up about all the trouble the folks around here are causing. They're not backing down on this here murder even if Calvin Smith needed it. You're going to have to go to New Berne. Maybe Penny's husband can help you out like he did John and Brett. But from what I hear, he's been assigned as prosecutor of your case. I'd say that's a problem if he is as good a lawyer as he's rumored to be."

The lady seated across from him when he boarded the train had gathered her skirts with an offended sniff when she saw he was a prisoner. She had relocated to the far end of the car much to Marcus's sardonic amusement. With New Berne just a few miles away, he shifted on the seat and tried to think of something less frustrating than his current predicament. It was obvious that any hope of sleep was finished for another long troublesome night. The manacles on his legs and wrists were not just an embarrassment they were damned uncomfortable. He tried to turn his thoughts to Lena but found when he did that his brain just circled back to his coming arrival in New Berne and the trial. When he thought of his trial, he remembered that Ryan Madison would be the prosecuting attorney. And then he thought of Penny. His heart still harbored a hollow place where once his love for her had been firmly lodged. He knew that no matter how hard he tried, she would probably always hold first claim to the secret most reaches of his heart. His courtship of Lena had not taken the longing to see Penny from him. The only bright spot in the whole mess was the chance that she would be able to see him due to the influence of her husband. He could only hope that she would want to after the angry words he had hurled at her when she announced her marriage to Ryan. He missed her. Penny had been such an integral part of his life for so long that having her gone was like losing his molar when his tongue just wouldn't quit worrying at the spot.

New Berne had settled for the night when he arrived. The citizens were tucked into snug beds leaving only flickering gas street lamps and the occasional hoot of a hunting owl to give animation to the still town. A soft cool breeze brought the scent of the water to him when he emerged from the train and walked to the waiting wagon. It was a pretty town even at night. The trees were draped with leaves of red, gold, and orange where the lamplight illuminated them along the quiet streets. He looked at the dark windows and deep shadowed lawns of the houses he passed on the way to the jail, envying the peaceful dreams of their occupants. Never had he so treasured the freedom that had suddenly been taken from him. He dared not think for how long that might be and how this might all end. He prayed it would not find him swinging on the business end of a rope.

It was nearing midnight before he was left alone in his small cell. He could pick out the details of his new abode by the dim light of the lamp in the hall. Other than a narrow cot furnished with a single threadbare blanket, there was only a small table on which rested a pitcher of water. Under the table sat a lidless chamber pot. The single barred window was too high to give more than a small glimpse of the night sky. Dejectedly he sat on the edge of the cot, rubbing his wrists made sore by the manacles that had bound him on the train. It was some time before he stretched out on the makeshift bed and fell into fitful sleep. He awakened at dawn, almost as tired as when he had fallen asleep. From the other side of the door to the hall where his cell was located, he could hear voices. It wasn't long before he was served a meager breakfast of rancid boiled salt pork and coarse cornbread. He pushed it aside with disgust and drank the coffee. At least it was good.

"Mr. Cauley, you have visitors." Marcus looked up at his jailor in surprise. At this hour of the morning he had expected no one. Hoping it was Penny he sprang to his feet and hurriedly combed his fingers through his hair. Without the benefit of fresh clothes and a bath, there was little more he could do to prepare himself for company.

He did not realize it but a momentary flicker of disappointment crossed his face when he saw Lena and her father standing outside his cell. But Lena saw it and her heart plummeted.

"Lena, Mr. Rouse. It is so good to see you. It means so much, so much that you would come all this way for me." Surprised and grateful that they had gone to such lengths to find him, Marcus stammered in his haste to assure them of their welcome.

"Of course, we came, boy. We took the train yesterday morning hoping that you would come in earlier. When you didn't, we checked into the hotel to wait it out." Lena's father reached through the bars to pat his arm reassuringly. "Don't worry. We're going to get you out of this mess."

Lena added, "We gave a sworn statement in Kinston that you were with us Saturday night. We plan to be here for your trial and try to find out who said that he heard you threaten Calvin. We know you didn't kill him, no matter what you might have said about wanting to."

Marcus shook his head, "You know how men talk when they're worked up. Brett, John Bartlett, and I all said he deserved to die and we would like to kill him but none of us would have. "

"I found a lawyer for you yesterday afternoon. He says he's an acquaintance of your former neighbor, Penny Kennedy Madison. I thought you might like to have someone represent you who at least knows some of the same folks you do. I'd heard kin of hers were held with you for a couple of days before they were released."

"That's right. Apparently the darkies or someone heard them making the same statement I did, but since that was all they had against them, they were released. At least Brett and John are off the hook for the time being. I guess you heard the widow is swearing I killed her husband and my kitchen knife was the murder weapon."

"Why on earth would she say such a thing? You were at our house Saturday night." Lena looked perplexed.

"The problem seems to lie in the fact that I was late getting to your house. I tried to tell them I stopped by the Tull farm on the way. I planned to talk with Joshua Dawson about an overseer's job. Since no one was there, no one can vouch for my whereabouts."

"Someone must have seen you over that way. I'll go over and talk to some of the folks along the road. There's bound to be somebody that we can get to come forward on your behalf." Wiley Rouse again gave him a consoling pat on the arm.

"Mama made you some cookies and ham biscuits, Marcus. We tried to take food to the Kinston jail but they wouldn't give it to you."

"Thanks, Lena. I appreciate the trouble, but to tell the truth, I didn't have much appetite the last few days. Those cookies and biscuits might help me perk up a bit, though. Do thank Mrs. Rouse for me."

"Nonsense, you know by now that cooking is no trouble to Frances. She would have packed a trunk full if we'd had the time," Wiley chuckled.

Lena put her hand through the bars and took Marcus's hand. "I don't intend for my ring to go to waste. We're going to get you out of here. I promise."

"I hope you're right." Marcus replied giving her hand a squeeze.

"That's it. You folks are going to have to leave now. That's all the time you can have with the prisoner." The burly guard waited impatiently for them to leave, jangling his keys as a reminder.

Still holding her hand, Marcus pulled Lena close enough to press a kiss on her lips through the iron bar barrier. He shook her father's hand and watched the two of them leave. Again he felt regret that he did not love Lena as much as she deserved.

The guard returned with his midday meal. The coffee he drank along with the biscuits and cookies that Lena had brought. The cold grits and fatback he left on the plate where they soon congealed into an unappetizing lard-encrusted mass. He decided the food alone was enough to drive a man crazy without the enforced idleness of the empty hours. He watched the day march across the ceiling of his room, the light changing with the passage of time. No one came again until the guard brought his last meal of the day around four in the afternoon. It wasn't much more appealing than the others had been but he forced himself to eat. He wasn't sorry when the dying light of the day brought night.

It was the following afternoon when he received his next visitor, John Harvey, the man Wiley Rouse had hired to represent him. John wasted no time in explaining the seriousness of the charges and the evidence against him. Marcus thanked him for his time and again explained that he had not been at home on the night of the murder.

"That just won't wash, Mr. Cauley. The prosecutor is just going to say that you had the opportunity to do it before you got to the Rouse's. You admit that it was bedtime before you got there. Ten, maybe eleven o'clock, wasn't it? And there are no witnesses to explain your late arrival by saying they saw you at the Tull farm."

"My fiancée's father, Wiley Rouse, is going to ride over to the Tull's to see if he can find someone that saw me in the area."

"Yes, he told me that when he approached me about representing you. The Rouse family seems to think real highly of you. I know from what Mr. Rouse told me that you are a neighbor of the prosecutor's wife's family. I don't know that will have much sway on Ryan Madison but I have found him to be a fair man. He is also a tenacious and smart lawyer. I would be happier, for sure, if he weren't the one assigned to prosecute your case."

"Just do the best you can. I'm innocent and I sure don't want to hang from the end of a rope, especially for something I didn't do."

"That's the God's truth." John Harvey stood to leave. "I'll do what I can to save you from that."

Except for his attorney, the next three days brought him no visitors. Marcus grew more and more frustrated at confinement and the inability to do something to prove his innocence and secure his release. He paced the narrow confines of the cell, asked for and received a copy of the latest newspaper, and picked at the unappetizing food they brought him. The boredom became almost overwhelming. Just when he thought he could take no more, the jailer walked down the hall and announced a visitor. Marcus was lying on his cot, listless and unhappy. He opened his eyes a slit, not sure if he even cared to get up.

"Penny, my God, you came!" He sprang from the cot and hurried to the bars of his cell.

Reaching through the bars, Penny patted his arm in reassurance. "Of course, I came. I've been trying to get a pass for days but they have done nothing but stall. It seems the military commander ordered that you receive no more visitors after the ones you had when you first got here. Except for your attorney, no one is supposed to visit with you. It was all my husband could do to get me in for a quick visit." Penny noted his cramped cell before turning sad eyes to his beard-stubbled face. "I'm so sorry, Marcus. I know you're not guilty and I have done everything I know to do from here to prove it. I just can't do much in New Berne. Somehow we have to make that woman admit she lied.   Ryan is going to Raleigh next Wednesday and I intend to ride the train with him as far as Kinston.   Maybe if I spend a few days there, I can learn something that will help you."

"Don't make problems for yourself. How is your husband going to take it if you go looking for evidence to free me?   After all, he's the one doing the prosecuting."   Marcus snorted in derision.

"He's fair. He doesn't want to convict an innocent man. The problem is all the evidence is against you. I have to find something that's *for* you. Can you tell me anything that might help?"

"Look, even the damned knife that killed him is from my kitchen," Marcus said with exasperation.

"Or from the overseer's, or from Lucinda's. I can swear to that and you know it," Penny shrugged dismissively.

"That still doesn't get around the fact that someone says they heard me say I would kill him, nor his widow's statement that I did it. Why she would say something so untrue, I don't know."

"No doubt, she was angry that you told them to leave. I hear you fired her husband because of the wrong that you accused him of doing to Lucinda. In their minds, Lucinda is just a lowly black woman who has no rights and no human dignity. Plus, I'm sure he told his wife he had nothing to do with what happened to Lucinda. I mean, what man is going to tell his wife he's guilty of something like that?"

"Penny, you make sense. But making sense is not going to be enough to get me out of this."   Marcus looked at her for a long moment, holding her eyes with his. Somberly he added, "Having you have come to see me and wanting to help, means more to me than you can know. If you only knew how I care for you. I was so frustrated and furious when you married another man, because I wanted you for me. Hell, I suppose I still do. Even so, I'm engaged to marry Lena Rouse come December. I just don't know if I can ever stop loving you enough to give my heart to her the way she deserves."

"Marcus, please don't. Don't say these things. I'm married now and I love my husband, even if I'm pretty upset with him for agreeing to prosecute your case. At least, I know he's fair and he won't railroad you. I care for you. I do. I want you to be happy and I want to help you. You're my good friend and you will always be. We just can't be more than that. At one time I did try. You know I did. I just couldn't, because I already loved someone else." Penny's eyes pleaded with him to understand and forgive.

"He's Rye's father, isn't he?" Marcus didn't wait for her answer. "You know you don't have to answer that, and I have no right to ask it. I'm sorry. That's none of my business."

Penny lifted her chin defiantly, "No, it isn't. But, I will answer you anyway. Yes, Ryan is his father. I fell in love with him many years ago, and I never stopped loving him and hoping that he would return to me. I wanted to love you. You're a good man, Marcus, just not the man for me. You deserve to be loved. Lena is a lucky woman. Be good to her and let her teach you to love her the way she deserves."

The jailer opened the hall door and motioned to her to leave. Penny squeezed his hand, "I'll see what I can do to help you. We all will. Just don't give up. Promise?"

Marcus nodded, then reached through the bars and grabbed her other hand. "Would you give me a good-bye kiss, please?"

Penny leaned close to the bar and kissed the cheek that he pressed against it. "God keep you, Marcus."

When she left, he felt as though the sun had sunk below the horizon never to shine again. Despite his joy at her visit, it left him aching to hold her and bleaker than before.

9

"Child, they for sure been some miseries here since you been gone." Mammy commented as she embraced Penny. "It mighty good to have you home again."

"It is so good to be home. I've missed you all so much." Penny looked around the kitchen, pleased to see all of the canned goods that Nancy and Mammy Rena had put up for the winter. "It looks like y'all have been some kind of busy canning and preserving. I'm so sorry I couldn't be here to help you."

"That's all right. Moses help out with it and Miz Nancy. That sure is a hardworking woman. She like doing it, too." Mammy looked at the store of food with satisfaction. "They's enough y'all can take some with you to New Berne when you leave."

"That would be wonderful. I'm afraid we had no time for a large garden this year. Ryan had only a small one planted, however next year I plan to enlarge it so we can preserve enough for next winter from the garden there." Penny laughed, "Rye didn't waste any time running to find Nancy. Is she in the house?"

"She just run up to her room. She say she got a surprise for Rye she got to get."

"If that's the case, he'll get to her room before she does," Penny laughed at the antics of her happy, ebullient child. Her voice soft with regret, she added, "We've missed everyone so much. I do hope I can go see Pa and he won't be so angry with me."

"He got more on his mind right now than you being married to a Yankee man. This here mess with Marcus and that dead man has sure stirred it up around here."

Penny patted Mammy's hand in comfort. The worry lines in the woman's face had deepened in the months since she had last seen her and more gray hair peppered her head. Penny noticed that she also seemed to be moving slower and suspected her rheumatism was bothering her again. She hated to see the woman, who had been as responsible for raising her as her own mother, becoming old and feeble. Moses also seemed exceptionally frail when he met her in the yard to help her from the buggy. Although Mammy said nothing about his condition, Penny could see the worry in her eyes when she looked at her husband.

"Mammy Rena, I'm so sorry about what happened to Lucinda. How is she doing?"

"She be doing all right. But that boy of hers got some problems dealing with it. He ain't said nary a word since it happen." Mammy eyes filled with tears as she added. "I do some fretting 'bout that young'un."

"Oh, dear. How very awful for him and Lucinda, too. I wish I knew what to do for him. I'll check my grandmother's notes on remedies and see if there is anything I could give him that would help." Although she knew that the offer of herbal remedies was small comfort to a woman as troubled as this one, she did not know what else she could do to bring relief.

Mammy shook her head sadly, "I spect he mostly just needs a little time to forget about what he seen that man doing to his mama."

"I wonder if some tansy tea or maybe vervain would help?" Penny mused.

"I already give the child some motherwort, and it ain't done nothing. I done tried rosemary, too. I just don't know what else to do for him 'cept for waiting it out."

Penny puzzled how to bring up the subject that she was determined to broach with the woman without causing additional pain. Both Lucinda and her parents had a strong motive for killing the overseer. While Penny didn't believe that either Moses or Mammy would have done it, she was less sure about their daughter, Lucinda. Regardless, she decided, she still had an obligation to Marcus to help him if she could. "Mammy, do you know who might have killed that good-for-nothing overseer? I know your people talk among yourselves and often know a lot of things before the rest of us. Anything that you know or can find out to help Marcus, I'd really appreciate."

Mammy looked uncomfortable and was quiet for several long moments before she answered, "I don't know nothing for sure, but I got my suspicions."

"Do you think you could ask around and see if you can learn anything for me?"

"You knows I will. I don't want Mr. Marcus suffering for what he ain't done," Mammy said grimly. "He and Mr. Brett trying to help Lucinda and our children with that schoolhouse they built. That's a fine thing. We darkies ain't going to forget that."

"Mama. Look what Miss Nancy made for me." Rye ran into the kitchen holding up a gaily-colored patchwork snake with button eyes. A smiling Nancy was on his heels as he barreled into the room.

"My goodness, that thing is big enough to ride." Penny grinned at her son as she swept Nancy into her arms. "Thank you so much. He's going to love it."

"It was fun to make. I got to use up a lot of those scraps I've been saving, not to mention about half of this year's cotton crop just to stuff it," Nancy laughed. It was obvious that she was delighted with the joy that Rye was receiving from her gift. With no prospects for children of her own, Rye was surrogate for the son she would never have.

"For goodness sake, I didn't think we had any cotton this year."

"Just what came up voluntarily is pretty much all."

"Well, I'm going to have to get someone to run this place and get it producing again. I just didn't have opportunity to do much this year. I guess Marcus and I both need to find ourselves a good overseer."

"I kept meaning to write you about that. I have someone that I think you'd be right pleased with. My nephew, Jeremy Davenport, just got married and he's looking for a farm to sharecrop. With his family as big as it is, the other brothers have just about taken care of all the farming to be done on the family place. He could use a good farm to run until he can afford to get something of his own. I know the boy is a hard worker and his daddy has for sure trained him in farm work. His wife is a real nice young woman from Pink Hill, one of the Turner's. I'd be mighty pleased to have them living here and helping me out with this place provided it would suit you."

Penny offered a silent prayer of gratitude. "Dear God, Nancy! I'd be thrilled to have Jeremy and his new wife come here. What is her name?"

"Tillie. She's as pretty as a speckled puppy and a good little cook. You're going to like them both."

"Perfect. Let's ride over to his daddy's place tomorrow and talk to them."

"No need. I already wrote him and he's going to be coming here. He says he might know someone that would work for Marcus, too. Until Marcus can get back here, he's going to need someone to run things."

"That's for sure. It doesn't look too promising for him at the moment."

Nancy hesitated, "Penny, your brother and father asked if they could come over for supper. Mammy and I have kind of planned a nice supper for y'all tonight and set things up in the dining room. I hope you don't mind?"

"Mind? I'm thrilled. I have so missed Pa." Penny felt like

twirling for pure joy. Having been the apple of her father's eye for most of her life, the last few months laboring under his censorious behavior towards her had been more than difficult. She grabbed Rye and swung him in a circle. "Grandpa and Uncle Brett are coming to see us, darling."

"Grandpa and Uncle Brett. That's great, Mama." Rye beamed with joy as he scooted off to play with his patchwork snake.

The meal proved to be a joyous reunion for her family. Her father held Rye on his knee for most of the evening. Constantly he pressed kisses on the child's head. Penny smiled her silent thanks to Brett. She wondered if he had told their father that he was to marry Isabel in December. Since Isabel had been a Southern sympathizer along with her mother, Penny suspected she would receive dispensation that had not been extended to her brother. Their wedding was planned for New Berne and in the same church where she and Ryan had said their vows. She promised herself that her father would be their houseguest when Isabel and Brett married. Chiding herself to just let go of past difficulties and accept his tolerance of her marriage, Penny relaxed and enjoyed the evening.

The clock was striking ten o'clock when Nancy yawned with fatigue. "Y'all are just going to have to excuse me please. I confess I am plumb worn out."

Penny smiled at the woman, "Nancy, you are an angel and I know you're tired. Thank you so much for planning this supper for our first evening home. And thank you again for finding me a sharecropper."

"What's this about a tenant?" Brett sat up with interest. "Who've you found? Anybody I know?"

Nancy resumed her chair before replying to the question, "He's Jeremy Davenport, a cousin of mine. He's newly married and looking for something to do to support himself and his new wife. I suspect y'all know his family. Also, Brett, his cousin,

Hardy Brown is looking for a sharecropping or overseer's job. I wondered if Marcus might be interested?"

"I'll talk to Hardy and see if he suits. Marcus wants me to find someone to keep things going until he can get back. Whether or not he wants a long term tenant I don't know, but he can for sure use an overseer." Brett grinned, "Lord, salvation cometh. I thought I was going to have to run all three farms: Pa's, yours and Belle Terre. That sure would be a problem for a young married man."

John Bartlett laughed at his son, "Brett, somehow I think you would manage not to neglect that bride-to-be of yours. Penny, you have to tell me if she is the angel, the beauty, and the paragon of all virtues that he claims. If she is, I swear, I may go after her myself."

"Mercy, Pa. If you do that, I don't know if I'll stand a chance. Why don't you leave her to me and find yourself a nice widow woman. In fact, I know just the one." Brett caught Penny's eye before adding, "What about you, Penny? Can you think of a nice widow for Pa?"

"I think we should keep everything in the family, don't you Brett? Perhaps Ryan and Isabel's mother Martha would do. She is a Rebel through and through and a fine looking woman to boot," Penny teased.

"You two just hold your horses. I'm not looking for a replacement for Sarah. I intend to grow old with a grandchild on my knee and good memories in my head. No sense looking for trouble at my age."

Penny asked her father, "Do you still visit her grave every day?"

"That I do. I visit just to think about the day's events. Somehow it brings me peace and helps me to find answers. That's one reason I'm sitting here tonight. She wouldn't want me to be angry with you for following your heart, Penny. Sarah and I made a mistake pushing you into marriage with Daniel. I swore I'd never do that again. Besides, who am I to judge your husband for his honest opinions? There were a lot of good men in that fight from both sides of the Mason-Dixie. From what Brett tells me, he's a fine man despite being a Yankee."

"That he is. I'm looking forward to you getting to know him when he stops back through to get me. Do come to New Bern and visit with us soon, too. And I insist you stay with us for Brett's wedding."

"Thank you. I will take you up on that. As for soon, I suppose it depends on this trial thing with Marcus. I sure as the devil plan to be there for that."

"Oh, Pa, I wish we could find some evidence to prove he didn't do it." Penny shook her head in frustration.

Brett commented, "Pa and I are asking around and I know that Marcus's fiancée's father is doing the same thing. If we can find a witness who can say that he was on the other side of town when Calvin was killed, that will go a long way toward getting him off. In the meantime, we're nosing around here. The darkies act like they know something, but none of them will talk to me."

"I asked Mammy Rena to keep her ears open and let me know if she hears anything. She says her people are all grateful toward you and Marcus because of the school. That should help."

"The problem will be getting one of them to come forward against one of their own kind if it was a darky that did it." John Bartlett shook his head, "You know as well as I do, they stick together. If it wasn't a darky, then they are just as afraid to point the finger at a white man. Either way, they're not talking."

"I can't say that I blame them considering how they have been mistreated by white people," Penny commented, daring to risk her father's disapproval on a topic that they had quarreled about in the past.

Hastily Brett changed the subject, "That Lena Rouse Marcus is engaged to marry is one fine looking woman. She seems like a real nice one, too."

"Oh, how did you meet her?" Penny asked in surprise.

"I ran into her in the post office the other day when I went into town. She was there with her father. They were putting up a poster offering a reward for information on the killing."

"That's good. Hopefully it will help," Penny glanced at her father who harrumphed at the news.

He remarked with dismissal, "Most of the ones who might know something can't even read. So, I don't know how much good it will do."

Brett interrupted, "That may be, but word still ought to get around."

Nancy, who had been quiet all evening, remarked, "From what I hear through the darky-grapevine, the news is out that there's a reward. I know they're afraid to talk, though."

"Who do you suppose did it?" Penny asked without really expecting an answer.

"The first person I would suspect is Lucinda. She certainly had cause to want him dead, but listening to Mammy and Moses, I just don't believe she did it," Nancy said emphatically.

"Nor do we, Penny. Both Pa and I have talked to her, and while she admits to despising the man, she swears she didn't kill him. She told me she suspects who might have, but that's all I can get her to say."

Penny looked at Rye softly snoring in her father's arms and knew that it was time to draw the evening to a close. It had been a long day for her, as well. She was ready to go to her own room and climb into the bed where she had spent the brief years of her troubled marriage to Daniel, and those few glorious nights of illicit love with Ryan that had resulted in the child she so adored. It had been an evening of contentment for her and for the others, despite the concern they all felt for Marcus and for Lucinda and her child. For Penny, the greatest joy was the renewal of her relationship with her father. If he did not exactly welcome the idea of her marriage, at least he had lost the anger that had divided them.

Despite John Bartlett's frequent irritation with Lucinda, after listening to him that evening, Penny knew he still felt an obligation to protect her. Both Lucinda and her parents had been his slaves until he had deeded them to Penny and she had set them free. As John saw it, he still had a duty to them. He knew Brett still thought of Lucinda as the childhood playmate who had studied her lessons along with Penny and him at their mother's knee. He, too, felt a commitment of honor to prevent the darkies that served his family from coming to harm.

While both he and his father had initially attended a couple of the KKK meetings, for Brett the violence and anger were too much a reminder of the hostilities of a war that he was trying so hard to put behind him. For John, while a dyed-in-the-wool states-righter and supporter of the lost Confederacy, innate decency compelled him to find another path forward. There were certainly troubles and hardships stemming from military control of the South, but for different reasons both men had decided that vigilantism was a poor answer. Both felt more inclined to take the path of their longtime friend and former sheriff, R. W. King, who was now in Raleigh along with Ryan, working to resurrect a lawful State government operating under home rule. Wisdom dictated that the rule of law and organized government was the only real and sustainable path to recovery for the defeated land and her people. For men like them, the polar extremes represented by the military and vigilante mobs, the needs of poor and uneducated Negroes, and mendacious and grasping carpetbaggers and scalawags, meant that the road to normalcy would not be an easy one.

During the coming days of Penny's stay, it became routine for her father and brother to join them for the evening meal.

Once Rye was tucked into bed, conversation invariably turned to the many concerns that beset them from all sides. Finding seeds, tools, and fertilizer for the crops that they would need to plant come spring was a priority. While the supply routes that had existed prior to the war were being restored, things were still not as efficient as before and goods were often difficult to come by due to pent up demand caused by four years of paucity. There were rumors of taxes on their land being increased to levels too prohibitive for them to pay. They saw it as nothing more than a legalize ploy for carpetbaggers and scalawags to wrest their farms from them. While Penny and her father had survived the war with some funds, they had earmarked those resources for restoring their fields to productivity. Were that money spent for exorbitant property taxes, nothing would be left for crops and replacement of worn out tools. And they were the lucky ones. Many farmers had no cushion of funds to pay taxes, exorbitant or otherwise. Too many widows with hungry children and no man to care for them were faced with the poorhouse or worse. Ragged and disenchanted blacks, without the skills and education to survive on their own, were beginning to return to the farms of their former owners. Hungry and miserable, they pleaded for housing and food. Sympathetic owners took in those they could support as they still needed the labor, but too many were turned away. For those the path to survival was indeed grim and often illegal. Gangs of such desperate men were posing an increasing threat to the countryside. Encouraged by those actions as well as unsubstantiated rumors, the KKK committed ever more aggressive acts of retribution.

Underlying these concerns was the worry that Marcus would not be able to prove his innocence. They had heard nothing of the Rouses' search for a witness to Marcus's trip to the Tull farm on the night of the murder. Despite all of their efforts and questions, both direct and those delivered more subtly, the darkies were saying nothing about what they might or might not know. Penny and her family were at a loss to find a way to help him.

As each day drew to an end, lying alone in her bed Penny looked forward to Ryan coming. Even though she missed him and her home in New Berne, it saddened her that her visit was drawing to a close. These days of renewed closeness to her father had reminded her of just how much she had always depended on the security of his love and support. At least with the estrangement of the last few months ending, her father and husband could at last get to know one another. Now both could be a part of her life and that of her child who had missed his grandpa terribly. Cuddling Rye close to her, she closed her eyes in cozy contentment. Beyond her window, a lone owl hunted in the dark shadows of the pine trees that lined the perimeter of her land. The last thing she heard was his mournful hoot before she drifted into slumber.

The week flew by. Brett rode with her in the buggy to collect Ryan from the train station for the trip back to Pleasant Glade. Penny hoped that supper with her family would provide the opportunity for her father to get to know Ryan whom he had refused to meet prior to her wedding. She had been nervous and on edge for the entire morning, fretting that something would go wrong and spoil all her plans for a pleasant and conciliatory evening.

"Calm down, Sis. Pa has already come to grips with your marriage. He's missed you and Rye more than you would believe. He will do everything he can to make the meeting with Ryan go well." Brett looked at his sister and smiled. "You certainly have turned into a worry wart. Is it something about New Berne? I sure hope it's not infectious. I'd hate for my bride to have caught it, too."

"The only thing Isabel has caught is a rash," Penny remarked with deceptive calm.

Brett's face fell. "What do you mean? What's wrong?"

"Well, she's rash enough to marry you," she teased her brother.

"Christ. And I thought you were serious."

They were sitting in the buggy laughing when the train pulled into the station. Penny was the first to spot Ryan waving to them from the window. "Look, Brett, there he is."

Penny jumped from the buggy, not waiting for Brett to tie old Polly to the hitching post. Running down the crowded trackside platform, she met him when he stepped from the train carriage. He caught her in his arms and swung her in a circle, laughing as he did so. "I've missed you, darling. I'll show you just how much first chance I get."

Before she could respond, Richard King stepped down beside Ryan. "Well, hello Miss Penny. I've not laid eyes on you in a coon's age. Looks like time's been a lot kinder to you than it has me."

"Thank you, Mr. King. It has been a long time."

"That's a mighty fine husband you landed yourself, despite him being a Yankee and all. He made some real good points in the debate we all had up in Raleigh. I must say, I was pleased to meet him. I already had heard some good things about him from my friend in New Berne, John Harvey, before we bumped in to each other in Raleigh."

"Oh, yes. He's the attorney and good friend of our neighbor, Mrs. Caroline Framingham."

Brett stepped up and shook hands with Mr. King, "Good to see you, sir. I'm going to be marrying into my sister's new family come December. I'd be mighty pleased if you could make it to the wedding in New Berne. It'd give Pa someone to talk politics and crops with."

"It would be my honor, sir. Be so kind as to let me know the date and I'll try to make it. I thank you for the invitation." Richard King shook hands with Ryan and kissed Penny's cheek before leaving them to make his way to the substantial home he had erected on the corner of King and Queen Streets.

Dinner proved awkward in the beginning, with both Ryan and her father searching for words, fearful of committing a faux pas that would make any kind of friendship impossible. Penny found herself wanting to translate between them and interjecting nervous comments when the moment seemed ripe with tension. Finally Brett interrupted to announce that Rye looked ready for bed. Hesitant to leave them, Penny fished for an excuse to stay but could find none. Giving Ryan a warm smile, her eyes lit with promise, Penny bade these men she loved goodnight.

'I'll come with you, Penny. Please excuse me, gentlemen. I confess I'm tuckered out this evening." The three men rose as they left. Before the women reached the stairs, the men had settled back into their chairs for the enjoyment of their brandies, the cigars and conversation.

When they reached Nancy's room where Rye would spend the night so Penny and her husband could enjoy a private reunion, Nancy took Penny's arm. "I'm so worried about Moses. Have you noticed how frail he looks? Mammy cries about it sometimes but I can't get her to say much. She says he has bad stomachaches and can't take much food. I don't know if there is something you can do for him, but I think you might want to see about him."

"Thank you for telling me. I've noticed he looks pretty awful, but when I ask Mammy about it she just changes the subject. I'll ask Brett to take him to see Dr. Miller. I'm afraid if my herbal remedies would help, Mammy would already have tried them."

Penny had almost fallen asleep when sometime later Ryan crawled into the warm cocoon of their bed and began to make languorous love to her.

10

*D*ammit, Marcus thought as he sat listening to the case Ryan laid out against him. *I would convict myself if I believed this shit.* He could not help but admire the rational and dispassionate way that Ryan presented the indictment. He could only hope that John Harvey was as good. Otherwise, the outcome was going to be grim.

He glanced around the crowded courtroom, chilled by the cold day. His nose was running and he was miserable but pleased to see that the Rouses, as well as, Brett and John Bartlett were there. He caught Penny's eye as he stared at her where she sat with her family. She smiled her encouragement. In response he felt a glow of warmth begin in his toes and emerge as a radiant smile. With that smile still lighting his face, he continued glancing around the room coming to rest on Lena Rouse. Her face had gone white and still when she saw the smile that Marcus had given Penny. Marcus knew that Lena in that moment realized the woman that laid first claim to his heart. Trying to lessen the impact of that knowledge, he forced himself to give Lena an even more beaming smile. The cool look she gave in return told him that she was not deluded by his effort. Somehow he knew he would have to convince her that not only was she the woman he wanted to marry but that he loved her. He wished he could convince himself as well.

"Will the defendant please *rise*?" Marcus heard the judge's rising tone of voice at the same time that John Harvey poked him in the ribs. He had been so focused on contemplating the complications of his personal life that he had tuned out what had been happening in the courtroom. Belatedly he rose to his feet while the judge continued to glare his way. "I'm sorry, Your Honor."

"I asked how you plea, Mr. Cauley?"

"Not guilty, sir." Marcus settled into his seat as the hearing against him began. It frustrated him that Harvey could present little in the way of refutation based on any kind of facts. He had no witnesses to swear he had been elsewhere. The knife was a match to others he owned. He had told the victim he deserved killing and the victim's wife was sitting in smug arrogance in the front row prepared to testify that he had indeed followed through on that statement. He could only wonder at the seeming confidence of his attorney and surmise that he was a fine actor indeed. Were he in Harvey's shoes, he knew he could not have presented himself with the same calm assurance.

"You've heard the charges read against you and you have an attorney to represent you. Mr. Harvey, are you prepared to proceed with the trial on behalf of the defendant?"

"Your Honor, we intend to prove that the defendant is innocent of any and all charges, however we have not been able to reach all potential witnesses that can attest to his whereabouts at the time of the murder. Therefore, I am requesting a reasonable delay and ask that the defendant be released on bail."

"Mr. Madison, have you any objections to granting a delay to the defense?"

"No, sir. The prosecution has no problem with a reasonable delay, however, considering the seriousness of the charges, I must recommend that we continue to hold the defendant without bond."

"Very well. Mr. Harvey, I will grant you a three-month delay, but Mr. Cauley will remain in jail until such time as the trail is resumed. Court is dismissed."

"I'm sorry I couldn't get you released, Marcus, but at least this gives us some more time to try to figure this thing out."

"Don't worry about it, Mr. Harvey. I know you're doing what you can." Marcus turned to see who had touched him on his arm. Lena was at his side looking as though her heart would break. He was shamed by the unshed tears in her eyes.

"I'm sorry, Lena. It looks like I won't be there for our wedding day. Will you wait for me?"

"Am I the woman you really want to marry or just the one you choose to marry since the one you want is taken? I have to know, Marcus. I know you don't feel the same way about me as I do about you, but I hoped you had put the past behind you and were ready to move on," Lena whispered. She stared into his eyes demanding the answer she deserved. He saw she was determined not to back down, determined to risk losing him if need be.

"Lena, you are the only woman in this world I want to marry. Believe me and trust in me. I'm going to be a good and loving husband to you, I promise. Will you wait for me?" Marcus paused, looking down at his feet. He knew what she needed to hear him say. Despising himself for the lie and the expediency of it, he raised his head and looked deep into her eyes, "I love you, Lena. You're the woman I want for my wife."

"Thank you, Marcus. Someday I hope you really and truly can say that with all of your heart and not just part of it. Yes, I'll wait. The minute you are free, I'll marry you." Suddenly she laughed, "I've no objections to a jail house wedding if you don't?"

Marcus beckoned his attorney nearer. "No time like the present then. Mr. Harvey, do you think you could get that judge to do a little ceremony before they haul me off?" he exclaimed on reckless impulse.

Lena's father stepped up and placed a restraining hand on John Harvey's arm. "Marcus, Lena, I know you mean well, but I want you to wait. I intend for my daughter to walk down the aisle in a wedding gown to marry a man that is free to be with her. A few more months aren't going to matter when you have a long life ahead of you. And God forbid if you should be found guilty, what kind of life would you have left for her? I'm sorry, Marcus. I like you and I look forward to your wedding to my daughter, but I will not have it done this way."

"He's right, Marcus," John Harvey quietly added.

The sheriff walked up to remind Marcus to come with him. His time for visiting was over. Quickly Marcus hugged Lena goodbye. Looking over his fiancée's shoulder he caught Penny's eyes and smiled in sad farewell. "Take care, Lena, I'll be waiting."

"Me, too, Marcus. Me, too." The tears that had welled in her eyes, spilled silently down her cheeks in twin rivulets of salt-laden sadness.

Mr. Rouse halted the sheriff, "Do you mind telling me where you plan to hold him?"

"I suspect he's going to be sent to Fort Macon. Most of our prisoners who are going to be held for any time get sent there. It's a lot more secure and bigger than what we have here. It's late enough now he ain't going to be taken anywhere tonight though. You might ask tomorrow. I'm sure Mr. Madison will know."

"Thank you, sir. I appreciate it. Take care of yourself, Marcus. We'll be visiting and I'll keep looking for those witnesses around Kinston. Mr. Harvey or I will be in touch the minute we learn something that might be of help."

"I appreciate it, sir. Thank you for all your kindness and for still believing in me." Marcus turned to walk out with the sheriff, feeling the eyes of both of the women in his life on his retreating back. He sincerely prayed that they went their separate ways. It was complicated enough without the two of them establishing any kind of acquaintance. He was relieved to see a subdued Lena follow her father to a waiting carriage eliminating the opportunity for any contact between Penny and her.

Ryan quietly escorted his wife from the courtroom. He could tell from the knit of her brows and the stiffness of her spine that a storm of some proportions was in the making. Hoping to waylay her anger, he commented, "I hated to have to recommend that Marcus be held without bond, but that was the only choice the military government gave me. I'm sorry that he can't go home and work to exonerate himself, but he's fortunate that he has so many loyal friends to help him."

John Bartlett just harrumphed. He looked as angry as his daughter. Hoping to avert unpleasant confrontation, Brett took Penny by the arm and demanded, "Okay, Penny, I want to see that store where Ryan said he bought your ring. I think it is time that Isabel had a pre-wedding gift from me. Pa, come along with us. I'd like your opinion on something suitable for my bride to be."

Grateful for the change of topic, Ryan took his leave to return to his office. As he walked he pulled his jacket close. The wind blowing from the water had a pronounced chill. Despite the reputation of the area for its mild winters, the low gray clouds looked a lot like the promise of snow. He wondered what a snowy Christmas would be like in New Berne. Not really watching where he was going, Ryan suddenly plowed into a soft and pliant body.

The low laugh told him who it was even before she said, "My goodness, you certainly have your head down in a determined gallop."

"Lizzy, I do beg your pardon. I hope I haven't hurt you." Ryan had caught her in his arms to steady her but quickly stepped back from her nearness.

With eyes dancing, she teased, "Is this the only way I can get a hug from you?"

"I'm afraid so. My hugs are reserved for my wife and child these days. Now if you will excuse me, I have pressing business to attend to." He made his voice as cold as the day hoping that she would take the hint and spare him further conversation.

Lizzy pouted at him, "We haven't talked in ages, so why don't I just trot along with you?"

Ryan struggled to remain courteous. "Please don't. We really have nothing more to say and I have no time to dally in idle chatter."

"Maybe you don't. But I do," Lizzy said with a saucy toss of her head.

"Lizzy, it's a free sidewalk. You can walk where you please, but I don't have to get into a needless conversation with you. Now, you must permit me to bid you a good-day." Ryan stopped and doffed his hat.

Not to be put off, she took the opportunity to quickly kiss him on the cheek. Looking over his shoulder, she lifted her chin and tossed a saucy grin at Penny who had seen the kiss from the opposite side of the street. Her father and brother had their backs to them, engrossed in the jeweler's window display. As smug as a cat lapping cream, Lizzy purred, "Maybe you should turn and wave to your wife. I don't think she likes me, do you?"

"The devil take you. Just leave me alone for Christ sake." Ryan was beyond annoyed. With Penny already irritated with him over his earlier motion in court, this was not going to improve the temperature at home. "Leave me alone, Lizzy. I love my wife with all of my heart. I don't need or want any other woman in my life. Now, would you please see if you can find some other man to focus your attention on? Please."

"Hmm. We'll see," she flung over her shoulder as she sashayed away, hips undulating in an ages old invitation.

Malicious tease, Ryan thought to himself. He turned to wave to Penny but saw that she deliberately turned away to join the men looking in the shop window. He knew there would be hell to pay later for that kiss. He could only hope that she had seen that he was not the one to instigate it. He rued the day that he had ever kept company with Lizzy. He had been drawn to the effervescent nature she exuded at a time when he was miserable with longing for the woman he loved and thought he would never have. He had not seen the vindictive side of her personality then and wondered if it were some new facet, or if she had just been successful in hiding it from him in the past. He did remember that she had been a flirt and a tease, and single-minded in her intention to marry him despite his stated lack of interest in that particular goal. He wondered if her pride was so wounded that she was simply trying to make him suffer for the loss of face that he had cost her among her circle, or if she held out a genuine hope that he would leave his wife for her. He knew well enough from the days half-hearted courting her, despite her seductive teasing, she would hold out for marriage before bestowing her favors. He was glad that he had a stack of paperwork waiting on his desk. His brain was tired of dealing with women.

"Penny, is something wrong? You look kind of funny." Brett peered intently in his sister's face.

"Don't be silly. I'm fine. Just still upset that Marcus is going to be in jail for Christmas and for who knows how much longer. It really is unfair." Penny did not want her father and brother to suspect the reason her face had blanched and her hands were shaking. Hoping to avoid having them notice, she wrapped her cloak close to her body and looked at the sky. "It sure is a nasty day. I wouldn't be surprised if we get some sleet or snow."

"As long as I've got a warm fireplace and a sweet woman to hold, I think I can take the weather." Brett peered at his sister. It was obvious she was trying to hide something from him and now was the wrong time to approach her about it.

"Well, boy. Do you want to go in and buy those pearls or not?" John looked at his children with pride. Penny and Brett were both healthy and attractive people. He was happy that they had found someone to love even if he might have preferred a Southerner for Penny's husband. Daniel might have been Southern but he had never made her happy. Again he rued the way he and Sarah had pushed Penny to marry their neighbor and old friends' son. He wished, as he did at least once daily, that Sarah were still with them. "Did I tell y'all about the day I bought the pearls for your mama?"

Penny glanced at Brett as they groaned in unison. Penny laughed, "Pa, you've told that story so many times I can recite it myself, but it's such a good one, I'd love to hear it again. Maybe you could save it for tonight, though. Isabel, Martha and Caroline are all joining us for dinner and that would be an interesting conversational topic in light of Brett's surprise pearls for Isabel."

"Well, I know a polite brush off when I hear it, young lady." Smiling, John took her arm and they entered the jeweler's shop, "I'll just tell my story to fresh ears later, Missy. Besides, Rye hasn't heard it and he needs to. Family tradition, you know."

Brett and the jeweler were soon in deep negotiations. When he learned that Penny was the Mrs. Madison married to Ryan Madison, the discount became even more appealing and a deal was quickly made. Penny and John bracketed Brett on either side and hastened to assure him that the pearl necklace with diamond clasp in the center would be perfect for Isabel. Judging from the beads of sweat that had sprung up on his forehead, Penny and her father knew that the necklace was an extravagance for him. Even so the deal was soon concluded and a smiling jeweler ushered them from the shop, asking to be remembered to Mr. Madison.

Pulling their wraps about them, they looked up anxiously at the moiling clouds. Penny was glad to have reached the buggy when the first pelting drops of sleet began to dance on the cobbles. She prayed they would reach the safety of her home before the roads became treacherous.

"We'd best get a move on." Slapping the reins on the

horse's back, John nodded his head at his son, "Don't worry, Brett. I know this stretches you a bit thin financially at the moment, but I've paid the taxes and made enough from the crop to help you out until we can get next year's crop in. Might as well make a good impression on this girl from the git-go, I say."

Somewhat abashed, Brett replied, "Thanks, Pa. I hope it won't be necessary to borrow your money, but it's good to know in case it is. I plan to be a bit more careful with money for a while anyway. We're just going to Baltimore to move the rest of her mother's things here, so that's not much of a wedding trip for her. However, it's the best I can afford at the moment. I must say I feel rather badly about it, though."

Patting him on the arm, Penny added, "It isn't where you go that will matter to her. It's how you treat her. Ryan and I didn't go anywhere, as you recall. He's promised to take me to Europe someday, but as busy as he is, heaven only knows when that will be."

His eyes distant with memory, John added, "Penny's right, son. Sarah and I moved into Pineview with the paint still drying on the walls and spent our first night right there in our new home. The furthest I ever took her was New York and that was just before she got pregnant with you. In fact, I have always believed that was where you were conceived."

"I just hope and pray that we will have as good a marriage as you and Mama. I'd like to know that on my dying day we were still as in love as when we married. Y'all could say that when Mama died. Penny and I were fortunate to grow up in a home like ours."

John snorted, "Don't go thinking it's all going to be peaches and cream. No matter how much you love one another, you're two different people. Sometimes you rub along real well and sometimes it purely chaffs. You just have to get through the rough patches knowing that they're just a temporary hitch. But through it all, I never went to bed without telling her I loved her and kissing her goodnight. That takes the sting out of a heap of things."

They fell silent as they rode through the town. The shopkeepers were beginning to close their doors and those about in the streets quickened their steps, eager to be at hearthside should a real winter storm set in. As her father drove the buggy through the town, Penny admired the New Berne she had come to love and was grateful that the Yankee occupation had at least spared it from the destruction that so many towns in the area had endured during the war. The citizens that had fled had mostly returned, except those who lay in the soil in other locations where they had been scattered by the war. The biggest hardship that New Berne had endured was the Yellow Fever epidemic that swept the town in the summer of 1863, killing large numbers of locals along with many of the occupying soldiers.

Penny stared in distraction at the glimpses of gray water that appeared between the trees alongside the road. She tried to put the image of Lizzy kissing Ryan from her mind, but the more she tried, the more securely it took residence. And the longer she dwelt on it, the angrier she became. She reminded herself, it was Lizzy who had done the kissing and Ryan had made no move to invite it. However, the quiet fury didn't dissipate no matter how she scolded herself not to make an issue of it. She had sensed from the first meeting with Lizzy at their wedding that the woman was out to cause trouble. Whether from sheer spite or a broken heart, Penny couldn't say for sure, but the former motive seemed the likely reason.

"Will you look at that," John exclaimed as they turned into the drive leading up to Penny's house. "Ryan sure did himself proud when he built this one. That is not only one beautiful house, but the view about takes my breath away."

"Thank you, Pa. I hope you and Brett will both be

comfortable here." Brett and her father had come for the trial and had met her at the courthouse, so this was John's first introduction to her home. Brett was also staying with them until his wedding on Christmas Eve. While he had campaigned to stay at Caroline's, the women there had united in opposition to that ambition. With the festivities just a week away, there was a flurry of activity at Caroline's house, where the wedding reception would be held just as Ryan's and Penny's had been. They had no need of a groom underfoot to impede preparations.

When the buggy pulled up to the porch, Rye burst from the front door followed by a panting Isabel. Running to his grandpa who had just climbed down, he leaped into his arms.

"Easy, little feller. I'm just a poor ole grandpa and you're getting to be a mighty big little man."

"Oh, Grandpa. I'm still littler than you."

Isabel laughed, "I feel as though I've been trying to hang onto the tail end of a tornado. He's has more energy in a day than I have in a week."

"Oh, I do hope he wasn't too much for you?"

"No, Penny, not at all. You know I adore him, besides Mother and Caroline were over here for a good bit of the afternoon to help rile him up and spoil him in the process. Right, Rye? Tell Mama what you got today." Isabel beamed at the boy.

"I got a toy horse and buggy that belonged to my daddy. Grandma Martha said I could have it."

"That's wonderful, darling. You take good care of it so someday you can give it to your little boy, too." Penny turned back to Isabel, "Isabel, did you...? Never mind," Penny laughed. Judging from the kiss that Brett was giving his fiancée, any further conversation would need to wait.

"Look's like we might as well go on in the house, Pa. It's two cold for the rest of us to stand around out here. I don't think those two are going to feel the cold anytime soon, though."

"For their sake, I hope not. That's the way it should be. However, in all this hubbub, I don't believe that girl was ever introduced to her future father-in-law." The twinkle in his eye was enough for Penny to know that he was not in the least miffed by the oversight.

"Lord, Pa. I forgot." Brett's sudden blush matched the red of his bride-to-be's face. "I'm really sorry. Miss Isabel Madison, allow me to introduce you to my father, John Bartlett. Pa, meet Isabel."

"Oh, my goodness gracious, Mr. Bartlett. I am just mortified. Please forgive us?"

"You don't worry one bit about it. If I was marrying you, I'd be doing the same thing my boy was. And call, me Pa. You're one of mine now, or soon will be at any rate."

"Thank you, I will." Isabel took his hand and that of her fiancé and led them into Penny's house. A glowing fire, evergreens on the mantle, and warm mulled cider greeted the chilly group.

11

Once again Marcus found himself on a train bound for incarceration. This time it would be even further from his home and with the likelihood of many months before any chance for freedom. His destination was Fort Macon, the pentagonal fortress on the outer banks of North Carolina across the sound from the harbor town of Beaufort. Converted into a prison following the war, it served the entire eastern part of the state. With constant dampness from the sea air penetrating porous brick walls, the dark chill days of winter, and the lack of any nearby friends or relatives to bring him extra food and comfort, he knew that the days would be long and grim. Instead of lying in bed at Belle Terre nestled in the arms of the woman who should already have been his wife, his lot would be a narrow bunk in a cell with other hapless prisoners.

Marcus worried about his plantation. He had no choice but to trust that Brett and John Barlett would find someone to oversee it in his absence and keep check on his affairs for him. He fretted about the school he and Brett had started for the Negro children. His prolonged absence made his property even more vulnerable to the Regulators and KKK who were roaming the countryside. Meant to keep order, they more often than not created mayhem for both whites and freedmen. The countryside was in chaos. Fear of riots by the resentful white populace had led to the removal of Negro soldiers from Kinston in September but that had not brought an end to the problems. Bands of marauding freedmen, desperate for food, struck fear in the hearts of the white populace. More than one man went to bed at night with a loaded gun at hand.

He had to rely on John Harvey and the charity and good graces of Lena's father to find a way to exonerate him. And he had to believe that Lena loved him enough to wait. Beyond that, he would have to find some way to endure the loneliness, discomfort, and despair of months behind bars. When he thought of it, cold sweat beaded his forehead. Marcus having always loved the freedom of roaming the woods and fields, the feel of fresh air and wind in his face, the caress of warm sun on his skin, wondered if he had the strength to endure it.

Ever the farmer, he noted the land that slid past his window had become much lighter and sandier than the dark fertile loam of the land around Kinston, sixty some miles to the west. The trees were shorter, too; now the forests were more scrub pine than the tall loblolly pines, cypresses, maples, sweet gums and water oaks that grew near his home. The sleet of the previous day had glazed the shrubs and weeds along the track with a thin coating of ice that sparkled in the feeble light of the winter sun. The day was bleak and cold, matching his mood. The whistle of the train, announcing that the station in Beaufort was just a short distance more down the track, broke his revere. There he would board an army boat that would take him across the sound to the fortress-prison. He had a fleeting vision of himself escaping his guard and dashing to freedom. Despite the temptation, he had enough presence of mind to realize that would only worsen his plight. Heaving a sigh, he gathered the sparse belongings he had been allowed to take with him and prepared to debark.

Descending the steps onto the platform, Marcus was jostled by his guard causing him to stumble before he could right himself. "Daggumit, watch it! It's hard enough to keep my balance in these chains without you making it worse."

"Shit, I ain't done it on purpose. You'd best git that chip off your shoulder or you ain't going to be real happy in that there prison over yonder. Smart-asses git took care of real quick like." The guard shrugged his shoulders and pointed towards the waiting boat where the relief guard was already seated.

"Sorry, I've got a short fuse right now, but thanks for the warning. I'll keep it in mind." Marcus figured he'd didn't need anymore going against him than he already had.

The biting wind that swept from the sea had him shivering before he and his new guard had left the harbor. Once they were in the open sound, spray from the white capping waves dampened his clothes, adding to his discomfort. Judging by the guard's chattering teeth, he was as miserable as Marcus. In the gray distance, the guard pointed north to a small island, home to wild horses whose ancestors had been shipwrecked there. They squinted to see if they could catch sight of one of the stocky little ponies. Ahead lay the low dark outline of Bogue Banks. Fort Macon was situated at the north end of the long sandy barrier island that protected the mainland from the sea. Garrisoned in 1834, it had stood as the main protection for the North Carolina coast and Beaufort from both enemy forces and pirates. Beaufort was the State's only deepwater ocean port,. The other major port at Wilmington lay inland on the banks of the Cape Fear River. By the outbreak of hostilities in 1861, the fort was in need of renovation and badly outdated against newer weaponry. Repairs necessitated by the 1862 Union bombardment to recapture the fort from Southern forces had helped, but the fortress was far from a comfortable post.

Indicating their destination the guard commented, "Right yonder is the pier we're aiming for. You can't see the fort 'cause it's got a topknot of dirt and grass and shrubs growing on it. But, it's in there. It sure ain't my pick for no comfortable garrison, but I been assigned here, so I reckon I gotta make the best out of it. It is one miserable day, ain't it? I swear it's cold enough out here to shrivel my balls up smaller than fly shit." The guard pointed at his pocket, "You got any backy in your pocket? I'm plumb out and I could sure use a smoke for my pipe."

"Help yourself. I not only grew it, I cured it. It turned out right good, if I say so myself," Marcus remarked shifting his eyes to his pocket to grant permission of access.

Stuffing his pipe with a redolent wad of tobacco, the guard nodded and returned the bag with a smile, "Appreciate it."

"Don't mention it. I think I'll light up my own if you'll take these cuffs off and give me a match." Considering his situation, Marcus sized the garrulous guard up as a good one to be friends with. Where he was going having a friend among the guards would not go amiss. "Where you from?"

"I was raised in the mountains up around Valle Cruces. I didn't much cotton for fighting the Yankees for a bunch of slaves I never had no truck with and the Rebels up my way didn't appeal to me neither, so I joined up with the Yankees and got myself stationed here following the capture of the fort in '62. I been stationed here ever since."

The man seemed nearly as tall as one of the straggly pines that grew on the edge of Marcus's fields and not much bigger around. His uniform hung from his gangly limbs and smelled decidedly worse for wear. His eyes were as gray as the winter sky with radiating creases at the corners that bespoke a merry temperament. Long, lank strands of oily hair shadowed a gaunt face. "Not the best place to get stuck, I imagine," Marcus remarked as he studied the man on the opposite bench.

"It sure ain't come winter, but it ain't so bad in summer except for the humidity and goldurn squeeters. I git to do some fishing for the cook. And on a hot day, that ocean makes one mighty fine spot to jump around in. I can't swim a lick but I sure do like to kick around in them waves along the edge."

"I swim a little in the millpond at home but I ain't ever swum in the ocean." Marcus paused, "I'm Marcus Cauley. But I suspect you already know that. What's your name?"

"Percell Brown, Marcus. Pleased to meet you. My friends

call me Shine, 'cause I made the best moonshine in the mountains."

"Lordy, Shine. You and I have a lot in common. I ran the best liquor still in Lenoir County during the war. Supplied every drunk around and a goodly portion of the Rebs, too," Marcus laughed.

"Shit fire! Is that a fact?" Percell grinned with new respect, "Don't worry about this here prison. You got any problems, you let me know."

They sat smoking in a companionable silence until the boat bumped the dock, reminding Marcus these moments of relative freedom were about to end. The guard stood, "Best git those cuffs back on you 'fore it harelips one of them tight-assed guards in yonder. Watch your step now. This here dock's mighty durned slippery when it's wet like this."

"I appreciate the kindness. Those moments without the cuffs and sitting out here under God's own sky made me feel right normal for the first time in days." Marcus smiled, "I guess I'll be seeing you around the fort?"

"That's a fact. Don't worry none. I'll see to it things don't go bad for you. You going to be in with some tough customers though. Three of 'em is responsible for hanging some darky over near Dover during a KKK raid and two murdered a man they was robbing. Just don't let 'em buffalo you none and they'll back off."

"That's mighty good to know." Marcus took a last look at the distant shore before marching behind Shine across the paved parapet and down the wooden gangplank into the prison. He paused in the center pentagonal parade ground that duplicated the shape of the surrounding red brick walls. A quick glance around assured him the walls averaged at least four and a half feet thick. In one corner, near a stairway to the earthen-work roof that surmounted the fort, stood a well. Cannon balls were stacked in a neat pyramid not far away. A few soldiers were standing around smoking on the opposite side where another entry led to the second gangplank access. Marcus looked up at the sky and took a deep breath.

"We got to git you over there to the commander's office and git you checked in, then I'll be taking you to your cell," Shine informed him. "Captain Charles Gaskill ain't a bad man, real fair like. Just talk respectful and you'll do fine."

Marcus blew out his breath, squared his shoulders and walked into the captain's office. When Captain Gaskill had finished laying down the rules and expectations and duly registered Marcus, he stuck out his hand. "Mr. Cauley, Madison Ryan is a friend of mine. He told me about you, and I know he isn't happy about having to represent the State against you. I feel certain your attorney will find the information he needs to assure that you get some justice. I'll do the best I can here to see to it that these thugs leave you alone."

"I would appreciate that, Captain Gaskill, sir. And I thank you for your kind words. It means a lot to me right now. I confess I was feeling mighty low on the way here."

"I'm sorry to do it, but I've got to put you in casement twenty-six with some other boys from down your way. They're not the nicest sorts, to say the least, so watch your back until you can establish yourself with them. Being from the same general locale should help some, as well as the fact you're white. They are some real Negro haters. I heard about that school you started on your farm. If I were you, that's the last thing I'd go telling them." Gaskill paused, "I understand you're a friend of Madison's wife and her family. In light of your affiliations, I've endeavored to make things a little easier for you by assigning you to fishing duty with Sergeant Brown here. Other times you can assist the surgeon, Dr. Elliott Coues, in the hospital. We have an inordinate amount of illness here among prisoners since conditions are not very good. When someone is seriously ill, you will bunk in the infirmary, in a real bunk, overnight to attend him. You're going to be mighty grateful for that when you can get to do it. Your bed at the moment will be on the brick floor. The floor is damp and in winter, damned cold. I've requested lumber to construct bunks, but it's not yet forthcoming. Try to stay as healthy as you can under the circumstances. That's the best I can offer. As a prisoner, it would create even bigger problems for you with the others if I were to do more for you."

"I understand, sir. Anything and everything you can do is most welcome. What you can't do, I understand."

When they were well beyond earshot, Shine commented, "Well, sir-ree, that went mighty fine. I'll be pleased to have you to do some fishing with. It's about the best thing going on 'round here in the way of duty, 'cepting when it's raw like today. Then I manage to find a way to stall it off to another time. Infirmary duty ain't so bad neither as long as you can keep from gitting whatever shit's going around." Looking a trifle embarrassed, Shine worked his mouth, "Maybe, you would like me to hold that backy for you. You take it in that cell and the others are going to take it off you for sure. All I ask is that you let me have a smoke now and again. I'll keep your pipe for you, too, and let you have it when we go out fishing. Then it won't be nobody's nevermind, 'cepting ours."

Marcus stood at the threshold of his assigned casement, while Shine fumbled with his keys. Finding the right one, Shine inserted the key in the old iron lock. Marcus could hear the click of the tumblers that spelled the end of his momentary sense of freedom. Five pairs of resentful, wary eyes glared at the intrusion.

Shine stepped aside and gave him a rough shove through the door. "I got another goldurn murderer to keep you sorry-asses company."

Marcus stood just inside the door, too stunned to move further. He heard the loud clank of the door slamming behind him and still he stood motionless. Vaguely he wondered if Shine in his own way had offered him some kind of protection. It was the only thing that made any sense to him of the guard's words and actions.

A short man, made powerful by a heavily muscled frame, slow rose from his pallet on the brick floor and walked up to him. Starting at Marcus's feet, he let his eyes inch their way to Marcus's own, obviously intending to intimidate, "Who the hell are you?" he snarled.

"Who the hell wants to know?" Marcus challenged, working the muscles in his jaw.

A skeletal gray haired man uncoiled himself from his squat on the floor and flicked off a louse he had mashed between his nails. "Looks like we got ourselves a live one." Pointing, he continued, "That there's Jethro Williams. I'm Smitty Wilson. So, who the hell are you, boy?"

"Marcus Cauley. I'm from Woodington vicinity down near Kinston. Hear you boys are from over my way."

"Williams there is from the edge of Tracey Swamp just off Lower Trent Road. My farm's on Dover road just west of Dover. Over there by the window is Roger Jones. That good for nothing in the far corner is Cephus Jones, his brother. They's in here for murdering a man they was relieving of some property they took a shine to. Other one over yonder is my sorry-assed cousin, Jimmy Wilson. Jimmy's from British Road east of where you are. Jethro, Jimmy, and me ain't done nothing to warrant being here. All we done was string up some uppity nigger. So who was it you done kilt?"

"Sorry-assed thieving fucker that worked for me got himself murdered. Caught him screwing my piece of ass and I was sure aiming to kill him, but somebody else beat me to it." Marcus was glad that those who knew him could not hear him speaking with such vulgarity.

"Your wife?"

"Ain't married. I said my piece of ass." Marcus hoped his lying bravado was sufficient and they would soon tire of him, allowing him to orient himself to his new circumstances. Looking at the sorry state of the others, he could only hope it was their natural condition and not the result of their incarceration. "Accommodations sure ain't much, are they? No beds, no tables, no chairs, nothing but some blankets on the floor?"

"These daggummed Yankees ain't going to make it too nice-like for us Rebs. What did you think you was gitting, a fancy hotel?" Jethro snorted. "Shit, we're lucky to git three squares a day and bread that ain't full of weevils." He motioned to the corner, "They brung you a bedroll. That's the end of any hospitality from that bunch."

Marcus walked to the window and peered into the dry moat that surrounded the fort. Across the way, he could see windows in the opposite wall surmounted by the parapet he had crossed earlier. "What's in that section over yonder and why ain't there better bars on these windows?"

Cephus spoke up, "That's storage and stuff over there. I hear it's full of water half the time. As for the bars, I'm real grateful they ain't much. We're kind of figuring on gitting the hell outta here real soon like. Seeing as how you're just about a neighbor of ours, you can join up with us."

"Hell, man. This is a damned island. How you planning to get off of it, if you manage to get out of here?"

"Remember, the folks on this here island are Southerners. They ain't gonna sell us out to no Yankees. I heard they helped out some other men that decided they didn't like it here none," Jimmy explained.

"Well, I'm hoping I can get out of here the legal way. I've got a lawyer working on it for me. They ain't got nothing but circumstantial evidence, so there's a chance. I'm certainly not interested in swinging for something I didn't do." Marcus shrugged and walked over to his bedding. He picked up the roll and shook it out. The blankets were of the poorest quality to begin with and years of use had succeeded in wearing them even thinner. He could only pray they were not infested with vermin. "Hell. How do you keep warm in this place?"

"We sleep in our clothes. It's too damned cold to take'em off," Jethro laughed uproariously. "Besides, it keeps us from looking too good to one another. Course, it don't do nothing for the aroma in here."

Marcus grinned, "Yeah, I didn't want to mention that." The five men chortled appreciatively at his humor.

The men seemed to accept him, and while they were not the sort that he would seek out for company, the presence of someone to talk to would help pass the time a lot better than in the lone cell he had occupied in New Berne. He played a game of cards and made sure the others won, allowing them to rib him about his lack of skill.

By four it was so dark in the cell they could no longer see, bringing an end to the card game. At five they were marched to the mess hall for a supper of cornbread, fat back and dried black-eyed peas swimming in clotted grease. Afterwards, due to lack of light, bedtime was early. Breakfast was bread, and the noon meal a repeat of the supper of the previous night. Marcus learned that the fare varied little. An occasional sour pickle or raw onion to prevent scurvy, or a sweet potato, added some variety. After a week, he longed for the opportunity to go fishing. He salivated just thinking about a mess of fried fish.

The tedium was broken by his daily work in the infirmary from eight in the morning until five at night. In the middle of the day, following dinner, he was allowed to exercise in the parade area provided the weather allowed. After another week, the weather dawned sunny and mild. Marcus's prayers were answered when Shine came to him in the infirmary and announced that they were going fishing.

Despite a brisk wind that swept over the chill February waters of the Atlantic, the sun provided ameliorating warmth. The day was an exceptional one and more than welcome after weeks of gray gloom. Marcus sucked air into his lungs with all of the avidness of someone who had been deprived of oxygen. To be free and a part of nature once again was a privilege he gave fervent thanks to God for providing. Not to mention the intervention of more earthly forces such as the Captain and Shine. "Shine, I have to tell you, this day is a rare gift and I appreciate it more than you know. I am sick to death of walls around me all of the time."

"Just help me catch a mess of fish for the Captain's dinner and with spring a coming, there'll be some more days like this'un. I brung your backy and your pipe. We might as well git this fishing trip started off right, I say."

"That suits me just fine," Marcus grinned. His pipe was just a small, added bonus. It was the freedom to be outside that he craved. Taking the pipe, he allowed Shine to light it for him from the Lucifer match used to light his own. Marcus commented, "Damned Lucifers stink something awful but they sure are a convenience."

He looked around with satisfaction as he lowered himself into the small rowboat that they would use. From the vantage point of the boat, he could see the area around the fort was covered with low growing oaks and cypress trees. Gnarled and distorted by the winds from the sea, they leaned toward the sound that separated the long, sandy island of Bogue Banks from the mainland.

Rowing from the lee of the island, the two men oared the boat into Bogue Sound and allowed the tide to push them along as they prepared their lines with bait consisting of pieces of an old fish that was too bony to be worth human consumption. Half rotted chicken baited crab pots that Shine had anchored to buoys two days previously. The first order of business was to check the crab pots once the lines had been cast from the boat and drifted behind them. Shine oared the boat to the first pot, "I'll pull this one in and show you how to git the crabs out. Then I'll do the rowing and let you git the crabs while I hold the boat to the wind." Pulling in the pot, he showed Marcus how to extract the crab and put it in the croaker sack that lay in the bottom of the boat. "Be right careful now, these critters'll bite the pure fool outta you with them claws."

"Hey, I think we got something on that line there," Marcus pointed.

Shine busied himself getting the fish into the boat. He held it up for Marcus to admire before giving it a careless toss into the bucket. "That's damned fine mackerel. Captain Gaskill is gonna be one happy man tonight. I intend to git enough he ain't the only one enjoying a mess of fish and crabs. If there's time, we'll do some oystering and claming along the shore. I could sure use a mess of this myself after that slop we been gitting to eat. Damned if that cook can't mommuck up a piece of beef or pork something terrible. But give him some fish and he'll do'er up right. "

"Is there any chance I can have some of our catch for my own supper?" Marcus looked hungrily at the fish and the jittering sack.

"Don't worry. I'll see to it the cook takes care of us. Long as we git enough for the Captain, cook and me and you come next. After that, the officers, then the soldiers git some, and if they's any left, the prisoners."

"That seems like a good arrangement to me," Marcus said as he hauled another crab from the pot and into the sack.

The two men worked at a steady pace during the hours that followed and soon the sack was bulging and the bucket filled. Additional fish flopped feebly in the wash that trickled around their feet. Neither looked at the sky and the clouds that hung in dark angry tatters along the horizon. Soon the wind was rising and the waves were throwing cold spume across the bow of the boat. Wet with spray and eager to get back to the safety of the small pier behind the fort, both manned the oars and struggled to fight the rising fury of the storm that was sweeping down on their small craft. Shine, despite the chill of the wind-blown rain, broke into a nervous sweat.

"You okay?" Marcus asked anxiously.

"Yeah, but I shore don't like this weather none." Shine responded.

Just as he finished speaking he turned his head and gawked at a large wave that had formed on their stern. Panicked by sudden fear, he dropped his oar and watched as it spun away from him. He made a desperate lunge for the oar just as the wave lifted the boat at an angle. With arms wind-milling, Shine overbalanced and plunged head first into the stormy sea.

Fighting panic, Marcus maneuvered the boat to where Shine had fallen in and secured his oar in the bottom of the boat. Ripping his shoes from his feet, he prepared to dive into the sea to rescue Shine. Taking a deep breath, he said a prayer. This wild water was a far cry from the placid millponds of his swimming experience.

12

John, Brett and Isabel stood beside the carriage in the Madison's yard. Their bags were lashed on and they were ready to be on their way, the newlyweds going to Baltimore to finalize the shipment of the last of the furniture from the former Madison family home to Isabel, Martha and Ryan, each having pre-determined their favorite pieces. Brett didn't mind the secondary mission, as long as the primary one was enjoying his new bride.

John was accompanying them to the pier in New Berne, where their ship was even now waiting, and then he would begin the drive home. He had talked with Penny prior to leaving to say that he felt that his family, despite his anger and initial rejection of Ryan, had been reunited. He even admitted without reservation that Penny's choice had been a good one. After all, he reminded her, Ryan had been raised in a "Southern" family despite his later defection to the Northern cause. As for Isabel, she reminded him so much of his dearly mourned wife, that he could not help but love her from the first moment he had met her. He assured both Penny and Brett that he was happy in the knowledge that both of them had given their hearts to good people and would be the progenitors of more grandchildren that he would know and love, just as he already did Rye.

Penny smiled at the threesome and wondered what it was that Brett was whispering to Isabel that inspired the sudden infusion of blood to her face. It warmed her to see the warmth and rapport between the newly wedded couple. Her father was watching them as well, and beaming with pleasure. Studying

Isabel, Penny suddenly saw the similarity to her mother. It wasn't so much the facial features as it was a matter of a sunny, joyous, serene personality. For the first time since she had announced her wedding to a former Union officer, Penny felt loved and at peace with her father. Christmas celebrations following the wedding had been merry and once again the table bore the imported seasonal holiday foods such as cranberries, pineapple and oranges they had enjoyed prior to the deprivations of war.

As for her husband, she admitted she was less than pleased at the moment. Standing by her side, Ryan felt the distance between them. He knew the unsolicited kiss from Lizzy still rankled, as did the incarceration of her friend and would-be-lover, Marcus. He had been tempted that day to buy a gift of jewelry for his wife, just as Brett had done for Isabel, but he had not. He was afraid that his good intentions would have been misinterpreted as the actions of a man acting out of guilt rather than loving generosity. Later, when the air had clear, he would still buy her the diamond drop earrings that the jeweler had reserved for him that bleak afternoon. As for now, he struggled to find a way to reassure his wife that she was the most important thing in the world to him, that no other woman would ever own his heart, and that he was actively trying to find an excuse to free Marcus. In his own mind he could not believe the man capable of the cold-blooded murder of which he was accused.

When the buggy turned onto the road and was lost to sight, Penny took Martha and Caroline by the hand and invited them both inside. Both women were going to miss Isabel badly. When they were seated on the damask divan in the parlor, Penny began, "Ryan and I need to ask a favor of the two of you."

"That's right, ladies. I have to go to Raleigh for another legislative meeting and I would like to take Penny with me.

You see, we have never had a trip together and with Isabel and Brett off on their own, I think it's high time we had a trip, too." Ryan gave Penny a merry wink. Watching the sudden sparkle of the women's eyes, Penny realized they had guessed where that wink and his explanation were heading.

"Well, if you need to escape for a few days to work on another grandchild for me, I'll be happy to take care of Rye. I can come here if that would make it easier for you?" Martha offered, shocking them all by the unaccustomed candor.

"You most certainly will not," Caroline interrupted. "He may not be my blood but he's a grandson to me, too. Besides, it takes both of us old biddies to keep up with him on one of his slow days."

"Of course, Caroline, dear. I didn't mean to offend and you're quite right about both of us being needed," Martha hastened to assured her before she could become any more incensed.

Remembering the rivalry that Ryan had told her existed between the two women when his mother first arrived in New Berne, she could not help but marvel at the close friendship they now enjoyed. Isabel had done much to bridge the rough seas between them. Their mutual fondness of gardening had also helped. The fledging gardens surrounded her new home had profited from both their enthusiasm and Caroline's generosity in sharing her plants. Penny's need of herbs for her remedies had given both of the older women a new arena to explore in fulfilling her specific garden needs. Rye had also worked his own brand of sunny magic to weld them all into a close family unit.

Penny blushed at the mention of another child. Recently, for the first time in their marriage, Penny had shunned Ryan's amorous advances. She knew he was puzzled and saddened by her rejection. Had she been asked she doubted she could have explained the complexity of emotions that boiled below the tranquil surface she struggled to project. Despite loving her new home and friends and the extended family she had gained, she still yearned for the comfortable nearness of her familiar childhood friends, family, and home. She missed Nancy, Mammy Rena, and Moses. When he had first mentioned the trip to Raleigh, she had rejoiced that it would give her the opportunity to visit Pleasant Glade for a few days. She began planning in her mind what she would take with her and whom she wanted to visit. However, when Ryan continued to explain his own vision for the trip, she realized that her plans would have to wait. Not wanting him to suspect her disappointment, she pretended an eagerness she did not feel and agreed to the trip. After all, she reasoned, she loved her husband and they had never been away together. She wished she could rejoice that he wanted to spend time alone for the two of them to enjoy one another.

That night in their bed, Ryan turned to her and pulled her into his arms. She lay unresponsive when he first began to make slow gentle love. Soon her body awoke to the passion he elicited in her. Afterwards, she knew that he sensed a part of her mind was in another place, when he asked, "Tell me what's troubling you? You're not yourself these last few days."

"I'm sorry. I really don't mean to be difficult. I just feel out of sorts somehow."

"Penny, I think you're homesick. You didn't say much when I mentioned taking you to Raleigh with me, but you didn't react with as much happy surprise as I had anticipated. Maybe you were planning to use my trip as an opportunity to visit Pleasant Glade. Before we married, I promised you we would spend a lot of time there. I have been so busy I haven't kept that promise. It's just that I didn't expect the government to appointment me to prosecute all of these cases. I also didn't envision that the district would elect me to represent them in the legislature. If you'd like, I'll have Mother bring Rye to

Kinston and meet us there on the way back from Raleigh. Brett and Isabel will be back from Baltimore and I know Mother wants to see Isabel's new home. This gives her the perfect opportunity. We'll spend some time, too, so you can visit friends and neighbors, see your family and check on things at Pleasant Glade."

"You're right. I think I am a little homesick. I didn't realize how much I had missed Pa until he was here for the wedding. That visit home sounds wonderful right now." Penny nestled into his side, "Do you think Miss Caroline might like to come as well?"

"We'll ask both of them in the morning," Ryan promised. He breathed a deep sigh of relief, admitting to himself that he had been really worried about her and their marriage. He had found himself wondering for the first time if the relationship with Marcus had been more serious than she had told him. He realized that at moments he had felt an irrational jealousy that had made him almost glad that Marcus had been charged with murder and might well hang. Chiding himself for his rancor, he had endeavored to be even more considerate and loving towards his wife. Finally he seemed to have broken through the icy reserve between them and regained the warmth of their previous relationship. At least he hoped that was the case.

Although Penny had been peaceful and relaxed when she fell asleep, sometime in the night she began to toss restlessly, panicked at the vision that played across the stage of her mind. She saw Mammy Rena brewing something she knew to be evil and intended to cause harm. Poison? A woman dressed in black and as sinister as a demon from hell floated just in the periphery of her vision. Was the poison to kill her? Why would mammy want to kill someone? In her vision she heard a child screaming and then the glint of a knife gleaming in the light of a full moon. The vision dissolved in a field of blood, leaving her whimpering with fear.

"Penny, wake up. You're having a bad dream." Ryan touched her arm gently and then gathered her to him. "It's just a dream, darling."

Groggy, she sat up in bed and muttered, "It wasn't just a dream."

"No?"

"It was a warning of something sinister that's going to happen. I don't know why, but Mammy and a child are involved in it. There's someone else too, but I can't see who, anymore than I know who the child is."

"You haven't had a vision in a long time, not since the one of the boat wreck. That proved to be nothing and I'm sure this will, too. We all have dreams and most of them are just that, not visions."

Penny's voice tensed with repressed anger, "I know the difference. I've dealt with this all of my life and I know the difference. I tell you this was no dream. And just because the shipwreck didn't happen yet, it doesn't mean that it won't. I know you don't understand this thing I have, but it's real. You have to trust me enough to know that."

"I do trust you. Now try to relax and go back to sleep. There's nothing you can do about it tonight. When we visit Pleasant Glade, you can talk to Mammy and see if there's something that you need to concern yourself about. All right?"

She offered a grudging, "All right." When she felt sleep reclaim him, she eased from the warmth of their bed and paddled barefoot across the cold cypress floorboards and down the stairs to the smoldering fireplace in the parlor. Poking up the dying embers and adding fresh fat lightwood and a log, she tightened her robe and sat huddled before the fire. Sparks chased one another up the chimney as she drowsed. Again she felt danger gathering around her. She knew the shivers that raced down her spine were not from the chill of the January night. She could feel the darkness of evil descending into their midst. Although she replayed the vision in her mind, she could not discern why Mammy was pushed to the point of committing murder. Nor could she determine the other shadowy figures, the woman in black and the screaming child. The knife glinting with dripping blood, she recognized. But who had been stabbed?

Just before daybreak she climbed the stairs to her bed and slipped into the warm cocoon created by Ryan's slumbering body. When thin morning light crept through the French doors that opened onto the balcony overlooking the river, Ryan pulled her close and kissed her into awareness. Again they made love.

Ryan rode into his office that morning in a happy frame of mind. It was quick to be dashed by Colonel William Wheeler, commandant of the New Berne District, who stopped by his office for a misery session.

Wheeler informed him, "I just fired off a letter to Governor Jonathan Worth. I feel it's time someone advised him that New Berne is in danger of being swamped by people from outlying areas. They keep flocking into the town for protection from those damned bands of freedmen who are terrorizing area farms. I hate to be pessimistic, but I just don't anticipate any relief unless the governor gets prodded. Perhaps, while you're in Raleigh, you could emphasize to Governor Worth the importance of additional troops to keep peace in the district."

"Of course. I'll do what I can to help. I wish I could offer you assurance that your pleas will be heeded. I don't see much action of that kind coming from Worth though."

"Nor does anyone else from what I hear. It doesn't hurt to try I always say."

As soon as they were ensconced in their hotel in Raleigh just down from the Greek Revival-style Capitol, Ryan walked to the governor's office and requested an appointment. After an hour of fruitless waiting, he had just risen to leave Governor Worth's office, when the man emerged from the door behind his secretary's desk. Ryan wasted no time introducing himself. Obviously Worth was in a hurry to be elsewhere and had no time to spare. Not to be put off, he swung into step beside him and hastened to state his business.

The governor shrugged. "Wheeler's letter will be referred to Brigadier General Thomas Ruger, commander of the military occupation. I leave it to him to handle the situation. Now sir, I must excuse myself. I have more pressing matters to attend."

"Sir, need I stress..." Ryan began.

The governor cut him off with a curt, "I said I'll see to it."

Less than satisfied by the governor's remarks, Ryan left him to walk back to the hotel. He planned to treat his wife to a nice dinner and present her with the diamond drop earrings that nestled in the breast pocket of his gray serge suit. Since the promise of a visit to her old home, Penny seemed to be more of her usual self. Ryan hoped that the time in Raleigh, the earrings, and some concentrated attention from him would help erase any residue of anger that she might still hold towards him. Heaving a heavy sigh, he walked into the opulent lobby of the hotel. Just inside the door, he ran into R. W. King, his counterpart in the legislative assembly who was representing Lenoir County.

"Mr. King," Ryan hailed him, "Penny is going to be delighted to know there's a fellow townsmen here."

"Madison, good to see you." King said as they shook hands.

"And you as well, sir. But please, call me Ryan."

"So your wife's with you? If I had known, I would have brought my own." King smiled affably. "So, do you have dinner plans already?"

"I'm sorry, for this evening we do. However, perhaps tomorrow night you would be kind enough to join us?"

"That would be my pleasure, sir."

Ryan liked the man and would have asked him to join him for dinner that evening, but he wanted no change in the scenario of seduction he had planned. Tonight his attention and any charm he could muster were going to his wife.

The following morning Ryan walked from the hotel to the Capitol with a detour by the governor's mansion. He watched in amazement as a cow ambled across the area that had once been a beautifully landscaped garden but now resembled a neglected pasture. The house itself stood unoccupied: windows like blind shattered eyes, shutters broken from hinges and dangling like dirty underwear from the skin of the house, and the once grand home, devoid of furnishings and uninhabitable. He shook his head sadly at the reminder of the folly of war, and walked on to the Capitol. There he sat half listening to the bureaucratic droning of the morning session of the General Assembly and allowed his mind to drift to the evening before. Penny had been delighted with her gift and the passionate lovemaking afterwards was the stuff of his dreams. He felt his body quicken at the remembered passion.

The rising of strident voices around him brought his pleasant musing to an abrupt halt. Shaking himself to alertness, he sat forward in his chair. As he sifted through the cacophony of shouts to try to make sense of the turmoil, he became more and more alarmed. The outcome of the furor was the creation of a series of laws governing the rights of freedmen that would come to be known as the "Black Codes."

The secretary read the new regulations in a monotone that belied the gravity of what the assembly had created. "Gentlemen, as we have agreed. Black children that are orphaned and abandoned or whose parents are deemed unable or unsuitable to care for them may be placed in apprenticeships. Freedmen are forbidden to testify in court against whites. They may not serve on juries. Should a black man rape a white woman, it will be a capital offense."

This became the only instance in North Carolina law for which conviction for rape resulted in death. Ryan listened as the secretary continued to detail the new laws controlling weapon ownership, racial intermarriage, contracts and the right of mobility. As he saw it, all were discriminatory.

Growing ever more furious, Ryan could no longer remain quiet. Springing to his feet, he exclaimed, "Gentlemen, I must object. These laws in essence will relegate Negroes to much the same position they held under slavery."

A chorus of "No's!" from the cronies of the new governor drowned out Ryan's protests. He sat frustrated and helpless convinced that the Federal government under the new Congress would retaliate with vigor against States that passed such laws.

That night at dinner, Penny and Ryan sat in the dining room of the hotel basked by the light of candles on the table and gaslights in the chandeliers overhead. The excellent dinner of mountain trout, brought in fresh from Boone by train that very afternoon, and fine French champagne did nothing to lighten the mood at the table.

R.W. King, who had joined them at dinner, brought up the subject that weighed on Ryan. "Well, sir, I gather from your remarks in the assembly that you are dismayed by the actions today. As we struggle to reestablish ourselves, what ramifications might we expect from these new codes?"

Ryan looked into the older man's eyes, "Sir, if Southern legislatures continue the subjugation of Negroes it can only prolong the military occupation you despise. Furthermore, it will delay the South's emergence from what has been an essentially feudal society. I fear the congress will give President Johnson no option but to crack down on us following the actions here today."

"Can it become even worse for us than it is now?" Penny asked in alarm. "Mr. King, do you think Ryan is right?"

"I suspect your husband has a greater understanding of Washington and what we may expect than we do. I just hope to God he's wrong."

Ryan squeezed Penny's hand, "I hope I'm wrong, too."

He did not foresee that North Carolina would soon find itself dealing with the freedmen's response to the Black Codes, the Equal Rights League, a secret organization of freedmen. Whites, while wary and uncomfortable before, now feared massacre in the night at the hand of this new menace. As Ryan foresaw, the shortsighted actions from the various factions would bring challenges in the coming months and years that would further stress the fabric of the newly mended federation of states.

Ryan sat in thoughtful silence as they rode the train the following morning. It was a cold and gloomy day. On the way to Goldsboro Penny was content to look out the window at the passing countryside made austere by winter. There they would change trains in order to continue on to Kinston. Smoothing her moss green skirt across her knees, she idly picked at a piece of lint. She touched the earrings that swung gently from her earlobes and smiled with pleasure at the memory of the evening Ryan gave them to her.

Seeing the gesture, Ryan reached over and squeezed her hand, "I think you like my present."

"I love the earrings, but most of all, I love you. I'm just so grateful that we found a way back to one another after the war. I was remembering another time I took the train between Kinston and Goldsboro. I was pregnant with your child and desperate to reach my husband in the Richmond hospital in order to allay any suspicions about who had fathered my baby. With Daniel away in the war for so long, it could have been a disaster." In retrospect, she could not help but wonder if that had been the best course of action. It was almost a miracle that it had not cost her the husband that now sat beside her.

He lifted her hand to his lips and kissed it. "I'm glad that's all behind us. I cannot image life without you."

They rode in companionable silence for several miles before

Ryan said, "I've been mulling it over and I've made up my mind to resign my seat in the legislature. The whole process sickens me and it takes time from the life I want to build with you. I promised you we would spend more time at Pleasant Glade and it's a promise I haven't kept. It's important that Rye grow up knowing his family, the ones in New Berne, as well as, those in Kinston. With Isabel in Kinston, I know she will appreciate having us visit and bringing Mother as well."

"That would be wonderful, darling. However, are you sure you want to give up your legislative seat? You were so proud to be elected and so many people have put a lot of faith in you and the kind of representation you can provide. For me, I would be happy to see you relieved of that burden, but I worry that you will regret that you gave it up." Leaning against him she snuggled into his side, "Think about it a little longer. I don't want it to be a rash decision that's the result of your disappointment in Raleigh this week. We can work around it if it's something you decide you really need to continue doing."

"Are you sure you wouldn't resent the increased demands on my time?"

"I miss you every minute you are away from me, but I know we both have things we need to do in our lives that are separate from what we are together. If you decide to continue, we'll find a way to make it all work, so please don't factor worry over me into your decision."

"Penny, it isn't worry about us that leads me to this, but rather, frustration that I'm not as effective as I would like and disappointment that it takes so much time from my family. I hear what you are saying and you have a point. I had thought I could make a positive difference for a place I have come to love and now call home. I'm just not so sure anymore that this is the best use of my time and energy." He shook his head sadly.

Penny murmured, "I know, sweetheart. This whole business makes me sad too. I had so hoped that once the war was ended we could just get back to living in some kind of peace and harmony. Maybe someday..." They could only wonder how long that might be.

A healthier looking Moses met them at the station and helped Ryan load their bags into the buggy. On the drive to Pleasant Glade, Penny kept him busy answering questions about the farm and the happenings in the community. He commented on the new overseer she had hired and what a positive addition he and his wife were. He laughed as he recalled the return of an ebullient Brett and his new bride. He described the arrival of Martha, Caroline and Rye and their first day at Penny's home. He talked freely about the neighbors, but when Penny asked him about his own family, he grew reticent. Other than commenting that Lucinda and Jeremiah were staying with him and Mammy to help out with their visit, he provided nothing more. Wondering what he was holding back, Penny decided not to press him, but to wait until she could get Mammy Rena alone for a long chat.

It was so late when they arrived she knew it would have to wait until the following day. Deciding to leave the unpacking and visiting until morning, the travelers were quickly bedded down.

"Ryan, wake up. I thought I heard a scream." Penny shook her sleeping husband.

Instantly alert, he asked, "Where do you think it came from?"

"Listen, do you hear something?"

"It sounds like someone running. I wonder what Rye's doing up?" He pulled on his robe and hurriedly tied the sash. "I'll see what he's up to and get him back to bed."

Penny sat up in bed and wrapped her arms around her knees to await Ryan. After several minutes he still had not returned. Growing concerned, she had just started to climb from bed, when she heard him call to her from the open door of their bedroom. "Penny, come quick. I need you in Mother's room. She's been stabbed."

Running on bare feet, Penny reached the guest room on her husband's heels. "What on earth happened?"

"I don't know. Rye and Miss Caroline are both sleeping peacefully but when I checked on Mother, I saw a dark spot on her sheet that didn't look right. When I took the candle closer, I could see it was blood. It looks like she was stabbed in her neck. Can you do something to help her?" His voice rose with concern.

Penny rushed to the unconscious woman's side. "Bring the candle closer and then light a lamp so I can see how badly she's injured."

She whipped the sheet from the unconscious Martha's upper torso and leaned down to staunch the blood spurting from her neck. "This is a serious wound. We can only pray that the artery isn't punctured. There is just so much blood. Wake Nancy and ask her to get me some bandages. And, darling, please hurry!"

13

Sputtering, Shine lifted a gritty face and turned to look up at Marcus, "Goddammit, ain't I near enough dead already to suit you? If you don't quit that durn pounding on my back you're going to stick your fist plumb through me."

Marcus laughed, "Welcome back. I thought for a minute there you were a goner. By the time I pulled you in the boat and got us to shore, you were just about done for. That's why I faced you down in the sand and started pushing on your back. Now that some of that water has come up and you've got enough wind to cuss, I know you're going to be right as rain."

"I thought I was a goner myself when I fell out the boat. I reckon I owe you my life, for sure." Shine sat up and extended his hand for Marcus to pull him to his feet. Shine brushed away the damp sand that clung to him and glanced at the boat, asking, "Well, did we manage to save any of them fish and crabs?"

"All but maybe a couple of fish that washed overboard when I was hauling you in. Looks like we're going to have a fine mess for dinner. As for the clamming and oystering, haven't you about enjoyed all of this you can stand for one day?"

"Give me a minute more to git my land legs and let's give'er a go." Quietly Shine added, "And thanks, I won't be forgitting I owe you my life."

"I'm just glad we both lived through it. When I jumped into that water, I thought I was probably about to march through ole St. Pete's gate alongside of you. I don't think I've ever swum that hard in my life. Hell, I know I haven't. It's enough to make me turn religious," Marcus laughed. "That would probably be a welcome change to my fiancée and her family. They're right religious like and have made it plain I'm a little too casual in my church-going."

Pulling the clam rake from the boat, Shine waded into the calm surf along the shore. The storm clouds, having dumped their load of rain and wind over their hapless heads, were just tatters on the horizon, but the wind that now blew across the outer barrier island held a decided chill and the water was cold.

Marcus stood watching Shine for a moment, "That air's got a little bite to it. Are you sure you want to mess with this now when we're both soaking wet? We've got enough fish and crabs for the Captain, the guards and us, too. I'm tired after that swim. Let's just call it a day." He started gathering the fish and crabs from the boat. In a minute, Shine shrugged and left the surf to help him. By the time they had finished, their teeth were clacking like castanets and their shaking hands were making them clumsy.

"Lord, I am pure aiming to plop my behind by the fireplace. I intend to set with my feet baking pure tee done as a turkey soon as I can get shed of this stuff." Shine mumbled as they trudged through the gate toward the kitchen.

"Not me, sir. I'd just as soon stick kind of close to the kitchen fire and protect my rights to some of that fish I worked so hard to get," Marcus stated with emphasis. He was so sick of fatback, tough and frequently gamy pork, and dried peas he wasn't about to risk losing a chance at fresh seafood just to change clothes.

"You ain't got to worry about it. I'll see to it you git enough to eat 'til you're plumb ready to bust. After I tell the Captain how you saved my sorry ass, I 'spect he's going to think you deserve a treat. After all, you could've left me to drown and skedaddled with the boat. I sure would've considered it in your shoes. Let's dump this stuff and git into some dry clothes then I'll take care of it for you."

"Thanks, Shine. I suspect my carcass will warm a lot faster in if I ain't soaking wet." Marcus shivered uncontrollably as he stumbled into his cell and fumbled for some dry clothes. His cellmates had already gone to the mess hall for the daily fare of fat back and dried peas. Despite the dunking he'd taken, he considered it worth it to have something decent to eat for a change. For a moment his conscience prickled that his fellow prisoners might not have the benefit of his day of toil. He draped his clothes over the new slat-back chair that sat by the window and cast a rueful glance at the cold brick floor and thin blankets that would be waiting for him following dinner. An involuntary shudder racked his frame followed by an explosive sneeze.

"Hustle it up, Marcus. I want to git myself in some dry clothes real quick like. I'm going to take you to the kitchen and then do just that." Waiting in the doorway, Shine hugged himself against the wind that whipped around the parade ground, circling like a trapped beast. "Tarnation if that wind ain't some kind of fierce."

"Sorry to keep you, Shine. Let's get our bones to some warm food." Marcus remarked as he followed Shine towards the kitchen.

"I meant to tell you and I just plumb forgot. The warden has a package that come for you yesterday with quilts and food and some letters. He gave it over to be searched and recorded or you would already have it." Shine grinned back at him. "Don't worry about that floor tonight, I'm going to see to it you get a bed in the infirmary. I'll tell the doc you swallowed a bunch of seawater saving my ass and you need to be coddled for a day or two. I also aim to see if the warden can't do better by you and maybe git you into a cell with a bunk."

"Lord, that would be as welcome as rain in a drought. That

brick floor is so cold and miserable I've been tempted to try hanging from the ceiling like a bat. At least it's warmer up there. What little heat that fireplace in there puts out never makes it down to the floor. It's a pure wonder we ain't all dead of pneumonia."

"You ain't lying about that." Shine snorted, "I could sure as hell use some of that moonshine I used to make. It could light a fire in your gut that'd burn for a day. Lord, I can taste it now...smooth as Chiney silk on my tongue, warming to a purr going down my throat, and then building to a furnace in my belly."

"It would sure be welcome," Marcus agreed. "I don't think I've been warm and totally dried out since I came here. It's a damned wonder my skin ain't as mildewed as my shoes."

With his stomach filled with the best food he'd eaten in months and the warmth of the kitchen wrapping him in a cocoon of comfort as nurturing as a mother's womb, Marcus sighed with satisfaction as he slipped into sleep slumped over the worktable in the back of the kitchen. He dreamed of Lena and the children he would give her. In his sleep he found Penny's face trying to replace that of his fiancée. He stirred drowsily and forced his mind to find Lena's image again.

Listening to Marcus' sibilant snores, the cook shook his head and chuckled as he moved about his domain, readying the space for the morrow's meals. He couldn't recall every having heard such effusive praise from anyone for his admittedly sparse culinary skills as that heaped upon him by a grateful Marcus.

While Marcus slept, Shine was doing his best to plead for special dispensation for the man who had saved his life. The warden listened as Shine elaborately described the day's events and Marcus' heroic efforts to save him. Exhausted from the effulgent pleas, he held up his hand to stem another round of importuning. Shine left with a new assignment for Marcus:

permanent duty in the infirmary including night duty as a standby attendant. Marcus would have a bunk in the infirmary and a locker for the meager possessions allowed him. When Shine returned to the kitchen with the news, he also carried the package that had arrived the previous day.

Marcus was elated at the prospects of a bed awaiting him at the end of each monotonous day and he reminded himself that compared to the other prisoners, he was privileged indeed. However, he should have remembered the old adage, 'be careful what you wish for.' But his delight in the news accompanied by the letters from Lena and the package she included containing two quilts, some cookies, and three books were absorbing enough to allow no time to contemplate any negative import to his change of quarters. At the bottom of the letters, he picked up a final envelope expecting another letter from Lena. It was with a flush of guilty pleasure that he saw Penny had written him. He tamped down the upwelling of joy that a letter from her could still bring him and reminded himself that particular road led only to the land of heartbreak. She was his past, an unrealized one at that, and Lena his future. He reread Lena's letters and acknowledged once again that he was fortunate to have the love of such a good and steadfast woman, one that was as beautiful in her own way as Penny. He looked with longing at the letter from Penny and debated shoving it unread into the fire that still burned brightly in the cook's stove.

Marcus closed his eyes and munched thoughtfully on one of the oatmeal cookies Lena's mother had made for him. For the first time in months, he felt as though there might be some light at the end of the tunnel. Lena related how her father had found a witness who could attest that he had seen Marcus leaving Henry Tull's farm the Saturday night of the murder. Although the man was unsure about the time, he at least provided a partial corroboration to that portion of Marcus' story. If only the man could remember some clue that would give a time to his sighting, Marcus would have a good defense against the circumstantial evidence mounted against him. Lena's father was as persistent as a bulldog, so Marcus could only trust that he would continue looking for some proof that would exonerate him.

He held Lena's letter to his nose and inhaled the faint aroma of the rose perfume she wore. He smiled remembering the words of devotion and love that she had written him. Aware he had done little to deserve such devotion, he vowed to be worthy of it, should fate give him the opportunity. Determined to think only of her love for him and the life he would create with this good woman, Marcus slipped Penny's letter into the bundle. Perhaps later, he would read it. For the moment he wanted to forget the feelings he still had for her, and concentrate on Lena instead. He did not trust his heart to be able to block Penny out if she had written anything that would feed his love for her. In his rational mind, he knew that his only option was to get on with his life, but his heart was not a rational organ. It wanted him to spin daydreams where his fondest desires would all be realized. Reality was but a momentary inconvenience. Marcus snorted at the very idea. Current reality was a hell of a major inconvenience to the realization of anything that he might desire.

Shine tapped Marcus on the shoulder, "I'm about ready to turn in. Let's go git your stuff out of that cell and git you moved to the infirmary."

"Right. I'm about ready to get some sleep, too. It has for sure been a long day," Marcus said, as he stood to follow the guard.

When he entered the cell, he was grateful to see that his cellmates were sleeping. Moving with care so as not to disturb the others and guided only by the dim light from the dying embers in the fireplace, he collected his scant belongings and departed the cell. He was happy to see the last of it. In the infirmary, he put his things in the locker that Shine indicated.

"Thanks, Shine." Marcus stuck his hand out to shake the guard's. "I sure do appreciate your help getting me a bed in here."

"Aw, don't mention it. I told you I owe you my life. This is small payment. And you remember, I'm a man who ain't forgitting what he owes and who he owes it to. That's a promise."

"You're a friend for life, Shine. Soon as I can get my sorry behind out of here, I intend to see what I can do to make things better for you and that's a promise."

"I can deal with that," Shine grinned as he left the infirmary.

Marcus patted the corn-shuck mattress on the cot he had been given. He turned it over and checked for bedbugs, the ubiquitous tormentor of such quarters, and smiled when he found none. Shaking out his quilts, he quickly made his bed and stripped down to his long-johns. For the first time since his arrest, the night brought a sound and peaceful sleep.

The morning sun was sending silver ribbons of light through the casement window when he opened his eyes to find the doctor peering at him with a quizzical expression on his face. "What seems to be the problem, Marcus? I can't see anything wrong with you and you don't have a fever."

"I'm sorry, sir. I guess no one told you that I have been moved here to sleep. The warden made the change last night so there will always be someone on duty in here."

Dr. Coues worried his cheek with his tongue for a moment before commenting, "I see." He studied Marcus a moment longer before adding, "If you want breakfast, you'd better hustle on over there before they quit serving."

"Yes, sir. Soon as I can get some clothes on, I'll do just that. It appears I over-slept. I'll try not to do that again because I know you like to get organized in here first thing in the morning."

"With no patients at the moment, that's not a problem. Now, run along to breakfast."

Marcus wasted no time getting into his clothes and vacating the infirmary. Judging from the less than enthusiastic reception the doctor gave the news of his new assignment, it was a good time to give him a chance to adjust to his morning surprise. Things weren't much better in the mess. Although most of the prisoners had eaten and left for their morning chores, his previous cellmates were among those remaining.

He ambled over to their table and began lowering his tray only to be halted by a snarled admonishment from Smitty Wilson, "Why don't you just move your sorry kiss-ass, cock-sucking self on somewhere else. You're too damned high-falluting to be setting with us anymore since you got to be the warden's little pet."

"I sure wouldn't want to inconvenience you boys any, so I'm happy to move. However, for your information, I'm assigned to night duty in the infirmary and that's the reason for the move. It's certainly not because the warden needs me for a pretty boy. Besides, I hear his wife is a sight better looking than I am." Marcus attempted a laugh, hating himself when it sounded forced.

"Whatever. Just move on. You ain't welcome here," Jethro said as he looked at Marcus, his saurian eyes colder than an artic winter. "You might better watch your back. We don't take much to suck-ups."

"I can handle your shit. You mess with me, you'll know we tangled." Marcus picked up his tray and moved to a far table by the window where he ate in solitude. Despite the tough and confident words, he felt uneasy.

The room had gone quiet and frozen, as though waiting for a spark of anger to warm it back to life. He was glad when the other prisoners finished eating and sullenly abandoned the room to him. Appetite ruined, the breakfast he had relished now tasted like bilge water. Feeling bitter bile rising in his throat, he dropped his fork and deposited his dishes by the counter. He didn't want to go to the parade ground for his morning outing and he didn't want to go back to the infirmary to face the doctor, but he couldn't stay in the kitchen. He couldn't stand the smell of food either. Taking a deep breath, he pulled his coat around his chest and fastened the buttons. Better to just find a quiet corner of the parade ground and give things time to settle down.

During the coming days the isolation from his fellow prisoners left Marcus with nothing to occupy his free time except reading and then re-reading the books and letters that Lena had mailed. He awaited the next sporadic batch with impatience, wondering why the mail service was still operating so inefficiently. He had understood poor service during wartime, but had little sympathy for continued problems during Reconstruction.

His days in the infirmary and the occasional night duty, gave him time to observe Dr. Coues and to learn from his skill. Most of the time, treatment was for minor injuries and the constant plague of colds and ague bought on by the damp chill of the fort. The most serious injury occurred when a soldier on duty on the ramparts, stepped too close to the edge and lost his balance falling some twenty feet into the moat. The rainy winter had turned the moat into a muddy quagmire essentially cushioning his fall and sparing the man injury except for a broken leg.

Marcus assisted Dr. Coues in getting the man onto the table and prepped for treatment. The break was a serious one. Despite Corporal Reginald Hollis's frantic pleading for the doctor to save his leg, Marcus knew enough about broken limbs to tell that the doctor's first impulse was immediate amputation. The risk of infection from the foul water and mud in the moat was not something he could ignore. Fortunately for the soldier, the doctor was sufficient moved by Hollis's emotional entreaties to delay surgery.

"All right, son. It is against my better judgment, but I'm going to try setting this leg. The danger is infection and there's not much we can do for that except pray hard you don't get enough of one to cost you your life. Do you really understand the risk you're taking?"

"Yes, sir, I do," Hollis said. "I don't want to live my life as a cripple. I don't want to go home to my girl one-legged. You do what you can to save it."

"Marcus, get the alcohol, some boiling water, and some chloroform. Then I'm going to need your help with him." The doctor began assembling the items he would need while Marcus hastened to comply with his directions. They worked in tandem until the limb was cleaned, set and neatly bandaged. When they had finished they set about cleaning the work area while the chloroformed soldier continued a soft snoring. Marcus tucked a blanket around him and prepared to spend the night watching for any signs of a fever.

Coues patted Marcus on the shoulder, "I appreciate your help, Marcus. You've learned a lot during your time here."

Marcus thanked him and the two sat chatting amiably. Marcus told him about Penny, her gift for healing and the herbs she had prepared for the people of the neighborhood. The doctor listened with quiet interest. "You ever considered studying medicine?"

"No, sir, I'm a farmer and that's the life I love. I aim to get back to it as soon as this mess can be worked through."

Giving him a level stare, without preamble Dr. Coues asked, "Did you kill that man?"

"No, sir."

"I suppose if you had, you wouldn't tell me," the doctor muttered. Louder he added, "I don't think you're a murderer, either. You've got too much self-control. I've watched you with the other prisoners when they taunt you: you don't back down, you just quietly hold your own. They respect you enough they don't push but so far, but even if they did, I don't see that kind of brutal rage in you."

"I appreciate that more than you know. It's hard sitting here, penned up like some animal and accused of something I didn't do. I confess I despair at times. I've got a fiancée waiting for me. I want to get out of here before she gives up on me."

"That Penny must be some woman. I can see your eyes light up when you talk about her."

Marcus looked down at his feet. "Penny's married to Colonel Ryan Madison in New Berne. But you're right. I sure did love that woman for a long time. The woman I'm engaged to is Lena Rouse from the Falling Creek area near Kinston. She's a fine, deserving woman and I aim to marry her the minute I'm free. If it hadn't been for this mess, I'd already be a married man."

Weary from the long day, Dr. Coues stood and stretched, "Well, I'm going to turn in for the night. Keep an eye on our patient here and if he starts running a high fever, let me know."

Marcus didn't dare fall asleep. He owed it to the boy and to the doctor, to maintain watchful vigilance. Several times during the night, Corporal Hollis asked Marcus for water. By morning it was obvious that he was running a fever but not one of sufficient degree to alarm the doctor. It was fortunate for Hollis that the low-grade infection gave way to healing and soon he was limping about on crutches, his splinted leg distended at a stiff angle. He cried with gratitude when the doctor removed the splint and allowed him to stand. In time, the only evidence of the injury was a slight limp when he was tired.

Gradually the relationship between Marcus and the doctor developed into one of mutual respect and genuine liking. Having an intelligent, interesting man to talk to and learn from was a genuine boon to Marcus who had never gone much beyond the confines of Lenoir County and knew little of the world beyond that of a farm. For the first time, he felt his boundaries expanding and with it a greater appreciation for his own abilities.

For the doctor, while skeptical, it was a chance to learn as much from Marcus as he could about the herbal remedies that he had seen Penny use. Since his knowledge was sketchy at best, Marcus wrote her that Dr. Coues was interested in learning about the various medicinal herbs indigenous to the area and would like her address to write for information. Listening to Marcus described the life of a farm: the joy of watching a calf rise on shaking birth-wet legs, the pride of looking out across newly greening fields, and the pleasure of eating food grown on your own land, taught the doctor something of the rewards of a pastoral life. A bookish city-bred man, he had never spared much attention for nature other than an occasional remark on a particularly glorious sunset. Now he determined to go with Marcus and Shine on their next fishing trip, provided the day was a fine one.

The time in prison that had previously weighed so heavily on Marcus now became one of new friendships with bonds strong enough to endure for a lifetime and of an introspection that gave new knowledge of the man he was and the one he wanted to become. Although he would never have desired the path that brought him to this crossroads in his life, he was nonetheless grateful that the ill wind had indeed blown some modicum of good.

14

Penny had never before been frightened of the world around her. Even during the war she had not felt as threatened as now. Martha's stabbing and subsequent death changed that. The fog of evil that hung over them all after Martha's murder was so dense and pervasive that Penny choked on the very air in the rooms of her house. This home where she had felt safe was no longer a refuge. Mammy Rena, who had been like a mother to her, was strangely silent and remote. Nancy walked through the rooms like a wraith, not speaking, her face covered with noiseless tears. Ryan and Isabel held one another with stunned faces, their grief deep and unrelenting for the mother that they had lost. Even Caroline, who efficiently stepped in to help her organize for the laying out and to see to Rye's needs, acted as though she was floating on an alien sea. Penny held Ryan and murmured words of sympathy as he struggled with his grief. Merely smiling with great sadness, he offered no suggestions as to how to bury his mother and asked her to do what she thought best. This was perhaps most frightening of all, as she had always looked to Ryan as a tower of immutable strength, yet now he seemed so sunken in despair that he barely responded when spoken to. She knew he also wrestled with feelings of guilt that he had been remiss in assuring the safety of those around him.

It was her father and brother who arranged for the coffin, a preacher, and train transportation of the coffin to New Berne following the funeral services. Caroline had insisted that Martha be buried in the Framingham family cemetery on the knoll behind her house. Ryan, knowing that his mother had been happy in the last years of her life living with Caroline, did not demure. Isabel smiled through her tears and agreed that the formerly querulous woman had made peace with her demons while living there and thus the site was a good resting place for her. They were both grateful they could look back on their mother's life and hold close the memory of her final years. But gratitude that her last years had seen a positive change in her personality did nothing to ameliorate their shock at how she had died.

Penny found herself increasingly grateful for the quiet efficiency of the Davenport couple, Jeremy and Tillie. Together they had scrubbed the lasted vestiges of blood from the floor in Martha's bedchamber. While Tillie worked in the kitchen helping Lucinda and Mammy prepare food for the funeral, Jeremy rode into town to get the sheriff.

Sheriff Kennedy, after interviewing each of them in turn, shook his head and commented with puzzlement, "It just don't make sense. I can't figure out any motive for someone doing this to the woman. After all, she's never even been here before."

No one could disagree with Jesse Kennedy's assessment of the situation. Other than Martha's scream and the running feet that had awakened Penny and Ryan, none of them had heard anything.

Ryan prepared to leave following the funeral service, and a day spent plaguing the sheriff who had finally tossed him out. Jeremy drove the wagon holding his mother's casket to the back steps where the family had gathered. Caroline and Rye were returning to New Bern with Ryan and his mother's body. Despite his adamant objections, Penny had pleaded to be allowed to stay a few days in order to spend some time with her family and the people on her farm. Before Ryan climbed into the wagon to begin the sad journey home, he turned to Penny, "I have real misgivings about leaving you behind. Not knowing who murdered my mother, you must understand how worried I will be for you until you're safe at home."

"I know, darling. Pa is going to stay here with me until I leave and I promise I'll keep my bedroom door locked at night. We all will. Rye will be fine with Miss Caroline during the day and I know you'll manage at night. Kirby and his wife will do all they can to help you. Just don't let Gertie spoil him by cooking too many sweets." Penny was well aware that it went beyond "misgivings" as he had been furious the night before when she had told him she was staying behind and planned to keep Rye with her. He had made it coldly clear that if that was her choice, he couldn't force her but she "damned well" would not endanger Rye by keeping him there. Penny agonized about staying. She knew Ryan was still mourned his mother's death and wanted her with him. She wanted to leave, but her responsibility to the people on her farm also weighed on her.

"We will be fine, Penny. It's not us I'm worried about." Ryan was struggling to repress his anger. The tight set of his mouth gave ample evidence that he was still very annoyed with her. "I'm miserable enough that I couldn't prevent my mother from being murdered. How do you think I would feel if the same killer came for you, too?"

"I promise I'll be careful. I would just feel too awful to leave Nancy just now. She's a nervous wreck and threatening to go back to her parents. I would so hate to have her leave, especially with Mammy and Moses in such poor spirits. The Davenports are wonderful, however they're young and don't know things here that well yet. Give me just a little while longer, then I promise I'll come home. I'm going to miss you and Rye so much that I can't stand to think about it. However, maybe if I stay I can help the sheriff find out who did this."

"Oh, for God's sake, Penny! Do you think that is any kind of reassurance to me when I am already worried sick for you?" Ryan had to stop himself from raising his voice in frustration. Clenching his fists, he stood rigid for a moment collecting himself. "Look, I don't want to leave either, but I have to. If it weren't for getting Miss Caroline and Rye home safely, Mother buried and the court case that's waiting for me, I'd be staying here to look for the killer and sending you to the safety of our home. You promise me you'll not go meddling in this. It's too dangerous. You don't know what kind of hornet's nest you might unwittingly stir up. Dammit, your brother and father can sort things out here. Why is it you think you can do what they can't?"

"I promise I won't do anything foolish and I won't meddle in the sheriff's business." Penny smiled at the man she loved, "Do you think you could give me a goodbye kiss?"

Trying a final ploy to get her to go with him, he whispered into her ear just before he kissed her, "Come home with me and I'll do better than that."

"With a promise like that, I won't stay long. I love you, Ryan. Please try to understand."

"I love you, too," but there was a defeated chill to his voice when he said it. Ryan lifted Rye to kiss Penny goodbye and then into the wagon. "If we're going to make the train, we'd best get going."

Penny, Mammy, Moses, Nancy and Tillie stood in the yard watching them until they were lost from sight. Caroline and Rye turned to wave good-bye as the wagon drove away, but not Ryan. Penny knew from the rigid set of his back he was leaving furious with her. She could only hope that she was doing the right thing by staying. Caroline promised she would talk to Ryan and take good care of both her husband and her son until she could return. Penny wasn't sure how much that would help as Caroline also questioned the wisdom of her remaining behind. She had not hesitated to tell Penny she was making a mistake that Ryan would be slow to forget.

From the corner of her eye, Penny could see Lucinda standing in the doorway of the kitchen with Jeremiah peering around her. She resolved that Lucinda and her son would not leave until she had the opportunity to sit the coolly reserved woman down for a long talk. She was worried about not only about Lucinda's parents, the skittish behavior of her son, but Lucinda as well. None of them seemed comfortable around her. Something was troubling them and she intended to delve into what it might be.   Nancy also needed to be placated and soothed before she bolted. The Davenports deserved some kind of heads up to the atmosphere that Penny found so unsettling. She didn't think it emanated from them, but she had to be sure. And she wanted badly to discover who had murdered Martha and the overseer. It seemed too coincidental for two murders to have occurred in such proximity to one another and in such a short time. Was there a connection? Were others in danger if some one as innocent as Martha of any connections to the area could be murdered?

Penny was grateful that her father was in the house that night. She also felt comforted by the loaded pistol that rested beneath the snowy pillowcase on Ryan's side of the bed. Without him there to comfort and protect, even the presence of her father in the bedroom across the hall would not have been enough to allow her the sense of security she needed to sleep. As it was, she slept, not soundly but enough that when she awakened at first light and made her way to the dark and cold kitchen, she was more rested than she had been for several days. Soon she had coffee brewing, biscuits in the oven, ham sliced and sizzling in the pan, and eggs whipped and resting in the bowl ready for scrambling. Churning in the pantry for preserves to go with the biscuits, Penny reached to remove a jar of huckleberry jam from the shelf. Squinting in the half-light, she could see a small package stuffed behind the jars.

Curiosity aroused, she picked it up and carried it into the kitchen where she dropped it on the table. She could tell by the aroma coming from the cast iron skillet, that the ham was ready.

Speared the slices before they could burn, she moved them onto the platter she had placed near the stove. Sliding the skillet from the heat, she turned back to the table. The roughly sewn flour-sacking bag looked innocent resting on the scrubbed pine tabletop. Despite feeling a sense of guilt that she was prying into someone's secret property, Penny did not feel sufficient compunction to refrain from opening it. Dumping the contents onto the table, she watched as several small bones, a black hawk's feather, a pebble, a clump of hair, and a crude doll fell onto the surface of the table. She surmised it must be Mammy Rena's as she had heard her when she was a child talking about the witchdoctor of her village and his magic conjures. The old woman had to be very upset to consider casting a spell on someone. She was so absorbed in pondering the significance of the items and what Mammy intended to do with them that she did not hear the kitchen door opening.

"You don't be messing with my things now, Miz Penny. That stuff ain't for you." Mammy walked to the table and wasted no time scooping the items back into the bag.

"Mammy, something is going on around here that I don't like the feel of. Bad things have happened, both here and at Marcus' farm. Whatever is wrong and is affecting the ones I care about is something I can't just leave alone. I intend to get to the bottom of it. Now is not the time to talk about this bag and all of the rest since the others will be down any minute for breakfast. But, whatever it is that's troubling you we need to find a better way of dealing with than that bag of hokum."

"Ain't hokum. That's serious conjure magic I learnt as a child in Africa." Mammy mumbled rebelliously.

Penny halted a sharp retort when her father and Nancy entered the kitchen. "Hello, sleepy heads. Give me a minute to scramble these eggs and we'll have breakfast."

Following breakfast, John Bartlett left to return to his own plantation for the day. Nancy excused herself to work on a dress she was sewing on upstairs in her bedroom, leaving Mammy and Penny busy putting the kitchen in order and planning what to pull from the pantry for the midday meal. Judging by the tight set of the old woman's mouth, Penny knew she would get little from her until Mammy's wrath had subsided. Taking the damp kitchen towels, she walked out to the clothesline and began pinning them up to dry. Startled by a noise that did not belong in the quiet morning, she spun around, her nerves already on edge. She could see the figure of a woman partially obscured by the large camellia tree in the edge of the backyard. There was a striking familiarity about the woman. And then it hit her. Feeling as though she were looking at the ghost of her mother-in-law, incredulously Penny cried, "Martha??"

The woman stepped from behind the bush. Penny stood, mouth agape and trembling as the woman drew near. This woman was slovenly, not at all like the meticulously groomed Martha, nonetheless there was an uncanny similarity. "Who are you?"

"You must be Miz Kennedy? I been wanting to talk to you," the woman said in a flat twang, not bothering to respond to Penny's shocked inquiry.

"My name is Madison now. I repeat, who are you?"

"I'm Abigail Smith, Calvin Smith's widow woman. He what was murdered by Marcus Cauley," she whined.

A combative Penny replied, "Let's get one thing straight, Mrs. Smith. Your husband was not murdered by Marcus."

"I ain't come here to argue none about all that. I come 'cause I got five hungry children to feed and no man to provide us nothing. We could sure use a mite of help and a place to live," she wheedled.

"I can give you some money to buy some food for your children, but there is no place here for you to live. You wait. I'll be right back." Penny left her standing in the yard and entered the house to retrieve her reticule from her bedroom. Ryan had pressed an extra roll of bills in her hand when he left in case she needed supplies for the farm so she had more than she knew she would need. Penny halted in mid stride, recalling the woman had testified at Marcus' hearing. At the time she had paid her no mind, as her attention had been focused on Marcus. Thinking back to that day and the woman's damning testimony, Penny regretted her ready charity. Were it not for the children, she would have changed her mind about the proffered money.

Descending the stairs, Penny saw Mammy waiting at the bottom, arms akimbo and her face a mask of fury. "What that sorry trash wanting around here? She got no bizness here, Miss Penny!" Mammy spat the words.

"Don't worry, she won't be staying. I'm just giving her some money so she can feed her children."

"That ain't your worry. She just be a coming back for more if you give her money."

"Mammy, this isn't like you. Why do you dislike this woman so much? I doubt that you even know her more than passing well."

"I knows enough to say she nothing but trash." Mammy gave Penny a hard stare, "It be best if she don't come 'round here no more."

"What on earth has she done to you to make you feel this way?" Penny was genuinely puzzled. "Her husband may have molested Lucinda, but neither she nor her children can be held to blame for his sins."

"I got my reasons," Mammy declared.

Penny sighed, "We'll talk about that later. Right now I'm going to give her this money and be done with her."

"Ain't seen the last of that trash, no 'am. Sure ain't." Mammy stalked into the kitchen, slamming the door behind her.

"Lordy, the way these darkies carry on, you'd think it was me what done something wrong," Abigail simpered at the slamming door.

"Mammy isn't one to be upset for no reason. Take this money and get some food for your children, and don't come back here for anything else. Is that clear?" Penny turned on her heel without waiting for an answer.

Abigail called to her retreating back, "Yes 'am, I hear it. I reckon theys others who ain't so snippety."

Annoyed by the Smith woman's attitude and dreading the coming conversation with Mammy, Penny veered away from the kitchen. What she needed at that moment was a walk to calm herself before venturing into what was sure to be a verbal fray with her old and much loved servant. Although there was a November chill in the air, the sun was warm enough that her shawl would suffice for a short amble into the woods behind her house. Craving a watercress salad for her dinner, she hastened her steps through lush Long Leaf Pines to the creek bank where a stand of cress grew in rampant profusion. Penny was so absorbed in collecting the cress that she did not at first hear the strange whimpers that seemed to be emerging from a clump of woods further down the path. Clutching her skirt to make a basket to hold the cress, she stood and followed the sound.

Creeping softly in the direction of the whimpering, she moved a low branch of glossy green Carolina jasmine. Huddled behind the bushy vine, Jeremiah sat rocking and crooning, his face wet with tears and mucus. Penny looked through the trees to see what had so upset him. In the distance, she could see Abigail Smith making her way through the woods back to wherever she had come from. Penny wondered if there was some connection between Jeremiah's agitation and the woman.

"Jeremiah, where's your mama? Does she know you're here? Let's go find her, shall we?"

The boy didn't acknowledge her presence in any way. "Jeremiah!" She said more sharply. "Is something wrong?"

Unable to arouse him from his rocking stupor, Penny

hurried back to the house shouting for Lucinda. Lucinda rushed from her mother's cabin just as Penny ran into the yard. "What is it?" She cried in alarm.

"Lucinda, Jeremiah is down near the creek bank and is crying and upset. I tried to get him to come but he just ignores me. I don't know what else to do."

"Just show me where he is, please. He hasn't been right since he saw Marcus' overseer violate me. And for some reason, his widow terrifies Jeremiah."

As they ran back the way Penny had come, she asked Lucinda, "Is he still not talking."

"I'm afraid not. Your brother finished building the school and I've started teaching a group of students. I take him with me thinking that being around other children will help, but so far nothing seems to get through."

"He's over there behind that jasmine."

"I think perhaps you should leave. He'll come with me if no one else is around." Lucinda paused, "Thank you, for your concern. I'm grateful."

"You're welcome, Lucinda." Penny returned to the house alone, carrying the cress she still cradled in her skirt. She could not imagine what it was about that slattern Abigail that would so terrify Lucinda's son. Hoping that Mammy would be in the kitchen so she could talk with her about it while they washed the cress for supper, she was disappointed to find only Nancy drinking a cup of coffee left from the morning's pot.

"What happened to Mammy?"

Nancy shrugged, "I don't know where she was off to. She picked up her shawl and left when I came in. I didn't ask her where she was going. Is something wrong?"

"I get the feeling she either knows or suspects where some of the problems around here are coming from. I know she despises that overseer's widow and Jeremiah is terrified of the woman. What Abigail Smith has done to create such animosity,

I don't know. I can understand why they would hate the man who hurt Lucinda, but Calvin's dead. Why would they feel this way about the widow? After all, she's not responsible for what her husband did, even if she isn't particularly pleasant."

"I don't know either, but somehow they all seem to think that she is responsible for Jeremiah's continuing silence." Nancy took a sip of her coffee before continuing, "I worry about him. That child was always sullen and difficult but now it's something more. I confess he gives me the creeps. He's just not a normal child. He's evil somehow."

Penny was shocked, "Nancy, that's not at all like you. He's just a frightened child. I know he's been a bit of a problem, but he has been through a lot watching those men do that to his mama."

"It's not just that. If you think about it, you know Jeremiah was always different. And now he's always sneaking around and just watching. I just don't know how much more of it I can take. I'll be glad when Lucinda takes him on home. My nerves were already on edge and now with Martha murdered in her bed in the room next to me, I'm just about undone."

"I know. It's a hard thing to fathom and deal with. If it made some kind of sense, it would be different."

"I wish I knew why it happened. I might sleep better if I did." Nancy shuddered involuntarily. "Mammy's acting weird, too. I've tried but she just won't talk to me."

"I noticed as well and I planned to talk with her about it if she were here." Penny snorted, "That's probably why she left. Plus, she's furious I gave Abigail money."

"I also gave Abigail some the other day," Nancy remarked. "For some reason she's been hanging around the neighborhood. Tillie told me they think she's living in an abandoned shack over on the Whaley farm. I wish someone would run her off. She's nothing but trouble, for sure."

15

Lizzy did not intend to wait. The minute she heard that Ryan's mother had been murdered and he had returned to town without his wife, she dressed in her most alluring dress and walked to his office praying that he would be there. Luck was with her. Ryan sat at his desk pushing papers about. Try though he might, he was having no luck focusing. Just as he slammed his fist on his desk in frustration, a quiet knock at his inner office door was followed by Lizzy's cheery hello.

Ryan's invitation to enter sounded grudging at best. She snickered at the tone.

Confident she looked her best, a provocative Lizzy sauntered into his office. Composing her face into one of sober commiseration, she cried, "Oh, Ryan. How truly awful! I just heard what happened to your poor mother and I am so very sorry. During the time we were courting I came to love her like my own. This just breaks my heart." Lizzy squeezed tears from the corners of her downcast eyes.

"Thank you, Lizzy. I appreciate your condolences. I must confess, I find it difficult to deal with the whole mess." Ryan grimaced then shuffled his papers. She refused to take the hint.

Always sensitive to his moods, Lizzy realized what he wanted, but her own plans were the priority at the moment. "Oh, poor Isabel and dear Miss Caroline, as well. I know she is devastated. Those two had become like sisters. I must pay her a call."

"That's kind of you. Yes, Miss Caroline is very saddened by what has happened. After years of living under the same roof, she had grown very close to my mother. At the moment, my son is with her during the day which helps keep her mind from what happened."

Lizzy wasn't about to divulge her prior knowledge that he had returned from Kinston without his wife. "Oh, my goodness," she gasped in feigned shock. "I'm so sorry. I can only imagine how much you need Penny with you at a time like this. And poor Miss Caroline with the added responsibility of an active little boy at her age." Walking closer, she leaned across the desk and patted his hand. "Do you think it would be terrible, if I were to stop by and spend some time with them. It might relieve Miss Caroline of some of the burden of dealing with Rye. Oh, I know he is a darling child and no trouble, but she is quite old, you know."

"If you wish to call on Miss Caroline and express your sympathy at our loss, I don't think that would be amiss. However Rye is not only in Miss Caroline's charge, but her housekeeper and mine are also helping and of course I'm there at night."

"You dear man, my heart goes out to you." Lizzy edged around his desk as she said it and caressed his cheek with a light kiss. "If there is anything at all I can do to help, I'm only too eager. You must let me out of my obligation to you for our past friendship. After all, you're still the most wonderful man around and I still consider us friends." She quelled the giggle that threatened as she watch him becoming uncomfortable by her nearness and the pressure of her breast against his shoulder as she leaned over him.

Ryan cleared his throat and rose from his desk. "Please excuse me, Lizzy. I have to get over to the courthouse to check on the status of a case that I'm working on. Permit me to see you to the door."

"Oh, but of course. I'm sure you're busy. Please don't allow me to intrude on your schedule." Lizzy smiled sweetly, "If there's anything at all I can do to make life easier on you all right now, just let me know. Again, I am so very sorry for your loss."

"I appreciate your stopping by," Ryan responded in dismissal. He did not want Lizzy complicating his life. Just because he was without Penny for the present did not mean that Lizzy had an opening to re-enter his life. His was annoyed with himself that a small frisson of remembered desire sparked to life, when hips swaying seductively, she walked from his door to the sidewalk. Pushing the image from his mind, he returned to his office and resumed work on the papers that had piled up on his desk during his absence. If only Ryan had known the declaration of war that had just occurred.

Lizzy walked down Pollock Street with a smug, self-satisfied grin on her face. She had only just begun to fight. Passing a shop window displaying an appealing toy train, she altered course and entered the store. A few moments later she emerged carrying it in her arms. *My admission ticket,* she declared. Now she had only to borrow her father's carriage and ride out to Caroline Framingham's for the sympathy call. Again she thanked her lucky stars that her parents had always allowed her exceptional freedom unlike most young women she knew.

The next afternoon Lizzy went to Caroline's to express her sorrow at the loss of Martha. She found Caroline sitting in the sunroom exhausted. A still energetic Rye was urging her to go outside and play with him. Seeing her opportunity to ingratiate herself, Lizzy insisted that she take him out. Grateful for the relief, Caroline was more than happy to oblige. Lizzy waited a day and then went again to take the little train that she had purchased for Ryan's son. Again she took him out to play. Over the coming days, she began to establish a pattern with her trips. From time to time she took presents for Rye and less frequently a sweet or some other trifle for Caroline. Caroline was guarded with her at first, but slowly began to relax. Having Lizzy to occupy some of Ryan's time made it much easier on the aging woman. Although she felt a bit guilty allowing a growing relationship to develop between Lizzy and Penny's son, she was reluctant to say anything to Ryan, nor did she mention it in her letters to Penny.

At the end of three weeks, Lizzie and Rye were walking by the river in front of Fair Bluff when Ryan arrived home. Racing ahead of her, Rye ran to meet his father who joyfully swung him into his arms. "Hello, Lizzy. I see you've been keeping this little fireball busy. I'm sure Miss Caroline is grateful for a breathing spell. Where is she, by the way?"

"She's lying down in her sunroom. I think she has a headache and since I had nothing else to do this afternoon, I volunteered to play with Rye. We've become good friends the last few weeks and I do so enjoy him."

"Miss Lizzy gave me a ball, Papa. And another toy, too," Rye squealed. "She plays fun games with me."

"Thank you, Lizzy. I appreciate your help." Ryan hesitated to invite her in, fearing that she might presume more than he was free to offer. "Be so kind as to allow me to escort you back to your buggy. If you don't get going, it will be dark before you can get home."

"Heavens, no. I'll just pop over and get my shawl and be off. Rufus will help me with the buggy." Waving merrily, she called, "Bye, Rye. You, too, Ryan."

Watching her leave, Ryan reflected on the breezy personality and physical beauty that had first attracted him to her during the period that he was certain that he had lost Penny forever. Shaking his head with bemusement he walked into his house with Rye chatting happily in his arms. Ryan was far from happy as the absence of his wife for nearly a month was beginning to weigh on him. He had given her more than ample time to visit with her family and take care of her responsibilities at Pleasant Glade. He and his son needed her now. Following dinner, he sat at his desk overlooking the river and penned a letter to her. Although he tried not to show his irritation, he could not prevent some of it tingeing the tone of the letter.

Ryan pushed open the French doors onto his veranda and walked out to sit in the early evening light. The sun was just setting turning the river to a sea of molten gold with streaks of vermilion. Wheeling gulls flashed white against the colors of water and sky. Despite the chill of the night air, he sat there until his limbs stiffened from the cold. It was still early and he was restless. With Rye settled for the night, he asked Gertie to watch him while he walked over to visit with Caroline. He needed some human comfort.

"Miss Caroline," he greeted her when she opened the door. "Do you think you have time for a drink with a friend. I just can't stand the nighttime quiet in my house any longer."

"Lordy, don't you look down in the mouth. Come on in the parlor, I was just pouring myself some Sazerac. I know you don't want that, however, I can get you some wine or whiskey as you wish?" Caroline called over her shoulder as she walked to the liquor cabinet. "So, you're missing Penny are you? That son of yours has missed her, too. He's a happy adaptable child and I've enjoying having him during the day, but I know I'm too old to be good company for him. From that standpoint, that conniving little baggage, Lizzy, has been a blessing. I worry though that she is getting a little too chummy with Rye. You know Penny is going to like that about as much as a cocklebur in her bed sheets. Not only that, but she's going to be mighty put out if she thinks Miss Lizzie is sniffing around you again."

She paused, "What did you say you want to drink? I was so busy running off at the mouth, I didn't hear you."

"I didn't say, but a whiskey is fine." Ryan said, not looking up from the patch of carpet he was studying.

"Well, as I was saying, I think it is high time Penny came on home for any number of reasons. Having you moping in my parlor with your chin just about raking the floor is surely one of them. Not that I mind the company. I'm an old woman and it's not often I get to have good-looking gentlemen callers. Of course with your mama gone, John Harvey is calling on me again; not that I would call him good-looking mind you. Lord, I have missed Isabel and Martha. Despite getting off to a rocky start with Martha, I came to love her. We were a good match, both of us feisty old women. My house gets mighty quiet at night now just like yours. Mercy, I'm just running on and on and not giving you chance to get a world in edgewise."

"I don't have too many words to get in. I miss my wife and at the same time, I'm aggravated with her. I know I should have put a stop to Lizzy long before now because Penny has no use for her at all. Of course, Lizzy made it a point to antagonize her from the beginning as though Penny stole me away from her."

"If I didn't know that you were in love with Penny long before you met Lizzy, I would think the same thing. Lizzy doesn't know the whole story so you can't blame her for feeling the way she does. After all, she had some mighty definite plans about a future with you."

"What Lizzy planned is Lizzy's business. I never asked her to marry me. Maybe I toyed with the idea in my mind, but I was never serious in my involvement with her. You know that. I was just lonely and she's a pretty woman and good company. It took some of the pain away from missing the woman I thought I would never have." Ryan shook his head, "What a mess when Penny finds out how *helpful* Lizzy has been and how much Rye has grown to like her."

"It's going to be trouble for sure."

"I wrote Penny pretty much demanding that she come home immediately. If she doesn't, I'm going to go get her and bring her back."

"I hope it's before Lizzy starts looking good again. You don't want to mess with that piece of skirt. She's a determined woman and I wouldn't put it past her to stir up trouble."

"Well, if I came here to get cheered up, I'm not sure this conversation is doing it," Ryan commented.

"Oh, pish. I never met a man that wasn't flattered to have two women fighting over him." Caroline chuckled before turning serious. "However, you have a wife and son. Lizzy needs to find herself another man to focus on."

"Believe me, I've told her that," Ryan remarked. "I'll ride by her house tomorrow and tell her Penny is returning and she doesn't need to come out any more."

"Now isn't that a brilliant idea? If you were stupid I could understand it." Caroline's eyebrow lifted in warning. "The last thing you need to be doing is going to that woman's house. If someone sees you, how do you think you'll explain that, especially since her parents and neighbors know the two of you kept company at one time? No. That is not smart. I'll give her the heave-ho when she comes tomorrow. That's one less opportunity for her to sink more claws into you."

"Thanks, Miss Caroline. I'd appreciate it."

"What have you heard from Kinston? Have they learned any more about who might be responsible for Martha's murder?"

Ryan sighed, "Penny wrote me after the sheriff's last visit. They don't have any clues at all what caused it. She says that Mammy has been messing with hexes and that grandson of hers is mighty troubled. She seems to think it might have something to do with the murder of her neighbor's overseer."

"With two murders so close together, you think there must be some connection, but for the life of me, I can't imagine what it is."

Ryan shook his head, "I agree and I have racked my brain but nothing makes any sense."

They continued chatting amiably for another hour. Ryan saw that Caroline was tiring and felt his own eyes beginning to droop. The conversation with his friend, her cozy parlor and the good whiskey had all served to take some of the tenseness from his body. Standing, he took her hand and kissed it. "Please excuse me if I overstayed my welcome. This visit has done me good though. I feel much better now than I did."

"My dear boy, you are always welcome here. I am sleepy, but then old people like me know that soon we're going to be getting a permanent sleep. It makes me want to stay awake so I don't waste a minute of the years I have left."

"Miss Caroline, don't you go talking that way even in jest. You are the youngest acting woman I know of any age."

"That's the pity. The body ages but inside we're still young, just trapped and confined by skin, bone and muscle that grow older every minute. My heart and my eyes still think I'm twenty. Mirrors and joints remind me I'm not."

"Lock the door when I leave. There have been some problems with Regulators to the west of here. Hopefully that won't get out this way, but we can't be too careful. In her first letter after I got back, Penny wrote me that a white woman had been gang-raped over in Snow Hill. Six Negroes and one white man were charged with the crime but a gang of outlaws broke into the jail, took the keys and removed the prisoners. They took them to a nearby creek and killed them. The rumor is outraged citizens were behind the executions. I can't say as I blame them. Things have gotten pretty lawless despite military efforts to control things. I don't see it getting better anytime soon either."

"Rufus keeps the pistol primed for all the good it would do and I make sure things are locked up tight at bedtime," Caroline laughed. "Goodnight and don't worry about me. I'll be fine."

Frost was already on the lawn when he crossed to his house. He could hear his footsteps crunching the crisp blades of grass. Looking back he saw his tracks, dark against the silver gleam of the frost. For a moment he stood and looked across the garden at the land he had loved from the first time he saw it. Again he blessed Caroline's generous spirit that she would give it to him. Sighing, he turned and walked into his house. Upstairs he heard Rye stirring in his sleep. Going to his son's bed, he bent low and kissed his forehead and then tucked his disordered covers more snuggly around him. That done, Ryan went to his own cold bed.

Miles away, Penny lay looking at the shaft of moonlight that sifted through the gap in her bedroom drapes. The fire in the grate had become glowing embers that were beginning to darken and die. She had slept fitfully before awaking. Listening to the sounds of the night and the creaking of the house as it cooled, she heard nothing to make her feel uneasy and yet she did. It was good to have her father sleeping in the bedroom next to hers and Nancy in the one across the hall. She wondered how comfortable Nancy would be in the house alone after she left. If only they could find the persons responsible for the two murders, everyone in the community would sleep easier at night. If they did not, Penny suspected Nancy would return to her parents' home. Even though the overseer's house was in calling distance, it was not the same as having someone in the house with her. She thought of asking the Davenports to move into the house with Nancy. As kin of hers, she might like the idea enough to be willing to stay. The only reservation for Penny was whether or not she liked the idea of someone living in her home and using the things that had been left to her by her grandmother, mother and father-in-law. Mulling it over, she could see no alternative. She would pack the things that mattered and take them with her to New Berne and ask the Davenports to move in. That resolved, she fluffed her pillow one more time and rolled onto her side. Soon she was snoring softly.

She couldn't decide if she had dreamed of Lizzy or if it was a vision: Lizzy with her child, Lizzy with her husband, Lizzy in her house and in her bed. She roused herself from her dream and rolled to the other side, but was unable to relax enough to go back to sleep. She knew she had been gone too long. It was time to go home. She trusted her husband, but she had never trusted Lizzy. She had seen nothing of the woman since the day that Lizzy had met Ryan on the sidewalk in town the day of Marcus's hearing. Penny scolded herself for her jealousy and determined not to let the dream be more important than what it was. Even knowing it was just a dream, she could feel her ire rise at the very thought of the woman. She wondered if the reason for her jealousy was a carry-over from her first marriage, when her husband had impregnated Lucinda. At the time, it had made her feel undesirable and incapable of holding a man's interest. It never dawned on her to wonder if the problem were perhaps issues that belonged solely to her husband, Daniel, and not some lack of sensuality on her part. Certainly Ryan had never given her any reason to think that she could not satisfy him in bed. Yet, some vestigial doubts remained.

With sleep elusive, Penny climbed from her bed and added more wood to the coals. Soon flames were leaping in the chimney. Using the firelight to see, she began packing her things. In the morning, she would talk to the Davenports, arrange for the things she would have delivered to her, say goodbye to those on her farm and make a quick trip to her father's house to bid her father, Isabel and Brett goodbye on her way to the train station in Kinston. She intended to be in New Berne before nightfall.

When Penny arrived at the depot in New Berne, she engaged a cabby to take her to her home. Although she had pondered going by Ryan's office first, she had finally decided just to surprise him when he arrived home. Musing to herself as the buggy rolled out of town and down the riverside road to Fair Bluff, Penny planned the evening. She would make sure that Gertie had a wonderful meal prepared, that Rye was fed and bedded down, the candles were lit and she was in a seductive dress before Ryan arrived. After a month away and his less than pleased departure from Kinston, she wanted to make amends and show him the best way she knew just how much she missed him. She felt a blush coloring her cheeks when she thought of the evening to come. So engrossed was she in her daydreams she failed to hear Rye's squeals of delight when the cabby turned into the driveway leading to her home.

Suddenly the driver jerked the buggy to an abrupt halt to avoid hitting Rye and the curvaceous blond chasing him. Penny looked up startled. Rye and Lizzy stood on the side of the drive gaping at the unexpected arrival of the buggy. Recognizing his mother, Rye cried out, "Mama, you're home."

Penny waved to her son and then looked into Lizzy's smirking face. "You don't waste much time do you?"

"I can't imagine what you mean. I've been doing my best to take some of the pressure off Miss Caroline. She is a woman in later years, after all, and not up to the games of a young child. Surely you must appreciate the undue burden you placed on her."

"I appreciate quite a lot. We won't be requiring any further services from you. I thank you for your time and consideration, but I suggest you leave." In her anger, Penny was unable to quell her hostility at seeing the woman in her garden with her son. She would have liked to be cool and unconcerned but she was too angry to do it.

"Of course. I never over stay my welcome. Until you arrived, I *was* welcome." Lizzy flounced off pleased about the angry woman she left standing in the driveway. *Well the cat is among the pigeons now*, she chuckled with quiet amusement.

Penny calmed herself as she paid the cabby and hugged her child to her. Carrying him to the house, she listened to his happy chatter about the game he had been playing with Lizzy. She wanted to ask him about Lizzy's visits but dared not. In time, the story would come out. She could not blame Rye, but she did blame her husband. Either he was stupid or blind she thought. That woman has not given up on him. And by allowing Lizzy to come to the house, Ryan was encouraging her expectations. Penny took several deep breaths to calm herself, remembering her mother's oft repeated maxim about catching more flies with honey than vinegar. She would carry on with the evening she had planned never letting Ryan know that she had met Lizzy on arrival. After being away for a month, she wanted her return to be as pleasant as she could make it. She just prayed she was a good enough actress to keep her anger hidden.

16

He was neither prisoner nor free: ostracized and suspected by his fellow inmates and only partially accepted by those assigned to duty at the fort. Marcus missed the card games and desultory conversation that had previously whiled away the long hours with his fellow prisoners. The only good things to come out of his change of quarters had been the bed that was much warmer and softer than the hard brick floor, his growing rapport with the doctor, and increased opportunity to leave the fort to gather seafood and whatever produce the locals might be willing to sell to the denizens of the fort. As a Southern prisoner, he was more effective in negotiating prices than Shine. Although a Southerner as well, Shine was yet a member of the Union army and thus more reviled for his traitorous affiliation than even the Yankee troops. The inhabitants of the island were slow to forget that the fort had become enemy domain and fellow Southerners were now incarcerated in the fort they considered their own. Marcus was the recipient of their sympathy. More than one Banker, emboldened by outrage at military occupancy of the island of Bogue Banks, had surreptitiously whispered to Marcus that they would help him escape any time he wished. Marcus made it a point to thank them for their kindness and assure them that when the time came he would remember the offer. He never intended to have to escape, but if worse came to worse and it looked as though he would be hung for a crime of which he was innocent, he knew he would have little compunction about slipping away into the wild, brambled and wind tortured woods of the island. He could survive there in the summer, and maybe even the winter, until he could find a willing Banker to row him to the mainland. No point in burning bridges with an outright refusal of their offers to help.

Pausing at the top of a dune, Marcus looked down at the pristine beach laid bare by low tide. Shallow waves broke on the northern section of the shore, increasing in volume and height on the more steeply sloped beaches south of the fort area. Rotating his head he could see the green grasses of the salt marshes surrounded by necklaces of black fertile mud, nursery for a myriad of sea life. He smiled at the beauty of the island where dunes had formed over the centuries by the sifting of sand through a thick interwoven canopy of branches. Horsemint, sea oats and cabbage palmetto spread low on the edges of the forest beneath the protective branches of cedar, yaupon, holly, and pine trees. Foxes, raccoons, deer, and squirrels scampered about in the woods. Overhead seagulls called raucously to one another as they performed aerobatic swoops. On the waters of the protected sound, ducks and geese floated serenely. A stiffly elegant heron stalked pray on the edge of the marsh ignoring fiddler crabs darting about at his feet.

Only a few wooden houses dotted the shore, well set back from the ocean. Skirted by wrap-around porches, these vacation cottages of a few wealthy mainlanders were built primarily of wood salvaged from shipwrecks, as were the houses of the few inhabitants of the island. Gillikin, the only village, was home to a few hearty families. A single dirt road ran past the fort to the village which some in the fort had begun to call Salter Path in honor of the saltwater fishermen that lived there.

Marcus stood savoring the view while the April sun spread welcome warmth across his shoulders and face. Marcus relished the sensation of freedom that these excursions provided. Beside him, Shine took a deep breath of the salt laden air.

"Lord, it feels good to be in the warm sunshine again. I thought my bones would plumb break from the cold. That ole fort is about as mizable as it can git in the winter," Shine groused.

"God only knows it's not where I want to spend another winter," Marcus commented with heartfelt passion. "I sure wish I could get this mess resolved one way or another. Damned if this waiting around ain't getting to me."

"I can't blame you none for that. If it'd been me, I would've already taken to my heels, I can tell you." Shine grinned at him, "Hell, I'll look the other way if you feel like gitting a little running exercise."

"Thanks, Shine, but I'll stick around. I'd miss your sorry hide if I ran away and I wouldn't want you to have to pay for letting me escape. Besides, when I leave why don't you come with me. I could use some help on my place. The Bartlett's found me a temporary overseer, but I'm going to need someone I can count on for the long haul. I got to save some of my energy for making babies once I get married. If I'm too tired and overworked, I just don't see how I can do justice to my bride. So, far as I'm concerned, you'll be doing a mighty important mission: helping me do what I can to repopulate the South."

Shine looked at him and grinned. "That sounds like a mighty good plan to me. And I sure wouldn't want you neglecting your bride. Hell, I'll even give you a hand with gitting her some babies if you'd like." Pointing towards the salt marshes, he indicated a grizzled old man bent low over a bucket. "That's ole Ben Dough. They say he's kinda teched in the head but I ain't seen it. I like him fine. He's real gentle like. He's got a little cabin back in the woods over yonder where he collects stray things and tends to 'em. If there is an injured bird or anything else on this island that needs taking care of, he does it. He's got a little garden too. I don't know if he's got anything worth eating this early in the season, but we can see if he has any extras. I could sure use a mess of fresh mustard greens. Hey, looks like he's gitting a pile of them oysters. Reckon we out to git on down there and see if we can't git some 'fore he hogs 'em all."

Shine introduced Marcus to Ben, who nodded acknowledgment before ducking his head in shyness. After Marcus made several failed attempts to talk to him, he shrugged in defeat and went about the business of gathering oysters from the mudflats that lay pungently reeking with the baring of the retreating tide. The three men worked steadily for another hour as the sun climbed towards its zenith.

"Whew, I could sure use a drink of cold water." Marcus announced in a wistful voice as he wiped sweat from his face.

"Come to my house, I'll get you a drink." Ole Ben invited.

"Thanks, we'll do that," Shine answered for them both.

As they walked towards his home, hidden by the stand of woods, Marcus listened to the lilt of the old man's speech. When he said *house* it sounded like *hoose* to Marcus. It was like no other accent that he had heard before and didn't seem to belong to North Carolina. "Where you from, Ben? I've been listening to you and I just can't figure it out."

The question seemed to please Ben. "I've been on this island all my life and my great-great grandparents before me. My great-great-grand-pappy was shipwrecked here and decided it was where the Lord meant for him to be. Many of us on the island got here that way. If we talk rather funny I reckon it's because we don't mix much with mainlanders. We still talk the way our families always have in the years since our ancestors came here from England a long time past."

Old Ben's house was so hidden within the circle of gnarled, wind-twisted trees, that had Marcus not been led there, he would never have found it. It was a rustic structure made of weathered silvery timbers that looked as though they had been there forever. In a simple enclosure made of tree branches interwoven to make a fence, a few chickens happily scratched about ignoring newborn pigs and a sow. A nanny goat walked around the little clearing looking for something to chew on. On the backside of the house, in a plot that opened to the sky, Ben had a garden where Shine happily noted a generous crop of mustard greens. In twig cages leaning against the house, a raccoon and gull suspiciously glared at their intrusion.

Ben nodded toward the cages, "They're just about fit again. I had to fix that gull's broken wing and the ole raccoon had been in a fight with something and ended up the worse for it. I thought he would die for sure when I found him, but he's going to make it after all."

The three men entered the small cabin. Marcus was surprised that it was spotless and neat even if sparsely furnished. Through the open door to the right of the fireplace, Marcus glimpsed into a bedroom centered by a spool bed covered by a colorful patchwork quilt. On the hearth, a cast iron covered pot sat in the edge of the glowing embers. On the mantle of the stone fireplace, fashioned from the ballast stones of wrecked ships, was a miniature painting of a woman and young child. The red hair of woman and child reminded him of Penny. Catching him looking at the painting, Ben remarked, "That's my wife, Esther and my daughter Catherine. They died of the flu twenty-five years past."

"I'm really sorry to hear it," Marcus said.

"So am I. Reckoning I'll mourn them until I can finally die and be with them. Old as I'm getting it won't be as long as it has been." Ben chortled when he said it. "Oh, well, let me get you boys some of that cold water you wanted. I got some oyster stew in the pot there, some bread that I bought from Lula down in the village, and some goat cheese. I'm happy to share with you fellers if you're feeling a mite peckish."

Marcus hastened to accept before Shine could decline. The more he was with the old man the more he liked him. It felt good to sit at a kitchen table and share a simple savory meal. It was the first food that he had eaten outside of a prison since November. He wanted to linger there the rest of the afternoon but they did not have that luxury of time. With reluctance he stood and thanked the man for his hospitality. Shine did as well and also asked about the mustard greens in the garden. Ben and the guard soon struck a bargain, and the two men left with the greens they had purchased. Ben called after them, "Don't be strangers, now."

"I like Ben. I don't see anything wrong with him," Marcus decided.

"He ain't never caused me no harm. I like him just fine. I was only repeating what I heard tole about him," Shine bristled.

"What else are we supposed to be getting for the fort? We've got some mustard, but not enough for everybody, and we've got a bushel of oysters which is enough for a stew."

Shine held up his rifle, "If I see a deer or a coon, I'm going to git us some meat. I ain't real partial to squirrel but if all else fails, I'll shoot 'em, too."

"What about ducks or geese? There's a bunch of 'em right there on the edge of the sound. You shoot 'em and I'll bird dog and bring 'em to shore for you."

"You planning on pointing and barking' too?" Shine snorted over his shoulder as they walked to the sound. "You better figure on getting wet, son. I'm gonna' shoot us a mess of birds."

Get wet he did. Shine managed to shoot six ducks before the others all wisely decamped further down the marshes. By the time Marcus had collected half of them, he was dripping wet but having a grand time frolicking in the shallow waters of the sound. Watching him cavorting as he gathered the ducks, Shine announced, "Aw, hell, I think I'll help you."

The two of them carried the ducks to shore and then sat with their feet stretched in front of them, shoes to one side in the sand. The smoked their pipes and waited for the sun to dry their clothes. "This sure beats the last time we went swimming," Marcus laughed.

His face suddenly serious, Shine asked, "Marcus, were you serious about the job on your farm? If you are, I can tell you I'm interested."

"Serious as a sober judge. When I leave this place, you come to."

"Damned if I ain't. I am plain tired of soldiering, especially now. Guarding prisoners ain't nearly as much fun as gitting shot at and shooting back. This guard duty gits damned boring. It'll be worse with you gone."

It was a tired but contented pair that walked down the gangplank to the prison at dusk that evening. Both looked forward to a good supper and an early bedtime. For Marcus it would not be. The doctor had a new patient. One of the guards was suffering through the final stage of consumption, a sickness that the damp cold winter in the fort had only made worse. Marcus worked with the doctor to get their patient settled and soothing syrup for his cough at hand. The best they could provide were palliative measures. They both knew the patient would die regardless. As he prepared to leave the infirmary for the evening, the doctor pointed to a stack of letters on his desk. "For you," he informed Marcus.

After he left, Marcus took his letters and carried the candle to the small table by his cot. Sorting through them, he found the expected letters from Lena, one from Penny, and surprisingly, his first letter from Lucinda. He opened Penny's letter first despite telling himself just to toss it onto the flames burning merrily in the hearth. In shock he read of her mother-in-law's mysterious murder. Penny described the events going on in the community since his incarceration, Isabel and Brett's marriage, Hardy Brown's efforts to oversee the plantation in Marcus's absence, and her concern for Lucinda, Jeremiah, and Mammy. She bemoaned the fact that she had given some money to Abigail, Calvin's widow, wishing that she had not as she had no desire to encourage the woman coming back to Pleasant Glade. Marcus suspected that her concern for the woman's children had solicited Penny's generosity. He sincerely doubted that ignorant witling had elicited any sympathy for herself. As far as he could see, Abigail was a stupid woman and a pernicious one. It permeated the very air around her. Laying Penny's letter to one side, he next opened the one from Lucinda.

Lucinda described the success of her new school and her pride in the growing number of children that came to her door each morning eager to learn the skills they would need to survive and prosper in a new South. Despite her happiness with the school, there was an underlying thread of sadness for Jeremiah who apparently had never recovered from the trauma of her rape. Almost too casually she wrote of the new schoolmaster of a freedmen's school near Snow Hill, Sidney Busbee, whose school had been torched as a result of a letter he wrote to the governor. Following the rape of a white woman, he had also advised his fellow freedmen to report Regulators that were committing crimes in the community. He went to Raleigh to request troops be sent to maintain some semblance of law and order. Troops arrived in direct response to his appeal, garnering the animosity of both whites and blacks. Lucinda expressed her admiration for the man and her joy that the community had collected enough funds to begin rebuilding his school. Almost as an afterthought, she wrote that she had met Sidney on her last visit to Kinston and that he had requested permission to call on her. Marcus laid the letter in his lap and smiled. He sat lost in thought for some minutes before opening the first letter from Lena.

Her steadfast love and support for him lit the pages like a beacon. Marcus reminded himself once again how very thankful he was that he had met someone like her and that someday they would marry. Although her letters brought him joy and hope, there was nothing to indicate that either she or her father had made any progress in finding a witness to corroborate his story or any facts that would exonerate him. Finished with his letters, he tucked them into the drawer in the table, blew out the candle and drew up his covers. Curling on his side, his back to the room, he tried his best to ignore the coughing coming from the other corner.

Marcus awakened the following morning with a groan; furious with himself for dreaming that it was Penny he had married. He had held her in his arms and made passionate love to her. The odor of semen spilled in his underwear told him that the dream had brought sexual release. He was ashamed that it was Penny who inhabited his dreams and not the woman he had asked to be his wife. Disgusted, he found his clothes in the weak dawn light and walked over to the patient.

The man was still, his eyes staring unseeing at the water-stained ceiling. One more thing to be ashamed of, Marcus thought. The man had died alone, his passing unremarked. Marcus closed the blank eyes and pulled the sheet over the soldier's face, then walked to the mess for breakfast. Once again, he sat apart from the other prisoners who made at point of ignoring him. He stirred his food about his plate repelled by the sight of it. Despite the joy of the previous day, that morning he was as depressed as he had been at any time since his arrest.

Marcus was not so lost in thought as to be oblivious to the vague undercurrent of anger in the room. Suddenly two prisoners were sprawled on the floor fighting. He considered trying to get them apart but hesitated. Leave it to the guards, he thought, I've got no dog in that fight. Leaving his food uneaten, he returned to the infirmary and the doctor he felt he had failed by sleeping through his patient's death.

17

John Harvey leveled a long hard look at Ryan. The men sat with eyes locked for long seconds more. "So, are you willing to postpone this trial for a little longer? The man's in jail as it is. What have you lost by giving it a little more time? I just feel like there is something out there that is going to break this case for Marcus. You know as well as I do that he's not the murdering type. Heck, I hear the folks over at Fort Macon think he's been a real positive addition. Why not let them enjoy him a little longer. I'm afraid if we go to court now, an innocent man will be tried and condemned on nothing but circumstantial evidence."

"John, I understand how you feel and I'm inclined to agree. If you want to petition the court for a delay, I won't stand in the way. Besides, Penny would divorce me if I did."

"And rightly so," John snorted. "All jesting aside, I do appreciate it. I think you've made the right decision."

"I hope so." Changing the subject, Ryan continued, "We're having Miss Caroline over to dinner Saturday night, we'd be pleased if you could join us. I thought I might invite the mayor as well."

"Thank you. I'll accept your kind invitation with great pleasure, sir." Ryan waited for him to leave, but John continued to sit. Obviously reluctant to broach the topic he wanted to discuss, he harrumphed several times. "I heard some rumors that disturb me. I hope that you can put my mind at rest."

Ryan shifted uncomfortably, wondering who had spread malicious gossip about him and Lizzy in Penny's absence. Taking a deep breath to steal himself for what was coming, he responded, "I'll do my best. Tell me what's bothering you."

"The rumor has it that you have talked about resigning your seat in Raleigh and are trying to find someone else to propose in your place. Is that right?"

Ryan was relieved that this was the topic that John referred to. "I have considered it and still lean in that direction. Why? Are you interested, John?"

"Good God almighty, no! At my age that's the last thing I plan to get myself into," he exclaimed. "No. A group of us have talked it over and they've asked me to intervene. The last thing we need to have right now is for you to resign. You are one of us now despite serving with the Union forces that occupied New Berne. Your ability to stand back and look at Washington's point of view is important. We need fairness and dispassion. You give us that and we implore you not to quit at this point. Washington is in a snit with North Carolina after that last assembly in Raleigh. We still have issues with the military occupying forces. You are the ideal one to deal with that considering your military background. And I don't have to remind you of the issues around the KKK and the Regulators."

"Those are all of the reasons that I have hesitated to discontinue serving. The problem is the time that it takes from my family and what is becoming a growing practice. Not only that but I confess to being more than a little frustrated by my last trip to Raleigh. My voice and that of others who feel as I did about the actions that passed the assembly were ignored in their haste to grab back some of what they thought the war had cost them. In the end they only cost themselves a higher price with the punitive actions from Washington."

"Yes, well, to that end, I can appreciate your frustration. As for your growing practice, why not hire an associate or perhaps merge with another attorney. I for one would be honored to have you come in with me. I'm getting old enough I'm trying to wind down. I've got a couple of fine young attorneys on staff to help with the legwork. Another senior attorney would not go amiss."

Ryan smiled, "That's an interesting offer. Let me mull it over for awhile."

"Take all the time you need. I'm not going anywhere." John paused, "And yes, I'm glad Penny is back so you can spend some time as a family. I heard some disturbing news concerning that snippy little baggage you use to court. Elizabeth Berkely...Lizzy, I believe it was. Gossip has it that she was ready to move in on you."

"I wondered when that nasty little tidbit would start making the rounds. Damned, sometimes living in a small town is a pure nuisance. This is one of them. Please inform all interested parties that I love my wife, I am faithful to my wife, and I have no intentions of straying: past, present and future. Lizzy made it a point to visit Caroline and help her with my son while Penny was in Kinston, but I never solicited nor encouraged her company." Ryan felt himself growing angry.

Standing he walked to the window and looked down the street towards the river. Of all the times to have done so, he thought, this was the worst. Coming down the sidewalk was Lizzy. When she saw him in the window she gave him a radiant smile and threw a kiss. Ryan could tell she debated coming in. He made a hasty retreat to his desk praying that she would just keep on walking. The last thing he needed at the moment was for her to march in after the conversation he had just had with John Harvey. Much to his annoyance he felt himself blush.

"No hard feelings, Ryan?" John stood and extended his hand to Ryan. "Thank you again for allowing the delay of Marcus's trial. I know he's impatient to get on with it, but a delay is in his best interest. Also, please do consider continuing to serve us in Raleigh."

"That I will. Thanks for stopping by." After he left, Ryan sat at his desk with his head in his hands. What a mess, he thought. He had not been alone more than five minutes after John left when he heard light footsteps cross the hall outside his office and enter. He knew who it was before he even looked up. Groaning he rose with his weight balanced on hands planted squarely on his desk.

"Forgive me the discourtesy of my bluntness, but what do you want, Lizzy?"

"Oh, Ryan, I'm just so upset. People are just saying the nastiest things about us all because I went to Miss Caroline's house and played a little bit with Rye. I mean I only walked around in your yard when I was playing outside with Rye. It's not like I went in your house with you when your wife was out of town." Lizzy managed to look upset.

"Lizzy, I always took you for an intelligent woman. I think I may have been wrong. Do you really think showing up at my office is going to squelch gossip?" Ryan demanded.

"Oh!" she squeaked, "I never even considered that. Silly me. You must think me such a goose." Lizzy pressed her hand to her bosom and heaved a sigh, emphasizing the lush swell of her breasts. He noted the smug expression on her face when his eyes strayed momentarily to where her hand rested.

"What I think is you should leave. Now. And Lizzy, don't come back here. Not for any reason. Just leave me alone. Go on with your life. I am not for you and I never was." He looked up and glared into her eyes. "Your games have gone far enough."

"My goodness! I've just tried to show some Christian kindness and this is the thanks I get. Really, Ryan, you know you're being unfair and nasty to me. Have I tried to do anything that would suggest I'm just some hussy looking to steal another woman's husband? I am just mortified and more than a little insulted that you of all people would think that of me. When we were courting, you know I never gave you a moment's reason to believe that I'm that kind of woman."

"No, you didn't and don't start now. Please, just leave. We don't need to debate all of this. I just want to live my life as simply and as well as I can. I don't need and don't plan to have unnecessary complications. I appreciate what you did to help Miss Caroline with Rye. He enjoyed your company. If helping Miss Caroline is the extent of your concern, we all owe you an apology. Right now, I feel your help has done nothing but stir up unwelcome speculation. Coming here does nothing to allay that. This is a small town. You've lived here all of your life. I don't have to tell you that. Furthermore, you might consider how it looks to your parents. Do you wish to cause them undue mortification by your actions? Understand you must not come to this office again."

"Of course, my dear man. It has never been my intention to cause you any harm for any reason. I'm so sorry that my innocent intentions have managed to do just that. Please forgive me." Lizzy batted her eyes, squeezing tears from the corners.

"Ah, Lizzy. Don't cry. I'm sorry, too." Ryan took her by the elbow and escorted her to the front door. "Just please don't come back here."

When Lizzy left, Ryan gathered the papers he had been working on and shoved them back into his desk. Locking the drawer, he pocketed the key and picked up his coat. He'd had enough for one day. There was no point in staying and trying to work; his mind would simply not stay focused. He wanted to go home, but that would only necessitate explaining why he was home early after he had told Penny he had much work he had to finish at the office by day's end. Walking to the stable where Windfall waited, he saddled his horse. He thought it was a good day just to ride.

Guiding the horse to the river, he trotted along the bank of the Trent passing behind the ruins of the colonial governor's palace. The flowers of the old garden still bloomed among the ruins. Ryan reined in Windfall and casually looped the reins over an oleander bush. Working his way through brambles and weeds, he began picking the irises, tulips, jonquils and daffodils that had spread in random profusion under the shading oaks. When he had a bouquet, he resumed his ride in the opposite direction to the Neuse shoreline. Swinging away from the riverbank to the river road that ran to his house, he began the short ride home.

The wind from the water was warm and gentle against his face. Overhead the white blossom-spangled branches of the dogwoods competed with the draping flags of wisteria blossoms. Cardinals flitted about above his head, singing him home. He clutched his bouquet and prayed that the closed and guarded look that Penny had given him since her return would be replaced by one of joy when she saw the flowers he had gathered for her. He couldn't decide if her suppressed anger stemmed from his frustration with her staying behind in Kinston or if she had heard the rumor of Lizzy's visits. She had not mentioned any knowledge of them, so he could only puzzle as to the source of her distinct aloofness. He only knew that despite a pleasant and polite homecoming, she had maintained an emotional distance from him ever since. Sighing, he could only ponder the mysteries of the female mind. He also felt unresolved annoyance that she had ignored his desire to return to New Berne when he brought his mother's body. Having resisted the attentions of an attractive woman and remained true to the woman who had refused him in an hour of emotional need, he felt far more entitled to rancor than Penny. After all, he was taking her flowers as a peace offering and spurning the obvious affection of another woman. He wasn't sure what more he could do to placate his wife.

Penny was on the veranda with Rye when he arrived. He walked up to her with the flowers outstretched. "For my beautiful wife. I am so happy to have you home."

"Oh, Ryan, they're gorgeous. Thank you." Her smile was genuine and the kiss that she gave him assured him that the flowers were a welcome gesture on his part. Ryan settled himself on the porch and played with Rye while Penny put the flowers in a vase and positioned it on the chest in the foyer.

"They're just perfect here," she called to him.

"Something smells good from the direction of the kitchen. I had little for dinner so supper is going to be much appreciated." Ryan reached over and tickled Rye, sending him into gales of laughter. "Are you hungry, too, little boy?"

Returning to the veranda, Penny said, "I asked Gertie to do dinner out here since the weather is so gorgeous. She says it won't be ready for another thirty minutes or more. Rye and I wondered if you might like to take a walk with us by the water before it gets too dark."

Holding hands they ambled along the water's edge. Rye raced ahead of them, constantly looping back to show them something he had discovered. It felt good to them both to watch their son's eager exploration of his world. Easing back into their usual comfortable rapport brought them both a measure of contentment. "Penny, John Harvey came by the office today. He accepted our invitation for dinner on Saturday night. I also agreed to postpone Marcus's trial so John can continue looking for evidence to exonerate him."

"Oh, I'm so glad. I know Marcus is going to be disappointed that he has to wait in jail just that much longer, but that's better than going to trial when so much is still stacked against him. Thank you for agreeing to wait."

"You're welcome. I just hope John can come up with something. I've bought him a couple of months and then, he's going to have no choice but to proceed."

"I know. I've been so worried. I just know someone out there knows something if we could only find out who they are."

"John asked me to reconsider representing New Berne in Raleigh. I confess having him ask me to continue gives me real pause. I hate to let down the people who put so much faith in me and asked me to serve to begin with. My pique that my concerns were ignored is part vanity I suppose. I just need to get over it."

"Ryan, knowing you as I do, I think that is the best decision. I'm proud of you and of your efforts to help us come through this period with the best possible opportunities for everyone in the community. I'm glad you're going to stay. If you have to go to Raleigh, we can always come with you or stop in Kinston for a visit. I know you're busy in your office but you can employ a junior partner if your clerk, Mr. Morgan, is not enough help."

"Speaking of that, an interesting proposal came up today." Ryan shook his head in amazement. "John suggested we partner and let his young associates take some of our case load and leg work from us. I must say it came out of the blue, but it is an interesting proposition to say the least."

"Oh, my. Are you considering it then?"

"I have not decided one way or the other, but I think I'll look into it. I hate being so tied to the office. The trips to Raleigh only put me further behind here. Plus, as I explained a long time ago, I don't need to work for financial reasons. It's good to be useful and to contribute to the community, but I also want time for us. I would love to take you to Baltimore and New York. I want us to go to Europe together, maybe even have Brett and Isabel come along. There are so many things we can do."

"I'd love it, too. Do you know, I have never been out of North Carolina except for going to Richmond during the war?" Penny halted, regretting that once again she had reminded him of that trip. Not wanting Rye branded a bastard, she had gone to Richmond to lie with her first husband so the world would think that it was Daniel who had impregnated her and not her lover.

Ryan saw the shadow that crossed her face and knew where her thoughts had gone. He didn't like that memory any better than she did. Not knowing that she was pregnant with his child and getting a letter from her telling him that she would not divorce her husband, he had assumed that he was being jilted because Penny did not love him enough to risk the social anathema of divorce. Had he known that she carried his child, he would have abducted her if necessary and convinced her to follow through with their plans. As it was, her decision had come close to costing them one another. Thank goodness Brett had intervened and brought them together again on that fateful day shortly after the end of the war. Looking at his beautiful son and the wife he treasured, he shuddered to think how close he had come to never having them in his life.

"Mama, Mama. Look there is my new train. I forgot I left it here" Rye called to his mother as he dashed across the lawn.

"Oh, what a pretty train it is, darling. I don't remember it. Did Miss Caroline buy it for you?" Penny exclaimed as she reached to pick it up from the pine straw that blanketed the ground under the graceful branches of a longleaf pine.

"No, Mama. Miss Lizzy gave it to me. She came to play with me lots and lots."

"That strumpet!" Penny muttered under her breath. She felt her face turn red with anger. Biting back the words that bubbled just below the surface, she turned back to the house. "I think dinner must be ready. Let's go see if Gertie is ready for us?"

"Penny..." Ryan began.

"Please, don't. I don't want to hear it." Penny picked up her skirts and ran ahead of them back to the house.

"Well, son, it looks like I'm going to be living in a doghouse. I think we might as well get ourselves a dog, too.".

"Oh, Daddy, that's funny. People can't live in doghouses."

"Well, let's hope I need one only from time to time and not for long."

"Could we still have a puppy, Daddy?"

"We'll see." Ryan took his son's small hand in his and walked back to the veranda. Suddenly, the hunger he had felt was replaced with a feeling of nausea at the evening's sudden decline into rancor.

18

"Dammit. You aim to tell me I got to sit in this place for another two months. It ain't that I don't appreciate getting a little more time to try to prove my innocence, but I have to tell you this is just about to kill me and I've got it easy compared to most of these men. At least I get to go fishing and get out of here from time to time and I have a decent bed, but it sure ain't home. I'm worried about my farm and my girl. I can't expect either one to be at their best without some personal attention from me. My neighbors are helping out with the farm and I'm mighty grateful for it, but it just is not what it would be with me there to see to things. Then there's Lena. She's one fine woman, too good to waste years hanging around for a jailbird to come back to her, innocent or not." Marcus walked to the casement and looked out into the moat. It was filled with water from the wet weather and would soon be a ripe breeding ground for the ubiquitous mosquitoes that made life miserable for everyone in the fort. He turned a grim face to John Harvey, "Thank you for going to the trouble to come here in person to tell me this. I suspect this is for the best. Forgive me if I sound a little ungrateful just now. I'm just so blasted tired of being cooped up here."

"We're doing all we can, Marcus. And don't you worry any about Lena. That girl is as loyal and true as they come. She'll wait for you."

"I surely am counting on it. I'm ready to settle down and start a family and make something of my life."

"You will, you will. I promise you the time will come. This

is just a temporary setback. It won't be forever, although it must feel that way at the moment."

Marcus tossed and turned that night. Sleep eluded him as he struggled to come to terms with the latest setback. The only bright spots he could foresee in the coming months were the trips with Shine to fish or purchase supplies from the locals. He was grateful for Shine's friendship and the camaraderie, and he promised himself that once freed, Shine would have a job that offered him a better life than that of prison guard. When dawn came, Marcus pulled a stool by the window and reread his letters from Lena and the one from Lucinda. Those from Penny he left in the bottom of the box that held his meager possessions. Daily he struggled to eradicate his feelings for her from his heart. Reading her letters only served to renew his hopeless longings. It would be Lena he would return to and with whom he would build a life. When the doctor came in that morning, he found Marcus asleep on the stool, his head cushioned on his arms on the casement ledge.

"Morning, Marcus. That's a mighty lame excuse for a bed you made for yourself."

"Good morning, Doc. I sat down here at daybreak. I couldn't sleep last night. I guess reading these letters finally relaxed me enough to get some shut-eye." Marcus tucked his letters back into his box and went to breakfast.

When Marcus entered the mess hall, the room fell into an expectant silence. He knew the other prisoners resented his special status. The fact that they were all convicted felons and he had not yet been tried and sentenced was of no concern to them. As far as they cared, he was a prisoner just as they were and they resented the favors he enjoyed and they themselves lacked. Ignoring the animosity that surrounded him, Marcus collected his breakfast and stationed himself as far from the others as the limited options allowed. He ate steadily without looking up until his plate was clean, then decamped with dozens of sets of eyes boring holes in his back. Shuddering despite himself, he went about his chores trying to forget a growing uneasiness. The day dragged on as so many had, but this time the tedium was overlaid with a feeling of dread. Marcus debated returning to the mess for dinner, unwilling to face the animosity that awaited him. Shrugging it off as mere jitters brought on by his depression, he finally walked to the mess to eat before they stopped serving. Most of the men had left and those remaining avoided him. Masticating on the fatback flavored black-eyed peas, Marcus pondered the wisdom of asking to be returned to a cell. That would remove some of the isolation from the other prisoners and perhaps abate some of their hostility. He absolutely refused to consider removal from the fishing excursions. Without them, his life would be total hell.

It was dark when he left to return to the infirmary. Lost in thought, he did not hear the soft rustle of clothing behind him until it was too late. Twisting to see who it was, the shift of his body caused the blade to move from the carefully aimed trajectory that would have sliced through his ribs into his body cavity. The blade ripped into his back just below the shoulder blade and sliced along the top of a rib. Marcus yelled and grabbed for his assailant, missing him as he stumbled. In the dark he heard running steps signaling there had been more than one of them. The last thing he heard before slipping into oblivion was the anxious voice of a guard summoning others to help.

The guards shouts brought the doctor at a dead run. As soon as Marcus was on the table in the surgery, he struggled to staunch the river of blood that streamed from the bone-deep gash. After bandaging the shoulder, he stepped back. "That's the best I can do. The rest is between him and God."

Shine looked down at his friend. Marcus was unconscious. His skin had turned pale and drawn. "He shore looks pitiful-like, Doc. Ain't there nothing else you can do fer him?"

"I wish there were. That was a long deep gash. Must have nicked an artery for him to lose so much blood. Then there's the danger of superation. We don't know what makes some injuries putrefy until they kill a man and others heal clean. Some think it's due to dirt that gets into the wound and festers until it causes a sickness in the blood. I wish I had something to give him to prevent that, but I don't. No one does. I used some alcohol to clean it as best I could. That's all I can do. Now we just have to wait. If he doesn't get a high fever and the wound starts healing, he'll be right as rain in a few days despite the blood loss. That will make him weak for a while until he can build it back, but it won't kill him."

"Well, Doc, do you think it would be okay if I jest kinda sat with him tonight to keep an eye on him and all?"

"That would be a big help, Shine. If he wakes, he's going to be thirsty. Give a little water at the time until you see he can keep it down. If his fever starts going up, you wake me up. Hear?"

"Jest as fast as my legs'll carry me," Shine promised.

Marcus tossed fitfully in the night. Over and over Shine retrieved his quilt and tucked it back around him. At daybreak, Marcus still had not regained consciousness and judging from the flush of his skin, Shine knew the dreaded fever was upon him. Alarmed, he ran for the doctor. Unwrapping the bandages, the doctor examined the already inflamed wound.

"Damn, this is what I feared. Well, he's in for it now. I'll do what I can for him." The doctor turned to Shine, "You're dead on your feet from lack of sleep. Go on to bed now and I'll take it from here."

Acknowledging his utter exhaustion, Shine agreed, "If you're sure I can't be of no help?"

"If you don't get some rest, you'll be the one needing help. Now, go."

"I'll be back soon as I can git a little shut-eye."

It was late afternoon before Marcus blinked his eyes against the light and asked for water. The doctor held a glass to his parched lips and monitored his sips, allowing him only a little. "I know you're still very thirsty. Let's give this a minute to settle then I'll give you a little more. I want to get some beef broth into you, as well, as soon as you're up to it.

"What happened?" His eyes closed wearily as he asked.

"Looks like you were jumped by somebody that took a knife to you. Judging by the size of the gash, it was a pretty large blade. Just a fraction off and it would have gone between the ribs. You're a lucky man you made it this far. Now we've just got to get you well."

"I'm so hot," Marcus mumbled.

"You've got fever. Have a little more of this water, then rest."

Marcus slipped in and out of consciousness for the next three days. Shine was with him every moment he could spare from duty and the doctor rarely left his side except to sleep. Even the warden came by to check on him. Marcus was at times vaguely aware of people around him. They came to him as though underwater, their faces out of focus and their voices undifferentiated buzzing. An occasional disjointed word or two penetrated the mist. He felt their concern and was grateful, but when he tried to talk, no words came.

When Shine could stand the waiting around no more, he walked from the fort to the beach and turned south on the hard-packed sand. He scuffed his toes against the sand as he walked. Bending down he picked up a shell that washed in on a wave and gave it an angry heave back into the water. Once he ambled too close to the waves and wet his feet when one caught him unaware. Cursing, he shook the water from his boots and continued trudging into the sunset.

"Hey, Shine," Ole Ben called to him from the top of a sea

oat-covered dune. "Where you headed this time of day?"

Shine stopped and waited for Ben to come up to him. "You remember that feller Marcus I go fishing with? Well he got hisself stabbed and he's doing real bad. His fever's up way high and the wound's infected. The Doc has just about give up. I tell you, I'm just about worried outta my mind about him. He's been a real friend to me and I'd sure hate to lose him."

"I'm mighty sorry to hear it, mighty sorry. He seems like a real fine man," Ben remarked. He swung into step with Shine and they continued toward the sinking sun, admiring the rays of gold and vermilion that cast a warm glow on the tops of the dunes. The sea oats glowed against the sky, contrasting against the purple and blue shadows they drew in the sand. To break the silence, Ben remarked, "Sure is a pretty sight ain't it?"

"It is that," Shine agreed. "But I reckon I best think about turning around and gitting on back to the fort. I want to see if that damned fever is going down any."

"Come with me to my house. I got some remedies that the Indians that used to live on this island taught my grandpa to make and then he taught me. They may help, and if he's as sick as you say, they dern shore can't hurt."

Shine waited while Ben churned through his shelves until he found what he was looking. "Come here, now, and listen up real good."

Holding up a bunch of dried leaves, Ben continued, "This here is horsemint. I'm going to make a compound for the doctor to put on the wound. The Indians used it to kill bad spirits that git into the flesh. This here is Snakeroot that I done pounded down. Boil it in water to make a tea then give it to him to drink. It'll help bring that fever down. Now let's go out to the back and git some poke salad. You going to need to boil it till the leaves is tender, then season up and fry'em. Feed him several messes of poke to help build him up and give him the pot licker to drink from where you boiled the leaves."

Shine concentrated on all Ben told him, determined to remember each detail. He left Ben standing in the doorway of his house, calling back a promise to let him know how Marcus was doing. It was dark when Shine reached the gates of the fort and entered the parade ground. He wasted no time reporting back, before making his way to the infirmary carefully carrying the precious bundle that he prayed would save his friend.

"Doc, you here?" he called as he entered.

"Back here with Marcus, Shine. Come on back."

"I brung you this stuff, Doc. It's from Ole Ben. He says the Indians used it to heal folks. He told me what it's for and how to use it. He says it's gonna help Marcus to git well again."

"Marcus, I'm sure you and Ben mean well. However, I'm doing all I know to do. He is too sick to tolerate a lot of experimentation. I do not believe that the Indian medicine you suggest can possibly be more efficacious than modern medicine."

"I don't know nothin' about that efficasus stuff. I just don't see where it hurts nothing to try this, too. It ain't like it's deadly or nothing and it ain't like what you're doing is working neither, beg pardon." Growing agitated, Shine continued, "I ain't trying to be uppity or nothing. I jest want to help Marcus git well."

"As am I. I do thank you for your offer, but I'm going to have to refuse."

Shine glared at the doctor and shook his head. "Well, you have the say so. It sure ain't me. I was just trying to help."

Coues gave a weary nod, "He's your friend. I would expect nothing less."

Shine looked down at Marcus' flushed face. "Is he still burning up with the fever?"

"I'm afraid so. He's unconscious again as well. I fear it's looking grim for Marcus." The doctor stood up and stretched his back. "If you're able, I could use some help tonight. Do you think you could sit with him? I have to get some rest. I'm just about worn out."

"I'll clear it with the duty roster and be right back here just as soon as I can do that and git a bite to eat for my supper."

Shine left the infirmary with the bundle from Ole Ben tucked under his arm. He decided it was up to him to take advantage of the coming hours to utilize the things Ben had given him, despite the doctor's objections. Maybe the Indian remedies would work and maybe not, but at least he would have tried. In the kitchen he persuaded the cook to prepare the pot liquor and poke greens for him. Together they mixed the horsemint with some honey to make a salve. That done, Shine ate quickly while the cook finished brewing the tea and sautéing the greens.

"Here you go, Shine. I did this as near like you told me as I know how. I sure hope it works." The cook smiled, "Did you know that three of Marcus's former cell mates escaped just before you got back tonight? The warden suspects they were the ones that stuck the knife in him."

Shaking his head in disgust, Shine said, "No joking? So, how'd they escape?"

"It's no secret the salt air here has rusted the iron bars on the windows so bad a puny baby could kick 'em out. Looks like they just knocked out the bars; crossed the moat and got over the parapet. Captain's planning to take some men and see if they can pick up a trail first thing in the morning." The cook snorted, "That ought to give them a pretty good start. It is passing strange to me that they couldn't get their sorry hides out there tonight while the trail is fresh."

"Either way, it's unlikely they're gonna git 'em. Folks on this island will hide 'em and then take 'em on to the mainland. Hell, they're probably already over there by now." Shine snorted, "I sure ain't sorry to hear they're gone. Elsewise, I'd be mighty tempted to visit a little divine justice on 'em all by myself. I wouldn't take too kindly to hanging for a deserved killing. But that wouldn't stop me from gitting the ones responsible if I knowed who it was."

"They sure wouldn't be worth hanging for, so it's a good thing they've gone," the cook agreed as he scooped the sautéed greens onto a dish. "I'm sorry about, Marcus, but I had a feeling he was in for some tough times from this bunch. There's nothing like jealousy to stir them up. Doc says his chances of making it are looking pretty bad."

"It shore don't look good for him right now." Thanking the cook for his help, Shine took Ben's treatments and returned to the infirmary, grateful that Coues had given him the opportunity to spend some time alone with his friend. Despite the doctor's objections, he intended to get as much of the brew and salad into Marcus as he could. The only thing that worried him was getting the bandage off so he could apply the salve and then properly back on so it looked the way the doctor had bound it.

Marcus was stirring in restless sleep when he returned. Shine dipped a cloth in water and sponged his face, then pulled back the suffocatingly thick pile of covers. Marcus's eyes fluttered open. He managed a feeble smile, almost cracking his parched lips, and asked for water.

Shine gave him a small sip and then sat in the chair by the bed. Picking up Marcus' hand, he said, "Ole Ben made me something for you to take. He says it'll help with the fever and I got some salve to put on that wound soon as I can git that bandage off you. There's some poke salad here, too, that you need to try to eat some of. The doctor ain't in favor of trying it but I can't see where it does any harm." Shine studied the bandage so he could remember exactly the way it looked. Then he began unwrapping the wound. When he saw it, he had to force himself not to gasp or reflect dismay in his face. Quickly he took the salve and spread it on the wound.

When that was finished he reapplied the bandage, checking

his work against the original wrapping. "I know that probably hurt you and I'm mighty sorry for it. Now, I'm going to hold you up so you can drink some of this here pot liquor stuff."

Marcus struggled to give his friend a weak smile, "It looks like you, Ole Ben, and the doctor are all wasting your time on me."

"Don't go carrying on that a way. You're gonna make it. Besides, you done and promised me a job. I'm aiming to leave here with you and I don't mean with you in no box."

All that night Shine fed him the pot liquor in small doses. By daybreak he thought the fever might have dropped. Marcus even managed to eat a small quantity of the poke leaf salad during the night. When Shine heard the doctor returning, he hastened to hide the things that Ben had given him.

"Morning, Shine. How's our patient?" The doctor walked over and placed his hand on Marcus's head. "Amazing. I think the fever may actually have gone down a little."

"I was thinking that myself." Shine fidgeted unsure whether to tell the doctor what he had done or just keep quiet. In a moment there was no need to dither.

"Shine, did you undo the bandage for some reason? This is not the way I do them."

"Now don't go gitting all riled up, Doc. I jest don't see that there was much to lose by giving Ole Ben's medicine a try, so I done it. I put some of his salve on that wound and I give Marcus some brewed stuff that's supposed to bring down his fever. It sure looks like the brew is helping him some. I don't know about the salve since I hain't checked it since I done it."

"You are one stubborn mule, aren't you, Shine?" The doctor shook his head and smiled, "From what Marcus has told me about his friend in Kinston using herbal remedies, I'm sure he doesn't object to what you did. I confess somewhat regretting I rejected Ben's remedies last night after I left you. I guess the important thing is whether or not we get results, not how we get there. Now, let's get this bandage off and see what the wound looks like."

"Let me help hold him; it'll make it a sight easier," Shine offered with relief evident in his voice.

The doctor scrutinized the exposed wound with great care, "I just don't know, Shine. It may look a little better, just maybe. I guess since we've got it unwrapped, we can put some more of that salve on it if you have any left?"

Hurriedly Shine pulled out the hidden package and handed the doctor the salve. "I got more of the greens, too, and some poke salad liquor. Ben says the liquor will help build up his blood."

"Poke salad liquid, too?" The doctor shook his head. "Is there anything else in that bag you want to tell me about?"

"Naw, ain't nothing else. But we got enough of this to doctor him with for a couple of days."

"That we do. Let's just hope it works."

Marcus blinked wearily. He gave the two men a vague look and fell back to sleep.

19

Penny awoke with a start; cold sweat beading down her face. Not wanting to awaken her husband, she scooted from their bed and tiptoed onto the veranda through the French doors of their bedroom. The night was mild but still she shivered. She hated the visions that had stalked her sleep since she was a small child. Invariably they were warnings of events to come, events she had no power to change. Tonight's vision had been confusing and disturbing. It had begun with an image of Marcus. He was lying in bed, moaning with pain and fever and then suddenly he grew quiet. No sooner had that ended than she found herself in the middle of a violent storm. She felt the wind and the waves pushing her further and further from their boat. She was holding Rye and struggling to keep his head out of the water. Then Ryan was with her and grabbed hold of them both. For a long time the three of them flailed helpless in the maelstrom that engulfed them before a huge wave swept her away and all became oblivion. The later part of the dream she had experienced several times before. The first part with Marcus was new. Penny paced the veranda and made a fervent prayer that it had only been a dream and not something more sinister.

"Penny, is something wrong? It's still night." Ryan yawned as he emerged from the doorway, rubbing the rough stubble of a day old beard.

"I was just restless. I'm sorry if I woke you." Penny hesitated to tell him the real reason she had left their bed. Despite a vision bringing them together, he still put little stock her visions. There was no point in instigating an argument she could not win. How could she prove validity to someone who lacked the same experiences and proof that she had.

"I wasn't sleeping all that well myself," Ryan said as he took her in his arms. "I hope you are not still angry about Lizzy. I understand how you feel and I'm sorry this all happened. If it had not been for Miss Caroline needing the help, I would have put a stop to her coming out here the moment I found out about it."

"Ryan, that woman is a predator. No wife likes having someone like her stalking her husband. It's even worse that she would manipulate Miss Caroline and our son in her little schemes."

"She's not as bad as all that. I think she's just bored and lacks something to do with herself," Ryan said soothingly.

"Are you defending her? I thought you said you understand how I feel and why."

"I do understand how you feel. I just think the reasons for feeling that way are a bit exaggerated." Instant regret washed over him for adding the second sentence. Even in the dim light he could see that she was furious with him.

"Are you being deliberately obtuse?" she demanded.

"That's not very nice, is it?" Ryan struggled not to become angry as well. "I have never in anyway betrayed the vows of our marriage. It is wrong to make me feel as though I must defend myself for something I would never do. We must trust one another or else we face a bleak future together. I know you see that and I know that you don't mean to offend me by questioning my faithfulness."

"Ryan, as I have explained before, it is not you that I doubt." Penny hated sounding like the jealous wife but couldn't stop herself.

"If you don't doubt me then it's unimportant. Just stop dwelling on Lizzy." Ryan hugged her closer. "It's you I want in my bed, right this minute, as a matter of fact, and the rest of my life as well. Come back to bed and I'll prove just how much."

Penny looked up and smiled at her husband. Taking him by the hand she led him back to their bed. He reached up and pushed her gown from her shoulders, letting it fall at her feet, before scooping her into his arms and tossing her onto the bed. It took only a moment to divest himself of his own clothing and climb in beside her. Much later, with the pale hint of coming day just pinking the horizon, Ryan fell into exhausted sleep while birds sang a paean to the new day.

When he awoke, he looked over at Penny and saw her lying quietly with her eyes focused on the ceiling, her brows knitted with worry. "Is something still troubling you, darling?"

"It's nothing. I was just having a bad dream again and it left me feeling unsettled. I'm fine. Really." Turning to him and putting her arm across his body, she said, "Ryan, I'm sorry I've been so hard on you. I don't mean to be. I guess this whole mess has left me jittery and confused. I also apologize that I was not more supportive of you when you needed me after your mother's horrible death. I can only imagine how terrorized I would have felt if it had been my mother or father I discovered that way. I know you have suffered that you could do nothing to prevent her murder. I feel guilty, too, that I couldn't stop the bleeding. It frustrates me to want so much to help someone and find that what little I know isn't enough to save them."

"No one could have saved her, Penny. Not with the vein in her neck sliced. You did all that anyone could do. Try to remember all of the people you have helped with your medicines. Even the best doctors can't save everyone. If they did, the Grim Reaper would go out of business." Ryan grimaced, "I feel guilt, too, and with a damned sight more reason than you. I should have kept her safe. I'm the one that should have stayed behind and looked for her killer. You could have brought the body here as easily as I. After all, it isn't as though Mother would have known the difference."

"You are not to blame. None of us could have anticipated what happened. Now, enough sad stuff." Penny beamed at him, "I think it's time I told you a little secret I've been keeping."

"Ah, so you're keeping secrets from your husband, are you?"

"I don't think I'll be able to keep it much longer anyway," Penny laughed. You're about to become a father again, unless I miss my guess."

"Oh, my God, Penny! That's wonderful! And this time I'll be with you all the way. This baby you won't carry with me far away not knowing what is happening or even that I have become a father. When do you think it's due?"

"Sometime in October." Penny looked troubled again, "Do you think Rye will be upset at having a little brother or sister? He is so used to being the center of everyone's attention that it may be upsetting for him to have to share."

"We just have to make him part of the excitement and assure him that we don't love him any less just because there is someone new for us all to love." Ryan tucked his hands behind his head and grinned with satisfaction. "I confess I've been hoping that round little tummy and full breasts might be the signs of something happening."

Laughing, Penny hit him with her pillow, "Why you scoundrel, you knew."

"Suspected, just suspected. After all, I have done all I can to accomplish it," Ryan grinned.

"Not without assistance and willing cooperation," she laughed.

"Hmm. Let's celebrate while we can," Ryan said as he began making love to her.

It was late that morning before they walked down the stairs for breakfast. Gertie was in the midst of making teacakes. When they entered, they both stopped and grinned at Rye who was standing on a kitchen chair at the table, a smudge of flour marking one cheek.

"Look, I'm making a snake teacake." He pointed with pride to the long roll of dough he had just placed in the pan. Gertie says I can make one for each of us, too. So, I'll have a mama snake, a papa snake and a 'me' snake."

"I'm going to look forward to that snake all day. I bet I get so hungry thinking about it, I won't even be able to work. Speaking of which, I going to be late getting to the office. Do you have something I can grab to eat on the way?" Ryan rubbed his growling stomach and looked around with anticipation.

"I kept some sausage biscuits warm on the stove for you two. There is some coffee I can pour into a mug if you want?" Gertie pointed with floured hands towards the biscuits.

"That's okay. Just biscuits are fine. I'll get some coffee in town." Ryan waited while Penny wrapped the biscuits, then kissed her and Rye goodbye.

Popping his head back in the door, he asked, "Penny, why don't you two ride in to town later. I have a special treat in mind."

"Wonderful. What time shall we come?"

"I think I'll be through at the courthouse early, so make it around three."

"We'll be there."

After Ryan left, Penny abandoned the kitchen to Gertie and took her son into the garden with her. "Let's go see Miss Caroline. We haven't been to see her for a couple of days and I have something I want to tell her."

Penny took the short cut through the woods to Caroline's house, stopping to examine various weeds and herbs that grew wild beneath the sheltering trees. Most of them she knew as they had grown in the woods of her home near Kinston, but a few were new to her. She took samples of the leaves to ask Caroline if she could identify them. Then she would research whether or not they might have medicinal properties. It gave her great satisfaction to reflect on how much her neighbors had come to rely on her healing remedies. Once again Penny wondered what she might have done had she been born a man. Would she have had the opportunity to attend a medical college and learn modern medicine? Would she have continued to use the knowledge passed down to her from generations of granny women, as well as the more formal knowledge gained in a school? She knew doctors mostly scoffed at her treatments, but years of self-reliance and the absence of doctors had created a vacuum in which women like her had provided a vital service in the backwaters of the South. Not only that, but with medical training sketchy for many practitioners, granny women were often more effective.

It was a glorious day. The weather was warm but without the heavy humidity and heat induced torpor of summer. Wildflowers made the air redolent with their perfume and the bloom of the huckleberries held promise of cobblers not far away. Overhead birds chirping in the branches of pines and oaks and the chattering of squirrels, accompanied their progression through the footstep-muffling blanket of pine straw. Penny took a deep breath of the honeysuckle-laden air and then picked up her son and swung him in a circle. She laughed with happiness that her life offered so much rich promise.

Caroline was working in her garden when they walked into her yard. Penny watched the elderly woman push her bonnet back and wipe the perspiration from her brow. The bonnet reminded her of the ones her own mother and grandmother had made using inserted slats of cardboard to stiffen the brim that

230 Betty J. Vaughn

shaded the face. Around the bottom of the bonnet a ruffle provided protection for her neck. When Caroline heard them walk up, she struggled to her feet holding her back as she did so.

"Mercy, I never saw so many weeds. If my flowers grew half so well, I wouldn't have to do anything but plant them. As it is, if I don't get these weeds out they're going to choke out everything," Caroline fussed as she tossed a wayward dandelion into the basket at her feet.

"It's really warm for so much work. Surely you have someone that can do this kind of thing for you?"

"Of course, I do. I just don't want them to. I want to do it myself. I'm not dead yet; old, yes. It just means I have to be a little slower. It doesn't mean I have to stop doing everything I enjoy. When that happens, I swear I will just plop down and die." Again Caroline mopped her face with her handkerchief. "What a beautiful day. It makes me happy to be alive."

"I feel the same way." Penny smiled and added, "I have another reason to be happy. I wanted Ryan and you to be the first to know. I told him this morning. Miss Caroline, I'm going to have a baby sometime in October. I just know it's going to be a girl and I want your permission to give her your name. I thought perhaps I would name her for both you and Martha, Martha Caroline or Caroline Martha."

"Oh Penny, you darling girl. If it's not a boy, I would be thrilled. I think that would be okay with Martha, too. The two of us old biddies actually became good friends. In the end, I truly loved her and I miss her so much. Butting our heads up against one another gave both of us energy. To tell the truth, I think I liked her more for being a little cantankerous. At least she had spirit. That's something to admire." Caroline chuckled, "Maybe a little too much spirit sometimes for tranquility. But when you have been alone as long as I have, tranquility begins to wear on you. Arguing with her added years to my life and zest to my days. I confess I miss Isabel, too, but she's been wonderful about writing. I wouldn't be surprised to hear any day that your father is going to end up with another new grandchild."

"I hope so. I know he has missed Rye since we moved here. It would be wonderful for him to have a grandchild nearby again."

Pointing to the assortment of leaves in Penny's hand, Caroline asked, "What is that you have in your hand?"

"I found these in the woods and I don't know them. I wondered if maybe you could help me identify them."

"Let's go up to the house and get some iced tea before I melt into a puddle. I'll check them out there. Rye, you little imp, give me your hand and help your old 'granny' to the house."

"Okay, Grandma Caroline."

Penny smiled at the two of them, "I see in my absence you two developed a new relationship."

Caroline's face went still for a moment. "I hope you don't mind. With Martha gone, I thought it would be good for him. God only knows, it's good for me. You know I love Ryan like a son. And now you and Isabel are the daughters I never had. I hope you don't mind if he calls me Grandma. With both of your mothers dead, he has no one else."

"Miss Caroline, I'm deeply honored and more than happy to have you for my children's grandmother. Ryan will be, too."

"Lord, who would have thought this late in my life that I would be the matriarch of a growing family. I just love it. I wish my husband could be here to see it. He always regretted that we had no children."

That sat on the veranda sipping their tea and looking at Rye play in the shadow of a huge magnolia whose branches of glossy green leaves nearly touched the ground. In the distance, a lone sailboat was gliding down the river. Caroline pointed to it.

"Isn't that a beautiful sight? I loved sailing as a child. Did you know that Ryan took me on a sailing trip during the war? We had a picnic and while we were eating he told me that he was in love with a woman named Penny whom he'd lost. I thought he meant you'd died."

"He never told me that," Penny commented with mild surprise. I'm sure he would take you sailing again if you want to go. In fact, he taught me to sail but I don't feel secure enough to go on my own."

Caroline picked up the leaves that Penny had brought to the porch. Carefully she studied each one, looking at both sides of the leaves and at the stems. Three she laid to one side, the other two she kept. "This one is false unicorn. It's named that because the root looks a bit like a horn. It's sometimes called colic root because it's used for colic treatment. I've also heard that it can be used to treat morning sickness. That might be handy for you to know at the moment."

"I've not been troubled with it this time the way I was when I was pregnant with Rye. Do you know what the other one there is?"

"This is white yam. Indians also used it for colic and irritable bowels. Those over there I'm not sure about. I think at least one of them is poisonous though." Caroline sighed, "That reminds me: I've been putting it off but I need to gather some blackberry leaves for tea to help with my digestion. It's been troublesome lately."

"Don't bother. I already have some dried leaves. I'll make you some tea and send Gertie over with it later."

"Thanks, Penny. I'd appreciate it."

They talked on for a few minutes more before Penny called Rye to say goodbye. She wanted to get home for a midday meal before taking the buggy into New Berne for the three o'clock appointment with Ryan. She smiled in anticipation of the promised surprised.

When they rounded the corner, Ryan was standing on the edge of the street in front of his office in animated conversation with the mayor. Before the buggy neared them, the mayor shook his hand and continued on down the street. Ryan turned to go into his office, but catching sight of them, waited by the curb for them to stop. He took Rye from Penny and then reached up to help her down.

"You're right on time. I've finished at the office for today so I thought I would give Rye his surprise first, then I have one for you."

Rye jumped in delight. He didn't care what it was; just getting a surprise was excitement in itself. "What is it, Daddy? What's my surprise?"

"Well, aren't you the eager one?" he teased.

Penny laughed, "I don't think we'd better waste anytime. He's been so excited all morning it was all I could do to keep him occupied until it was time to leave to come into town."

"All right then. Come with me to the ice cream store. They have a new flavor I think you're going to love. Fresh strawberry ice cream."

"Oh, I'm going to love that!" Rye skipped between his parents holding their hands.

"I visited with Miss Caroline this morning and told her our news. I also asked, if the baby is a girl, could we name it for both her and your mother. I hope that's all right with you?"

"Don't you fret. I think it's a grand idea. I suspect she was very pleased that you want to do this for her."

"She's thrilled. So, do you like Martha Caroline or Caroline Martha?"

"Either way is fine with me. You decide," Ryan grinned at her as he said it.

After the ice cream, Ryan took her by the elbow and led her back to the street. "Now your surprise: a thank you present for giving me such good news. The jeweler that sold me your earrings told me he has a bracelet to match. If you like it, I want to buy it for you."

"Oh, my. If I get presents like that every time, I'm going to have to keep on having babies."

"You can have as many as you want. I kind of like helping you make them," Ryan smiled at her over Rye's head as he said it.

Looking at one another, they failed to notice Lizzy who stepped from a shop into the street in front of them, nearly bumping into her before they saw her. Penny and Ryan both stifled involuntary groans. Neither of them wanted Lizzy spoiling their day.

Taking the proverbial bull by the horns, Ryan greeted her. "Hello, Lizzy. I'm just taking my wife shopping for a special gift. It seems I'm going to become a proud father once again."

Penny watched the woman's face turn a sick shade of green, before she recovered herself enough to say, "Oh my, congratulations to you both. How very nice," before abruptly crossing the street. Penny resisted looking at Ryan at that moment, but she couldn't help a small feeling of triumph. Maybe it was petty of her to relish Lizzy's comeuppance, nevertheless, she was delighted that it was Ryan who had told her and that he had done so with open pride.

Lizzy was angry, angrier than she had ever been. Clenching her fists into tight balls to hide her fury, she left them. She promised herself she would win in the end.

20

Marcus squinted against the painfully bright light that beamed from the casement across his narrow bed. He was too weak to lift his head. The room began a slow spin before coming to a tottering stop. Through parched lips, he begged, "Water."

"Lord have mercy, Doc. He's done woke up." Shine beamed at the doctor and then down at his friend. "I shore am glad to have you back with us, Marcus. I'll git you all the water I can carry if the Doc will let me give it to you."

The doctor walked over and lifted Marcus up as Shine gave him a sip of water and then another. "Marcus, I wouldn't have given you a snowball's chance in hell a week ago, but by damn, you're going to make it." He winked at Shine, "I reckon I owe Old Ben and you some thanks. That Indian treatment just may have made a difference after all, Shine."

It was another two weeks before Marcus could walk from his bed to the casement and look out at the sunlight shinning on the grass that dappled the swamp-like moat with patches of gold. Those few steps alone were enough to exhaust him for the rest of the day. After another week, he could walk to the mess for his meals but that was the limit of his physical strength. It was another two weeks before Marcus was strong enough to once again go fishing with Shine. He emerged into the late April sunshine, a wan and weakened man. He knew the limits of his ability and opted to sit on the sand in the warm sun for much of the day with a baited fishing pole to legitimize his time out. Shine, happy just to be out with him once more, did the fishing and oystering for them both.

Marcus felt his eyes closing under the soporific influence of the warming sun. Dark spots danced behind closed, blood-reddened lids. Soft wind rustled the golden sea oats that reached like embracing arms around his little spot of sand. The rhythmic slapping of waves against the crushed shells of the shore lulled him into the healing arms of Lethe. His eyelids twitched as he dreamed. He didn't feel the inquiring scamper of a fiddler crab brushing against his open palm. He didn't hear the triumphant call of a pelican rising with fish-filled beak from the shallow water. And he didn't see the scuttling clouds, like benign puffs of cotton, sailing across the enveloping sky.

From time to time, Shine looked up from his work and smiled. Marcus's recovery seemed little short of a miracle to him. He prayed that Ole Ben would come by before they had to leave so both he and Marcus could thank him for his life-saving remedies. Once he looked up from where he was raking oysters to see Marcus sitting up and watching him. He called, "If I keep on gitting oysters we're gonna have enough for all of us at the fort and the rest of the island, too. You just set yourself there and work up an appetite. We need to git some meat back on them bones of yours."

Marcus waved and then lay back against the sand once more. This time he turned his head so the lowering sun would not be in his eyes. He watched the marsh grass rustling in the breeze and pondered the route that had brought him to the shore of the ocean he had never before seen. Before he could become morose, he forced himself not to dwell on the 'whys' of his predicament, but rather to find more positive things to occupy the few hours left before the prison walls once again reclaimed him. In his pocket were the letters from Brett, Lena, John Harvey, and Penny that had collected during his illness. Both Lena and John had reassured him they were doing all they could to find a witness or some other information that would exonerate him. Lena had reassured him of her love and commitment. He had laughed as she described the tribulations of trying to find the right fabric for her wedding gown. She was determined it would be white satin and white satin was in short supply.

Brett told him that the new overseer at Belle Terre, Hardy Brown, had planted acres of corn and cotton. In a fit of industry, he had also decided to raise a larger acreage of tobacco on the black fertile soil of Marcus's farm, predicting that it would be North Carolina's cash crop of the future. With the appetite of the boll weevil growing and a blight that was beginning to affect local cotton crops, he conceded Hardy might have a valid argument for his decision. Marcus longed to see for himself the progress being made against the deprivations and neglect of wartime. He ached to be the one nursing his farm back to prosperity. In his mind he walked across the furrowed loam looking for the tender shoots that were beginning to grow tall and ripen. He smiled thinking about his land and the house that was waiting for him, his bride and the children she would bear him, children that would one day farm the land he had left to them. Idly he tested names for his unborn children.

He touched his pocket where the letter from Penny rested, separate from the others and unopened. He had struggled against his first impulse to shove it into the fire that warmed the damp evenings, even as he had refused to read it. He could banish her from his waking moments, but he could not stop her from haunting his dreams. Almost without volition, he found himself pulling the letter from his pocket. He looked at his name written in flourishes on the front. He lifted it to his nose and detected the faint smell of the perfume she always wore. He lifted the sealed edge of the envelope and extracted her letter. Marcus scanned the upbeat litany of the events of her daily life, all the mundane things that hold the bigger moments together. It was only when he reached the end of the letter that he felt a stab of pain grip his stomach like an iron glove. She was pregnant with Ryan's child...again. To stop the insidious creep of futile longing that seized him, he forced himself to stand and walk down to the edge of the water. "Shine, you going to take all of those oysters today or leave some for another time?"

"I was just finishing. You want to git the horse and wagon over here so we can load up or are you feeling too puny for that?"

"I think I can manage to lead that old nag over here without any trouble. It's the least I can do to thank you for bringing my sorry, worthless ass out here with you."

'You know I ain't goin' fishin' without you. Besides, the fresh air and sunshine done you good. You look fitter already."

"I think you're right," Marcus replied.

Shine loaded the bushels of oysters into the wagon and stowed his equipment. Climbing into the seat beside Marcus, he snapped the reins against the backs of the patient army mules. The weakening rays of the sun lit their backs as they plodded the sandy road back toward the fort. They had only gone a mile when they saw movement on the verge of the road, causing the sea oats to ripple back and forth. Suddenly Ole Ben stood in the road waving to them.

"Whoa, mules," Shine ordered, pulling back on the reins, and stopping just short of Ben. "Landsakes, Ben, you just about to git yourself run over."

"Sorry, I didn't mean to spook you. I just wanted to say hello to Marcus here." Turning to Marcus, he continued, "I am mighty glad to see you up and about. Shine was some kinda worried about you."

"I owe you a heap of thanks, Ben. The treatments you gave Shine may well have saved my life. Even the doctor gives credit to them for making the difference."

"My grandpa always went to the local Indian witchdoctor when somebody was sick. He said the medicine they were using was cheaper, easier to get, and more effective than what he could find elsewhere around here. Considering how remote the island is, that's not surprising." Ben smiled and waved, "I'll get on home now; Esther's waiting for me."

They drove on, puzzled by his last remark. Marcus shook his head, "I believe Ole Ben is getting a touched demented. Didn't he tell us his wife Esther died twenty-five years ago in a flu epidemic. You know, I feel sorry for him in some ways, but maybe it makes it less lonely for him to think she's still there."

"Well, if he thinks she's going to have a hot supper waiting on the table for him, I suspect he's gonna be a mite disappointed," Shine shook his head, a smile twitching at his lips.

"Did you ever marry, Shine?"

"Naw. I was sorely tempted once, but I guess she didn't have much use for me. Pretty thing she was. I sure did have a mighty yen for her, I can tell you. Tore me slap to pieces when she up and married my neighbor's boy. And him sorrier than an egg-sucking dog. Guess there just ain't no accounting for what women cook up in their heads."

Marcus pulled a wry smile, "Looks like we got more in common than moonshining, tobacco pipes, and fishing. I got my heart broken, too."

"Well, you at least got another woman waiting for you. I ain't got nothing and no prospects of nothing."

"Oh, I don't know about that. With so many fellows lost in the war, a prime specimen like yourself ain't going to be fancy free for long once they get wind of you. Right now the problem is there's nowhere to meet women stuck off out here. When you come home with me, I'll bet you won't last as long as a hungry preacher's Sunday sermon before some sweet little thing gets her hooks into you."

"Well, I guess I better start packing my wedding trunk the way the gals do," Shine laughed.

When they arrived back at the fort, the warden walked out

to meet them. "Marcus, I have a telegram from your lawyer in my office. He says he'll be on the way here soon with some news that is going to set you free. For your sake, I surely hope he's right."

"I assure you, Sir, you can't begin to want it half as much as I do. Although I appreciate the courtesies you've given me, I want to go home and get on with my life." Marcus found himself afraid to hope. He had been disappointed before. That disappointment was almost harder to live with than the daily tedium of prison. It weighed so heavily on his soul to have dreamed and planned with positive anticipation only to have those dreams trampled by the cold reality of the day. He needed an underlying foundation of hope just to sustain himself through the travails of his current life, but that soaring giddiness of joyful waiting was much too dangerous to allow into any corner of his mind. He also needed what strength he had left to continue to recover from the aftermath of a nearly fatal wound. However, he knew he had no extra strength left in him to deal with recovering from more dashed hopes.

"Shit, Marcus, I thought you'd be turning cartwheels. Ain't you tickled to death at the prospects of gitting outta here?" Shine asked incredulously once the warden had left them.

"I'm pleased for sure; but I figure I'll just bide my time until I see exactly what it's going to mean. I don't care to get all excited and happy if it means having to deal with the opposite feeling when the news doesn't work out the way I thought. I've been burned by that fire aplenty."

"I reckon I can see what you mean, but if it was me, I'd be happier than a sailor in a whorehouse." Shine grinned, "I 'spect I ought to git my resignation turned into the warden, so's I can leave when you do."

"That would be great, Shine, but I think you should wait until I know for sure whether or not I'm going to get out. If I don't, I'm selfish enough to want you still here. Without you to run interference, God only knows what would have happened to me." Marcus laughed, but he was only half joking.

"Hell, I wouldn't leave without you regardless," Shine reassured him.

The next two weeks crawled by. Despite his constant reminder to himself not to think about what John Harvey's visit might mean, he could not stop thinking about the possibility that he might soon be free. In the mess, the other prisoners left him alone. With the escape of his three former cellmates, the animosity toward him seemed to have abated. Or perhaps, he surmised, his fellow prisoners deemed the vicious stabbing sufficient punishment. Whatever the reason, he was grateful that he could eat his meals without watching his back the whole time. Whenever he thought about the night he had been stabbed, he thanked his lucky stars that he had shifted his body when he did and that Shine had convinced the doctor to try Ole Ben's Indian remedies. Perhaps, he told himself, his luck was on the rise. He could only pray that might be the case. And pray he did, as one day edged out another in that endless seeming progression into the future with him still a captive.

Three weeks after the telegram, Marcus was escorted to the warden's office. John Harvey, Lena and her father were waiting for him there, along with Penny's brother, Brett. Marcus looked at their smiling faces and for the first time, he felt a great upsurge of joy begin within him. Walking up to Lena, he gathered her into his arms and pressed a chaste kiss on her cheek, ever conscious of her father's watchful eyes. He shook the men's hands and then took the seat the warden indicated.

The warden began, "Marcus, I have an order to return you to New Berne. It seems there has been a break in your case that looks as though it will exonerate you of any guilt. I am releasing you into the custody of your attorney under advisement from the court in New Berne. You are to gather your belongs and be ready to leave within the hour as you must catch the afternoon train from Beaufort in order to be at the courthouse tomorrow morning." Standing, he walked over to Marcus and shook his hand. "I'm pleased for you. I never thought you were guilty. I just want to say that I wish you all the best and a speedy and fair conclusion to this whole mess."

"It won't take me long to get my things together, but I would like to have a word with Shine. He's become a real friend to me during my time here and I need to thank the doctor as well."

"I'll have Shine report to the infirmary immediately. You can gather your affects while you're waiting for him. I'll see to it the doctor is there as well before you leave. Good luck to you, Marcus."

"Thank you, Sir." Turning to the others, he said, "I'll be with you and ready to go as soon as I can get packed and say some goodbyes. And thank you all for believing in me. I had just about given up that this day would ever come."

Lena squeezed his arm gently, her heart on her face. John, Brett and Lena's father were all smiling broadly. He wondered what turn of events had brought them all here and assumed that they would tell him on the way to New Berne.

Marcus found himself strangely sad that he was leaving; at the same time, he celebrated his longed for release from prison. He knew that he would miss Ole Ben to whom he owed his life; the doctor that had watched over him and befriended him during the longs months of captivity, and until he could arrange release from service, he would particularly miss the man that had become a close friend to him. Shine was jubilant that the long awaited day had arrived and assured Marcus he would waste no time in asking the warden to release him from military service. He promised Marcus that he would visit Ole Ben and let him know that Marcus had been released and thank him again for his life-saving remedies. The doctor cautioned Marcus that he was still not fully recovered and to take it easy in the coming weeks. He was awkward with the emotion of the moment. Clasping Marcus' hand, the doctor pumped it with unaccustomed vigor. With his bag packed, Lena's quilt draped over his arm, and a parting smile on his face, Marcus nodded goodbye to both his friends and left the infirmary.

"Whooee!" He heard Shine call after him, "I'm gonna be a coming soon as I can. I'll git the Doc to write you when I'm gitting relieved of service here."

"Do it, Shine. I'll be waiting," Marcus called back.

On the boat trip to the mainland, Marcus held Lena's hand, while Brett explained what had transpired to affect his release from Fort Macon. "Lucinda came to me a couple of days ago and said that she knows who killed the overseer and she thinks she can prove it. It seems her son, Jeremiah, saw the murder happen. That coupled with the trauma of watching his mother's rape contributed to his months of muteness. A week ago he began to talk again and one of the first things he did was to accuse Abigail Smith, the overseer's wife of the murder. Because of his age, his testimony is kind of iffy."

John Harvey interrupted, "Even so, this gives cause for reasonable doubt and it reinforces the testimony of the witness that can verify you went to the Tull farm that night prior to going to Lena's house. Although the child is young, his testimony cannot be totally discounted unless the prosecutor makes a deliberate effort to confuse him in order to render his testimony worthless. I don't see Ryan Madison trying something like that, so I feel some confidence that this will carry sufficient weight to have them drop charges against you. If not, I will ask for bail and a trial date."

"So, what you're telling me is it's not cut and dried." Marcus heaved a sigh before continuing, "I sure hope this will be enough. I am so tired of dealing with all of this."

After several moments of uncomfortable silence, Marcus said, "I'm sorry. I don't mean to sound ungrateful. I'm just impatient to be done with it and get on with my life."

Mr. Rouse spoke up for the first time, "Son, we're ready for you to get on with it, too. My daughter's trousseau is about ready and the preacher's on standby. All we need is the groom. Then we're going to get you two married and started on what I pray will be a long and fruitful life together."

Marcus smiled and squeezed Lena's hand, "Well, Lena, did you ever get that white satin for a wedding gown?"

From the crestfallen look on her face, he knew the answer before she spoke. "I tried but I finally had to give up. Mama says she can make one out of batiste that will look just fine. After all, it's not the dress that's important."

"Wait a minute," Brett exclaimed. "We can fix that little problem. I'll see if Isabel or Penny will loan you theirs. They both wore white satin."

Marcus saw Lena flush. The offer of Penny's gown was the last thing he wanted, and knowing of his past love for the woman, Lena wouldn't want it either. He spared her answering, "Brett, that's very generous of you, but I'd rather see Lena in her own gown and not one she borrowed. Batiste will be fine. She's going to be a beautiful bride regardless of what she's wearing."

Lena smiled her gratitude and tightened her hold on his hand. "Thanks any way, Brett. Marcus is right. I'd rather have my own so I can save it for our own daughter to wear someday. Besides, I haven't had the chance to look in New Berne yet, so perhaps I may still find some white satin if I decide I really want it. If not, I'm going to buy lace to go on the batiste gown Mama's already working on."

For the remainder of the journey to New Berne, Marcus listened as the others caught him up with all of the news of the outside world. He was happy merely to sit in their midst and adjust to the reality of his longed for release.

21

The sharp bang of the gavel pronounced Marcus a free man. He gave a grateful handshake to John Harvey and then turned to Mr. Rouse and Lena who were sitting behind him. He pumped Wiley Rouse's hand before giving Lena an exuberant hug. Looking over Lena's head, he could see Penny sitting beside Brett and John Bartlett, smiling with happiness at his acquittal. Marcus nodded at Brett and his father before allowing his eyes to travel to Lucinda who was sitting uneasily on the next bench. She had her son's hand gripped in hers. Before his eyes slid past, he had not missed the perplexed look that Penny gave him when he ignored her. For a moment he was ashamed that he had slighted her, as she had written him and wished him well during his stay in prison. It wasn't her fault that he was having a problem putting his feelings for her behind him.

Ryan Madison walked up and shook his hand just as he was exiting the courthouse. Penny and her family were standing by his side.

"I'm glad this is behind you, Marcus. It's a pity that we could not have known about Abigail Smith prior to your arrest," Ryan commented.

"Well, what's done is done. I'm just glad that Jeremiah decided to start talking and told his mama what he had seen." Marcus forced himself to look at Penny, "I appreciate your letters. Yours and the ones from Lena and John Harvey helped keep my spirits up those long months."

He put his arm around Lena's waist, and smiled down at her. He was determined that Penny would not know, that no one would know whom he really wanted to be holding in his arm. "We're going to be having a wedding just as soon as we can get around to it. We've already invited your folks. I hope that you and Ryan will come as well."

"Thanks, Marcus, and congratulations. You've found yourself a beautiful bride, and a loyal one from what Brett tells me. We're happy for you both and wish you long, prosperous years together," Penny beamed at the two of them.

Lena bit her lip for a moment before replying with some asperity, "Thank you very much."

Marcus, realizing she did not want to linger in Penny's company, interjected, "I think we'd better get going if we want to make that train to Kinston. I confess I'm eager to get there. Are you folks coming, too?" He inquired of John and Brett.

Penny's brother responded, "That we are. I think Lucinda is going to be on the train, as well. She's mighty pleased about her school teaching job and that school we started. She's anxious not to miss too many days. I know she wants to tell you all about it, so try to talk to her during the trip."

"Good, I'll look forward to it." Marcus paused before continuing, "I hope it has changed some of her attitude. I was getting pretty worried about her."

John Bartlett spoke up, "Well, if you mean: *is she still chasing white men*, I think I can at least partially reassure you. It seems she's been carrying on a bit of a flirtation with a darky schoolmaster over near Snow Hill. Unfortunately that has still not completely taken the focus of the KKK away from her. I suppose you and Brett have to take the blame for that by starting this blamed darky school. I'm not saying I object to it, mind you, it's just that you can't expect the Klan to be thrilled about the whole idea. They think it's just going to create a bigger problem with uppity darkies."

Marcus bit his lip thoughtfully, "Well, I can't say that I'm surprised that's their take on it, but as far as I'm concerned, they can just get over it. That slavery stuff is done for. The south is never going to be like it was before the war. That's not all bad either."

"Well, let's save this discussion for the train, I need to say goodbye to Penny and Ryan, here." Uncomfortable with the conversational direction, John Bartlett turned away.

Marcus watched as Penny hugged her father and brother goodbye. Ryan shook their hands and then cuddled his wife against his side as they watched them leave. Marcus rested his gaze on her swelling belly and the look of proud possession on Ryan's face. Jealousy grabbed him by the scruff of his neck and held tight. He felt his groin throb just looking at her. He wanted to be the one holding her in his arms, kissing her, giving her children of his own. A low feral growl slipped from his clenched jaws before he could stop himself. He saw Lena had followed his train of thought all too well, as she stiffened and edged away from his hand at her waist. Hating himself for not keeping a tighter rein on his emotions, he turned away from Penny and climbed into the waiting buggy. Wiley Rouse gave him a thunderous glare as he helped his daughter climb into the buggy. She took the seat across from Marcus rather than beside him. Not only had Wiley caught the look that Marcus gave Penny, but it was an inexcusable breech of etiquette to enter the buggy without assisting Lena in first. Marcus looked down at the group still standing on the grass near the street. Ryan had noted the sudden flare of lust in Marcus' eyes and bore as hostile an expression on his face as the one Wiley aimed at him. All Marcus could think was 'what a mess, what a damned mess. What in the hell is wrong with me that I can't let this woman go?' It was going to be an uncomfortable few hours on the train to Kinston unless he could figure out a path to self-redemption.

John and Brett made a desultory effort at conversation during the first part of the journey then ignored the icy silence of Wiley and Lena, and the remote man that sat beside them.

John was oblivious to the reason for the pallor that hung over what should have been a celebratory occasion. However, Brett knowing Marcus's previous romantic ambitions suspected the cause for the sudden chill. Marcus had not gotten Penny out of his system and Lena knew it.

Lucinda sat apart from them in the back of the car in the area reserved for Negroes. Her son fidgeted beside her as he stared blankly out the window. The charm of his first train ride had worn off and he was once again withdrawn from the world around him. Closing her eyes, she wearily pondered how to help her son who had seen too much evil in his short life. Although he could once again talk, he communicated only when necessary providing little clue to what he was thinking and feeling. He had never been an easy child, never exhibited open affection, and rarely had he laughed and played like a normal boy. Even before witnessing her rape and Calvin Smith's murder, he had been remote. His cruelty to animals and his rejection of other children disturbed her. Underlying and surmounting it all was a growing suspicion of an even darker evil. Lucinda brooded that he had mistaken Martha Madison's similarity for Abigail Smith. She knew she should have done more to help him with whatever demons hid within his mind. It was so easy for her to work with the children she taught, to enjoy the interaction and their excitement at an expanding world of opportunity beyond that of their previously enslaved generation of ancestors. She suddenly realized that she preferred the company of her students to that of her own son. Guilt suffused her face before she carefully coached her features into a pleasant smile.

"Look at that tree there, Jeremiah. Do you see the big old owl sitting on that limb about halfway up?"

He did not shift his head to look either at her or the tree, and he didn't respond. Trying again, she asked, "Do you like riding on the train? It's a lot easier than going such a long way in a wagon, isn't it?"

Getting no response, she sighed with weariness and leaned against the slatted back of the seat. She was relieved when Marcus walked down the aisle toward her and dropped onto the opposite bench. An adult conversion on a topic other than her own worries was definitely welcome.

"Lucinda, I want to thank you and your son for going all the way to New Berne to testify for me. Without it, I'd still be rotting in prison and waiting for the hangman's noose."

"It's the least I could do. I owe you for giving me a chance to do something worthwhile with my life, something I would never have dreamed possible." She smiled with some of her old seductiveness, "I thought I was destined to be a jezebel until you and Brett built me that school."

"Lord, I thought so myself," Marcus chortled. "By the way, I hear you've got a schoolteacher fellow sniffing around after you."

Lucinda looked down at her hands that were suddenly twisted together in her lap. Her voice held an unaccustomed shyness when she replied, "His name's Sidney, Sidney Busbee. He's a good man. It's too soon to know whether or not he's all that interested in me."

Marcus noted that she didn't say that she wasn't interested in him. Smiling, he chided her, "Well, you can't tell me, if he is as smart and fearless as your letter said, that he's too scared of you and your charms to make his intentions known."

"Did you come back here just to tease me about a man?" Lucinda demanded with her old fire.

"Actually, I wanted to hear how that school of yours is doing. Since we have some time, care to tell me about it?"

"What's the matter; is it too chilly up front for you?" Lucinda regretted the barb the minute she said it. "I'm sorry. That was uncalled for. It isn't easy watching someone else holding the one you want, is it? Believe me, I know. I loved

Penny's husband Daniel and despised her because she could marry him when I never could have. He was too much old South to marry a Negro. He never loved Penny. It was me he wanted. I'm the one he gave a child. And Lord, did I ever love that man. It just about killed me when he married her. So, I for certain sure understand how it feels. I'm glad you found Lena, but she's not stupid. She's got eyes and she can see how you feel about Penny. When you talk to her, she knows from what you don't say how you feel. If you ever want her, if you want to make her happy, you've got to let Penny go, just like I had to let Daniel Kennedy go."

"Jesus H. Christ, am I wearing a sign or something?"

"Every time you look at her your face changes. You need to work at getting that look on your face when you see Lena. And I can't tell you how to go about doing that. The heart is a fickle and difficult to control thing. How you love one and not another that is equally attractive and desirable is a mystery. Maybe you'll never be able to feel as much for Lena as she deserves and needs. If you can't, can you live with her and truly make her happy?"

"You ask some hard questions. I know Penny is lost to me. I care for Lena and given time, I pray that she will become the love of my life. But it's going to take time. I know I spent too many years yearning after Penny. I'm trying to go on with my life now. I'm lucky I found Lena and she still wants me. And I'm blessed she stood by me through all of this."

Lucinda just shook her head, "White man, you shouldn't be telling me how lucky you are. You need to be up there, telling her and making her believe it. If you don't, you're going to lose that woman. We can talk about my school some other time. Now, you go and see if you can fix things with her."

"Thanks, Lucinda. I appreciate our talk. I never knew how you and Daniel felt about one another. I suppose I made the mistake of thinking, like so many others, that it was just a white man tasting a little of the other side. Lust is easier to understand than accepting that a white man can love a woman like you, particularly a man raised in the South, no offense intended. I'm sure a love that you can never have because of racial differences was a hard thing to face for both you and Daniel. It explains a lot of things that confused me about Daniel and Penny's relationship. And about you for that matter. Just don't let it make you bitter the way it made me."

"I'm working on it. It's not easy for sure, but meeting Sidney helps." Lucinda waved her hands at him, "Now, shoo. Get on back to your woman and convince her she's the only one for you. Convince yourself, too, while you're at it."

Marcus nodded his head and winked. Then squaring his shoulders, he walked back to the others. Lena watched him as he walked down the aisle toward her. There was no smile of welcome on her face. An overwhelming sadness consumed him for ruining what should have been a happy reunion for them both. He stopped for a moment and locked eyes with her and then he smiled.

"Lena, let's go sit in those seats over there a ways and have a little talk."

Wiley put a restraining hand on his daughter's arm. "I don't think so, Marcus. It's best you let things settle down for a while. You come on over to our house after dinner on Sunday. You and Lena can visit then."

Marcus waited to see if she would defy her father and go with him. With sad resignation, she lifted an eyebrow and merely shook her head before looking down at her clenched hands. At that moment Marcus realized he might well have lost her. Always before he had been invited for the customary Sunday dinner with the Rouse family. His pride wounded by having Brett and John Bartlett an audience to his rejection, his face froze into an icy glare. He turned on his heel and walked back to the seat where he had asked Lena to join him. After a few moments, Brett rose and followed him.

"Mind if I join you?" Brett didn't wait for an answer. He sat facing Marcus and said nothing for several minutes waiting for the other man to acknowledge him. It didn't take much to surmise that Marcus was uncomfortable, embarrassed and more than a little angry. Whether he was angry with himself or Wiley Rouse, Brett wasn't sure. "You sure do jump from one frying pan to another, Marcus."

"That's the God's truth." Marcus snorted, "It's a hell of a note to have a woman wait patiently for you for months while you rot in prison, and then when you're free, she's not sure she wants anything to do with you anymore."

"Be fair. It's not that and you know it. She's waiting to see if you can get that sister of mine out of your head and heart long enough to give her a chance."

Marcus worked his mouth in that way Brett had seen him do so often, before he finally blurted, "I'm a pure damned idiot. Your sister never loved me. I just refused to see it. Lena is a wonderful, beautiful woman and a good one. I don't know why, I can't just get on with my life the way I want to. I want to love her, God only knows I do."

"Maybe you need to stop trying so damned hard to force yourself and just let it happen. She's has to be pretty crazy about you to have hung in there all those months you were away. Cozy her along and make it up to her. Act like she's the most important woman on earth to you and in time, you just may realize she is. Mr. Rouse is another proposition. He's protecting his daughter from a man that he doesn't think deserves her. You've got to convince him you're worthy of her. I don't know how you're going to go about doing it, but you'd better figure something out pretty damned quick, or you're not going to get the chance."

"To tell you the honest truth, I don't blame Wiley Rouse. If that were my daughter, I'd feel the same way."

"Tell him that. Then tell him you're going to move heaven and earth to prove to him that you will be the best husband any woman ever dreamed of and you want the chance to prove it. Right now, you're not going to get the chance to say a lot. But at least he invited you to come over Sunday. Be respectful and attentive the rest of the time on the train. Get on back over there and apologize for walking off. Tell Lena she's the most wonderful woman God ever put on this earth and you are counting the minutes until you get to see her Sunday. I'll talk to Pa to get him off the scent while you do some making up with them."

Marcus looked up at Brett with a twinkle in his eye, "Someday you're going to have to tell me how you got to be so wise in the ways of women."

Brett laughed, "Isabel is giving me lessons. I have incentive to want to learn them real well. I've learned I prefer a warm woman to a cold shoulder when I climb in bed."

Marcus stood, "Let's do it."

Brett followed him back to their seats. Rather than sitting on the bench with him and his father, Marcus sat beside Lena. He dared to pick up her hand and kiss it. She did not attempt to retrieve it, so Marcus continued to hold it. They rode the next ten miles with their shoulders touching each time the train swayed on the track. Looking out the window, Marcus commented, "I never realized just how beautiful this piece of country is. I suppose some people would find all of these pine trees and the swamps a little boring, but they look good to me. I'm looking forward to walking my fields and looking at the crops growing. I can't wait to climb into my own bed in my own house."

Lena bit her lip before answering, "I can't imagine how awful it must have been to be locked up like that for something you didn't do."

"It's something I hope I never have to repeat. I don't know if I could do it again and I had it really good compared to the rest of the prisoners. It's just the confinement against your will, the inability to determine what you do with your day, and the knowledge that you are trapped that are so horrible. The boredom, the discomfort, the poor food, the lack of privacy just add to the misery."

Wiley cleared his throat with a tentative peace offering, "I hear the fellow you hired for an overseer is doing a fine job for you. You were lucky to find him."

"Indeed I was. I owe the Bartlett's a big thank you for that."

For the rest of the trip, while there was still an awkward reserve among the three of them, it wasn't the same icy silence as before. Lena permitted Marcus to give her a sedate kiss on the cheek when they parted at the station in Kinston but she kept her body rigidly away from him.

22

They were lying in bed looking at the moon rise over the water. For the last hour, Penny had been pleading with Ryan. Making a pouting moue he could not see in the dark, she begged, "Please, Ryan. Take me sailing this weekend. Let's pack a picnic and go sailing in the sound. The weather is gorgeous and it's not too hot. We could spend the night even. Besides, if we wait any longer, I'll be too big and clumsy to go sailing."

Ryan rolled over and tucked her into his body spoon style. "Penny, there is little that I can refuse you. You know that. I do wish you would think about it. You're over four months pregnant. We shouldn't do something like this until after you've had the baby. I would not even have told you about the trip to Beaufort and the judge's offer of his boat there, if I had known what an issue it would be."

"If we wait for that, it'll be ages before we can go again. I can't leave an infant to go sailing and we couldn't take one with us. Besides Rye has been begging to go. You know *you'd* like to. Come on, say *yes*."

Ryan agreed reluctantly, "We'll go if you insist, but it would make me happier to wait until after the baby comes. Once you are strong again, we can leave it with a wet nurse long enough for a sailing trip."

"By that time it will be winter and too cold to go. You're talking about waiting another year."

"All right, all right, yes." Ryan laughed, "Mercy, you are persistent. We'll go, but don't blame me if I say I told you so."

"Wonderful. Rye is going to be so excited. I've been taking

him sailing along the shore. He's really learned a lot. He loves sailing as much as we do."

"I'm glad he's not afraid of the water." Ryan smiled, "He is a brave little fellow isn't he? Just like his father..."

"Maybe like his mother," Penny teased.

"Wife of mine, could we go to sleep? I have to be at the office early to finalize documents that have to be filed at the courthouse by ten. I'll ask the judge if it is okay if we take the boat out Saturday. I'll also check train schedules to Beaufort for Friday. You and Rye will have to entertain yourselves in Beaufort until I can finish with the case there." Patting her fanny, he added, "And you need to rest. You're going to be busy organizing things we'll need for that sailing trip."

Snuggling in contentment, she murmured, "I love you Ryan Madison."

"I love you, too, Mrs. Madison."

Rye was dancing with excitement when Friday morning arrived. They rose at dawn to pack the last minute items for their trip and arrived at the station just in time to meet the train. Penny decided she was as thrilled as her child although she was trying hard to be sedate.

Ryan, sensing her inner excitement and her efforts to appear nonchalant, laughed at her and teased. "You know, darling, I've reconsidered the risk of taking a pregnant woman. I think it's better if you stay here and just Rye and I go."

Not realizing at first that he was joshing, Penny bristled. "You most certainly are not. This whole thing was my idea and you agreed. No backing out at the last minute."

Catching the twinkle in his eye, Penny smiled, "You're just pulling my leg, right?"

"Hmm, pulling on those legs of yours might be fun." Ryan remarked as the train blew its whistle for boarding.

"Later," Penny tossed an arch smile over her shoulder as she gathered the picnic basket and took Rye's hand. "Right now we have a train to catch."

It was late afternoon when Ryan finished with business and could meet them back at the Atlantic House Hotel for an early supper in the renowned dining room. Tired from the excitement and a day spent exploring the streets of the port town of Beaufort, Rye was soon fast asleep in a small cot near the window. After reading for an hour or so, both Penny and Ryan retired to their own bed. Moonlight played across the bedcovers as they made love, mindful of not waking the sleeping child. Afterwards they, too, were soon sleeping.

Saturday dawned with a muggy warmth and little wind. Ryan pulled back the lace curtain that covered the hotel room window and looked out at the street below. A strange yellow light cast a pall over the town. Penny was dressed and waiting when he turned back to her.

"We're all set to go," she announced.

When they walked out of the hotel and down to the waterfront. Ryan cast an anxious look around. A bank of clouds on the Southern horizon seemed low and heavy. They worried him enough that he debated canceling the trip. Continuing to watch the sky, he noted birds flying inland. Horses on the streets of the town seemed inordinately skittish. He too felt a vague unease that he could not name. "Penny, I just don't feel right about this. There's not much wind and it's going to be pretty hot out there by noon. You're already perspiring. Are you sure you want to go through with it?"

"Oh, don't worry so. As soon as we're away from shore, I'm pulling this skirt off. I have trousers on underneath so I'll be fine and much cooler without these layers. Besides it's clear except for a few far off clouds. We should be fine." Something nagged at the back of her own consciousness, but she refused to open her mind to it.

Carrying their gear, they walked onto the pier where the waiting boat was moored to a well barnacled pier. Ryan nodded to a grizzled old timer who was busy mending nets. Noting the picnic basket and the woman and child, the man commented, "Wouldn't go far if I was you. Weather's going to take a turn."

"We thought we'd just sail a bit in the sound and then have a picnic lunch. We should be back by late afternoon." Ryan had argued long and hard to confine the trip to a one-day excursion rather than an over-night one. Penny was still unhappy about it.

"Wouldn't go far," the old man repeated laconically, before turning back to his nets.

Ryan pushed off from the pier and maneuvered the boat toward the south. He planned to cross the sound and skim the sound shore of Bogue Banks, stop for a picnic lunch near the village of Salter Path and then return to Beaufort by mid-afternoon. Catching a little wind, they were soon well into the channel. A ripple of foam broke the blue of the water in their wake. Penny laughed with joy at the sound of the water rushing past the hull and the light flapping of the sails as Ryan maneuvered to keep the boat headed into the wind. In mid sound a stiffening breeze whipped her hair into errant tendrils that tickled at her cheeks. She tucked it back under her bonnet and then reached over to pull Rye's protective hat lower on his face so his nose was shaded from the sun.

Ryan began to relax and enjoy the experience, as well, while keeping a wary eye on the horizon. Rye swiveled about pointing out various landmarks on the shore. By eleven Ryan spotted a small beach with easy access and tacked the boat to take them ashore. When the boat was close enough to glide the rest of the way in, he dropped the sail and removed the centerboard. Swinging his legs over the side, he dropped into the waist deep water and guided the boat in. Penny and Rye followed him onto the beach where they spread the blanket and began to pull out the things they had packed. As his parents munched on fried chicken and corn on the cob, Rye chased fiddler crabs along the shore.

When they had finished eating, Ryan lay back on propped elbows and studied the sky. The horizon had grown darker and the wind was picking up. He was still not alarmed as the breeze was no more than was needed for a good sail. Closing his eyes, he half drowsed for a few moments as he listened to Rye's conversation about sand fiddlers and other denizens of the shore. He was content to be with his family and enjoy the peace of the moment. Even so, continued unease lurked at the back of his mind.

Penny called him back to the present with a question. "Ryan, have you noticed how quiet it is? There are no birds calling. Except for some sand fiddlers and a crab or two, I've seen no other living creatures."

"That is odd. I noticed the horses in town were acting funny. I wonder if that old-timer was right about the weather changing." He stood up and once more studied the sky. Dark scuttling clouds had begun to encroach on the blue of the sky. "Penny, we need to get back. I don't like the looks of this. I want to be well ashore before it turns bad. The wind is already rising a little. It could start getting rough out there soon. We can't afford to waste a minute."

"Do you think a storm's coming? I hear northeasters can be something fierce along the coast. I don't want to get caught in one. Maybe we should find someone to take us in until the weather is better."

"If we hurry, we should be okay. I'll grab Rye and the basket and you get the blanket. I'll stay close to shore until we get nearer Beaufort and then I'll cut over. That is the only time we'll be any great distance from land."

By the time Ryan had maneuvered the boat to the point that he had to either commit to crossing or continue on to the fort and ask for shelter, the wind had begun to pick up. The waves were just beginning to show an occasional white froth on their crests. "It's not that far across the sound from here. It looks as though the water's not so rough that the crossing will be dangerous if we hurry. However I think I'll take us on down to Fort Macon and see if we can stay there until this blows by. I don't want to risk anything with the two of you in the boat."

Penny was watching the sky with as much anxiety as Ryan and it did not seem that hazardous. "As long as it's like this, I think we're fine to go on across. Rye sit down in the bottom of the boat and hold on, okay?"

Rye looked up at his mother and without a word, settled into the bottom of the boat. Ryan glanced at his son and then at Penny, "If we're going to do this, you'd best hang on, too. You can help me by keeping your eye on that opening just to the right of the projecting land you see on your left. That is where we are aiming for. Once there the water will be calmer and we can go on into Beaufort without much problem."

"Goodness, I'll be glad when we get back. I'm sorry I pushed you to bring us but I had no idea the weather was going to be a problem."

"You couldn't know any more than I could. Besides, I wanted to come. I didn't have to agree."

Penny nodded her head, but she could not help feeling as though her stubborn insistence had endangered all their lives. Watching clouds boiling in from the south, she could only pray that they would soon find themselves back at the Atlantic House Hotel. Long before they had reached the halfway point in the crossing, sudden squalls began to push the boat and huge drops of rain pelted them. Ryan struggled to hold the tiller and reef the sail against the ever-stronger wind. White-capping waves began to slop water over the gunnels and into the boat. Watching the water collecting in the bottom, spurred Penny to dig in the basket for something she could use to bail.

"I have to bail this water or we'll sink," she cried.

Not hearing her but seeing the intention, Ryan nodded his head at her when he saw what she was doing. "Good girl!"

His words were whipped away by the wind. Together they fought the growing tempest. Ryan read the expression on Penny's face and saw determination mixed with growing fear, a fear that was beginning to infect him as well. Fear would render him less effective in combating the storm, he coached himself to relax and just deal with the battle the elements were delivering to him. He needed every ounce of strength and focus he could muster.

They struggled on for long minutes more, minutes that seemed like an eternity. Ryan could see that the storm was pushing them toward the inlet at the north end of Bogue Banks. His only choice was to alter course and make a run for the pier at the fort. If swept into the open sea, they would all die. "We have to try to get to shore fast!"

"What?" she cried. Realizing their voices were lost in the storm, he signaled Penny his intention to steer the boat toward the fort. She nodded her head in understanding, never ceasing to bail the growing volume of water in the boat. Her lips were moving in what he took to be a silent prayer. He cursed himself for not paying greater heed to the old man on the pier. As he watched the mounting waves, he remembered Penny's dream. Claws of dread gripped his gut.

Holding the boat on a course for the fort became ever more difficult as the wind kept trying to push them broadside to the waves. The water and the sky had become a matching turmoil of leaden gray fury. Screaming gales tore at their hair, clothing, and sails. Raindrops drove like nails into their skin, stinging them. Rye began to cry as he watched the storm building around their boat.

"Ryan, look out!" Ryan glanced at Penny and saw her point at him as she opened her mouth in a scream that was swallowed in the noise of the storm. He had no time to react to the huge wave that loomed behind him.

The boat climbed in dizzy ascent to the crest, hung there a breathtaking moment and then began a slow heeling. Ryan lunged for his son, just as the boat turned over and they were ejected into the water. Holding onto the edge of the boat, he looked for Penny. She moved toward him and yelled while pointing at a rope that was whipping in the water between them, "I'm going to try to tie the rope around you and Rye."

"Okay, but be careful. I can't help you, without letting go of Rye."

"I know. Just hold on to him."

Working with one hand in the brief lull between waves, Penny managed to get the rope around them. Then she hurried to tie it around her chest just beneath the armpits. Their only hope was to hold onto the boat as it tossed in the angry waves. Kicking with their feet they tried to guide it as best they could. Their destination was only a vague shadow in the lashing rain. At that point, any land was welcome.

Ryan managed to get Rye's body onto the hull of the boat; even so the child's lips were beginning to turn blue from the chill of the water and the howling wind that snatched at his light summer clothing. Trying to keep him warm, he worked his own body onto the hull beside his son's small body. The rope that Penny had tied around him was both safety and nuisance as it restricted his freedom of movement. Holding Rye with one arm and balancing his body against the motion of the boat, he reached a hand down to Penny to pull her onto the hull with them. Penny struggled to lift herself from the water enough to grasp his hand. Feeling his strong clasp pulling on her wrist, she struggle to lever herself onto the hull, placing Rye between them. The rope around her chest loosened during their efforts and dangled in the water.

"Help me get this rope back around you," Ryan called above the roar of the storm.

"Just in case I don't get another chance, I want you to know how very much I love you and Rye," Penny shouted through chattering teeth.

"I love you, too, darling. Now, hurry and tuck this rope around you and under your arms and then give the end back to me. I'll hold on to you while you get it."

"Just hold on to Rye." Penny prayed, "Oh, please, God help us."

She struggled to get the rope around herself and had almost succeeded when a powerful wave lifted her in the air and swept her into the roiling water. Penny screamed as she was swept away.

"Penny! Oh, my God. I'm coming." He struggled to free himself from the confining rope but knew if he did their son was lost. He could only watch in agony.

The last Penny saw of her husband was his anguished face as he struggled to hold himself and their son on the boat, his other helpless arm extended toward her as she was pushed further away. Fighting rising panic, as the vision she had so feared became reality, Penny began the struggle to keep herself from drowning. How long she battled the waves and the weary despair that threatened to steal her will to fight she didn't know. She didn't know many times she was pushed under only to claw her way back to the surface spitting water. She could no longer see the boat. She could no longer see shore due to the dimming of daylight and the dark of the clouds. A large piece of driftwood struck her side. Grabbing it, she wrestled to pull herself on top. There she wedged herself in the knurled branches and hung on with all of the strength she had left. She could feel her muscles tiring and feared they would fail, and a merciless sea would swallow her. Penny wept tears of despair. The sea was all around her, seducing her with the savage caress of hungry waves waiting for her to resign herself to the ultimate oblivion of their cold depths. The salt of her tears was lost in the salt of the sea and she knew she was lost as well. Penny closed her eyes and concentrated on enduring against a world gone mad. The storm seemed to go on forever as she fought to stay on the pitching driftwood. It plunged up and down in the waves like a thing possessed and still she held on. Her last conscious thought was a prayer that God in his mercy would spare her husband and child. The one she cradled in her womb would go with her into eternity.

Ryan wept, cursing himself that he could not protect both his wife and child. He railed at a God that would take her from him and their son. Kicking as hard as he could, he worked to angle the boat so that the waves would carry them to shore, or what he thought was shore, although the gray swirling maelstrom around him gave little clue where that might be. How long he clung to his son and struggled to keep them both on the tossing boat, he could not have said. Sometime in the early evening, he felt the upturned hull scrap against land. He dropped over the side and dug his feet into the sandy bottom to leverage the boat further onto the shore. Cradling his son against his chest to protect him from the flying leaves, twigs and sand that blasted their exposed skin, he began to walk into the shelter of the island. A limb flew from a small tree knocking him to his knees. After several seconds, he managed to regain his footing and forge onward until he reach the path that memory told him lead to the haven of Fort Macon. Fierce bursts of wind scoured the road and whipped the sand into grainy billows that took flight, joining the debris from trees and bushes. Hunched over to protect both he and his son, he braced himself against the battering wind and trudged in the direction of Fort Macon. When he at last stumbled onto the gangplank that led down to the fort, the lower elevation and the protective ramparts provided some relief from the ravages of the storm. Banging against the door of the fort, he prayed he would be heard above the screeching howl of the wind and crashing sea.

With his fist bruised by futile effort, he sank to his knees with exhaustion. Curling his son close, he faced the wooden barrier and fell into fitful sleep.

Morning dawned clear and still. The warming rays of the sun awakened him as he uncurled cramped limbs. Rye stirred in his arms, then blinked his eyes against the light. "Where's Mama? I want my mama."

Ryan choked with emotion as he replied, "I'm sorry, son. Mama was lost in the storm. We're going to find someone to help us and then we'll go look for your mama."

Rye's lips trembled and big tears rolled down his pale cheeks. "I miss Mama."

"I know, son." Swallowing the sob that threatened to choke him, he struggled to his feet and pounded on the door leading into the fort. This time he was heard.

After eating and settling his son in the infirmary under the doctor's care, Ryan went with a hastily assembled group of men to search for his wife. When the soldiers learned that Ryan's wife was from Kinston, one of them moved to his side and introduced himself.

"Sir, I'm Percell Brown, Shine to my friends. I'm a friend of Marcus Cauley from Kinston. He was a prisoner here until a couple of weeks ago. As soon as I can get released from service, I'm going to Kinston myself."

"I know Marcus. He is a friend and neighbor of my wife's family," Ryan said.

"I know this island pretty good. Now, don't you worry none. If your wife's on it, we'll find her."

"Thanks. I appreciate your help."

Over the next two days, Ryan and an escort of soldiers walked past Salter Path all the way to the end of the island. Back and forth they went eyes darting in every direction. Everywhere the destruction of the storm was evident. Trees were toppled, branches stripped clean of their leaves, shrubs battered flat, and bodies of tiny animals and marine life littered the sand. The sturdy island cottages had lost shutters here and there and shingles had flown off and buried themselves in the sand like so many lopsided tombstones. They asked everywhere they went if anyone had seen a woman wash ashore, but no one had and despite their diligent search, they did not find her either. On the return trip to the fort, they again searched the undergrowth and even ventured into the marshes, and stell there was no sign of Penny. Ryan felt mounting despair and an overwhelming sense of loss, mixed with an equal proportion of crushing guilt. He had not wanted to go. Now he could only blame himself for not heeding his initial gut reaction.

Trudging along the edge of the water as he scanned the reeds, Shine remarked, "I'm going to go check with Ole Ben. If anybody would of found her it would have been him. Ya'll go on and keep looking. I'll catch up."

Ryan nodded with dejection as he walked away.

Ben was in his cabin when Shine entered the clearing and called for him. Bursting from his door, he slammed it shut. "What you hollering about, Shine?"

"Just wanted to see if you came through the storm all right."

"Except for a messed up chicken coop and some lost shingles, everything's fine. We're just lucky the eye of that storm missed us and the island didn't go under water. I've seen the day when the folks here tied themselves in the tops of trees to keep from drowning. Yep, we were damned lucky with this one. Could have been a hell of a lot worse, for sure."

"Ben, have you seen a woman around here acting kind of lost? One got washed overboard by the storm and we've been looking along the shore for her body, but so far, we haven't found her. She could have survived and come ashore but no one has seen her. I guess the other possibility is she got washed out to sea."

Ben narrowed his eyes, "Why are you coming here looking for a woman? There ain't nobody here but me and my wife, now you git on."

"Now, Ben, you know your wife died twenty some years ago. You told me so yourself," Shine reminded him.

"Just git on, you hear," Ben turned and walked back into his cabin. The slap of the closing door punctuated the unaccustomed lack of cordiality.

23

Ben had walked the shore the morning after the storm in the time-honored tradition of those who make their livelihood near the sea. He was curious to see if the storm had washed up anything that might be useful. It was nearing noon and he was growing tired and ready to turn back when he spotted a flash of color caught in driftwood several hundred yards down the beach. Drawn to investigate, he walked closer. He shuddered when he saw it was a body. From a distance, judging by the pants, he had taken it to be that of a man. When he was close enough to bend down and examine the body that was trapped within the broken off branches of the driftwood, he realized that it was a woman, a woman with auburn hair like his Esther.

Falling to his knees, he cried, "Esther, Esther you came back to me. Please, Esther, please don't be dead."

The woman's hands were so locked around the driftwood that he had to pry each finger loose to tug her free. When he had her on the sand he rolled her over and took her wrist in his hand, feeling for a pulse. He thought he could feel it, reedy but still there. Clutching her to his breast, he begged, "Esther, hang on, honey. Let me get the mule and cart and I'll come back for you. Please, Esther, don't die."

Ben stood up, unbuttoned his shirt and wrapped it around her, positioning her so the warming rays of the sun could reach her body. Clumsily he patted her shoulder and then left at a trot. Panting from the unaccustomed exertion before he had gone even midway, he forced himself to stop, slow his pulse and steady his breathing. He leaned over, gripping his knees until he was recovered enough to breathe without gasping. Standing straight, he set off again at a more moderate pace. It would help no one if he had a heart attack before he could return for her. When he reached his stable, he fumbled with anxiety in his haste to hitch the mule to the small cart, but managed to get it done. He had already climbed into the cart to leave when he thought to fetch a quilt to wrap around her and a pillow to pad her head from the jolting. Dashing back into his cabin, he collected them and shoved them into the cart. Once more he clambered into his seat and picked up the reins. Realizing his upper body was bare, he remembered leaving his shirt with her. At the last moment, he ran back for another shirt before climbing once again into the rickety cart. Giving the reins a sharp slap, he set off to collect his "Esther."

When he had traveled as far as he could with the cart, he left it on the road with the mule tethered to a shrub and made his way through the dense stand of oak and cedar to the place where he had left her. Ben panicked when he emerged from the copse and saw nothing but sand and marsh. Forcing himself to rational thought, he began walking the shore. He soon spotted her, realizing that he had stopped short with the cart and would have to carry her further than he had planned. He could only hope that he was up to it. It had been years since he had tried to carry any real weight. Somehow, he had to do it. He had to save her.

She was lying as he had left her. Wasting no time, Ben bent down and struggled to get her on his shoulder so he could carry her to the cart. Her body was dead weight and he collapsed on top of the woman, unable to move her. Sobbing with frustration, he knelt on one knee and tried to lift her into his arms. He managed to gather her up, but then was faced with trying to stand. Trembling with effort, he stood with his burden locked in his arms.

"I've got you now, Esther. We're going to go home and I'm

going to make you well. Oh, Esther, I've missed you for so long." Tears streamed down his face as he tottered towards the tangled and broken thicket that he would have to cross to get her to the cart. He had gone no more than a hundred feet when he realized that he had to rest before he dropped her. Stopping, he lowered her to the sand and gulped air. His heart was hammering like a wild thing in his hoary chest. It had been years since Ben had prayed, but now he beseeched the God that had abandoned him so many years past. He could not endure losing his Esther again. Somehow he had to get her home and save her.

Ben lost count of how many times he stopped before he finally got her to the cart. During the entire trip she had not moved. He could only pray that the pulse of life still beat somewhere in that cold, still form. He wrapped the quilt around her body and tucked the pillow under her head. Then he climbed into the cart and urged the mule into a trot. He knew he had to get her into dry clothes and a warm bed. He would make some herbal tea that had restorative qualities and pray that she would take it, pray that some spark within her still wanted to live. As he drove, he babbled to her pleading with her not to leave him again. Fear caused him to turn every few yards to check on her as he hurried the mule home. Each time he looked, she lay insensate to the jostling cart and the world around her.

When they reached the cabin, he was exhausted from nervous tension and the unaccustomed labor. Ben gathered the dead weight of her body in his arms and staggered inside where he lowered her as best he could onto his bed. His arms gave out the last few inches and she dropped heavily. Her head rolled to one side. Alarmed, Ben cried out, "Esther, Esther, I'm sorry, honey. I hope I didn't hurt you more. I'm so sorry. You just wait right here. I'm going to get that pillow and quilt and I'll be right back."

Ben ran back to the cart and gathered the bedclothes. Glancing back at the mule still hitched to the cart, he yelled, "Don't you run off, damn you. I'll take care of you soon as I see to Esther."

Ben removed the woman's clothes until her body lay bare before him. She seemed uninjured apart from where her skin had been abraded and chapped by the wind, sand, and flying debris. Rushing to the cupboard, he churned to find one of Esther's nightgowns. Pulling the garment over her head, he worked her arms into the armholes and then smoothed it down her body, caressing the mound of her belly as he did so. That's right, he remembered, his Esther was pregnant with their daughter Catherine. With the bedclothes snuggled around her, he reached for the pillow and tucked it under her head spreading her salt-stiffened hair over the top of it. He reminded himself to wash it later. Ben stood up and studied her for a moment realizing that the bump he had felt on her head must be why she was unconscious.

"I sure do wish you would talk to me, Esther. You can't begin to imagine how bad I've missed you talking to me. Now, I'm going to go fix you up some good tea and see if we can't get you right as rain. You just rest. I'm right here and I'm going to fix you up just fine. Just fine, you hear?"

Ben worked at fever pitch to make the tea. Anxiety made him shake. Hot liquid sloshed on him when he tried to fill her cup, causing him to drop it. It broke at his feet sending tea running across the rough boards of the floor before seeping through the cracks. He fetched another and poured the tea with care. Stepping around the broken china, Ben inched toward the bed. He lowered the cup onto the small table that held his Bible and a lamp. "Esther, honey, I'm going to raise your head and see if I can get some of this tea in you. I need you to swallow, now."

Frustrated that the tea only spilled down her chin and

puddled in the hollow of her neck, Ben gave up on that approach. He fetched a spoon from the cutlery drawer and eased it between her slack lips managing to get a small amount of tea into her mouth. He massaged the muscles of her throat to encourage the swallowing reflex. When he saw her swallow the sip of tea, Ben felt that Heaven had shed its magic light on him. His Esther was alive. Sip by small sip, he succeeded in getting the healing tea down her throat. She still had not opened her eyes. He touched her eyelashes where crystals of salt had dried. "I'm going to take care of you, honey. Soon you'll be fine again," Ben said as he caressed her check. "You just rest for a minute while I go to unhitch the mule. I won't be long."

When he returned to the cabin, he made a light supper for himself and tea for his Esther. Again he used the spoon to feed her the tea. When he was finished he removed his faded clothes and pulled on a nightshirt. Folding back the covers, he slid into the bed beside her. Ben nestled his face against her shoulder. He could not resist touching her sleeping body, but when his hand cupped the soft weight of her breast, she struggled feebly and tried to push him away. "I'm sorry, Esther. I just wanted to touch you again, honey. It's been so long. I didn't mean to wake you up. Go back to sleep, I won't bother you again."

Ben sighed to himself as he drifted into contented sleep. He had not meant anything sexual by his caress. It had been years since his body had stirred with lust. He had touched her to reassure himself that a flesh and blood wife was back in his bed. For years he had fallen asleep at night with the last thing on his lips, a "goodnight, Esther." Now that she was back his good-night would fall once again on her ears rather than empty air.

Penny grew restless during the night, tossing and turning in the strange bed and vaguely aware that an alien body lay next to hers. She tried to remember what had brought her here, what had happened to her. She tried to remember who she was. Thinking made her head hurt so she stopped trying, even though not knowing left her frightened. She remembered someone calling her Esther but the name did not seem right to her. Her real name existed just beyond the fog. Moving to the far side of the bed, she moaned before slipping back into unconsciousness.

When she awakened, the sun was high in the sky. Across the room from the bed where she lay, a man of sufficient senectitude to be stooped and gray was working at a hotplate suspended over coals in the fireplace. She struggled to sit up but the movement made her head hurt and she moaned with pain. Ben heard her and crossed the room to her side.

"Esther, you're awake. I'm just making you some tea. I have some bread, too, if you're hungry?"

"I'm not Esther. I'm..." she looked up in confusion. "Just tea, please. I'm not hungry." She closed her eyes and lay back, watching him surreptitiously when he turned away. She did not know this old man that insisted on calling her Esther.

"Here, Esther. I made the tea just like you like it with lots of milk," he said as he sat the cup on the table and lifted her against the headboard.

"I'm not Esther. I don't care for milk in my tea."

"Of course you're Esther, honey. You just got a bump on your head. You'll remember soon," Ben soothed. "If you don't want the milk, I'll drink this cup and get you another one."

"Thank you. Just a little sugar, please."

When he handed her the second cup of tea, she studied his face, "I don't know you. What am I doing here?"

At that moment a loud holler in the yard distracted Ben. Without replying, he left the cabin, slamming the door shut as he exited. She could not hear what he was saying, but it was only a couple of minutes before he returned.

Agitated, Ben paced the floor, running his hands through his sparse hair until it stood on end.

"Please, who are you? Where is this?"

"Esther, honey, I'm *Ben*, Ben Dough. I'm your *husband*. That baby you're carrying is our daughter Catherine. This is Bogue Banks. You've lived on this island all your life and so have I. Don't you remember?"

She just shook her head. She knew he was wrong, but she didn't know what right was.

Ben's smile was placid. "It's all right, honey. You'll remember just fine when that bump on your head gets better."

"Why is there a bump on my head and why is my skin all bruised and sore?" Penny asked as she studied her outstretched arms.

"You got caught outside in a bad nor'easter. I found you and brought you home."

"Oh." Penny tilted her head to one side, studying this old man. "You said I'm your wife?"

"That's right, honey," Ben's face lit with pleasure.

"I am not." She was adamant in her denial.

"Now, now, you need to be calm. Don't go working yourself into a tizzy. As soon as you're healed you'll remember."

"I think I'm hungry." Blushing, she continued, "Please, I need to use the chamber pot."

"Let me help you," Ben said hurrying to her side.

"Just put it there. Then go away, *please*," she said. "I would like some privacy."

"Of course, Esther. Soon as you're done, call me and I'll take care of it and then make you something to eat. All right?"

She nodded her head.

When she had finished relieving herself, she crawled back into bed, exhausted from the effort it had taken. She tugged the covers primly up to her chin and then called Ben back into the room. She was thankful for the coming darkness that cast her face into shadow. It embarrassed her to have a strange man empty her slop jar, even if she was too weak at the moment to have any choice. But she would be well in day or two. She was young and strong. If only her memory would return, she would be fine. Needing comfort, she wrapped her hands around the child she carried and prayed it would be soon. Somewhere this baby had a father and it was not the man that called her Esther.

As her strength returned she grew fond of the old man that nursed her with such faithful care and tenderness. He was kind and patient. She knew he wanted more from her than she could give him. He wanted her to be the woman she was not. It irritated her to be called Esther and it disconcerted her to sleep next to a man she couldn't remember from before the accident. If there had been another bed, she would have used it. She considered asking him to sleep on the floor, but this was his house and he was old. When she suggested that she make a pallet in the floor, he had been appalled. So to avoid an argument, she had bitten her lips and climbed in the bed. She slept as far from him as the narrow sagging mattress would allow and waited with increasing frustration for her memory to return. After a week, she was able to help Ben around the cabin and with the garden. She began to cook and clean. The old cabin glowed from her feminine touch and with the fresh wildflowers she kept on the table it had a more welcoming aspect than the one she had awakened to that first morning.

She had seen the portrait that Ben had of Esther and the daughter he called Catherine. It puzzled her that he would think she was that woman even though she admitted their hair was much the same and there was some faint resemblance. It was when he mentioned the child she carried and called it Catherine, that she felt great unease. Something was wrong with him in his mind that he could not see the impossibility of it all.

That night when he reached over at the supper table and patted her stomach and referred to his Catherine, something in her snapped. "Don't call my child Catherine. I don't know a Catherine and I'm not Esther. I don't know what happened to your wife and daughter, but I do know I am not your wife.

You've got to see it, Ben. Look at that portrait. How can that old picture be Esther and Catherine and my belly have Catherine in it?"

For a moment Ben sat in shock. Then his lips began to tremble and slow tears rolled down his cheeks. "Esther, honey, don't be this way. You're just confused."

She heaved a sigh, then stood and gathered the dishes. There was no point in arguing with this sad old man. If only she knew her name and where she belonged, she would leave. A month had slipped by and still no memory nudged the corners of her conscious mind, she still had no clue about who she was, where she called home, who her family might be. When she had finished cleaning, she ambled from the cabin and down to the water. It lay like a sheet of silver beneath the shining rays of a full moon. Across the sound she could see the twinkling lights of distant homes. Something seemed to be tugging her across the water to the distant shore. She wondered if she belonged there on the mainland and not on the island at all. Holding her swelling belly, she patted it and talked to her unborn child, reassuring herself that someone out there must miss her and want her back.

During the coming weeks, they slipped into a quiet routine together, the old man and her. He was content, happy even. She was troubled and frustrated, but hid it as best she could while she waited for the day when she could tell him she was not Esther because she knew who she was once more.

One morning he woke her and told her he was going to collect some herbs for medicine to help her when their child was born. She gave him a quizzical look. Some memory stirred at the back of her mind. "Let me come, too. It'll only take a moment for me to get ready. I'm sure I can help. I don't know why, but I think I know something about herbs."

"That stomach of yours is getting mighty round. Are you sure you're up to it, Esther?" Ben asked with concern evident in his voice.

Ignoring the name she had come to hate, she responded, "I'm sure. Besides, how far can we go on an island?"

"This island is not very wide but it's a lot longer than you might think," Ben smiled. "Least ways, we don't have to go all the way to the far end."

They walked for hours in the shrubby undergrowth of the island, gathering the barks and herbs Ben wanted. She pointed at some of them and was proud when she could tell them how to prepare them and what they were for without his tutelage. Ben seemed amazed at her knowledge.

"Lord, Esther, I didn't think you knew anything about my concoctions. You always said that was my department and left it up to me. I'm right pleased you're taking an interest."

"I'm not...." she began, then stopped herself. It did no good to remind him Esther was not her name.

They had neared the road when she heard distant voices. "Oh, Ben, listen. Let's go see if anyone there might know who I am?" She turned in the direction of the sound, but was halted when Ben roughly took her arm and snatched her back.

"No! *I know who you are.* We're going home now, Esther." Despite his frailty the grip on her arm was strong.

The woman looked at him with surprise and mild alarm. He had never treated her with anything but gentleness until that moment. Not wishing to anger him further, she stooped to gather the horsemint and blackberry leaves that had fallen from her basket when he jerked her. "That's fine, Ben. We'll go home."

As they walked, she planned to slip away at the earliest opportunity and find someone on the island who might know her, now that she knew Ben would never willingly allow her to ask. Walking beside him back to the cabin, it struck her that Ben's face was the only one she had seen in all of the weeks since her accident.

24

Ryan sat in the front pew letting the last strains of the organ music wash over him. His eyes were closed to shut out the hostile, accusing faces of Penny's father and brother. He knew they blamed him for taking a pregnant woman sailing in the face of a tropical cyclone. His guilt was great enough as it was without taking on a bigger burden than he felt he could carry by allowing their anger to penetrate the shell he had built around himself.

His son sat beside him, unsure why all of the adults were so sad and not understanding the purpose behind the church service. He whispered to his father, "I want my Mama. Can we go find her now? Please?"

"We can't, Rye. Mama has gone to Heaven to be with the angels." Rye was having none of it. "Well, let's go get her back. I want my Mama here with us."

Ryan looked at his son. He felt helpless and lost. "I wish we could. Now, ssh. We mustn't talk during the service."

On his other side, Caroline sat like a pillar of granite, strong and solid. She had been there when he needed her, to comfort and to absolve him of the crushing remorse he felt when he thought of the ill-fated sailing trip. Through the open window of the church, he could just glimpse the top of the tombstone he had ordered for Penny. Her father was angry over that, too, and had assured him there would be another marker in the family cemetery at Pineview. Whether her husband liked it or not, he wanted his daughter's tombstone beside that of her mother.

Even Isabel seemed puzzled that he had used such poor judgment when he decided to sail into a storm that jeopardized them all and cost Penny her life. Marcus, who sat with Brett and John Bartlett, radiated almost palpable waves of fury. Mammy, in the back of the church with the other servants, refused to speak to him. She blamed him, too. He would have liked to explain that the only reason he had lived was to save his son. He had wanted to save Penny, but he could not and that knowledge was killing him. Nothing anyone could say about him, or reproach him for doing, came close to the anger he felt at himself.

Ryan had waited a month before declaring his wife dead. He had gone to the island once a week to ask if anyone had seen her or if her body might have washed ashore. Finally he had to accept that she must have washed out to sea and was forever lost to him. He had lost weight in that month and his eyes were sunken and shadowed. Her face, her mouth opened in a scream as she was snatched from him, haunted his nights, rendering sleep impossible. He ate little and had all but abandoned his practice, leaving it to John Harvey and Charlie Morgan to cover for him. If he had not had Rye to depend on him and to rear, he would have gladly thrown himself into the waves that had taken Penny from him. Oblivion was preferable to this living hell. He considered leaving New Berne, taking his son to New York or even Europe, but he knew no matter where he went the nightmare would travel within him.

When the service ended, he picked his son up in his arms and walked with Caroline to stand beside the stone monument commemorating Penny's short life. "Dearly beloved wife" it read. Taking a deep breath, Ryan looked up at the trees that shaded the cemetery. The leaves were as dark as raven wings against the bright blue purity of the sky. On the grass around the tombstone, shadows danced as the wind tossed overhanging branches. The shadows flitted across the face of the tombstone and the words inscribed on it. Although the day was warm, hot even, he shivered.

Caroline looked into his ravaged face, feeling pity well into her heart. She was wise enough to offer him, not her pity, but the courage to live in the face of a loss that was tearing him apart. "She loved you, Ryan. This was not your fault and she would not want you to blame yourself. None of us knows how our days will end. None of us can explain the reason why one dies and another lives. None of us can justify the workings of the universe when it seems so unfair and capricious."

"It's not the universe I blame."

Ignoring his comment, she continued, "You have a son that needs and loves you. You are still a young man; your life will go on. Mine has, although at one time I thought that it would not. When my husband died, I had no one and nothing but memories. He was the center of my world, the reason the sun rose in the morning. When he died there was no sun, just darkness. I wanted to die. It would have been easier by far if I had been the one to go first, but I wasn't. That was years ago and I'm still here. Have I stopped missing him? No, and I never will. He holds a special place in my heart that will always be his, but I have learned how to live without him and find good in my life. It doesn't feel like it now, but the day will come when the sun begins to shine again and you will rejoice in your life once more. Don't close yourself away. Your son deserves more than that and so does the memory of the woman you loved so dearly."

"I can't..." his voice trailed away, lost for words.

Caroline forged on, "As for the anger of her family and friends, it isn't aimed at you so much as at their helplessness in the face of a fate they cannot control and cannot accept. That will change too with time. Her family will get beyond this. You're Rye's father and the man Penny loved. They know that now, they've just forgotten that you are a part of their family, too. Give them time. They did not live through those last hours on that boat with you. They could have done no more than you. Remember you saved your son's life. If you had left him to go after her, you might all have been lost."

Ryan smiled at his old friend and nodded his head. He didn't know if he believed her words but he believed in the love behind them. "Thank you, Miss Caroline. I hope someday I feel differently. Right now I've lost too much to think of the future. Not only did I lose Penny, but I also lost the baby I will never know. I wanted so much to be there for this one, to hold that newborn child in my arms as I looked into the eyes of its mother. I missed being part of Ryan's first years. I didn't want that for this one. I owed it to Penny to be with her."

Caroline patted his arm with understanding. "I'll take Rye over to say goodbye to the others if that would be easier for you. I know there have been some harsh words between you all that have hurt."

"No, he's my son and that's all he has left of his mother's family. I can't run from them forever and I'm not going to start now."

"Good. Hold your head up and remember you've done nothing to be ashamed of. I'll be with you every step of the way," Caroline smiled at him. For her, Ryan Madison was the son she could never have borne, as her womb had been barren. To him she gave the love of all of those years of maternal yearning. Composing her features in a pleasant but dignified expression, she walked beside him. No one would hurt him further without finding himself on the receiving end of a very acerbic tongue.

Seizing the initiative when they approached the Bartletts, Caroline commented, "John, Brett, I'm sure you both want to bid your grandson and Ryan goodbye. This has been a painful loss for all of us. Isabel, I feel sure your husband will spare you at home for a week or so in order to help your brother manage his son during these difficult days of adjustment. I confess I would like to spend some time with you as well."

Isabel looked at the brother she loved and softly asked, "Ryan, may I be of comfort to you and Rye? I'm happy to stay if you want me." She did not look at Brett for approval.

Ryan was grateful to her for the offer, even if it had come at Caroline's urging. He smiled at her, "I would be so thankful if you could do that. I confess, I don't know how to go about picking up the pieces of our lives. Brett, I hope you will permit her to stay? You are all welcome at Fair Bluff. John, why don't you come, too? Rye loves having you near and it would be good for him just now."

For a long moment an awkward silence hung over the group. Caroline ended by saying brightly, "There's no need to decide anything right this minute, is there? Come on back to my house. We have food there for the mourners. There are so many who want to express their sympathies. John, you and Brett ride with me. Ryan take Isabel with you and Rye." Allowing no opportunity for a response, she took John's arm and turned him toward her waiting carriage, expecting Brett to follow. She depended on their innate gentility not to cause a scene. Penny's father shot her a glaring look that she met with blithe ignorance. She took grim pride in managing the situation. That left only Marcus who hovered near the gate with fists clenched. She knew he wanted nothing so much as to drive his fist into Penny's husband, the man who had taken her love from him.

"Well, Marcus," she began when they drew near, "You come on to my house, too. There's room in my carriage for the four of us. I know Penny, who loved you for a dear friend, would want you to express your sympathies to her husband."

For a moment he looked at her in confusion, then jerked his head in a curt nod and joined them. Caroline smiled to herself. She was old but she'd been born knowing how to manage men.

"Where is that beautiful bride-to-be of yours? Did she not come with you to the funeral service?"

Marcus shifted with discomfort, "Ah, I'm afraid I didn't get the chance to get over to Falling Creek to tell her I was coming." He did not want to admit that things had cooled with the Rouses since that debacle of a day weeks past.

As their carriage left, Isabel and Ryan walked to his buggy. Ryan saw Mammy standing abandoned on the front steps of the church. She looked frightened and confused. He suspected she had never been so far from home before. He knew that she had loved Penny like her own child, and although she was angry with him, his heart went out to her. "Excuse me for a moment, Isabel.   Would you mind holding on to Rye for me? "But of course," Isabel complied.   Comprehending his intentions when she saw where he was looking, she asked, "Would you like me to invite Mammy to join us?"

"No. I'll do it. I want to."

Mammy watched him coming. She had always liked him and if she had not interfered that time when he had come to Pleasant Glade looking for Penny, they might have had far more good years together. She regretted not telling him that Penny carried his child. If she had, he would have known years earlier that the trip Penny made to Richmond to see Daniel was not when she became pregnant. And there was an even bigger remorse in her heart, one that left her both afraid of him and knowing she deserved his damnation for keeping it secret. And yet, how could she tell him what she knew of her grandson? Despite the guilt she felt when she looked at him, she still blamed him for Penny's death. As far as she was concerned, he should have known better than to take a pregnant woman sailing. Even though she understood that had he known a storm was imminent he would not have gone out in the boat with his family, it did not stop her from blaming him. She caught her lower lip with her teeth, to bite back the words she wanted to hurl at him and waited for him to speak.

"Mammy Rena, the others are all coming down to Miss Caroline's house on the river. Penny would want you to be there, too. She loved you so much. She told me that in many ways, despite how much she loved her mother, you were just as much a mother to her. I know you are hurt and sad, just as I am. Come with Isabel, Rye, and me. You can visit with Rye a little while and see where Penny lived. When it's time to catch your train, I'll see to it you get back. Penny wouldn't want you to be lost from our lives even though she can't be here with us."

Slow tears seeped down her ebony cheeks and the lump in her throat blocked any words she might have uttered. Without a word she followed him to where Isabel and Penny's child waited. Rye extended his arms to her seeking comfort. With a full heart, she lifted him into her lap and crooned softly in his ear as they drove from the church. They had not reached the end of Pollock street to make the turn onto East Front before Rye was snoring in her arms. Ryan smiled at his son and sent a silent thanks to Mammy. Since the accident Rye's sleep had been fretful, fraught with nightmares that left him reluctant to go to his bed. His eyes were as circled from lack of sleep as his father's.

Watching her holding the boy, Ryan asked, "Isabel, please take him to Pineview when you leave. Perhaps Mammy will help care for him until I can arrange for a nurse. I'll miss him sorely but maybe it would be better for Rye to be with Penny's family until he learns to accept the loss of his mother."

"If you think that's for the best, of course I will."

It bothered him that Rye might think that his father had gone away, too. That would bear some pondering. He would not send his son to Penny's plantation, but rather to Pineview to stay with the Bartletts. Since his mother's death at Pleasant Glade he was averse to any of his family staying there, especially in light of the fact that the murderer remained at large.

Looking back, Ryan could not have said how he survived the coming weeks. Isabel had stayed for a week, as promised, and then had returned to Kinston taking Rye with her. After a month without him, Ryan was so lonesome for someone in the house, besides his housekeeper and her husband, he had gone to Kinston to get him. Although the Bartlett men had lost some of their animosity, the easy camaraderie he had enjoyed with Brett from the beginning was lacking. And while John was his ever courteous and affable self, there was a noticeable reserve. Mammy came to see him and to tell Rye goodbye, but was so nervous that it was a misery for them both. The Davenports came, as well, to report on the running of Pleasant Glade. While he was tempted to sell it and bank the money until Rye came of age, he hesitated selling Penny's beloved home. Under Jeremy's careful stewardship, the plantation was once again becoming a profitable enterprise. He was tempted to ride over and see some of the crops that Jeremy spoke of with such pride, but visions of his mother with her throat slit squelched the impulse.

The only bright moment in the short visit had been the ecstatic faces of Brett and Isabel when they told him he would soon be an uncle. Ryan was happy for them, but the image of his wife's swelling belly kept intruding itself into his brain reminding him of all he had lost. He was not sad to take the train back to New Berne where he had a new nurse waiting to care for Rye. He only hoped that the child would like her. Isabel had told him that he no longer went to bed at night crying for his mother and seemed to be accepting that she was gone forever. But then, he thought, how does a young child comprehend the magnitude and finality of death?

When they arrived at Fair Bluff, Mrs. Josephine Gwaltney was standing in the front door watching for them. She was a widow, somewhere in her mid-fifties, white of hair and red of complexion. Not more than five feet tall and on the decidedly generous side, she reminded Ryan of a red ball he had loved as a child. Her blue eyes sparkled with humor and she had a kind and loving nature. She had been the best that he could find for his son. He could only pray that it was enough.

"Son, I want you to meet a very nice lady. Mrs. Gwaltney is going to be staying with us. She once had a little boy, too, so she knows all about what little boys like."

Rye looked up for a long suspicious moment, "Are you my new mama?"

Leaning down to be nearer his level, Mrs. Gwaltney gave him a pleasant smile and reassured him, "I'm not your new mama. No one can ever take her place. I'm your new friend. It's all right to have a new friend, isn't it?"

His lower lip was caught in his teeth as he stared at her. He shrugged, "I guess so."

Ryan smiled at the woman appreciative of the way she had handled the introduction. As he walked back to the buggy to retrieve his portmanteau, he heard Rye ask, "So, where is your little boy? Will he live here, too?"

"No, Rye. He won't live here. You see, he's up in heaven where your mama is. Maybe she will see him there and they can be friends the way you and I will be."

Rye knit his brow as he thought about this last information. "Why can't I be there with my mama and your son be with you? I don't want my mama to have another little boy. I'm her boy."

"That's right, precious. You are her little boy and she loved you with all her heart. No one could ever take your place in your mama's heart."

Some days were better than others for Rye, but he gradually accepted the changes in his life. Caroline made it a point to visit each morning to take him on a nature walk if the weather permitted.

"I'm going to teach you about the plants your mother planted and how she used them to make medicine. Each day we'll visit a different plant and I'll tell you all about it." She didn't tell him that she had scoured books each night to learn as much as she could in order to teach him.

One morning as he held a fuzzy rabbit tobacco leaf in his hand, he announced, "I'm going to be a doctor when I grow up and make people well like Mama did."

"That's fine, Rye. I know your mama would like that." When she took his hand to walk back to the house, she heard a voice she recognized calling for them. Well, Caroline could not help but think, this was about what I thought she'd give herself in the way of a timeline. It's not so soon as to be vulgar and opportunistic, and not so long as to give someone else a chance to move in on the man she's determined to at last snare for herself. Pursing her lips she stood waiting for the younger woman to find them.

Lizziy ducked under a low hanging branch of a Rose of Sharon tree and greeted them brightly, "What a gorgeous day, Miss Caroline. I just love the weather in September when it starts to get cooler. Gracious me, I am just purely sick of hot weather. If summer lasted much longer, I think I'd just have to move up North with the Yankees."

"Hello, Lizzy. What brings you out this way? I haven't had the pleasure of a visit from you in months."

"I thought I'd come visit with Rye. I know he must be so sad now." Reaching in her pocket she pulled out a harmonica. "I brought you a present, Rye. I saw Kirby in town, and he says he knows how to play so maybe he will teach you when he's not busy working for your daddy. Would you like that?"

Rye reached for the harmonica and putting it to his lips blew cautiously. He squealed with delight when he managed to create a raucous screech. "Thank you, Miss Lizzy. This is a great gift."

"One day you'll be able to play songs on that, I'll just bet. When you do, I'm going to have you play all of my favorites.

Will you do that?"

"Yes, Miss Lizzy." Rye grinned, "I'll race you to the house."

"Well, maybe not today, Rye. It's still a little warm and I don't want to get all hot and perspirey."

"Heavens no, we certainly wouldn't want to get messy looking," Caroline blurted. She suspected Lizzy planned to stay until Ryan returned and she was determined to discourage her from doing it. "Let me take Rye back home and you come on over to my house with me. I think it's time we have a little visit."

Lizzy had no intention of allowing a meddlesome old woman to stand in her way. She smiled. Her voice dripped sugar when she said, "Oh, I am so sorry. I would just love to, but I have other plans for today. Maybe next time I drop by, we can have a nice visit?"

"Oh, no doubt I'll be seeing you again," Caroline allowed with subtle sarcasm. "I must say, I'm always quite amazed at the latitude your parents give you to travel about on your on. In my day it was not permitted of young ladies of quality. Only women of a certain sort went about alone. It would behoove you to remember that gossip can be most unkind regardless of its merit."

Lizzy ignored the sharp comment, replying, "Well, I really do have to go. Bye, now." She decided to take her buggy a little way down the road and wait for Ryan to come along. She could always say she was just picking wildflowers beside the road and act surprised at seeing him. She didn't want precipitous action to frighten him away. She intended to test the waters to see how he was doing and what his reaction to her might be. She would to be kind and sympathetic, a warm shoulder and a friendly ear when he needed it. Once he accepted that, she would start kindling a fire. She'd lost him once, now he was darned well going to be hers.

Lizzy was growing impatient with the wait when she finally

heard the clopping of horse's hooves coming her way. Snatching up the bouquet of wildflowers, she sprang from the buggy. After fluffing her skirt to shake out the wrinkles and smoothing her hair, she began picking the blooms of some Jerusalem artichokes growing on the verge of the road. Ryan reined in his horse when he was a few feet away. "Should you be out here by yourself, Lizzy? There's been some trouble in the area and it's not safe for a woman to be wandering around alone. I must say I'm appalled your parents are so negligent as to allow you to travel about without escort."

Lizzy was miffed that he too felt it necessary to remark on her unescorted state, but was not about to show it. "Oh, I was just so tired of staying around the house all the time, I needed to just get out. It's so lovely by the river, I couldn't resist driving out this way."

If he noticed she did not respond to the comment about her parents, she couldn't tell. If he only knew, she snickered. They had long since despaired of reining in their wayward daughter.

She looked up into his intensely blue eyes and sighed prettily, "I have been wanting to explain I didn't go to the funeral because I didn't feel comfortable, but I want you to know how very sorry I am about Penny's death. I'm sure it has just been so awful for you and Rye both. If there is anything at all I can do to help, you know I will."

"Thank you Lizzy. This has been the worst time of my life, for sure. I appreciate your sympathy and you should not have felt uncomfortable about attending Penny's funeral. After all, you are a friend."

"I'm so glad you think so. I want to go on being your friend and Rye's as well. He needs someone to mother him a little since Penny is gone. I hope you don't mind if I visit from time to time just to help with him?"

"It isn't necessary. Miss Caroline is wonderful with him and I hired an excellent nurse that he seems to have really taken to, but thanks for the offer." Ryan studied her for a moment, suspecting her motives. "Lizzy, right now I don't need any complications in my life. Do you understand what I'm trying to say?"

"Why, Ryan, I'm sure I don't know what you mean. I would never dream of 'complicating' things for you."

"Well, you best be getting back into town before it gets dark. Take care of yourself, Lizzy." He nodded his head and rode on.

In the coming weeks, Lizzy managed to run into him every few days. She groomed herself with care, dressed in her most flattering frocks and conducted her campaign with all of the concentration of a general. She was unfailingly cheerful and amusing. She sensed in his loneliness, he was appreciative of her light-hearted banter and flattered by her obvious attention.

Even so, Ryan cautioned her, "I do not intend to ever involve myself with you or anyone. I never will marry again. I can never love another woman the way I did Penny. That part of my life is finished."

Lizzy wanted more. There was no way she was going to risk losing him again. She paced the floor of her room seething at the slow pace of her pursuit. She needed to do something that would obligate him to her. There had to be a way to take their relationship beyond cordial, but reserved, encounters. Suddenly she stopped. It was a reckless thing to do, but she thought she knew how to secure a proposal from him. He didn't have to marry her right away. It was too soon to be decent, but she was determined he would at least commit to marrying her when a decent period of mourning ended. With a young child to rear, society expected men to remarry more quickly than those without that consideration.

She walked over to her mirror and studied her reflection with some satisfaction. Lizzy was going to use every weapon at her disposal. She had hoped to approach him through his son, but Caroline had managed to circumvent those efforts. Now, she would have to try another way. For a moment she was unsettled by the rashness of her plot. Gazing into the troubled eyes that stared back at her, she shrugged and turned away. She would not think about the ramifications of her actions. Nothing was going to deter her from getting what she wanted.

25

Marcus gave a vicious yank on the handle of the pump. Water coughed in the pipe and then began spurting out in intermittent splashes. He scooped his hand into the pail under the pump and splashed water on his face. He was hot, tired and definitely out of sorts. He'd worked all day hauling corn to the crib, where he would store it until he could grind it into meal or put it aside for winter feed for the cows, mules, chickens and pigs that depended on it for food, even more than the humans on his farm. Leaning back, he stretched tight muscles in his back that had begun to spasm from the unaccustomed labor. He thought about spending the evening with a jar of moonshine as he had often done of late, but knew he'd pay for it tomorrow if he did. He brushed irritably at the dirt and debris that had sifted down the back of his shirt tickling his skin. "Dammit," he swore under his breath, "I can't seem to get anything going right in my life since I got out of that damned prison."

He did not realize Brett had walked up behind him until he heard him laugh. "What in tarnation has you so worked up, boy?" Brett asked.

"God dammit, you are enough to turn my hair gray. Don't you have more sense than to walk up on a man with all that's going on right now? It's a plumb wonder I didn't kill you," Marcus demanded more frightened than angry, as he lowered the pistol he had grabbed.

"Sorry, Marcus. I was just riding by and thought I'd drop in to see how you're doing. I hope the darkies I loaned you were some help today, but judging by the looks of you, I think you worked harder than anyone. It wouldn't be hard to mistake you for an old boar hog that's been rooting around in the dirt." Brett shook his head before continuing, "It sure is a pity about the Miller murders. I guess you heard the man who did it was a former slave, John Miller and a band of other freed Negroes. Is that why you're carrying that gun?" John Miller, former owner of a slave by the same name had been murdered in his field. " I hear his wife Elizabeth, who witnessed the killing, asked the murderer, *'John, we have been good to you. Why do you do this to us?'* Sheriff thinks they murdered her because she could identify the assailants. It's a damned shame, fine woman, her husband, too." Some of the band had been captured and jailed. Soon after, they were freed from the jail and murdered by some of Miller's kin. The ringleader escaped. Tempers were high and folks were more trigger-happy than wary. With the Miller's killer on the loose, no one knew who might be next.

"Yeah, I heard. I suspect every family around here is wary at the moment."

Changing the subject, Brett asked. "What has you cussing and talking to yourself other than working your ass off?"

Marcus heaved a sign before answering, "Lena. I purely damn-lee give up on women. Some men seem to have all the luck with them and some don't have any. I guess I'm just one of the not-any."

"Ah, Lena's still pouting at you, is she?"

"When I told her I went to Penny's funeral without letting her know, she went crazy as an Indian on hooch. I never heard such a screeching in my life. Hell, you'd think I'd gone out and fucked every whore on Sugar Hill."

"She knows you were in love with my sister. She just feels threatened. You need to just reassure her a little more. That woman loves you, but she needs to know whether or not you love her. I mean, whether or not you love her *enough* and not just as a woman to bear your children."

"Well judging by the letter I got yesterday, she ain't going to be giving me any more chances to give her children or anything else. I have been 'requested' to give her 'some time to think on the future.' " Marcus jerked his head towards the house, "Come on in and set a spell. I have a little cure for what ails me that is purely calling my name."

Brett laughed, "If I go drinking that moonshine of yours before getting on home, there are going to be two pissed off women in Lenoir County tonight. I just stopped by to give you a letter I picked up in town today. Looks like it's from Fort Macon."

"Good. I've been waiting to hear from my friend Shine. As soon as he can be relieved from duty, he's going to come work for me as overseer. I tell you, if it hadn't been for that man, I couldn't have done it all those months in prison. He's as good a friend as you could ask for. I believe you're going to like him too, Brett." Marcus took the proffered letter and opened it. "It *is* from Shine. He can't write so the doctor penned it for him. Hell, it looks like he's not going to get an early release from duty."

"I'm sorry to hear it. Is there anything that anyone can do to speed things up?" Brett asked as Marcus continued reading.

"Hmm," Marcus continued to read. Looking up from his letter, he commented, "This is mighty curious."

Intrigued by his tone of voice, Brett asked, "What's that?"

"There was an old man on the island that I got to know while I was there. He was maybe just a little bit demented from old age, but harmless. According to Shine, he's been queerer than a three-dollar bill for the last few months. Won't let anybody get near his cabin, sneaks around the island, and is ornery as a mad hornet if anyone tries to talk to him. I was in his cabin right after I met him." Marcus paused, "Strangest thing, he had a portrait of his wife that looked enough like Penny to set me back for a minute. It was downright eerie."

"Where is his wife now?"

"She and his daughter died nearly twenty-five years ago." Marcus held up the letter, " Yet, Shine says Ole Ben told him that he has to stay close to home to take care of his wife."

"He sounds about as crazy as a bed bug," Brett laughed.

"I wonder..." Deciding it was too bizarre Marcus left the thought hanging. "What else is going on around here? You, John, and Isabel doing okay?"

"We're all fine. Isabel is having a little trouble with keeping her vittles down in the morning, but I hear that's not uncommon. Pa still mopes around about Penny and sits a lot in the graveyard by that new marker he put up for her. Between visiting her marker and my Mama's grave, he spends a lot of time down there."

"You talked to Lucinda? When I talked to her the other day, she seemed to be real worried about something."

Brett shrugged, "Not lately. School's doing okay and the KKK seem to be leaving her alone since Pa and I put the word out they'd better not come poking around here to stir up any more trouble. The one I'm worried about is Mammy. I've known that old woman all my life. I learned as a child when she was upset about something and when she wasn't. Something is for sure weighing on her mind, but damned if I know what it is. Those darkies stick together. If they don't want you to know something, you can just give up on it, because they sure ain't going to be telling you."

"That's the God's truth," Marcus agreed.

Marcus went to bed sober and sorry for it, as he did nothing but toss and turn until the sun had begun to pink the eastern sky. Disgusted at the wasted effort, he gave up the struggle and swung his feet out of bed. Something about Ole Ben had nagged at him all night. Mammy worried him, too. She knew something that was troubling her a heap. As for the Lena, he didn't know whether to try again or to just give up. The more

he thought about the whole mess, the more he wanted to just hunker down and forget the world existed beyond his own property   lines.
With the corn harvested, he had time to ride over to Sycamore Hill and see Lena, that is, *if* she would see him. She said she needed time to think before he came calling again, but as far as he was concerned what she really needed was some tall reassuring. Wiley Rouse was just about pissed off enough with him for trifling with his daughter's affections and staining the family honor, that he was apt to take a shotgun to him. At that thought, Marcus grinned and decided, *what the hell, I'm going.*

A hound sprang from behind the picket fence when he rode into the yard, baying like he'd treed a possum until he recognized Marcus. Marcus looked toward the house just in time to see the lace curtain on an upstairs window flutter shut. Someone had seen him arrive, now it remained to be seen whether or not they would let him in. When he swung off the horse to tie the reins to the hitching post, he heard the soft click of the front door opening and closing. He looked over his shoulder to see Lena walking his way, a determined look on her face.

"I think I wrote you that I need some breathing time. Didn't you get my letter, Marcus?"

"I did. I read it and that's why I'm here." Marcus jerked his head towards the road, "Come, walk aways with me. There're some things that need saying."

"Just for a minute. Pa's not going to be happy I'm even talking to you, much less leaving the yard with you." She cast a nervous glance in the direction of barn.

Lena walked beside him but far enough apart that there was no danger they would touch even by accident. It was obvious she didn't intend to make it any easier on him by starting the conversation. He was the one that had come to talk and she intended to let him get on with it without any help from her.

"Lena, I'm sorry I didn't write you I was going to the funeral. If I had thought it would matter to you if I went, I would have. You realize I have known Penny and her family for years. I used to work for her father; and I'm a friend with the whole family. It would have been mighty impolite of me not to even go. You understand that. Going to her funeral had nothing to do with you and marrying you. I told you I want to marry you a long time ago and I still do. If this mess over Calvin Smith's murder hadn't got me locked up for all those months, we'd have been married last November. Here it is the sixth of October almost a year later and we still ain't married." Marcus reached over and took her hand. Although she tried to pull it away, he held on with determination. "Lena, the question is: do we still love each other? If we do, then we need to get married. My feelings for you haven't changed. So, the thing I need to know is whether or not you have stopped loving me?"

"Marcus, my feelings are constant. I did not give you my heart lightly and it's hard to take it back. I suppose I hoped *your feelings* might have changed and that you would move on from the torch you were carrying for Penny. As long as she was alive, I could cope. But, how on earth do I compete with a dead woman? She will never grow old and gray, or frumpy from bearing children. She'll never have a bad day and snap at you out of sheer frustration. She'll always be a perfect memory of the woman you loved and couldn't have. I don't want that eating at me the rest of my life and I'm afraid it would." Lena removed her hand from his clasp. "Let's try being just friends for a while without the pressure to get married. Maybe in time, we will both reach the point where we want that to be the next step. I'll tell Pa to unload his old squirrel gun and let you come calling again. As for Ma, you don't have to worry about her. She thinks I'm being a sentimental, persnickety fool and I ought to just go ahead and marry you."

"I always did think your mother was a fine, sensible woman." Marcus laughed, "We're going to be friends, but do you think it would be okay to be kissing friends." He didn't wait for her answer. Pressing her body into his, he let her feel his need while he kissed her. At first she was stiff and unyielding, then she began to return his kisses with ardor.

"Have we been *just friends* long enough, do you think?" Marcus asked when he came up for air.

Lena managed a shaky laugh, "How do you expect me to think and act rationally when you kiss me like that?"

"Who says you have to? I'll do the thinking for you. You just agree to marry me. How about tomorrow?"

She smiled, "Go home, Marcus, and I'll think about it. You come next Sunday for dinner."

"I'll be here," Marcus promised. "It would be real nice if you would put my ring back on your hand. I like seeing it there."

"We'll see. Now, go." Her voice was soft when she said it.

Marcus rode away with a pleased smile on his face. She hadn't thrown him out on his ear and she had not moved away when his thighs pressed into her with proof of his response to her body and lips. She still wanted him and given a little more encouragement, he would persuade her to marry him.

It was a beautiful autumn day, crisp and fresh with a light wind scattering leaves that were beginning to take on autumn colors. Suddenly Marcus felt a lightening of his spirit. Somehow his world was going to right itself. Marcus had spent long years alone and he was tired of it. His had spent childhood neglected and poverty-stricken. As a young man he had worked as an overseer for Penny's father, saving every dime he earned for the day when he could buy his own land to farm. Thanks to Penny, he owned a fine home and fertile fields. He smiled to himself as he kicked his horse into a trot. He'd lost his chance with Penny the minute Ryan showed up, but she had still added both material and spiritual richness to his life. He owed her a debt of gratitude for that. With quiet determination he gave himself permission to let her ghost rest. Soon if he played his cards right, he would be married to a woman that loved him and that he had learned to care for, not with the same desperate passion that he had felt for Penny, but with a calm steady love. Perhaps, that would prove a better one for him. And if the stars favored him, in time he would have sons and daughters to sit by the fireside in the evenings with him and his wife. The empty days would be forever ended. When he crept into his cold bed that night, he felt more contentment that he had known in years.

The old fat rooster that stalked the barnyard with arrogant presumption began to crow the sun over the horizon, rousing Marcus from sleep. He stretched his limbs languorously, glad that it was the Sabbath and he could spend the day in idleness. Those long months in prison had taken a toll on his stamina and the last week of hard labor in the field had left him tired. Looking at the exposed places on his body, he was pleased to note a healthy tan now replaced the pallor of incarceration. Marcus took a deep breath of the cool morning air and slowly exhaled into the stillness of the day. He lay still for long minutes relishing the luxury of lying in his own bed after a productive week's work and the even more productive Saturday trip to Sycamore Hill.   Punching his pillow to prop his head up, he lay back and watched dust motes dancing in the light sifting through his window. He mulled over Shine's letter and fretted that it was taking so long for him to be released from duty. Something continued tugging at the back of his mind. It bothered him that whatever it was remained nebulous.

Marcus rolled over and tossed back the covers. It was frustrating for him to lie around leaving his affairs unresolved. He would go to Fort Macon and convince the warden to expedite Shine's release. If he left on the noon train, he could spend the night in New Berne and then take the early train to Beaufort. With the corn harvested, he could squeeze a few days from the needs of the farm to make the trip and be back in plenty of time to get to Lena's on the following Sunday. Marcus grabbed the clothes he would need and stuffed them into his battered old valise.

In the kitchen, Bessie had made breakfast and left it on the table for him while she went to gather eggs for the pound cake she planned for dinner. Marcus bolted his food and then walked to the coop where the cackling of hens marked his cook's progress.

"Hey, Bessie," he called. "You in there?"

"Well, if I weren't who else would be out here getting eggs for that cake you love?" Bessie hollered in answer. He could hear her grumbling as she made her way to the door.

She emerged from the coop with stray feathers caught in her hair and a thunderous expression on her face. "That dad-blamed rooster done spurred me again. I tell you the next time he come after me, we going to be having chicken stew."

"I just wanted to tell you I'll be gone for a few days so don't worry about making that cake on my account. Y'all are going to have to eat it for me." Marcus continued, "Keep a sharp eye on things around here. With that trouble over at the Miller's, things are kind of unsettled. You have any trouble or need anything, let Mr. John or Mr. Brett know. As a matter of fact, it would save me time if one of you let them know I'm going to be gone for the rest of the week. I should be back no later than next Saturday." He had to be if he wanted to ever have a chance with Lena. She would never forgive him for missing that Sunday dinner after she had softened enough to invite him again. As if in promise to himself, he repeated. "I'll be back no later than Saturday."

Marcus sat in his hotel room that night, staring out the window at the moonlight sparkling on the Neuse River. Quiet fury at Ryan Madison gnawed at him. He doubted he would ever stop blaming the man for Penny's death. Unbidden the thought popped into his mind, *if she had married me instead of Ryan she'd still be alive.* Disgusted that he kept returning to his old thought patterns, he stood up and slammed his battered felt hat onto his head. He hoped a walk would clear his mind and allow him to sleep. One of New Berne's taverns might provide some assistance as well, he decided.

26

An uncomfortable Ryan shifted in his chair as Caroline stared at him. She had arrived at his door the moment he came home requesting a private talk. He struggled to keep the guilt from his face as he remembered the night before. He could only hope Caroline hadn't seen or heard something to make her suspect him of a dalliance with Lizzy. He wouldn't put it past Lizzy to make sure Carolina knew she had been there the night before. Were that nighttime rendezvous public knowledge, societal expectations would demand he offer immediate marriage. Again he cursed Lizzy and his own culpability in the matter.

Ruefully, he replayed the previous evening. When Ryan had finished his evening meal and tucked Rye in for the night, he entered his bedroom with plans to read a book until sleep overtook him. He had not planned on the lit candles and a waiting woman when he swung open the door. He checked behind him and then shut the door. "What are you doing here? Your reputation will be ruined if anyone finds out that you were in my bedroom. Are you crazy? Do you realize the rashness of this?"

Lizzy didn't answer. He watched a sly smile play about her lips. Sliding her hands up her body she let them glide over her curves until they met at her throat. Then one by one she unbuttoned her blouse and shrugged the garment from her shoulders. Next she dropped her skirt into a puddle around her feet. As though mesmerized Ryan stood open-mouthed watching her, knowing he should stop her but he couldn't. Never taking her eyes from his, she stepped free of her chemise and stood before him in all her naked glory. Ryan's eyes traveled a concupiscent path down her ripe curves. He had sensed that the body under her clothes would be a good one; he just had not realized how very beautiful it would be. Against his will, he felt himself stir with lust at the blatantly lubricious offer presented to him. Almost without volition, he crossed the floor, sweeping her into his arms. She lifted her lips for his kiss and murmured encouragement as he carried her to his bed. He hesitated for a moment when he reached it, remembering carrying Penny in the same way. Pushing the thought from his mind, he dropped her onto the bed. With the practiced seduction of a whore, Lizzy tucked her arms behind her head. Her pose reminded him of a reproduction he had seen of the *Nude Maja*.

He quipped, "You look like a painting by Goya." It was obvious from her blank eyes and smug satisfaction that she had no clue to the reference but was pleased to be compared to a painting.

Ryan tore his clothes from his body before he could change his mind. He refused to consider the full ramifications of what he was about to do. She smiled at him, amused by his haste. However, the languid smile wobbled and her eyes blinked when she saw visible proof of his desire. Ryan saw the direction of her gaze and grinned. His voice was ragged when he spoke, "I'm sorry. It's been a long time since I was with a woman and my body is eager for the comfort. I know you are a virgin and I have no business doing this; but Lizzy, I so need some love and warmth in my life. Just be sure you know what you're doing. Once you lose your virginity, it cannot be reclaimed. How will you explain it to your future husband?"

"Let me worry about that." She was annoyed that he missed the obvious. Did he really think she was planning to marry someone else? "I want you Ryan. Now."

He lowered himself beside her and began to caress her body,

relishing the warmth that radiated from her and the promise of release. As much as he wanted to blot away everything but the pleasant carnality of the moment, Penny's face kept swimming before him. His mind took hold, squelching the demands of his body, and he found himself flaccid. Ryan pulled back and sat up, disgusted and embarrassed for the both of them.

"Is something wrong? Did I do something wrong?"

"God only knows it's not you. It's me. I can't do this, as much as a part of me might like to. It just isn't right."

Her voice was modulated to sound sweet and compassionate as she reassured him, "It's okay. I understand. As soon as it's right for you, I'll be waiting." Lizzy took her time leaving the bed. He knew she was making sure he saw what he was rejecting from as many angles as possible before pulling on her clothes.

He didn't realize it but she had left in a well-concealed huff of embarrassment and frustration that her plan had unraveled. If he would only sleep with her, she would see to it he married her. She promised herself she would be back.

When she left, Ryan had donned his nightshirt and picking up the book he had planned to read, hurled it at the fireplace. The previous night had been a long and restless one.

And now tonight had brought an unexpected visit from Carolina. Considering the thunderous expression on her face and that tell-tell raised eyebrow, he suspected he wouldn't sleep well tonight either. Ryan waited for Caroline to begin saying whatever it was that had brought her calling on him with such urgency. Refusing to begin the conversation, he watched her like a cat waiting for a mouse. Caroline caught her lip in her teeth and squirmed on the chair, sloshing the cup of tea she held in her hand. She lowered it to the table beside the settee. Lifting her chin, she met his eyes.

"Ryan, I've done some serious thinking of late and there are some things that I feel compelled to say to you, whether it's any of my business or not."

"Miss Caroline, my dear friend, you must always feel free to talk to me and tell me what you're thinking. I value your judgment above all others." Ryan struggled to keep his composure. Surely she had no way of knowing what had transpired upstairs the previous evening.

He choked back a groan when she began, "It's about Lizzy and you." Taking a deep breath she reached for his hand and held it.

"Ryan, if I were younger, I would chase you shamelessly until you were mine. Trouble is, I'm old and you're like a son to me. I don't blame Lizzy for wanting you. She wanted you before you married Penny and she never got over being dropped. Now that Penny is gone she's going to do her all-mightiest to get you back. This time she's determined you won't get away. Lizzy is a pretty girl and she can be amusingly good company, but there is a side to Lizzy I don't trust. I don't know if she loves you so much, or if she's just so competitive that she can't stand losing out to Penny. I do know that this is no time for you to get mixed up in something that you may regret once you have some healing behind you."

"I assure you I have no intentions of getting involved with anyone." Ryan crossed his legs and gave a pointed look at the clock on the mantle.

Ignoring the implied invitation to leave, Caroline gave him a skeptical snort and continued, "Penny deserves a period of mourning. You and your son need time to get over the immediate pain of her loss. Some day I hope someone comes along that you can make a life with and that will be a good mother to Rye.

"It's too soon to think of that, furthermore I don't know that I will ever remarry." Ryan shifted in his chair, impatient to finish the conversation.

"Well, if do you want a wife at some point, I don't believe

Lizzy is the one for you. She would want a child of her own and she would never love Penny's son the way he needs to be loved. I've seen enough of her with Rye to know that she resents that child. Furthermore, Lizzy was never someone you loved, was she?"

"You know not."

"Maybe I'm wrong, but during the war I think you went out with her to take your mind off Penny." Caroline grimaced, "I guess I'm asking you to not see Lizzy for a while. I know she's been seeking you out, but you can stop that. Will you do that? Don't do it for me, but for all of you before you do something you'll regret the rest of your life."

"You're right, of course. I don't disagree with anything you've said. It's hard because I'm lonely and the arms of a willing and beautiful woman can be a great comfort. It would be wrong to take that comfort, though, when I can't give love in return. I still love my wife. Just because she is dead it doesn't mean that I can stop loving her." Ryan squeezed her hand and stood up signaling an end to the conversation. "It's a pity you're not younger. If anyone could take my heart from Penny, I think it's you. You are one heck of a woman."

Caroline raised her eyebrow in amusement. Winking at him, she remarked, "I'm not so *very* old, so don't you go tempting me."

Laughing, he walked her to the door and kissed her withered cheek. Ryan watched her walk through the woods between their two houses. When she reached her house, he went back inside. Leaning against the closed door, he cursed under his breath. How right she was and how very close he had come to doing something that he might well have regretted for the rest of his life. Ryan walked into the parlor and poured himself a stiff glass of whiskey from the decanter that he had left there earlier. Taking his drink, he walked onto the veranda. A brisk breeze from the water reminded him that winter would soon claim the land. He stood staring at the water until the chill drove him to the warmth of his bed. As he blew out the candle, he recalled the old adage about playing with fire. He needed to throw water on that particular fire and be done with it. Fitting his pillow around his head, he reached over for the one that had held Penny's head. It still carried the scent of her. As he had done each night since returning home without her, he fell asleep with its comforting aroma pressed against his chest.

Miles away a cold wind was blowing from the sea, carrying the tang of salt before it and bringing it sifting through the cracks in the old cabin. The woman shivered from the draft. The candle on the table had burned low, guttering as it prepared to die. It was an unhappy evening for her. Across the table, Ben's eyes glistened with unshed tears as he watched her. "Esther, why don't you just leave it alone? You're going to be having that child in a few days and you don't need to go traipsing about upsetting yourself. As soon as Catherine is born, I'll take you to Fort Macon if that will make you happy. I just don't see what it is you want over there."

"I *told* you I'm not Esther. Things keeping coming back to me that tell me this is all wrong. I feel sure someone somewhere knows who I am. People that I know and that love me must be missing me and wondering where I am. I want to go home, even if I don't know where that is. This isn't home for me, Ben. I appreciate all you have done for me, but I don't belong here."

"Drink this tea, Esther. I made it for you to calm you down. You don't need to go getting all worked up. That's bad for you and the baby."

Penny shook her head vehemently. She was convinced he had been drugging her with the herbal tea to make her sleep. This constant grogginess wasn't normal. It also prevented her from giving form to the memories that were crowding the edge of her conscious mind. The next morning when he left the cabin, she pushed the cup of tea he prepared for her to one side. When she heard him ride off on the mule, she hastened to dress in one of the old fashioned gowns she had found in his wife's trunk. At the last minute she went back for a shawl to protect her from the cool wind that swept in from the ocean. Walking as fast as her cumbersome abdomen would allow, Penny reached the road and turned north in the direction of the fort. She had gone no more than three hundred feet or so when Ben stepped out of the woods beside the road leading the mule behind him.

"Esther, honey, where are you going?"

She refused to answer. She had a strong suspicion that Ben was determined she would not talk to anyone for fear someone might know her. Her shoulders slumped. With resignation, she turned and began the walk back to the cabin. Ben stood in the road watching until he saw her enter the path leading home, then he finished loading the driftwood onto his mule and followed her. Penny avoided him the rest of the day.

Now with supper done, the thought of having to crawl into his bed and feel his hand patting her body in the night made her shudder. She looked at him. He was a demented old man and she felt sorry for him, but not sorry enough to spend the rest of her life shut away from the outside world, never to know where she belonged. Holding her belly, she felt the movement of her child and made a promise to herself that she would find the father the minute she could escape.

She awakened in the morning to the sound of hammering. Ben was banging nails into the window to keep it shut. She sat on the bed watching him through the sandblasted glass of the window. When he had finished there, he moved away from her line of sight. She heaved her thickened body from the rumpled bed and pulled a shawl around her nightgown. He had left a pot of coffee on the stove. Penny picked up the battered pot and poured herself a cup of the bitter brew he liked, and sat at the table nibbling on a leftover biscuit wondering what he was up to. After several minutes, she heard him hammering once again on the outside of the cabin. This time he appeared to be banging near the door. Her head jerked up with alarm when she realized what he was doing. Ben was making the cabin so he could lock her in when he left. The thought of being locked in and alone, with her baby just a couple of weeks away, caused her toes to curl in alarm.

Running to the door, she banged on it with her fist, "No, Ben. Please, don't lock me in. I promise I won't go away anymore. Just please, don't lock me in." Her voice rose in panic when he didn't answer, "*Ben!*"

"This is for your own protection, Esther. I'm not going to leave you any longer than I have to; but when I have to go out to get something, I can't have you wandering off. You could hurt you and the baby both. Don't you see that, honey? I'm doing this for you," Ben wheedled. "I'll be back in an hour or so. I've got to go into the village and get some supplies. You rest yourself and I'll be back soon."

"Don't leave me like this!" she shouted.

Ben didn't answer. Shaking his head, he harnessed the mule and left. He hoped Esther wouldn't be so difficult once the child came. He smiled at the thought of having both Esther and Catherine in his little cabin once more. Clucking to the mule, he trotted down the road to the village.

Penny sat dejectedly at the table pushing crumbs around with a fingertip. She was too depressed to dress or clean the cabin. She looked around at what had become her prison and felt her heart sink. Unless she could figure out how to escape, the old man would keep her there until one of them died. She put her head on her arms and closed her eyes. How long she sat there she didn't know. Some noise interrupted her solitude. Penny bolted from her chair, straining to hear what it was. A voice that sounded familiar was calling for Ben. Penny ran to the window as two men rode into the clearing. The one whose voice she knew called for Ben to come out. They sat still for a moment waiting for a response and hearing nothing, nudged their horses to leave. Frantic to capture their attention Penny beat on the window and shouted at their retreating backs.

"Did you hear something?" Marcus asked.

"Can't say as I did. Set still a minute and listen," Shine ordered.

They both heard a woman's voice shouting from within the cabin. "I'll be damned, Marcus, that cabin must have his wife's ghost in it, or else Ole Ben's done found himself a woman."

"I've not seen many ghosts in my life; how about you? Let's go see what she's hollering about." Marcus remarked. When they were closer to the cabin door, he could see that it had been barred from the outside so whoever was within could not leave. He heard frantic pounding on the inside of the door as though someone were hitting it with something heavy.

"What in Sam Hill do you reckon is going on in there?" Shine said as he swung down from his horse.

Marcus followed him to the door as the banging within intensified. Marcus yelled, "Simmer down. We'll have this door open soon as we can find a lever to pry out these nails."

Shine trotted to the shed and returned with a crowbar. After several minutes of effort they succeeded in dragging away the wooden bars that had been nailed into the door and across the frame. Pushing the door open, Marcus stood face to face with Penny Madison.

"Jesus, God in Heaven! Penny! What are you doing here? Everyone thinks you're dead. Oh, my God, I ain't believing this."

Shine looked at Marcus in puzzlement, "Is this the woman that was supposed to have been drowned in that storm a while back? Do you know her?"

Jarred out of his stupor, Marcus walked forward and pulled

Penny into his arms. She still had said nothing. "Penny, are you all right? Your family is going to be so happy we found you. What are you doing here with Ben Dough?"

"Is Penny my name?" Penny felt frightened for a reason she couldn't have said. "Ben calls me Esther, but I know I'm not Esther."

Marcus realized that some injury from the storm seemed to have affected her mind, "No, Penny, you're not Esther. You're Penny Madison. You and Ryan went sailing and got caught in a storm. Ryan, your husband, thought you drowned. Both he and your son Rye made it to shore but they couldn't find you. People looked for you for weeks until they finally gave up. How did you end up here?"

"Ben found me. He saved my life. He thinks I'm his wife and he won't let me leave." Penny shifted her stare from Marcus to Shine. Pointing to Shine, she said, "I don't know you."

She stared at Marcus who was beaming at her, "Do you know me, Penny?"

She bit her lip in concentration, "Yes, you're... you're Marcus. Oh, my God. I know you. I *know* you." For the first time in months, Penny felt hope. She would remember her life, and with that thought came a burst of joy.

"We need to get you home real soon. Ryan will want to be with you when this baby is born. Forgive me the presumption, but it doesn't appear that it will be too much longer." Marcus was pleased to be able to refer to Ryan's child without a flash of jealousy behind the words.

"Ryan, that's my husband. I have a son, too?"

"That you do. Rye's the spittin' image of his pa," Marcus grinned. Looking around the cabin, he continued, "I hate to leave before telling Ben goodbye, but under the circumstances that might be for the best. He's going to be powerful upset regardless."

Shine and Marcus helped her onto the horse. Marcus swung up behind her and put his arms around her. It felt so good to hold her and know she was alive, but it didn't make his heart pound the way it once had when she was near. "Hold on, Penny. We're going to ride down to the fort and catch the boat back to Beaufort. It's too late to get the train today, so we'll spend the night in town. I'll send a telegram to Ryan letting him know which train we'll be on tomorrow. He's going to be one happy man."

Penny was nervous and hesitant when the train pulled into the New Berne station the following day. Although Marcus had filled her in on many details of her life and she had begun to remember far more, the idea of facing her husband and not recognizing him or her own child was a chilling one. Penny rose from her seat and with a tight grip on Marcus's arm, descended the steps onto the platform. Her eyes eagerly searched the platform for a face she would recognize but saw none. She could feel her heart sink, fearing that Ryan and her son were there and she didn't know them after all.

Marcus swore. It was not loud enough for her to understand what he had said, but from the tenor of his voice, she suspected he was angry about something. "What's wrong, Marcus? You sound upset."

"I guess there is some misunderstanding. I sent the telegram to Ryan's office so he would have it when he arrived there this morning. I thought if he had received it, he would be here. I guess we need to find a buggy and ride over there."

"I think it isn't far. Let's just walk."

Marcus glanced at her rotund figure, and quirked one eyebrow. "Normally I would agree but under the circumstances, it might be better if we rode. We'll wait here. Shine, would you see if you can find a buggy we can hire for a little while?"

Ryan had indeed received the telegram. When he opened it

and read the message, he felt his knees give way and would have fallen had his desk chair not been right behind him. For a moment he wondered if it were some bizarre hoax and then rereading the terse message from Marcus, he realized that the man would never have sent him something like this if it were not true. He felt a brief flash of jealousy that he had not been the one to find his wife and then he could only sit in stunned awe. The reality of the news seeped into his soul and he felt a great lifting as though he were soaring on wings. He looked up and closed his eyes, and prayed, "Thank you, God. This is the most miraculous blessing I could ever have asked for."

Ryan rushed for his hat, put it on his head, took it off and then sat back down. It was another three hours before the train would arrive. He could not decide whether to go home for Rye and Caroline, or just wait and fetch her alone so the two of them would have a few moments of private reunion before he had to share her with others. He decided to wait and go alone. To pass the time, he went to the church and arranged for the removal of the tombstone before Penny could see it and he stopped by the telegraph office to send Penny's family word of the joyous news.

When he had done all of that he returned to his office and started pacing the floor, too excited to settle down and work. He had just made the twentieth circuit of his office, when he heard the front door open. Turning, he saw Lizzy standing at the threshold smiling seductively. She walked into the office and closed his door. Lizzy had taken great care choosing a dress that flattered her figure and coloring, a dress that was provocative but still demure. Leaning back with her hands holding the knob behind her back, she smiled, well aware that the pose enhanced her breasts.

"Hello, darling. I've missed you. Since the other night all I've done is think about you and long for the day when we can be together like that whenever we'd like." Ryan stood as though he were carved from stone causing her to become nervous at his lack of reaction. Archly she inquired, "Well, did you miss me?"

"Lizzy, don't ever come to my office again. It's over. It was over long, long ago. I will never leave my wife for you. I don't love you. Find someone else."

"I don't know why you're talking about not leaving your wife. She's dead," Lizzy knew she had become shrill and cautioned herself to be non-confrontational. "I'm sorry. That sounds so harsh, but it is true."

An enormous smile creased Ryan's face with unalloyed joy, "No, Lizzy, she's not dead. I just received a telegram this morning saying that Penny is safe. She's been found and is on the way home to me. You need to leave now. I have just enough time to get to the station to meet the train."

"You're lying," she tried to make it sound a statement of fact but the uncertainty in her voice gave her away.

"Why would I lie about something like that?" Ryan shook his head, "I don't know what your plans were Lizzy but they were far different from any I might have had."

Her face blazed with sudden humiliation and anger, "You unmitigated cad. You didn't mind me showing up naked in your bedroom and lying in that bed you shared with your precious wife."

"That was a mistake I'll never repeat. Now leave before we both say things we'll regret later." Ryan took her elbow to escort her to the door.

Jerking free, she sat in the chair in front of his desk. "Don't think you are going to use me like some whore and then just toss me out. I won't have it."

"If you will recall, I didn't invite you to my bed. You came on your own volition. If I treated you like a whore, maybe it's because you were acting like one."

"How dare you talk to me this way. How would you like it

if I told Penny, or Miss Caroline, or my father how you have behaved with me? I'll bet you wouldn't be so arrogant about it all then. You act like you and Penny are so perfect. Hah! Something tells me that son of hers, that looks so much like you, wasn't fathered by her poor dead first husband."

"Lizzy, you do what you need to do, but remember it only tells the world the kind of woman you have become. I will live with it. Now get out of here before I throw you out."

"Damn you, Ryan Madison. I hope you die. "You aren't the first with that sentiment and I doubt you'll be the last. Now, goodbye. I'm going to meet a train."

Lizzy abruptly stood, jerked her nose into the air and swept out. "You've not heard the last of this," she threatened.

Livid that Lizzy had delayed him, Ryan grabbed his hat and ran down the street desperate to reach the station before Penny's arrival. He heard the train pull into the station when he turned the corner. Cursing at his inability to move any faster, he panted onto the platform. Standing near the train, he saw Marcus holding Penny around the waist as they looked for him.

Waving his arms in the air, he called as he ran, "Penny, here. I'm here."

And then she was in his arms and he was hugging her, laughing and crying at the same time. "Thank God, you're safe. I will never let you out of my sight again."

When Penny looked into his eyes she felt an overwhelming sense of rightness and a happiness that welled up inside. "I'm home, Ryan."

"Yes, darling, you're home. Let's go see Rye. He's never accepted that you were gone for good. He is going to be so thrilled you're back. Oh, my God, I love you. I have missed you so much. You cannot know how very much." Ryan turned to Marcus, "I owe you a debt I can never repay for bringing her home to me. Come with us, if you have the time, and tell me all about how you found her."

"Ya'll go ahead and I'll come later. I sent my friend Shine for a buggy. We'll follow in that. You two need some time to yourselves right now." Marcus felt a release from all of the years of frustrated longing that he could stand in front of this man and say those words. His steps were light as he went to find Shine.

EPILOGUE

Ryan's heart swelled with joy as he gazed into the face of his newborn daughter and the mother who had returned from the dead. Penny caught his warm look and smiled tiredly. She closed her eyes, squeezing the hand that he had slipped into hers. She was happy to be back in her home with those she loved around her. Her memory had made a steady return during the three weeks she had been home, leaving few blank places.

There was so much to learn of the time she had been gone, but she hesitated to ask for fear he would want to know about those long weeks when she had lived with Ben Dough. How could she tell her husband that she had slept with another man, albeit an old one, who called her his wife and touched her with a passion he could not fulfill? The memory of those nights she had lain beside the old man feeling his hesitant stroking of her body filled her with an embarrassed disgust. She blamed herself for not stopping it, but how could she have, when she did not know to begin with, whether or not Ben was her husband? Once she suspected her name was not Esther, she warned him never to touch her again. Yet, in the night she had wakened to feel him tentatively caressing her flank. He had never gone beyond a touch of affection, assuring her that his days of lusty lovemaking were but a memory. Still she could not bring herself to tell Ryan of these things.

Ryan said something to her that she didn't hear, lost in thought as she was, "I'm sorry, what did you say?"

"I was just saying that your father and brother are downstairs; Isabel and Caroline, too. They would like to see you and the wee one, if you're up to it that is?" he asked solicitously.

"Yes, do have them come up and bring Rye, too. I want all of the people I love with me." Penny peered down at the little face of her daughter. She pushed the lace trimmed swaddling blanket away from her face and studied it. "Do we call her Martha Caroline or Sarah Caroline or Sarah Martha or Martha Sarah? I know Pa wants the name Sarah in honor of my mother and we both want to honor Caroline and your mother, too. I just don't know what to call her."

"We could always have a Martha, a Caroline and a Sarah and then two more boys we could name for our fathers." Ryan grinned at her, "I don't mind trying to make them all."

"At least give me a day or two to recover before you start planning more." Penny laughed, even though it hurt the tender places that had been torn by the birth. "That still doesn't resolve the name of this one. I would like to name her before the others come up. Help me."

"I think I like the name Caroline Sarah. We could nickname her Carah. We'll name the next one for my mother. Besides, Isabel has already said she wants to name her baby Martha if it's a girl." He felt his mother would approve Isabel's baby bearing her name rather than this one. He might never know who had killed his mother, but he had made peace with her death. Ryan stood, "I'll just fetch the others."

When he left, Penny shifted her weight to find a more comfortable position and gently rocked her sleeping baby. For a moment she felt guilty that she had not named the baby Catherine. Poor Ben. She felt such pity for him and mourned for him in losing his 'Esther' a second time. In his mind, she knew he thought that his wife had returned to him and the baby she carried was the lost Catherine. Perhaps one day, she and Ryan would visit him and thank him for saving her life. She did not know if that would be a happy thing for him or a greater wound in an already wounded soul. As soon as she was up from childbed, she resolved she would find a way to tell Ryan of her time on the island. To keep secret what she had lived through would only create a barrier between them. She wanted no secrets from the father of her children.

For a moment her thoughts flashed back to the ride with Marcus from Ben's house to the fort. His arms around her had been a safe haven and his tender care of her on the journey home had warmed her heart. She could at last look at him with genuine warmth and friendship untangled by regret for leading him on all those years when she thought Ryan had been lost from her forever. She sensed a change in him as well. He loved her she knew, and probably always would, but it was a gentle, undemanding affection and she knew she loved him in the same way. When he left to return to Kinston, he had smilingly told her he was on his way to go-a-courting. At last, he was ready to allow another woman to claim his heart and she was happy for him.

She was smiling to herself when they all crowded into her bedroom to admire the new baby. With Ryan sitting on one side of her and Rye on the other, she felt surrounded by greater love than she had ever known. "I'm so happy we made it home to you all, Carah and I."

Bibliography

Bradley, Mark L. *Blue Coats and Tarheels, Soldiers and Civilians in Reconstruction North Carolina,* Lexington, Kentucky: The University Press of Kentucky, 2009.

Lenoir Co. Historical Association *The History of Lenoir County,* Winston-Salem, NC: Hunter Publishing Company, 1981.

Mussey, Barrows *A Book of Country Things,* Brattleboro, Vermont: Stephen Greene Press,1965.

Rouse, F. L. Woodington and Vicinity, Lenoir Co. NC *Families and History, Kinston, NC,* 1991.

Rouse, F. L. *The Rouses of Southern Lenoir County and Related Families,* Kinston, NC, (undated.)

Thomas, Mai *Grannies' Remedies.* New York, NY: Gramercy Publishing Co. (date not given.)

Wiggington, Eliot, Editor *The Foxfire Book,* Garden City, New York: The Doubleday Company, 1972.

About the Author

Ms. Vaughn holds a BS degree in art from East Carolina University in Louisville, KY, and she studied art history and Italian at Scuola Internazionale di Grafica in Venice, Italy while supervising a study program there under the auspices of Columbia University. She currently resides in Raleigh, North Carolina.

Other titles by B.J. Vaughn

The War Between the States has come to eastern North Carolina, bringing hardships, pillaging, and fear to the local residents. For those left at home, the struggle to procure the needs of daily life is all-consuming; for those serving in the armies of both North and South, death is a daily companion. Against this backdrop, an unlikely and forbidden love affair between a local woman and a Union officer leads to difficult choices for them both—choices that will tear them apart and force them to deal with the abandonment of their dream of a life together.

Despite broken hearts, misunderstandings, and missed chances, Penny and Ryan strive to survive the dangers and ravages of war and make the best of their separate futures. With the surrender of the South at Appomattox, Penny realizes she has one last chance to either find the man she loves or settle for a life alone.

- **Paperback:** 236 pages
- **Language:** English
- **ISBN-10:** 0874260795
- **ISBN-13:** 9780874260793

www.ingramcontent.com/pod-product-compliance
Lightning Source LLC
Chambersburg PA
CBHW020330120726
47904CB00002B/354